White Rose Ensnared

Anne hissed in Rosamund's ear and would not be denied. She wrestled her flimsy gown over her head, revealing her naked body. Her nipples were erect, standing up pert and proud from her little breasts. She twisted the fine linen into a thick rope and caught at Rosamund's hands, dragging them behind her back and roughly binding them together. Rosamund knew that she should struggle, but she did not want to. A heavy aching languor filled her body as she looked down at Alice tormenting their captive across the other side of the room. Anne called over to the young man. 'Come on, Piers. You want her, then take her. Don't wait, you silly fool. Swive her!'

Other books by the author:

Crash Course
Hand of Amun
Forbidden Crusade
Down Under
Dreaming Spires

White Rose Ensnared
Juliet Hastings

BLACK LACE

Black Lace books contain sexual fantasies.
In real life, always practise safe sex.

This edition published in 2004 by
Black Lace
Thames Wharf Studios
Rainville Road
London W6 9HA

Originally published 1996

Copyright © Juliet Hastings 1996

The right of Juliet Hastings to be identified as the Author of
the Work has been asserted in accordance with the Copyright,
Designs and Patents Act 1988.

Printed and bound by Mackays of Chatham PLC

ISBN 0 352 33052 X

England, the fifteenth century.

On the throne sits King Henry VI, head of the house of Lancaster. Henry is a saintly man but unfit to rule: his mind is turning towards insanity. Powerful nobles now take the law into their own hands. The times need a strong King. Richard, Duke of York, supported by his handsome son Edward, is eager to fight the Lancastrians for the Crown.

The nobility of England is split into factions supporting the houses of York and Lancaster. Violence is rife. Safety comes from personal strength or adherence to a powerful patron. The Wars of the Roses have begun.

Rosamund: from the Latin *Rosa Mundi*,
the Rose of the World

Prologue

June 1456

*T*he torches flung a ruddy, jumping light over the tapestried walls. In each corner of the great wood-panelled hall stood a tall candlestick bearing more than a dozen heavy beeswax candles, so that the huge room was filled with glowing light and warmth and a heavy, sensual, waxed-honey smell.

At one end of the hall there was a long, narrow gallery, reached by a creeping staircase in the thickness of the stone wall. On it stood a handful of musicians, playing for all they were worth. The recorders shrilled to the painted rafters and the tabor beat a pulsing, insistent rhythm. The minstrels' gallery also bore two people who were not musicians: two young women, who stood in the shadows by the staircase door with their heads bent together in earnest, secret conversation, shielded from prying ears by the sound of the music.

'Well, Isabella,' said one, 'now you have been married for two whole days, what do you think of it?'

'Two whole days?' said Isabella, with a sly look from under her heavy white eyelids. 'Two whole nights, Rosamund. God have mercy on me, what nights!'

'Oh, Isabella.' Rosamund, Lady de Verney, turned

away and put her hand to her throat to conceal a blush. 'You never change. I do not wish to hear about your bed-sport. Henry would be shocked to hear you talk so.'

'He would not,' retorted Isabella cheerfully. 'He is as lusty as I am, Rosamund. Can you imagine it? You are married to such a crusty old stick, what would you know about it?'

'What indeed,' murmured Rosamund wistfully. She folded her arms upon the carved balcony of the gallery and looked down into the hall. There below her stood her husband, Lionel, Lord de Verney, all of sixty years old, stooping and sparse-haired and becoming unsteady in his movements. He did not see her above him, looking down. A little way from him stood a man Rosamund did not know, and as she leant forward this man looked up. He had odd, dark eyes below a leonine shock of dark hair sprinkled with white, and thin, sensual lips which curved into an admiring smile as he saw the Lady de Verney above him.

'You will have all the men looking at you in a moment,' said Isabella. 'Look how you show off your breasts, leaning forward like that.'

Rosamund looked at herself and registered with a start that Isabella was right. Her breasts were high and deep, too large for the fashion, and when she folded her arms thus the cleft between them was dark and inviting above the soft ruddy fur that edged the low neck of her dark-green damask gown. She stood up hastily, unfolding her arms and stepping away from the balustrade.

The minstrels reached the end of their piece and drew breath. Beneath the gallery the brilliantly dressed dancers separated and made their way towards the edges of the hall, calling out to one another and summoning servants with glasses of cool, flowery wine. Isabella said, 'I shall go down soon and dance with Henry again. The last time we danced I touched him beneath his doublet and I swear he grew hard on the instant. The power of a woman's hand, Rosamund!'

'You are incorrigible,' Rosamund said. She had known

Isabella since she had married Lionel two years before, when they were both just sixteen, and even then Isabella had been fascinated by men and the act of love. Soon Isabella would be leaving Lincolnshire for far-distant Dorset, where her new husband Sir Henry Eynsham had his lands, and sometimes Rosamund thought this was just as well: for her friend never ceased to plague her with thoughts about men that were entirely unsuitable for the virtuous wife of an elderly nobleman.

'Oh, Rosamund,' Isabella was saying, her eyes bright with eager remembrance, 'if you could have seen our wedding night. He is so strong and handsome, and he was gentle too. I have to admit I was a little afraid. But he kissed me and touched me, and soon I wasn't afraid any longer. When he held my breasts in his hands I thought I would faint: the tips grew all hard and when he touched them it was as if he put a dagger to my breast. And then, and then when he put himself inside me I thought – '

'Bella, how can you? Please!' Rosamund sounded genuinely angry. Her dark eyes flashed as she swung on her friend, and she set her full lips into a taut, pale line. 'I don't want to hear it. What good will it do me?'

'Rosa,' Isabella demanded, 'how can you bear being married to Lionel, with all this pleasure just awaiting you? How long is it since he lay with you?'

'Not long,' said Rosamund, conscious that she sounded defensive.

'How long? You daren't tell me. Now, Henry – '

Rosamund set her jaw and put back her shoulders. She stood nearly a head above the little slender figure of Isabella, and her high head-dress, a lofty glittering cone of stiffened silk to match her gown, made her taller still. The translucent chiffon which hung from the tip of the head-dress swirled in the air as she shook her head. 'How often have I told you?' she chided Isabella. 'You will not understand: or you just don't listen to me. My guardian found me a splendid match when he married me to Lionel. All I had was money, and he married me

3

to a lord! And Lionel is good-hearted and generous: look how he dresses me.' She gestured with one long-fingered hand at her beautiful gown, as fine as could be found outside the London court. It was gathered below her deep breasts with a narrow jewelled belt, and the décolletage descended almost to the belt before and behind, revealing Rosamund's smooth, white shoulders, her elegant back, and her breasts almost to the nipple. Close-fitting sleeves outlined her shapely arms and the pointed cuffs fell over her white hands to the beginning of her knuckles. The long, heavy train of the gown was edged with a wide band of the same russet fur that trimmed the neck, and it lay behind her on the wooden floorboards in careless splendour. 'He denies me nothing. I owe it to him to be a virtuous wife, and that means in my thoughts as well as my actions.'

'Oh, your thoughts!' scoffed Isabella. 'Rosa, one day Lionel will be dead, and then you can do as you please. Why shouldn't you know what young men are good for?' But Rosamund fixed her with a stony eye and after a moment she flung her hands in the air. 'Oh, very well, then. But can't you admire them at a distance? Look, what do you think of Edmund Bigod there?'

This was a game the two girls had often played, and Rosamund had managed to convince herself that it was harmless. 'Edmund Bigod,' she repeated eagerly, falling into her normal role of innocent. 'I haven't seen him before. Where is he?'

'Look, down there.' Isabella pointed out a young man below them, blond and broad-shouldered, dressed in a white satin doublet so short that his well-fitting scarlet hose left nothing at all to the imagination. 'Don't you think he's handsome?'

'He has a good figure,' Rosamund admitted, 'but I think his face is insipid.'

'Oh, you're so fussy,' complained Isabella.

'Since I may never indulge myself,' said Rosamund with a caustic edge to her smoky voice, 'I can afford to be as fussy as I choose.'

4

One of the musicians began to strum gently on his little gittern so that the others could retune. Rosamund cast her eyes over the guests and saw again the man with thick greying dark hair. He was standing alone, still looking up at her with those odd, emotionless black eyes. His face was harsh, with heavy, straight brows and a strong, solid jaw which spoke of immovable determination. His well-cut doublet was made of plain, unadorned black velvet. It was pleated on the shoulder and padded, as was the fashion, and the effect on the man's already massive frame was one of almost unnatural strength and power. His steady unwinking gaze made Rosamund uncomfortable and she drew back a little into the shadows.

'Who's that man there?' she asked, pointing surreptitiously downwards. 'The man with greying hair in the black velvet?'

Isabella looked and recoiled, her hand to her mouth. 'Oh, Rosa, don't look at him,' she said quickly in earnest. 'That's Sir Ralph Aycliffe. He's a vicious knave, everybody hates him. Father only asked him here because he is powerful, we're afraid to cross him: he goes everywhere.'

'What do you mean, he is vicious?' The man's dark stare now seemed ominous and threatening. 'What has he done?'

'Oh,' Isabella began, leaning forward conspiratorially. But before she could say another word there was a commotion on the little staircase and in a second the young Sir Henry Eynsham appeared, all glossy curled brown hair and brilliant teeth, demanding that his wife descend and dance with him. Isabella did not protest, and as Rosamund followed them down the stairs she saw that Bella's hand was resting, as if by accident, directly on one of the taut eggs of Henry's buttocks. Her small white fingers squeezed and shadows pooled around her finger-ends. Henry chuckled beneath his breath and turned to his wife, lifting her chin in his hand to plant a kiss on her lips which was nothing short of

5

lascivious. As Henry put his arm around Isabella's waist and led her through the door at the bottom of the stairs Rosamund saw that her friend's words were true. Beneath his skin-tight hose, escaping from the confines of the little pouch that held it, Henry's penis was noticeably swelling and thickening. Rosamund stared, then looked quickly away, blood creeping into her white cheeks. How could they be so shameless, flaunting their lust before a whole house full of guests? She followed them through the little narrow door, wishing she had a fan to cool her glowing face.

People swirled about her in the hall, preparing for the next dance. None of the young men approached her: they knew that their pleas were likely to fall on deaf ears. Although Lionel's age and infirmity meant that they rarely attended social events, Rosamund was already well known as the fairest, coldest lady in three shires, immune to the blandishments of love-lorn gentlemen. If only her husband would dance with her! But he was deeply engaged in conversation with Isabella's father, an old friend of his, and did not notice her hopeful looks. Henry led Isabella towards the centre of the hall to lead the dance and Rosamund sighed, envying her friend her happiness.

'Lady de Verney,' said a deep, gravelly voice at her elbow. Rosamund started and turned to see before her the man who had been looking up at her, the knight that everybody feared, who went everywhere. His black eyes looked into hers, then left her face and passed slowly down her body, lingering on her bare shoulders, appraising her high narrow waist and the ripe fullness of flesh that lay below the heavy train of her gown. No man had ever looked at Rosamund in such a way. She felt cold with shock, then suddenly hot and confused. What was she to do, what should she say, when he stood in front of her and stripped her naked with his impenetrable eyes?

'Sir,' she managed at last, sounding cold and dismissive, 'your servant.' She was going to turn her back on him, but before she could move he had reached out and caught hold of her hand and was lifting it to his lips to kiss. This was bold, but not unforgivable, and Rosamund stood meekly and permitted it.

The knight's hand was cool and hard. Rosamund's long fingers lay within his unresisting and he held them gently, but even so she felt a presentiment of latent power that brought back the strange, chilling sensation that had gripped her when he had first set his eyes on her. He stooped forward a little to put his lips to the back of her hand, just below the fur edge of her pointed cuff. His lips were thin, but unexpectedly soft. He withdrew and Rosamund expected him to release her, but he did not. Instead, to her confusion, he turned over her hand as it lay in his and for a moment seemed to be looking at her palm as if he would read her fortune there. Then he lowered his lips again towards the hollow of her hand where the flesh was warm and tender. He hovered for a moment, not touching her, while he drew in his breath through his narrow nostrils, inhaling the scent of her hand. Then his lips opened and caressed the very centre of her palm where the skin was exquisitely sensitive and between his parted lips his warm tongue just touched her, pressing firmly and delicately.

For a moment Rosamund stood spellbound, wrapped in the sensation of the stranger's kiss. Her lips slackened and her breathing was cold between them: her heart pounded. Then sense returned and she snatched her hand away, protesting, 'Sir!'

The thin, sensual mouth was smiling. 'My lady,' said the dark, rough voice, 'I was intending to ask you to dance with me.' He gestured towards the floor, where the couples were already parading in a stately bransle. 'But it appears that I have left it too late. Allow me to introduce myself instead: Sir Ralph Aycliffe, at your service.' He made her an elegant, courtly bow, and before Rosamund knew what she was doing she had dropped him a little automatic curtsey in return. Sir Ralph smiled still, she could almost have thought that

7

he was mocking her. 'I am astonished,' he said, 'that I have not seen you before. I would remember you if I had.'

'We do not go out much,' Rosamund said nervously, looking at the floor. It felt very odd to be exchanging social niceties with this broad, powerful man. Her eyes flickered up to Sir Ralph's face: he was not terribly tall, but he seemed to fill the space that a much bigger man would have needed.

'Ah, of course,' said Sir Ralph, his dark eyes shifting briefly to Lord de Verney. 'Your husband's health precludes it, I imagine.' One corner of his thin mouth lifted in a smile that looked almost hungry. Then he turned his attention to the centre of the floor. 'Ah,' he said evenly, 'we may dance.'

He held out his hand with such simple, assured command that Rosamund had taken it and allowed herself to be led towards the delicately pacing couples before she considered what she was doing. People turned and stared as Sir Ralph bowed to her and she curtsied and they joined the dance. They looked startled, shocked, disapproving, and Rosamund felt a sudden spur of excitement that tingled from the peak of her hair to her feet. Let them stare! It was not often that she danced. Near her Isabella was making faces, trying to catch her attention, but Rosamund ignored her. She lifted her head and stepped through the motions of the dance with even greater precision than normal, enjoying the knowledge that all eyes were on her. Sir Ralph danced well, with a controlled energy to his movements which was shamefully attractive. Rosamund found herself wishing earnestly that she was married to such a man, rather than her doddering, crumbling husband. Sir Ralph was not a young man, he must have been all of five and thirty, but his strength and virility were so obvious that it was easy to forget his age.

The bransle gave way to an estampie and still Sir Ralph danced with her. When the movements of the dance brought them close to each other he would reach

8

out and touch her, just brushing his fingers across her arm or her shoulder, even, once, tracing the line of her delicate jaw. As they continued to dance he grew bolder, and at last his strong fingers strayed onto the white curve of her breast where it swelled proudly above the tight confines of her exiguous bodice. Isabella came close to Rosamund as they turned beneath their partners' lifted hands and she leant over and hissed, 'For God's sake, Rosamund, don't let him treat you so.'

The whispered warning brought Rosamund to her senses. As the dance ended she freed herself from Sir Ralph, saying, 'Pardon me, Sir Ralph, but I must take some air.' She pulled away and headed for the door, catching the eye of her maid, Margery, and going as fast as a lady might walk towards the door to the garden.

'My lady,' said Margery through her teeth, 'how could you? With that man? I have never seen you behave so. My lord will be so wrath with you.'

'Whatever are you prattling about, Margery?' demanded Rosamund, speaking fiercely to try to hide her guilt. 'I was dancing, that is all. Am I not to amuse myself?'

Margery began to say, 'The Magdalen knows what that sort of dancing leads to,' but Rosamund did not listen. The sun was just setting and the gravel walks of the garden were sweet with the scents of flowers. Red and white roses arched over the paths, and on the mellow brick walls the apricot trees were twined with honeysuckle. Rose and woodbine strove with each other to perfume the air and the cool of the sunset began to strew the trees and flowers with gentle dew.

The damp air kissed Rosamund's bare shoulders with cool lips and she shivered. 'Margery,' she said, utterly ignoring her maid's remonstrances, 'fetch me my cloak before I perish with cold.'

'If you had not got yourself as flushed as a bantam cock, you would not be feeling the cold now,' muttered Margery, but she went obediently off to do as she was bid. Rosamund sighed with the relief of being left alone and lifted her face to draw in the sweet, heavy scent of one of the arching briar roses that overhung the path.

'One white rose holds another,' said a deep voice close behind her. She started and swung around, her hand to her bosom, breathing fast.

It was Aycliffe, he had followed her. She had enjoyed his improper attentions in the hall, surrounded by bright lights and safety, but here in the twilit garden it was another matter. 'Sir,' she said, trying to make her voice sound cool and imperious, 'I wish to be alone. Leave me.'

'But, My Lady de Verney,' said Aycliffe smoothly, 'you seemed to be enjoying our dancing almost as much as I. How could I not follow you? You have enslaved me.'

He spoke with a smile. What was she to make of him? If a young man had spoken thus she would know to dismiss it for the merest flattery. But this man, with his shoulders like a labourer and his dark, dangerous face, showing his teeth in a mocking grin even as the words left his lips – what did he mean? Rosamund turned her head aside in her bewilderment and distress.

'Let me accompany you as you walk,' said Sir Ralph. 'The Rose of the World should not walk in a garden solitary.' He reached out and took her hand. 'I swear to you, my lady, you are the fairest creature I have seen in longer than I can remember.' Again he pressed his lips to her hand, and now his fingers began to travel up her arm, moving dexterously over the folds of her tight sleeve, pressing against the tender skin inside her elbow. His touch stiffened her spine with a sensation that she did not understand, a churning in her stomach as if she were afraid. Did she fear him? Should she? His hand had reached the fur edge of her gown and now it continued upwards onto her naked shoulder. Against her cool skin his fingers felt as hot as fire. She was filled with consciousness of his impropriety and she lifted her head to chide him, but suddenly his mouth was above hers, sinking down towards her lips, ready to kiss her.

10

She wrenched her head away, horrified. 'How dare you?' she demanded. 'How dare you, you villain?' She clenched her fists with rage, rage at him for attempting her and at herself for half wanting him to succeed. 'If I had wanted to kiss a man,' she blurted, 'I should have chosen someone younger than you!'

At this his dark eyes kindled with fury. She could almost have believed that little flames lit within them. 'You impudent bitch,' he said, and before she could protest at his language or withdraw or call for help he had caught her by both shoulders and was forcing her backwards. Her back jarred against the brick wall beneath the arching stems of the rose, knocking the breath from her, and her head snapped to and fro as he shook her. It was as if a sleeping beast had woken and pounced on its prey. Rosamund desperately tried to catch her breath to scream, but even as she filled her lungs Sir Ralph seized her chin in his hand and plunged his mouth down onto hers, smothering her cry. She strained against him and he grunted in satisfaction and thrust his tongue deep into her mouth, exploring the softness of her lips, driving the breath from her again with the ferocious intensity of his kiss. Her hands beat at his velvet back, but she might as well have tried to wrestle with a mountain: her blows had no more effect on him than the fluttering of a captured dove's wings. Sir Ralph made a strange sound, half way between a gasp and a growl, and his hand moved from her face onto the skin of her shoulder and on down to her breast. Rosamund let out a little moan as his hard fingers slid beneath the edge of her gown, and she shuddered and writhed as they fastened on the tip of her breast and trapped it, squeezing until the tender flesh rose into a hard peak.

He lifted his lips from hers just far enough to speak, so that his words vibrated against her quivering mouth. 'You like that,' he hissed. 'Feel how your breast rises to my touch! What else is eager for me, my virtuous lady?' And then he was kissing her again and his other hand was grappling with the heavy folds of her gown, raising it so that the cool evening air kissed the bare flesh of her thighs above her garters. His fingers explored the tight ribbon of the garter and then slithered upwards, pressing and squeezing the delicate skin of her inner thigh, swiftly approaching the warm, secret nest between her legs.

One strong finger dexterously slid through the curls of dark hair and parted the soft, damp lips with casual skill. Hot pincers seemed to grip at Rosamund's flesh, making her moan deep in her throat beneath his stifling lips. He laughed as he kissed her and lazily moved his finger to a place just beneath her triangle and stroked there. She jerked involuntarily against him as if he had stabbed her. His finger moved again and she struggled, not knowing herself whether she struggled to escape or to force him to touch her harder, harder. The pressure of his heavy body held her pinioned against the wall, helpless and defiled, and his working mouth gagged her. The hand on her breast squeezed suddenly, sharply, making her writhe, and for a second his lips lost contact with hers. She twisted her head to the side and caught in a deep breath and screamed.

'Bitch,' he hissed furiously, pushing his body against her so that she gasped. 'Be silent, bitch.' Beneath the hem of his doublet his body was hot and swollen, a rigid pole of flesh straining against the fabric of his hose. His strength and violence terrified her and she screamed again. Suddenly there were hurried footsteps crunching on the gravel and torches bobbing as people rushed towards her. Sir Ralph hissed a curse and drew back, breathing quickly. His thin lips were curled in a snarl back from sharp, strong white teeth.

In a moment she would be safe. Rosamund found herself panting as if she had run a race. Her heart sounded in her ears, louder than a drum. Sudden anger filled her and she said through her teeth, 'Isabella was right. You are a vicious knave.'

He smiled at her words and her anger flared into fury. 'Do you mock me, sir?' she demanded, and spat in his face. The red light kindled again in his eyes and for a moment she thought he would spring at her, but then they were surrounded by people and the moment was past.

'My lady!' That was Margery, hastily wrapping Rosamund in her cloak and pulling her away from the still, silent figure of Sir Ralph. 'Oh, my lady, your shoulders are all scratched. That brute.' She stared accusingly at him.

'Lady de Verney.' Sir Henry Eynsham, looking very pale in the light of the torches. He was carrying his sword and the blade gleamed in the jumping glare, but he looked apprehensive, as if he feared Sir Ralph even though the man was armed only with his dagger. 'Lady de Verney, madam, are you well?'

'Perfectly,' Rosamund managed, though it was a lie. She could not take her eyes from Sir Ralph's face. The shining trickle of her spittle marred his dark cheek.

'Sir Ralph,' said Henry in a taut, strained voice, 'I must beg you to leave.'

Still Sir Ralph did not move. His eyes were fastened on Rosamund's. When at last he spoke his voice sounded like heavy frosted stone. 'Lady de Verney,' he said, 'I enjoin you to remember me. You can be very certain that I will remember you.'

He turned and was gone. Rosamund tottered, and Henry dropped his sword and ran forward to catch her and support her. 'Rosamund,' Isabella whispered earnestly, 'oh, Rosa, I warned you! Are you all right?'

'I feel faint,' Rosamund whispered, entirely truthfully this time. 'Please, Sir Henry, ask my husband if we may go home.'

Henry led her to a seat and hurried off to find Lionel. Margery and Isabella hung over her, twittering in concern. She sat staring into the dark, deaf to their anxious words. Why did she feel so strange? Her breasts were aching, their hard tips chafing almost painfully against the rigid fabric of her bodice, and the secret flesh between her legs was warm and swollen and seeping with moisture. Why? She had feared Sir Ralph, not desired him. She had tried to pull away from his invading, insulting fingers, and yet she was melting like hot honey. Could fear be so close to lust? She closed her eyes tightly, trying to shut out the image of his dark, threatening face, clothed in its ironic smile as a dagger is hidden by its silken sheath. Remember him? How could she forget him?

Chapter One

Twelfth Night, 1461

*I*n Rosamund's opinion, nothing could compare for pure, exquisite boredom with embroidery. She was energetic by nature, and at this time of year she expected to be out in the clear cold air, riding to visit one of their acquaintances for the Christmas festivities, or at least hunting in the forest with her favourite hawk. But Lionel had been summoned by his patron, the Duke of York, and he had ridden off to the north with all the men he could raise. Their household had been stripped, and her husband had forbidden her in his absence to leave the confines of de Verney manor. 'It would be dangerous,' he had said, wagging his finger in her face, 'very dangerous, for you to go out without a retinue to protect you. That knave Aycliffe might fall on you and kidnap you, God save your virtue. He will not attack the manor for fear of my lord of York: but do not tempt him by going vagabonding about the countryside.'

Rosamund had sat with her hands folded before her as meekly as a novice and said obediently, 'Yes, my lord.' She could not disagree, for everyone knew that Sir Ralph was a Lancastrian, an enemy of all adherents of the house of York and of the de Verneys in particular. It was not entirely Rosamund's fault, although her behaviour on that fateful summer's evening four years since had no doubt done its part. Sir Ralph desired her husband's lands, which adjoined his and were rich and tempting. He had overrun many smaller landholders in the district without compunction or remorse and doubtless would have accorded the de Verneys the same treatment if he dared. But Lionel was rich in money and men, and this and his allegiance to the powerful Duke of York had caused Aycliffe to be circumspect.

It was not comfortable to have such a belligerent neighbour. Rosamund had often counselled Lionel to be rid of him, to seize the initiative and attack him while he could. But Lionel would rather rely on the strength of his royal patron than take risks himself. And now he had been summoned to support the very lord that he relied on and left her alone, defenceless, shielded only by the name of York.

Rosamund leant her head against the mullioned window-frame and looked out onto the grey winter garden. It was no use day-dreaming, but sometimes she could not help it. It was pleasant to be a great lady and have riches at her command, but now the splendour of de Verney manor was no more than a well-appointed prison. Sometimes Rosamund thought she would gladly change the manor's dozen rooms and high windows for a simple farmhouse or a merchant's shop, if only –

She took a deep, cross breath and put down her embroidery hoop on the window seat. She was fretting through absence of exercise. A book, she would read a book, something dull and improving to keep her mind from her captivity. If she had called a page would have come running to fetch her whatever she desired: but she had sat still all the grey morning and went now on her own feet towards her bedroom, where her little library had a shelf to itself.

The house was quiet, for nearly all of its men were gone with the Lord de Verney. Rosamund hurried through the silent corridors, running where she could and jumping around the corners, filled with angry energy. Her bedroom was at the back of the house, looking out over the herb garden and the fields beyond. It was quite small, for it needed to house only Rosamund herself and her maid Margery. When she had first married Lionel she had spent several nights in the lord's bedroom, a great tall chamber at the front of the house, but now Lionel sent for her so seldom that she could barely recall the colour of the bed hangings. And the last two times she had gone there the poor man had been able to do little more than fumble and grope, an experience almost as embarrassing for her as for him. If he had not been desperate to breed an heir, she doubted he would even have attempted it.

She put her hand to the latch of her bedroom door and was about to go in when she heard sounds from within, whispers and giggles. Rosamund stopped at once, her heart in her throat. She knew well what the sounds meant. Lionel did not approve of female servants, and the only woman in the house beside its mistress was her maid, Margery. Margery was a hypocritical little besom, always vociferously shocked by misbehaviour in others while being herself given to every indulgence of fleshly lust that she could imagine. The predominance of men in the household gave her plenty of scope to experiment. Rosamund knew this because Margery had also set herself the task of tempting her mistress to adultery, on the grounds that it was a waste for such beauty to wane in the possession of one old man.

In six years of marriage Rosamund had never been swayed by Margery nor succumbed to the temptation of watching her at her sport. She had kept firmly to her resolution of being a good wife to Lionel and had done her best to forget the strange, hot sensations that had consumed her when Sir Ralph handled her so villainously in Isabella's garden. But now the devil sat on her shoulder and whispered in her ear. She was bored and restless and filled with undoubtedly sinful curiosity. Breathing quickly, she placed both hands gently on the closed door and leant forward, setting her eye to the hole where the latch-cord ran.

She could see her bed, a tall bed with a cover and hangings of embroidered Italian silk, and beyond it her clothes-press, and nothing else. But she could clearly hear the voices and she knew them.

'Matthew, you mustn't. Oh, you mustn't.' That was Margery, insincere as ever, her soft voice breathless. 'If my lady finds us – '

'Why did you let me come in here and close the door, then?' demanded a deeper voice. Matthew was one of the household men, a big strong young man with a good looking face. He limped, the relic of a childhood illness, and so Lionel had left him behind when he marched away. Rosamund pressed her face closer to the door.

'Margery,' murmured Matthew's deep voice, 'sweet Meg, let me.' Then there was silence for a moment, broken at last by a series of little helpless moans.

Rosamund swallowed hard. Her heart was beating fast. She was about to see what Margery and Isabella had told her of, a man and woman coupling, doing the deed of darkness, *swiving*. The obscene word flashed vividly through Rosamund's brain. What resemblance would the act bear to Lionel's pathetic grapplings?

Then Margery and Matthew came into her sight, their mouths pressed tightly together, swaying slowly towards the high bed. Margery was a little, slight creature, with a girlish figure that Rosamund often envied, and Matthew stooped over her like a giant. She had both her hands in Matthew's thick tawny hair and she was moaning as he kissed her. Their eager tongues twisted in their open mouths. Matthew's big hands were pulling at the lacings across the bosom of Margery's gown: the ribbons tangled and he pulled free of her clinging mouth, cursing, and tugged at them until they broke.

'Matthew, don't!' Margery cried, her voice almost a squeak. 'You've broken them. Stop, stop – ' But Matthew ignored her. He pulled open the front of her gown and pushed down the neck of her shift and exposed her

18

white breasts, small and shallow as saucers, and whispered with delight as her rosy nipples came into view. His mouth covered Margery's again and he put his hand onto her left breast, covering it completely, the nipple just showing between his strong fingers. The soft white flesh was dented as he squeezed and fondled and Margery became suddenly limp, leaning against him with her head tilted up and her mouth open so that his tongue could thrust and dart between her loose, softened lips. His fingers closed on her nipple and she cried out.

Rosamund found she was panting, hardly able to catch her breath. Her tight bodice was like a prison. Her own breasts felt swollen and tender as if a hand were touching them. She pressed her upper body against the door and whimpered inaudibly.

Now Matthew had both his hands on Margery's breasts, pinching and pulling at her nipples, stroking and teasing them with the horny balls of his thumbs until they were dark and tight and all the rosy flesh round them was swollen with desire. Margery was gasping with lust, her body undulating as she thrust herself towards him. Her clever hands were reaching up under his doublet. She was dexterously unfastening the points that held Matthew's hose, releasing them so that she could slip her hand inside and –

'Ah,' Matthew gasped, shutting his eyes in sudden ecstasy. 'Ah, you witch.' Margery smiled up at him as her hand moved within his clothes, stroking some invisible object. Matthew's closed eyes tightened and his breath hissed as at last she pushed his hose down from his muscled belly and revealed his splendid, surging penis, rampantly erect, a column of flesh so magnificent that Margery's small white hand would barely meet around its scarlet thickness.

Rosamund's mouth was suddenly dry and she clamped her teeth down on her lower lip to stop herself from crying out. She had never seen a young man naked, and this wondrous member was like nothing that she could have imagined. She watched greedily, fascinated,

19

as Margery slipped her hand very gently up and down the hard length of Matthew's eager cock, drawing back the soft skin from the bulging, purpled head. What could it feel like? Was it cool or hot? Was it as smooth and satiny to touch as it was to the eye? Lionel's wizened flesh had never attained such wonderful, taut elasticity, such swollen readiness. Rosamund breathed quickly through her wet, open lips, longing to do what Margery was doing.

Matthew groaned and suddenly caught hold of Margery and pushed her backward until she was lying on the bed with her legs hanging loosely down. He reached down to her ankles and caught hold of them, spreading them wide apart, then lifted her skirts, bunching them up around her slender waist. Her stockings were tied above her knees and above them she was naked, her thighs gleaming white and soft. Matthew's face changed as he saw the delicate dark fur curling crisply in the hollow of Margery's tender loins and the damp flesh between her legs, like a pink satin ribbon laid on white linen. He gave a little moan and dropped to his knees, setting his lips to her soft abdomen and then kissing gently down and down until his head was buried between those slender thighs.

God in Heaven, Rosamund thought, what is he doing? His big, dark hands were holding Margery's white haunches firmly, digging into the soft flesh, and she thought that his mouth was moving. Margery gave a sudden cry, so loud that Matthew lifted his head and whispered, 'Hush.'

'Oh God,' Margery whimpered, and she put her arm over her mouth, biting at her own flesh to keep herself silent. Her other hand moved to her exposed breasts, tracing the rosy outline of one nipple, flickering across the taut, aching peaks, and she gave a smothered moan.

'That's better,' said Matthew softly. He lowered his head again and this time he spread Margery's tender thighs further apart so that Rosamund could see the gleam of wet pink flesh between them. She shuddered and clutched her hand across her bosom. Matthew's long, thick tongue was lapping delicately at those soft folds, stimulating them, teasing them, and Margery was crying and crying into the gag of her arm. Rosamund clamped her thighs together, feeling her own sex empty and aching, longing for a man to caress it, to worship it as Matthew worshipped Margery's.

Matthew licked and sucked gently at the tiny bud that stood clear of the fleshy lips of Margery's vulva. It grew beneath his caresses, swelling and darkening. He smiled as he lapped at it and gently he fondled the flesh of Margery's inner thighs with his strong hands. His fingers stroked at the quivering lips of her sex and she moaned again: then he pushed two fingers deep inside her and withdrew them glistening with pearly moisture. 'Christ save me,' Rosamund whispered, staring. She almost moaned with pleasure just to see those thick fingers sliding in and out.

But now Matthew was standing up, leaning over Margery's quivering body, his massive member thrusting eagerly towards her. 'Ready, sweetheart?' he whispered.

'Yes,' Margery whimpered, lifting her hand from her mouth and reaching up eagerly to pull him down on to her. 'Oh yes, Matthew, please, push it up me now.'

Rosamund winced, shocked and astonished to hear her own maid speak so lustfully, so lasciviously. But Matthew did not seem to be shocked. He guided the broad glistening head to the soft lips of Margery's eager sex, found the notch, and with a gasp of pleasure thrust with his muscular hips until the whole hard length of him was sheathed inside her.

Margery moaned, her head rolling on the soft bedcovers. Her light brown hair began to escape from under her prim white wimple and she gasped with frustration and pulled the headdress from her and shook her head so that the soft hair spilled around her shoulders and onto her naked breasts. 'Please,' she whimpered, 'please, Matthew, please. Do it to me, swive me.' She lifted her thighs as if she would wrap them around his waist and he gave a breathless chuckle and caught hold of her under her knees, lifting her legs up and apart until it seemed that he would split her open.

'Feel this,' he said, and he pulled his hips back, slowly, agonisingly. The great gleaming shaft withdrew, inch by inch, shining with the moistness of Margery's welcoming flesh, and the juicy lips of her vulva clung to it as if she were desperate to keep him within her. Then inch by inch he forced it back up her, all the way in, until the tight purse of his balls brushed against the white skin of Margery's buttocks.

'Don't tease me,' Margery begged. 'Matthew, please.' And Matthew lowered his head to kiss her and took hold of her breasts in his hands and began to swive her in earnest, thrusting with all his strength, his naked flanks tautening and hollowing with each lunge. Margery cried out into his smothering mouth, her hips twisting and heaving as she lifted them eagerly to meet him, to take more of his wonderful thick shaft into her ravenous body. Then she tensed suddenly and her back arched and she hung back rigid from his strong hands, crying out in the ecstasy of her pleasure as he plunged himself into her, faster and faster, driving himself to a glorious, shuddering climax.

Rosamund leant helplessly against the door, shaking. Her heart was pounding and the secret flesh between her legs was wet and aching. So that was how it should be. How could she have known?

But now through the latch-hole she could see nothing but Matthew's bare buttocks and Margery's naked thighs wrapped around his waist, and gradually the hot eager arousal that had possessed her drained away, leaving her angry and frustrated. Her position was unchanged, she was still Lionel's wife, and now she would be frustrated by the knowledge of what she was missing. How dare they? How dare they, on her own bed? Suddenly her lips folded together in stern decision. She lifted the latch and walked boldly into the room.

'Holy Virgin!' she exclaimed, as if she had only just seen the couple lying sprawled in post-orgasmic exhaustion on the silk coverlet. 'Margery!'

Matthew leapt to his feet, crying out at the sudden shock of his withdrawal from Margery's warm wetness, and stood huddled over his naked crotch, trying to pull up his rumpled hose. 'My lady,' he stammered.

'Matthew,' said Rosamund, with cold fury in her tone, 'begone at once.'

Margery struggled to a sitting position on the bed. 'My lady,' she cried, fighting with her skirts, 'oh, my lady, I –'

'Matthew, get out,' Rosamund ordered. 'My lord shall hear of this.'

'My lady, I beg you, don't tell my lord,' gasped Matthew, looking as if any moment he would fall to his knees at her feet. 'He'll turn me away for sure. Please, I beg you –'

'Get out,' Rosamund repeated, and at last Matthew went, limping across the floor with his head hanging like a guilty dog and fumbling with his points.

'My lady, don't tell my lord. Please, please, don't tell him.' Margery had thrown herself from the bed to the floor. 'You know he was angry with Matthew before. He'd turn him out. In the name of God –'

'How dare you use the name of God when I have found you rolling on your own mistress's bed naked in a man's arms?' demanded Rosamund. 'How dare you be so abandoned?'

'My lady, we did no harm.' Margery crawled back to the bedcover and stroked at it, trying to smooth out the creases in the crumpled silk. 'No harm, my lady.'

'That is not my opinion,' said Rosamund coldly. 'You should both be punished.'

'Don't punish Matthew,' said Margery with sudden eagerness. 'Not him. It was my fault, I asked him here. I am a little whore, my lady, you know it, you know I cannot resist a fine young man. Punish me, if you must.'

'All right.' Rosamund spoke with sudden decision.

She really wanted to hurt Margery for having shown her so clearly the pleasure that she was missing. 'Very well. You have behaved disgustingly and I will beat you for it.' Margery looked up at her with bright eyes, not seeming the least bit afraid. Rosamund was angry that Margery should hold her so light. 'Get up,' she ordered. 'Hold on to the bedpost and bend over. Lift your skirt.'

Without a word Margery obeyed. Rosamund went to her clothes-chest and drew out a long, slender leather belt. Her jaw was tight with anger. She would make Margery smart: that would teach her to be so impudent! She stood behind her and drew back the belt, then hesitated. Her maid's skirts were hauled up around her waist, her buttocks were exposed to her mistress's gaze, naked and perfect like twin moons, and between them her secret flesh was gleaming wet, seeping with white juice like a fruit that is ripe to bursting. Rosamund's tongue seemed to swell in her mouth: she said in sudden wrath, 'I can see his seed dripping from you, you wanton hussy!' and she cracked the belt down across Margery's white flesh, as hard as she could.

Margery gave a little sharp cry and her naked hips shook. Her clothing was in disarray, her bodice still open so that her small breasts hung down freely, quivering as Rosamund struck her. Another blow fell, and another, and with each blow Margery thrust her buttocks lasciviously upwards like a she-cat that longs for the tom and the swollen damp flesh between her legs opened, gaping, asking to be filled. 'My God,' Rosamund cried at last in desperate frustration, 'anyone would think you enjoyed being beaten!'

Margery looked over her shoulder. Her tumbled hair fell around her flushed eager face and her tongue ran quickly around her red lips, moistening them. 'Don't you think that pain is very like pleasure sometimes, my lady?' she asked softly.

'That's stupid,' retorted Rosamund angrily. But the red stripes across the pure whiteness of Margery's delicate skin caught at her eyes and drew her closer, hesitating and fascinated.

'Hit me again,' Margery murmured. Rosamund felt her throat catch with hot excitement. She took a step back and cracked the belt hard across her maid's quivering skin. Margery cried out, throwing back her head, and with a spasm of shameful arousal Rosamund brought down the stinging leather again, turning it so that the end of it just fell onto those wet, turgid folds of flesh. Margery jerked, her back arching, her mouth open and gasping. 'Oh, my lady,' she moaned, 'if you could have seen what he did to me, you wouldn't want to punish me for it.'

For a moment Rosamund almost confessed that she had seen everything, but then she too would be revealed as a hypocrite. She stared at the enticing curve of her maid's white buttocks and the soft mound between them, glistening in its nest of brown fur, and ran her tongue quickly over her dry lips. 'That's enough,' she managed to say, her voice taut and husky, like a stranger's.

Margery straightened, letting her skirts fall, and tossed back her loose tumbling hair. Her eyes were gleaming and the delicate skin above her shallow bare breasts was flushed rose-pink. 'My poor lady,' she said, 'you've no idea. Don't you think you would like to know?'

'I am a married woman, Margery,' Rosamund said, trying to instil withering scorn into her voice. 'I'm not a novice fresh from the cloister.'

'I should think you know as little as any nun,' Margery said, 'married to that old stick for seven years. Try a man, my lady. I don't mean a rough lad like Matthew: find yourself some young lordling to show you sport. Do it soon, my lady. Beauty doesn't last for ever.'

Rosamund turned hastily away and went over to the window, dropping the belt from her trembling fingers. She reached out and caught up her mirror, a lovely thing of carved and gilded wood set with silvered glass, a little miracle to hold in her hand. It had been a betrothal gift from her husband. She lifted it and turned her face to the light, anxiously examining her smooth, creamy skin for signs of creeping decrepitude. Her own dark eyes looked back at her, wide and clear, fringed with long straight lashes that made them glitter like stars. 'I am not getting old,' she whispered protestingly.

'No, no, my lady.' Margery was standing behind her, gently caressing her shoulders, comforting her. 'No, in faith, that's not what I meant. You are the loveliest lady in three shires, everyone says so. You could have the choice of all the young gentlemen around here, any one of them you like.'

Rosamund lifted her eyes and met Margery's bright gaze in the silvered gleam of the mirror. 'I'm sure,' she said coldly. 'And then what? Whichever one it was would be off riding to the hunt the next day with his friends, and he would tell them of his latest conquest, and in less than a week everyone would know and they would laugh at me behind their hands and call me a whore. I won't do it, Margery. Lionel has not deserved to be made a cuckold.'

Margery's fingers just stirred against the pale skin of Rosamund's neck, making her shiver. 'Well, then, my lady, why not just take it in to your head to go out for a ride? If what my lord says is true, Sir Ralph Aycliffe will be down on you like a hawk on a hare, and he won't ask for your permission.' Rosamund's eyes widened and she watched herself in the mirror, seeing a hot shameful blush begin to stain her cheeks as Margery whispered in her ear. 'You know what they say about him, my lady, that he's the greatest whoremaster between York and London. They say he has a prick on him would make Matthew look puny. And you liked him, my lady, didn't you, when you met him at that party? Just think, he'd drag you down from your horse and have your legs spread wide before you could even scream. Why, he'd push that great thick cock right inside you – '

The mirror slammed down onto the table, almost breaking. 'Don't,' Rosamund said, whirling to face Margery and breathing fast. 'Don't, Margery, you make it sound almost pleasant that a wicked villain like Aycliffe should – should rape me! Don't talk about it.'

The two young women stood looking into each other's eyes. Margery very slowly smiled, her face like a mischievous child's. She took a step closer to Rosamund and said softly, 'If I go on talking about it, my lady, will you – beat me again?'

The skin between Rosamund's shoulder-blades was hot and cold with a confusion of anger and desire. She remembered Sir Ralph's fingers, strong and cool, probing between her legs and making her moan. She turned her head aside. 'I don't want to beat you again,' she whispered.

'You are flushed,' Margery said softly. 'Look, my lady, see how your skin blooms.' She reached out and touched the soft swell of Rosamund's breast above the tight bodice of her gown, where the white skin was rosy-pink and warm with the blood surging beneath it. 'Ah,' Margery whispered, 'you are hot, my lady. The humours burn you. Let me open your gown and cool you.' She lifted her hands to the silk laces that held the gown closed and began deftly to untie them.

Rosamund could not move. Her hands were heavy and limp and she stood very still as Margery unfastened the stiff gown and pushed it down from her shoulders. For a moment there was a sense of blessed relief as her breasts lifted and fell, freed from the tight, rigid bodice that had pressed them upwards, but then she gasped with shock as Margery's little hands slipped down inside her linen shift, touching her breasts, stroking them so that they ached with sudden sharp desire. She closed her eyes and shuddered with pleasure and disbelief and then she felt warm breath on her cheek. Gasping, she turned her head, and Margery's lips touched hers and pressed upon them and her little nimble tongue slipped gently into Rosamund's open mouth and flickered there, sliding in and out as Matthew's thick penis had slid in and out of her body.

Nothing had prepared Rosamund for the pleasure of it, the warmth and moistness that seeped through her whole body and gathered between her legs, waiting. Margery kissed her again, lustful and expert, and although she tried to keep silent she heard herself give a little moan of pleasure.

'Come, my lady,' Margery whispered, 'come,' and she was leading her towards the bed, pulling her shift from her shoulders, exposing her white body. 'Lie down,' she hissed, and Rosamund lay obediently back onto the cold coverlet, gazing up at the canopy with wide astonished eyes.

Margery left her for a moment, hurrying around the bed to throw the bolt on the heavy door. 'I should have done that a little while ago, my lady, and then you wouldn't have walked in on us,' she breathed, and then she pushed her own dress and her shift from her shoulders and crawled naked onto the broad bed, slender as a wood-nymph. She looked down at Rosamund's body: it was full-fleshed, opulent, with proud, heavy breasts and thighs like marble. 'My lady,' she whispered, 'I've wanted to give you pleasure so many times, but I never dared. But your body is so lovely, it asks to be loved, and with my lord gone – ' She stooped, her little breasts quivering with her movement, and laid her lips again on Rosamund's full, soft mouth. She pushed her tongue between her mistress's lips and as she did so reached down with her hand and gently, very gently, touched her between her legs, in that warm, secret spot where Sir Ralph had touched her, where the flesh was hot and aching with desire.

Rosamund moaned, lifting her round hips helplessly towards Margery's searching hand, and the maid drew back her fingers in surprise. 'Why, my lady,' she said softly, 'you are wet already, sweet as a honeypot.' She lay down beside Rosamund, pressing her little lithe body against her and smiling teasingly. 'Sweetheart, are you sure that you did not see what Matthew and I were doing?'

Helplessly Rosamund licked her dry lips with her tongue. The touch of Margery's hand had set a fire burning inside her: she felt hollow. 'I did – I did see something,' she whispered at last.

'What did you see?' Margery's voice was gentle, caressing. She slid a little way down Rosamund's body and drew the nipple of one of her breasts gently between her fingers. The coral-pink flesh tautened and swelled as she touched it and Rosamund gave a little whimper of pleasure. 'Tell me,' Margery insisted, pinching and pulling at the stiffening nipple, touching it with her sharp nails so that Rosamund's breath hissed through her teeth. 'What did you see?'

'I saw him – ' Rosamund's eyes closed and her lips drew back from her teeth. Margery had licked her taut nipple, flickering her tongue across it like a snake. 'I saw him – put himself inside you.'

'You saw him swive me?' Margery was smiling impishly. 'You saw his wonderful prick? Oh, don't wince, my lady, words won't hurt you. Didn't he shaft me well? He filled me up.' She lowered her head again and caught the rigid teat of Rosamund's breast between her lips, sucking wetly at it. Then she withdrew and pursed her lips, blowing a stream of cold air over the tight damp flesh so that her mistress moaned in an agony of pleasure. 'What else did you see?' she whispered softly, and blew again.

'He – kissed you,' Rosamund whispered. Her hands were moving as if they were not under her control, creeping up her naked body to rub and fondle her swollen, tormented breasts. Her eyes were closed: she could see again Matthew's head bent between Margery's pale thighs, his long, thick tongue licking and stabbing at her, his fingers vanishing inside her. 'He licked you, he touched you.'

Margery was lying on top of Rosamund now, one of her mistress's legs caught tightly between her slender thighs, rubbing her moist vulva wantonly against the soft white skin. 'He did,' she said. She caught both of

Rosamund's full breasts in her hands and pushed them close together then flickered her tongue over each of the taut nipples in turn, her little narrow fingers catching the rosy buds as they lifted, squeezing them so tightly that Rosamund arched her back with delicious pain. Then she slid further down the bed, her slender boyish body fitting easily between Rosamund's loosening thighs, and she reached out with her agile, probing tongue.

'Ah, God,' Rosamund cried, thrusting her breasts desperately towards Margery's chafing hands, her long white throat twisting as she writhed with pleasure. She could not believe the unbearable sweetness of the sensation, the liquid delight as Margery lapped and lapped at her, scratching at her nipples with her sharp nails. A glowing, heavy bliss grew in her loins, filling her with quivering fire, and she cried out. The pleasure concentrated at the front of that secret cleft, building and building, and her hands clutched helplessly at the silk coverlet as she lifted her hips towards her maid's searching mouth, blindly seeking even more intense sensation, even greater pleasure. She cried out again, lifting her hands from the sheets to touch herself, her thighs, her belly, her shoulders, feeling everywhere the echoes of the hot delicious ecstasy that arrowed through her pulsing, hidden flesh. Margery held her legs wide apart, caressing the soft skin on the insides of her thighs, then pressed her face close and opened her mouth and sucked, drawing between her moving lips the little pearl that was the epicentre of delight, pressing on it, rubbing it with the delicious roughness of her quicksilver tongue. Rosamund gave a single helpless cry and flung back her head, her lips parted and quivering, every inch of her body stiff and shuddering as a great convulsion of pleasure seized her and racked her and left her limp and breathless.

Margery crawled up the bed and lay down beside Rosamund, her head propped on her arm, looking into her mistress's face and smiling to see it drowned in

30

ecstasy. 'There, my lady,' she said. 'There you are. Long years I have waited for that.'

Rosamund slowly opened her eyes, feeling her fingers tingling still with the fading echoes of her first orgasm. She tried to speak, but could not make words. Margery smiled again and leant forward to kiss her and she returned the kiss languidly, pushing her tongue between Margery's lips and into her waiting mouth. They lay pressed together, exchanging warm lingering kisses, and Margery's little hard nipples dented the white softness of Rosamund's full breasts.

When she could speak at last she said, soft as a breath, 'Margery, Margery, I never knew.'

'Poor thing,' whispered Margery, kissing her lovingly. 'Poor darling. Seven years of marriage and never to know.'

Rosamund hesitated, then shivered. 'And with a man,' she said, her chestnut-brown brows contracting anxiously, 'with a man, is it – better?'

'A man!' laughed Margery. 'Do you have to ask? Women can please each other like this, my lady, but only a man can shove a great hot rod of flesh inside you. Oh, I know there are other things you can use, but nothing is the same as the real thing. A man's hard shaft feels so wonderful, there's nothing like it.'

Rosamund sighed and pursed her lips ruefully. 'Well, Margery, I shall have to wait to discover that joy until I am a free woman.'

'You mean until your husband dies. My lady, don't wait! He could linger for years. You would waste your youth.'

'Don't.' Rosamund laid her finger on Margery's lips. 'Don't tempt me. You're wicked, Margery. You shall make me glad that I beat you.'

'I am glad you did,' said Margery, smiling as she laid her tousled head on her mistress's breast.

Chapter Two

*T*he day was cold and grey, with snow lying in the hollows and more snow threatening. A party of gentlemen, a score or so, rode at a sharp pace over the muddy, rutted track. The pack ponies that trotted at the rear of the group, burdened down with shields, helmets and plate-armour, marked them out as soldiers. They carried banners bright with coats of arms, but their faces were tense and pale beneath the hoods of their heavy cloaks. Some of them were wounded, their hurts salved and bandaged or open to the cold air.

About half way back in the group rode three young men together. They looked tired and their faces were rough with several days' growth of beard. They were dressed fairly in well-made hose and short pleated doublets that showed off their athletic figures to advantage, but the good clothes were stained with mud and blood. Their cloaks were fastened with clasps of metal, not of gold, and the simple harness of their horses showed that they were squires, well born young men following their lord to serve him in arms and learn to be gentlemen. At present their faces were set into blank masks, presumably to conceal grumbling discontent at the length of their ride in the cold, bitter wind.

'Going a bit out of our way, aren't we?' said the tallest of them under his breath. 'Or are we lost?'

'Not lost, Geoff,' said his neighbour, a slight, fair young man with one arm tightly bound in a sling and hair that shone like gold even in the grey winter light. 'Not lost. My lord has a native guide up there. We're taking a message to some house, I believe.'

'Taking a message?' said the third, sounding disbelieving. 'Who told you that, Will? Why should my lord go out of his way to deliver a message?'

'It's not far out of the way,' said golden-haired Will. 'We'd have to come down the North Road anyway. A courtesy call, if you like. Some acquaintance of his was killed at Sandal, and we're off to tell his wife that she's a widow.'

The tall one, Geoffrey, frowned and shook his head. His face was well made, with sharp bones and bright-green eyes beneath light-brown brows that were shaped like the wing of a hawk in flight, a sharply angled arch that made him look both stern and quizzical. His left cheek was bruised along its high ridge and into the hollow beneath the bone and he had a long cut across his brow, jagged and roughly scabbed. Thick, tousled hair, silver-brown and glossy, showed beneath his hood. 'That doesn't sound like the sort of task I relish,' he said. 'Why are we all traipsing off for it?'

'As I said, they were acquainted,' said Will, 'and it's not far out of our way.'

'Filthy weather for it, anyway,' said the third, whose name was George. He was thin faced and black haired, with sallow skin and dark eyes that gave his expression a devilish gleam.

'Cheer up,' said Will, lifting a small leather flask from his belt and putting it to his lips. He swallowed, then juggled the reins into his immobilised hand and passed the flask on to George. 'Everything comes to he who waits. I heard my lord say where he meant to stop tonight: it's an inn we went to once before, when I was

33

travelling with him without you two. It had the prettiest, willingest wenches I have ever met.'

'Really?' asked Geoffrey, leaning forward with eager attention. He was a young soldier with all the predilections of young soldiers the world over, and willing wenches were for him the highest recommendation an inn could have. George tossed him the flask and he caught it nimbly in his gauntleted hand. 'Really? What were they like?'

Will reclaimed his flask and lifted it to his lips then lowered it, scowling, and held it upside down. A few melancholy drips trickled from its mouth. 'That's the last time I offer you any of my drink. You finished it, you bastards.'

'Will,' said Geoffrey eagerly, 'come on, tell us about the girls.'

Will cocked his head at George with a cheerful grin. 'Listen to the Lusty Bachelor here. Are you looking forward to adding a few more notches to your dagger handle, Geoff? When did a wench at an inn ever say no to you, anyway?'

'Come on,' said George impatiently. 'I want to hear about them as well.'

'Well,' said Will, leaning forward with a conspiratorial air, 'I'll tell you the truth, lads. That was the only time in my life that I ever had two women at once.'

Geoffrey's brows drew down hard, making his eyes glitter like birch leaves rustling in the sunlight. His mobile mouth widened into a disbelieving smile, but he said nothing. It was George who exclaimed, 'Two at once? What for? You've only got one prick.'

Will flushed, looking suddenly uncomfortable. 'Well,' he said, then broke off. 'Oh, to Hell with it. You don't really want to know.'

'I do,' protested George.

'Look at Geoff there,' exclaimed Will angrily. 'Looking so damned superior. Who do you think you are, Geoff?'

'I want to know what you did with two women at once,' Geoffrey said calmly, still smiling.

34

Will hesitated, looking into Geoffrey's bright eyes with an anxious frown. He licked his lips and swallowed, then said, 'It was amazing. I had one of them underneath me, I was shafting her, and the other one lay on top of us both. I could feel her all down my back, her tits pressing into me, squeezing me, and she put her hands around me and stroked me all over. I came like a gun going off. It was incredible.'

'Did you have her too?' asked George breathlessly. 'The one on top?'

'What do you take me for? I – '

'Hush,' Geoffrey said suddenly, and the other two squires fell silent. Geoffrey jerked his head towards the front of the group of horsemen and they saw their lord gesturing, pointing towards a tall stone-built manor house not half a mile distant.

'That must be it,' said George.

'De Verney manor,' Will said. 'Fine looking place.'

They swiftly drew closer to the manor, admiring its traceried windows and tall chimneys and elegant oriels. It was a modern house, handsome and well appointed, built for comfort rather than for defence. In front of the manor was a gravel-strewn courtyard, and the horses trotted in and milled there while the squires' lord Sir Thomas Parr ordered one of his pages to dismount and knock at the great oak door.

'Not even dismounting?' George whispered in disbelief and disappointment. 'I'm clemmed, it's freezing. Won't Tommo even let us go in to warm up and have a bite of something?'

'He's in a hurry,' Will whispered back. 'Just a short diversion, remember?'

There was a brief turmoil at the door. Geoffrey frowned, leaning from side to side and setting his heels to his horse to try to see what was happening. Then he very slowly lifted his hands to his hood, pushing it back so that it would not block his view, and became very still, his lips parting and the breath whispering through them as he stared.

A lady had appeared in the doorway, dressed in a long gown of velvet the colour of red wine. Her hair was hidden beneath a white headdress. She clasped the gown in both hands, lifting it clear from the gravel and mud, and came forward to stand by Sir Thomas's horse, looking up in silence. She was tall and well made, with high deep breasts and curving hips that the heavy folds of velvet could not quite hide. The hands holding her gown were long and white: and her face! Geoffrey felt his heart beating faster as he gazed at her. Her skin was smooth as cream, closely moulded to fine bones, and beneath soft feathery brows her wide eyes were as dark as jet, pools that a man could drown in. Her nose was straight and her parted lips were full almost to a fault, curved like a bended bow and glistening with the fresh colour of a peony.

'Geoff! Geoff!' He shook himself and turned his head quickly to stare wide-eyed at Will. His friend was grinning. 'In love again?'

Geoffrey shook his head impatiently and looked back to the lady. She had spoken some meaningless words of courtesy; now she was asking Sir Thomas his business. Sir Thomas sat straighter on his horse, discomfort showing itself in every line of his taut back. His cultured Southern voice said, 'My lady, I am Sir Thomas Parr, a friend of your husband's. I have come from the Duke of York's castle at Sandal. I am going westwards now to join forces with the Duke's son Edward, Earl of March. I came to bring you news.'

'News?' said the lady. She had a low voice, breathy, like a murmuring dove. 'That is kind of you, Sir Thomas. News of my husband?'

'No kindness,' said Sir Thomas, shaking his head. 'My lady, I am very sorry to tell you that a battle has been fought at Sandal, a disastrous battle for us. The Duke was killed with his son Edmund, and I am very sorry to tell you that your husband, Lord de Verney, also fell with many of his men.'

Lady de Verney's red lips parted and she took a step

36

backwards, her white hand clenching into a fist below her long white throat. She stretched out her other hand behind her and from the door ran forward a little slender maid who caught her mistress by the arm and seemed to support her.

'I am very sorry to bring you this ill news so roughly,' said Sir Thomas again, 'but our business presses. Forgive me, my lady.' He bowed to her from his saddle and then laid the reins to his horse's neck, preparing to go.

For a moment Lady de Verney stood still, clinging to her maid. Then she leapt forward, catching at the horse's rein, her great, dark eyes turned upwards. She was so lovely in her distress that Geoffrey felt as if a mailed fist was squeezing his throat, choking the breath from him. 'Sir Thomas,' she gasped, clutching at the rein, 'did you say the Duke of York was also dead?'

'His head is on York gate,' said Sir Thomas grimly.

'God help me,' exclaimed Lady de Verney, twisting her white hands into a knot before her face. 'God help this place. My lord, I beg you, do not leave us. When this news becomes known Sir Ralph, our neighbour, will fall on this manor like a hungry wolf. He has coveted it for years. There is no one to defend it! In God's name, my lord, do not leave us.'

'My lady, what can I do? The kingdom has need of me and my men. I am sorry, there is no choice.' He pulled at the horse's rein and turned it, lifting his arm to summon his men to follow him. They came willingly, ashamed to stay where those dark eyes might fall on them and pierce them with guilt.

'Sir Thomas,' called Lady de Verney desperately, hurrying after him across the churned gravel, heedless of her wrecked skirts. 'I beg you, stay just a few days, just until my husband's men return from Sandal.' Sir Thomas set his jaw and looked at her without a word, and her pale face grew gradually paler still. 'Jesu have mercy,' she whispered, 'how many of them are left? When will they come?'

For a moment Sir Thomas seemed reluctant to reply.

Then he grated, 'Only a handful are left. God knows when they will return to you. I am sorry.'

'Sir Thomas!' Lady de Verney ran to him and caught his rein, staring up. 'What will make it possible for you to stay? Is it money you require? You shall have all I can command!'

A dark-red flush crept up in Sir Thomas's cheeks. In a very low voice he said, 'Do you take me for a mercenary? Am I some *condottiero* to take your gold for my sword? Let me go, Lady de Verney. My honour lies with the Earl of March.'

He pulled the rein from her limp fingers and turned his horse again to ride away. His men followed him, not looking behind them. Geoffrey's horse tossed its head, wanting to follow its fellows, but his hands tightened unconsciously on the rein and drove it a little closer to the house. He was gazing at the lady's face, unable to draw his eyes away. She stood wringing her hands as the horsemen began to move across the gravel. Then, as if she felt his eyes upon her, she turned and looked straight at Geoffrey.

He felt a sense of shock. Lady de Verney ran up to his horse and stood below him, looking up. She was breathing fast and as he looked down he saw her white breasts above the low neck of her gown rising and falling, the silky crease between them deepening as she breathed, and suddenly his own breath was coming in quick short pants and he could feel himself growing tight and hot with lust beneath his stained, muddy woollen hose. He shook with desire for her, for the round white orbs of her breasts and the tender flower of her soft mouth. Her lips were parted as she looked up at him and suddenly his mind filled with a white-hot image of her kneeling before him, her full white shoulders bare to his hungry eyes, leaning forward to encircle his throbbing penis with those red soft lips. He stared at her spellbound.

'Sir,' she said in a low voice, 'I beg you to ask your lord to stay. Ask him to protect me.'

Geoffrey shook his head helplessly. His tongue felt

heavy and dry in his mouth, but he made it speak. 'My lady, I am sorry. There is nothing – '

She reached up with her white hand to catch hold of his thigh above the cuff of his long boot, saying earnestly, 'I beg you.' Then the words froze in her mouth and she stared up at him in silence. Her slender fingers had brushed against his groin and felt there the thickening length of his phallus as it burned and swelled with desire for her. Her lovely face was pale with fear and desperation, but as they looked into each other's eyes it began to flush, the scarlet blood staining her white cheeks like wine poured into a glass. She did not move her hand. Geoffrey's breath shuddered as he felt her touching him, the lightest touch possible, like a butterfly's kiss, driving him mad. His eyes saw nothing but her trembling scarlet lips and he leant slowly towards her.

'Geoff!' said an urgent voice behind him. He jumped like a stag and jerked upright. The lady drew back her hand from his thigh as if scalded. He turned his head, feeling hot blood burning in his cheeks. Will was behind him, gesturing fiercely. 'Geoff, are you mad? My lord is waiting. Come on!'

Geoffrey turned in his saddle to look down at the lady's face. She was pale again, pale as death, and those great, dark eyes seemed to suck out his soul. 'I'm sorry,' he said, shaking his head. 'I'm sorry.' Then he dragged at his horse's reins and dug in his spurs and the gravel flew up in spumes from the churning hooves as he galloped to catch up with the others.

'My God, Geoff,' hissed George as Geoffrey drew up beside him, 'what were you thinking of? One pair of dark eyes and you're lost! If my lord had seen you – '

'Shut up,' Geoffrey said viciously, his lips trembling as he glared at George. 'Shut up. How do you feel, George? Do you feel like a real man, riding off and leaving a lady defenceless? Is that knightly? Is it chivalrous? My lord deserves to be whipped for it.'

'Don't talk to me about chivalry,' said Will with a

laugh. 'You wanted to swive her. And her only three days a widow.'

Geoffrey made his hand into a fist and pressed it to his mouth to keep in the angry words. He said nothing else, no more at all, until as darkness fell they reached the inn that Will had spoken of with such approval.

In the inn yard Geoffrey swung off his horse and ran to catch his lord's stirrup and hold it steady while he dismounted. Sir Thomas looked at him for a moment from under his grey brows, then said sternly, 'A disapproving face, Geoffrey.'

'I am sorry, my lord,' Geoffrey said stiffly.

'You squires have worked hard the last few days,' said Sir Thomas in a resolutely cheerful voice. 'It was a hard fight, and it has been a difficult journey. The service at this place is good. Take the evening off, I will not need attendance. I will see a room and dinner is bespoken for you and your friends.'

'Thank you, my lord,' Geoffrey said, but his voice was still very cold.

'Our own room!' exclaimed George excitedly as they entered the inn. 'A night off! Heaven!'

'And pretty, willing girls,' added Will.

Perhaps they should not have had quite such high expectations. The room that was shown them was small and cramped, with only one narrow bed and three pallets made of straw, and the person who brought them their meal was both male and elderly. Will and George were greatly disappointed. But at least there was a bright roaring fire, and the old man brought them a large flask of good red wine as well as a decent dinner. George and Will drank and ate and presently grew very cheerful. George pulled his dog-eared pack of cards from his saddlebag and they tried to interest Geoffrey in a game, but he sat on the edge of the bed with his hands clasped loosely around his wine cup, staring silently into the depths of the fire. He saw again the lady's face, those soft, red lips that begged to be kissed, those eyes like jet, starred with long lashes. And they had abandoned her, left her helpless. He choked down the wine, his throat half-closed with shame and wretchedness, and bowed his head.

Janet had worked at the inn for the last year and a half and she knew why the patrons came. It was not for her master's table, but for his stable of fine looking, willing girls, of whom she was one. It was not a bad life, but sometimes she felt put upon. She was the most recent of the landlord's acquisitions and she always seemed to draw the short straw: just as now, when she had been sent to clear away for three, count them, *three* young men, nobodies, mere squires in the service of a knight, hardly likely to be generous with tips.

She opened the door by barging it with her full hips, since her heavy tray took both hands. As the door opened she heard laughter. Two of its occupants were chuckling over some wager. They looked up and she saw that they were both very attractive: one of them was blond, with his arm in a sling, and the other had a face like the Devil himself, thin and dark and wicked-looking. Perhaps this would not be so troublesome after all. Janet said cheerfully, 'May I clear away, my young lords?'

The pair of young men by the fire jerked to their feet, swaying slightly and grinning like a pair of fools. 'Clear away?' said the blond one. 'Sweetheart, you can clear us all away with a glance.'

Janet laughed merrily and came boldly in, swaying with her wooden tray on her hip. She was a fine looking girl, big-breasted and voluptuous, with a mass of fair hair held above her head with twists of coarse cloth. She hummed as she stooped to pick up some dishes from the floor and the dark devilish-looking young man came up close behind her and grinned as he pushed his hips up to her taut bottom. She jumped and frowned at him. 'I have work to do, my young lord,' she said, sounding cross.

'Don't be cruel,' smiled the blond one, catching hold of the tray and pulling it out of her unprotesting hands.

41

'All the way here I told my friends how beautiful the girls at this inn are. Don't disappoint us.'

'I'll be in trouble if I'm late to the kitchen,' said Janet. But her eyes flashed as she looked at Will's golden hair and she ran her tongue significantly around her plump lips. So much for them laughing at her in the kitchen. She had not seen a better-looking pair of gallants in her whole time at the inn.

'We'll make excuses for you,' offered the dark one. 'We'll say we kept you busy.'

'I hope they won't be just excuses,' Janet said archly. She put back her shoulders expectantly and lifted her hands to her hair. As she untied it she looked around the room, wondering where the third one was; she was sure her master had said that there were three. Yes, there he was, sitting on the bed. Janet saw with a frown that he was not looking at her. He had a cup of wine between his hands and he was turning it to and fro so that the dark liquid inside it glistened in the light. All that she could see of him was a mop of heavy, glossy brown hair, falling forward to hide his face. She scowled, for she was unaccustomed to being ignored, and worked faster to release her hair. When the action started she would make this one look up, and join in too, if he was as good-looking as his friends.

Presently her hair fell onto her swelling breasts, a lion's mane of tumbling tan curls. The dark one came up behind her and took it in his hands, breathing into her ear. 'Lovely,' he whispered. 'What's your name, sweetheart?'

'Janet,' said Janet softly. 'And you, my lord?'

'George,' said the one behind her. 'Will,' said the blond one. 'And that's Geoffrey, sulking over there. Don't worry about him.'

'The more the merrier,' Janet said. The dark young man behind her, George, was breathing on her bare skin, making her come out in goosepimples. She let her head loll gently back until it lay on George's shoulder and he set his lips softly to her plump neck. He kissed her and put his arms around her, sliding his hands up the front of her body until they reached her pouting breasts. Her taut nipples were standing up through the coarse fabric of her gown and she shivered and sighed as his fingers brushed over them.

'Geoff,' said Will in a voice that was low and taut with excitement, 'Get off the bed, we'll need it.'

Geoffrey got to his feet and dashed his hand over his wounded brow. 'Don't mind me,' he said. 'I'll go and doze in the common-room.'

Janet opened her eyes to look at him, wondering if she should let him go. The sight of him made her mind up at once, for he was as fair to look on as both of the others combined, tall and broad-shouldered and slender, with a face so strong-featured and lovely that she did not want to take her eyes from him for a second. She wriggled with delight as George's dark hands pushed inside the linen shift beneath her gown and began to tease and fondle her heavy breasts. 'My lord,' she gasped, 'don't go. I'm sure there'll be room for you.'

The young man seemed to hesitate. He took a step towards the doorway as if he would leave, then stopped, staring at Janet with burning eyes. She caught her breath in excitement as the squire behind her roughly pulled down the sleeves of her gown and dragged back her white shoulders. Her breasts were thrust forward, eager and lustful, their long, dark teats begging attention. She knew that she had lovely breasts and she arched her back, offering them to the young man where he stood irresolute, half way to the door. She narrowed her eyes to dark slits of desire and could not suppress a triumphant smile as she saw that within his tight hose the lovely young man's cock was moving, swelling with lust for her as the soft sac of his testicles tautened. He swallowed thickly and put his hand to the collar of his doublet, beginning to unfasten the clasps.

Suddenly the blond one, Will, was standing between Janet and her quarry, smiling into her flushed face. 'I've only got one arm working,' he said mournfully, gesturing at his sling. 'Battle damage. You'll have to be kind to me.'

The girl looked around the room, seeing the three handsome young men converging on her, and she shivered with delicious anticipation. 'I'll be kind to you all, she said, 'I promise.'

'One after the other,' George whispered in her ear, 'or all together?'

'All together,' she gasped, her head rolling back. 'I'd like that.'

'Hot little wench,' George hissed, his breath warm on her neck. He pulled her arms behind her and tugged at her gown, coaxing it over her full white hips and off, leaving her naked. She was all curves, shoulders and breasts, belly and thighs, and the thick bush of hair between her legs was appealingly fair, just showing the tender pink lips through its glistening curls.

The three squires stood close around her, pulling at their clothing. She breathed quickly, watching with eager attention as the third one, the beautiful one, tugged off his doublet and dropped it to the floor, finished unlacing his points and with one swift movement pulled his shirt over his head. His bare torso gleamed in the light of the candles and the blazing fire, broad shouldered, lean and smooth. The muscles tightened in his flat belly as he moved towards her, dressed only in his hose, and she gasped with simple lust. She caught hold of him by his hair and pulled down his mouth to kiss her. The other two were frantically unfastening, stripping themselves. Soon they were naked and they pressed closely around Janet, pushing themselves against her. George was still behind her, rubbing his hugely erect prick up and down the cleft of her generous bottom, reaching around in front of her to tug at her nipples. Will stood in front of her, fondling between her thighs with his unbandaged hand, his fingers probing and stroking until she whimpered. And beside her stood tall Geoffrey, holding her face in both hands while he kissed her. His mouth tasted of wine and honey and sweet spices, and as they kissed her hands fumbled at his hose, pushing them down and reaching inside to find his taut cock and stroke its hard length, sighing with approval as she weighed the velvety bundle of his balls gently in her hand.

All of them were naked now, their flesh undulating and glistening in the light of the fire. Janet's hands roamed from one man to the next, feeling the heat and life of their quivering erections, her face rapt with anticipation at the thought of those three gorgeous members taking her, filling her up. The one with his arm in a sling and the one that looked like the Devil were giving her their full attention. She moaned with delight to feel their hands touching her, their mouths slipping deliciously over her warm skin. But the tall one, the one with green eyes and a cut on his brow, seemed to be only half there. This did not please Janet: it was insulting not to have him all to herself. She dug her fingers into his hair and thrust her tongue into his mouth and with her other hand fondled his stiff, quivering shaft.

'Sweetheart,' whispered Will, lifting his head from the girl's jutting breasts, 'come on, don't keep us waiting.' Janet allowed them to manoeuvre her over to the narrow bed. She let them push her where they wanted, her plump flesh shivering under their hands. 'Lie down,' said Will, and she obeyed him. He placed her round hips at the edge of the bed and spread her legs wide, pushing his hand between her thighs, approving the slick receptivity of her flushed, swollen sex. Then he grinned at his friends and said, 'Worst wound gets first choice.' He dropped to his knees between Janet's legs and took hold of his straining prick. He rubbed the dark engorged head gently against her protruding clitoris and she jerked and moaned, anxious for him to fill her. Then he frowned with concentration and thrust, sliding his stiff cock up her until he was sheathed inside her to the hilt.

Janet lifted her wide hips eagerly towards him, whispering, 'Oh, that's so good. Oh, my lord, don't spare me.' The other young men were standing on either side of her, their erections thrusting rigidly forward, begging for release. The tall one still had that far-away look: she would save the best for him. She gasped as Will slid his glistening cock vigorously in and out of her and ran her fingers up the dark one's thigh. He leant forward eagerly and she put her hands to her opulent breasts and pushed them together into a silky, welcoming mass, smiling up at him. 'Here,' she whispered, 'wouldn't you like to feel them?'

George did not hesitate, but quickly straddled her heaving body. He rubbed spittle quickly over the stiff shaft of his splendid penis and then buried it between Janet's turgid breasts, groaning deep in his throat as he felt the clinging silkiness around him. His hands pushed the ripe globes of flesh close together, embracing his pulsing shaft, and he rubbed and rubbed at her long, dark nipples.

Janet's hands were free again. She convulsed with pleasure as she felt Will penetrating her deeply and George thrusting his lovely hard prick between her aching breasts. She reached up, longing for the smooth, silken column of male flesh that stood up so proudly from the soft nest of hair in Geoffrey's groin. He came and stood over her, letting her encircle his hot shaft with her clever fingers and dip it towards her mouth. A teardrop of eagerness stood on its satiny tip and she stretched out her long tongue and delicately licked it off, delighted when he shuddered and closed his eyes. Then her lips gently framed the taut, velvety glans, and he sighed and thrust himself into her mouth as deeply as he could. She took him in willingly, flickering her tongue around the quivering head, her lips fondling the delicate ridge of skin below the glans, her hands lifted to cradle his tight balls and caress the broad base of his thick shaft. He tasted musky and wonderful. The feel of him moving in and out of her mouth filled her with sharp, abandoned pleasure. Three of them, three strong young men servicing her with their sturdy weapons, filling her sex, squeezing her breasts, thrusting into her mouth: it drove her mad with delight.

Between her legs Will was pumping into her like a rutting beast, ramming her with delirious strength, yelling in pleasure as his climax came closer and closer. The man in her mouth was moving faster too, she could hear him gasping as he drove himself towards orgasm. She yearned to feel him coming inside her mouth, squirting his seed between her willing lips. He put his hand in her tangled hair to hold her head still and she moaned with submissive ecstasy as he shoved himself deep and cried out as his penis pumped and quivered, filling her throat with salty, delicious liquid. At the same time Will gave a final desperate thrust and groaned, pushing his hot spasming shaft as far into her as he could. Janet trembled on the edge of ecstasy, penetrated and filled and almost, almost there, her body tightening and twitching as it prepared to tumble into orgasm. Then, quite suddenly, the thick penis was gone from her mouth and she gasped and whimpered with disappointment. The golden glow of pleasure moved away, leaving her empty and aching, and she moaned.

'What?' whispered a voice above her. 'Not there yet?' The devilish dark young man, George, leant forward over her and smothered her faint protests with his lips, thrusting his hot tongue deep into her mouth to taste his friend's seed. 'Nor am I,' he whispered. 'What a shame. Turn over, sweetheart.'

Turn over? Janet wondered why she should bother. Why not just put his body over hers and push himself inside her? But she did not argue, only rolled heavily onto her front, her tight nipples rubbing against the rough linen of the bed sheets.

'Not like that,' said the dark voice behind her. 'Kneel upright. Will, come and pleasure her, come on.'

Strong hands caught her by her shoulders and pulled her up, dragging back her arms so that her breasts were thrust forward. The empty air caressed them; they yearned to be touched. She sensed movement before her and opened her eyes to see the blond young man sitting down comfortably on the bed. He reached out with his unbandaged hand to slide his fingers between her spread legs and stroke her quivering clitoris, so gently and persistently that she wanted to scream.

'That's it,' said the dark voice. 'Now, sweetheart, are you wet?' There was another hand between her legs, gathering fluid from her moist lips and stroking it back and back, along the dark, secret crease between her buttocks. 'Wet and lovely,' whispered the voice as the hand returned, sliding two fingers deep inside her so that she gasped, then trailing back, smearing the creamy juices liberally around her secret passage.

Suddenly she realised what he was going to do. Yes, the very Devil, taking her up her arse like a witch! She wriggled in protest and whimpered, 'No, don't, sir, don't.' But he held her shoulders firmly and she felt the hot blind head of his thick cock prodding between her buttocks.

'No,' she whimpered again, clenching her anus to refuse him and trying to pull away. But then the young man in front of her leant forward and set his lips to one of her hard nipples, catching the rigid teat between his sharp teeth, and at the same time swiftly caressed the trembling bud of her clitoris. She gasped with the pleasure and forgot her resistance. The thick stiff phallus of the man behind her slid at once between the tight puckered lips of her bottom, forcing its way up her, impaling her with shameful directness. She shuddered as she felt him push deeper and deeper until the whole length was sheathed inside her forbidden passage, throbbing and ready.

The young man pleasuring her continued to suck and lick at her nipples and gently, gently stroke and rub her exposed clitoris. Janet's head fell back and the muscles of her buttocks clenched in sudden, furious need. The devilish figure behind her gasped as she clutched at his engorged penis where it lay deeply imbedded in her, then began to thrust. She moaned and shook as he took her. He moved slowly at first, pulling out almost entirely and then returning, penetrating her to the hilt. A terrible dark pleasure grew and grew as his stiff shaft slid in and out and eager fingers stimulated her quivering bud of pleasure. She felt her orgasm coming as if from a long way away, unstoppable, building and building within her until it broke and burst and filled her brain and her body with hot, red ecstasy. She convulsed and cried out and the man behind her forced her shoulders down onto the sheets so that her white bottom was thrust obscenely up towards him, her secret cleft glistening with her juices, open to his abuse, her buttocks clenching and shuddering in climax. He snarled with victory and plunged his ravening penis in and out of her tight silken arse with terrible strength until at last he roared and quaked with the force of his own orgasm.

After a moment he withdrew and Janet subsided slowly to the rough sheets, collapsing like a pricked balloon, sated and astonished. One of the young men came over to her with a cup of wine and held it to her swollen lips, encouraging her to drink. In a little while she managed to sit up and smile, saying cheerfully, 'Will there be anything else, my lords?'

Two of them were already rolling themselves in their cloaks, ready for sleep. The tall one was standing leaning on the fireplace, the jumping red light illuminating his beautiful body. He glanced at her as if he was very weary and shook his head.

'I can stay the night if you like,' Janet offered, wanting to hear him speak. But he only shook his head again and then looked down into the fire. The flames flickered in his bright eyes. Janet shrugged, then picked up her shift and gown and wrestled them on, feeling her flesh still tender and trembling with the remains of her pleasure. She gathered the dishes onto the tray and went to the door, already imagining what she would tell the girls in the kitchen and how jealous they would be.

* * *

Geoffrey heard the door shut and turned his head slowly to look around the room. His friends were already asleep, breathing heavily, flushed and sated with wine and sex. He rubbed his hand over his face, remembering. As he thrust his eager cock deep into the kitchen-girl's willing mouth he had thought of Lady de Verney, of her red lips, of the lifting swell of her white breasts above her scarlet gown.

What could one man do to protect her? But he could not live with himself if he did nothing to try to save her from whatever danger it was that made her face grow as pale as linen and her breathing quicken. Geoffrey's mouth set with decision and he reached for his clothes, dressing swiftly. His friends did not stir. They misunderstood him: they would believe that he had gone for lust only, because he wanted to have the lady. They could not be more wrong. He would go alone to save her from whatever nameless evil threatened her, and he would go as pure as Sir Galahad, single-handedly redressing Sir Thomas's insult to chivalry.

He rummaged in his saddlebags for a scrap of paper and a quill and wrote, 'Tell my lord I have gone back. Don't wait. G.' He looked around for a moment in puzzlement, wondering where he could put the message, then smiled. He stooped down and tucked the scrap of paper into Will's sling. Then, with a final look around the little firelit room, he went swiftly to the door and out into the night.

Chapter Three

*R*osamund lay alone in her broad bed, shivering a little between the cold sheets. Tears hovered on the edge of every breath. She had never felt so helpless and afraid. Her husband was dead, killed on some remote battlefield, and with him the men who should have returned to de Verney Manor to keep it safe from attack. Rosamund knew how fast ill tidings travel. Before the day was out she was sure that Sir Ralph Aycliffe would have heard the news and be readying his troops of ruffians to attack her home.

She could not keep her mind from thoughts of Sir Ralph. She knew more of him than she had done when he had grappled with her at Isabella's wedding feast. Everybody in the neighbourhood knew and feared him. He lived unmarried in a castle, not a manor house, an old place, high ceilinged and damp. Those who spoke of him said in whispers that he kept the stone walls of his fortress well stocked with whores of both sexes who satisfied his disgraceful, gargantuan appetites in ways that had always been unclear to Rosamund. And Margery had said that he was a formidable lover, massively equipped.

Rosamund turned and twisted on the slick sheets, wishing that Margery was in the room. But her maid had made some feeble excuse and vanished, no doubt heading for a quiet corner where she could again be serviced by the ever-eager Matthew. Rosamund covered her face with her hands, trying to shut out the sight she had seen that morning, the thick stem of Matthew's flesh driving deep into Margery while the girl writhed and cried out. Perhaps, said Rosamund's fervid mind, perhaps Sir Ralph would come and take the manor and would do that to her, hold her down and spread her pale thighs and lie between them, crushing her with his weight, penetrating her with his great male member.

'No,' she said to herself, hopelessly trying to close her mind against these shameful thoughts. 'No.' She lay suddenly still as she heard the striking-clock in the manor hall cough and chime the hour: eleven. Eleven of the clock on a winter's night! No decent woman should be awake at such a time, let alone wriggling like a worm in her cold bed, wishing for a man.

A man. Suddenly Rosamund lay still, her dark eyes gazing unseeing up at the heavy canopy of her bed. She thought no more about Sir Ralph, but about the young man she had seen that day in the train of the lord who had come to her with such terrible news. She remembered how she had felt his eyes on her and how when she had turned to look at him his beauty had struck her like a physical blow, robbing her breathing so that she gasped.

She pictured him now, painting his portrait in the shadows of the bed. Tall on his horse, lean and broad-shouldered, with strong arms unconsciously flexing as he held in his curvetting mount. His face, clean-boned beneath a shading of dark stubble, with lips whose perfection of cut would rival many a woman's and bright glittering eyes beneath his wonderful sweeping brows. Such beauty, made more piquant by the jagged scab on his forehead beneath his heavy ash-brown hair and the dark bruise down one cheek. Who had dared to hurt him, she wondered, feeling fiercely protective.

And she had touched him, laid her hand on the hard

muscle of his lean thigh. She had meant no more than to get his attention, but she could remember exactly how it had felt to touch that warm hard flesh above the leather of his boot and feel his thickening penis pulsing beneath her fingers, knowing as she looked up into his brilliant eyes that it was for her that the blood throbbed and leaped, for her that the spongy flesh swelled to iron hardness. His clear eyes could not have lied to her.

He had leant towards her, his eyes brighter than emeralds. He had not spoken, but the heat of his expression and the hunger of his parted lips had told their own story. He had meant to kiss her. She caught her lower lip in her teeth, imagining how it would have felt if he had kissed her in truth. His beautiful mouth would have been as soft as down, as sweet as spun sugar. As he pressed his perfect lips on hers she would feel the delicate prickle of his two days' beard, sharp and delicious against her tender skin.

Rosamund had never in her life touched herself lasciviously, but now she could not stop. She turned her head on the pillow, arching her neck as if she reached up for a kiss, and slid her white hands down her long throat and onto her breast, pushing open the neck of her nightgown. The skin of her breasts tautened with eagerness and she lifted their full roundness into her hands, squeezing, weighing. Her hands were his, the beautiful young squire's, and she whispered softly, 'Kiss me, sweetheart, kiss me,' as she imagined his face hanging over hers, waiting. Yes, he would kiss her, his tongue in her mouth, his hands chafing at her aching breasts, and his long body would press against her, close and hard. How would it feel? Would he be heavy? Would she sigh to feel his weight above her, pressing down upon her?

Her delicate hands lifted the hem of her linen gown, exposing her naked thighs and the soft, yearning flesh between them. She ran her tongue over her lips, frowning in concentration as she delicately parted the moist folds of her sex with one trembling finger, trying to discover the little bud that had throbbed and leapt beneath Margery's delicious, searching tongue.

A shudder of pleasure ran through her as she found the spot. With one hand she softly drew back the folds of flesh around it, exposing the stiff peak and shivering with pleasure as the cold air kissed it. Then with the utmost gentleness she stroked the tiny shaft and whimpered with the surge of bliss that ran through her limbs.

The young squire would do this. He would spread her white thighs and lie between them, flickering his tongue over her secret parts, moistening them with his saliva, sucking and licking so that she moaned with joy. Would a man do that to a woman? Yes, of course he would: he was her dream. He would caress her with his mouth until she was limp and helpless, melting beneath his touch. Then he would lift himself over her and open her legs wide and push himself inside her, stretching her so wonderfully with the thick hot rod of flesh that she had felt beneath his tight hose. It would be bliss, sweet ecstasy, a Heaven of pleasure.

She gasped as she touched herself and unconsciously her hips began to move, lifting her juicy sex towards her searching fingers. Both hands were busy now between her parted thighs, stroking and touching, and with a sudden spasm of excitement she thrust first one finger then two into her slippery tunnel, pushing them deep and then withdrawing them, trying to imitate the thrusting movement of a man's body.

As she did so the images that filled her mind changed. The ardent tender lover evaporated and in his place was a faceless figure, sturdy and strong. It laughed to see her afraid and caught at her flailing arms and held them down, pinning both of her wrists above her head with one big square hand so that the other was free to run over her quailing body, pinching her nipples, driving three strong fingers up between her legs so roughly that she cried out. She struggled and writhed, but she could not escape. The dark figure leant over, lowering its shadowed head, and set its strong white teeth to the soft skin of her neck, biting so hard that she wailed in pain and bitter delight. She drove her fingers deeper and deeper into her wet hungry flesh as she imagined that faceless body wrestling her down, holding her helpless with its effortless power. He would ravish her, impale her on the fierce blunt spear of his flesh and thrust it deep into her again and again until she died, quivered and cried out and died from dark aching pleasure.

'Ah, God,' Rosamund whispered, her head thrashing from side to side as her fingers worked desperately between her legs. She imagined over and over again the helpless, delicious abandonment of feeling herself utterly conquered, subdued, taken and defiled. The strong, heavy body would drive into her, arching as it thrust, and at last, at last, she imagined the sharp white teeth gripping the nape of her neck while the muscular buttocks tensed and hollowed and shook as her faceless possessor spent himself inside her. She heard his groan, a cry of desperate release, and she cried out herself, helplessly, her fingers sunk deep into the moist juicy flesh that gripped them as she spun into shuddering orgasm.

Afterwards she lay very still for a few minutes, shaken and frightened by the ferocity of her own fantasy. How could she dream of force and savagery, of rape? She was exhausted but too afraid to sleep, and she clutched the pillow close against her and shivered. Then the image of the young squire returned to her: he leant over her, strong and gentle, stroking her shoulders with his big long-fingered hands and whispering soft comfort in her ears. She held the pillow tightly, as if it could return her love, and smiled a little. She had heard his voice and she knew it was like him, firm and strong, tender and beautiful. She closed her eyes tightly, imagining his kind hands, his soft voice, soothing away all her fear and the violence of her pleasure, and soon she was asleep.

She slept sweetly, but woke to worry and trouble. Her husband had taken all the manor's best men to fight for the duke of York and with them most of their store of weapons and gear. Now she sent what men there were scurrying here and there to look for bows and spears, but with little hope of success. The people were afraid, and one by one the peasants who worked on the manor farm slipped away towards their own homes.

Just before noon she stood with her husband's aged steward in the hall of the manor, looking unhappily at the meagre pile of weapons which they had gathered. The steward wept as he stood: he had served the lord Lionel since he was a child, and could not believe that his friend and master of so many years would never return to the manor.

'Hugo,' Rosamund said gently, trying not to sound exasperated, 'surely there must be more? This cannot be all?'

Hugo shook his head mournfully. 'If there is, madam, it is hidden from me.'

'We cannot defend ourselves with this,' whispered Rosamund, shaking her head. 'If he comes what shall I do? Shall I surrender the manor to him?'

'Surrender it?' repeated Hugo, staring. 'My lady, you could not. You would not. Surrender de Verney manor to that wolf's head? We should fight him to the last drop of our blood.' And the pathetic handful of Lionel's men who remained to her, the old and infirm, those who had not been fit enough to serve Lord de Verney in arms, all nodded their heads and muttered, 'Ay, ay.'

'You're all mad,' exclaimed Margery, clutching a cloak tightly around her as if it could protect her against Aycliffe's attack. 'A bunch of old men and cripples to hold off that devil? He'll lay us all out in the time it takes to say the *Ave!* We should run as fast and as far as we can and leave this manor to him, if that's what he wants!'

'Shut your mouth, you impudent quean,' snapped Hugo, rounding furiously on Margery. 'What do you know?' He turned again to Rosamund, saying urgently, 'My lady, remember your lord. Do him justice, my lady. Remember his will.'

'His will,' Rosamund repeated. Hugo had shown her

the will that morning, stained with his tears. It had astonished her. Lionel had little family, but she had expected him to leave his lands within it. Far from it. He had left everything he possessed, land, money and jewels, to: 'my faithful wife, the lady Rosamund, who has never given me one moment's cause to regret my marriage to her: that she may live in comfort with a husband who is better suited to her.' Remembering the words, Rosamund felt tears stinging her eyes too. Lionel must have loved her, and his generosity to her in death pierced her as sharply as a spear. She swallowed hard and said resolutely, 'Hugo, don't fear. I will not give up the manor without a fight.'

Hugo smiled sadly and opened his mouth to reply, then broke off as Matthew hobbled swiftly into the hall. 'My lady,' he called, 'a soldier is coming up the road.'

'A soldier? One?' Rosamund darted to the heap of gear and caught up a crossbow, which she tossed to Matthew. 'Wind that, Matthew. Follow me out. Perhaps he is one of my lord's men returned.' She did not dare to give voice to the alternatives. She ran to the great front door of the manor, which stood open to the cold winter air, and out onto the gravel.

One rider came towards her, a tall man on a good horse, wearing a heavy cloak that was drawn up around his face. Rosamund said quickly, 'Matthew, come here, stand by me.' She raised her voice. 'Who are you?' she demanded. 'What is your business here? Show yourself!'

The rider pulled his horse to a stop and pushed back his cloak. Rosamund's lips parted and she gazed in disbelief into the beautiful face of her dream. The squire said nothing, only looked into her eyes. His face was rapt, ecstatic as a martyr's, pale as an ivory statue set with jewels for eyes beneath the heavy swathe of his shining hair. For long moments there was silence. Then his perfect lips opened and he said in his tender caressing voice, 'My Lady de Verney, I have come to do you what service I can. I could not stand by and see you abandoned.' He smiled, a glinting smile like the sun through leaves. 'I would not have expected to find a lady challenging visitors herself,' he said.

Rosamund could not keep herself from glancing beyond the young squire's shoulder, hoping against hope that others had come with him. He caught the movement of her eyes and his head turned slightly. His smile became rueful and said, 'No, alas, my lady. I am alone. But what one poor pair of hands can do for you, that I will gladly do.'

'Thank you,' Rosamund whispered. She could almost have laughed: what could one man do to stem the tide of violence that Sir Ralph would pour against de Verney manor once the news of Lionel's death was known? But to come alone, offering himself for her, was so quixotic that it wrung her heart. All her fear and misery drained away from her as she stood looking up into his face, lost in the glittering brilliance of his eyes, knowing nothing but that he had returned for her.

After a long moment he said diffidently, 'My lady, will one of your people show me where I can stable my horse? He's tired, I set off to ride back here almost as soon as we stopped for the night.'

'Oh,' exclaimed Rosamund, startled back to courtesy with a speed that was almost comic. 'Oh yes, of course. Matthew, take Master – Master – ' She broke off, looking up at him now with a disbelieving smile. 'Sir, I am sorry, but I do not know your name.'

'Lymington,' said the squire, smiling brilliantly back at her. 'Geoffrey Lymington, my lady, and your most humble servant.'

'Matthew,' said Rosamund, 'take Master Lymington's horse to the stables. Master Lymington, will you come inside? Will you take refreshment?'

The young man swung down off his tall horse with thoughtless, animal grace. Rosamund could not take her eyes from him. 'That would be most welcome,' he said. 'I have not eaten since last night.' He walked towards her and she stood very still, feeling his approach tingling in her blood and bones. He had leant forward from his horse to kiss her and the hot flesh of his phallus had been hard with desire for her. He would teach her, he would show her the way of love, take her hand and guide her gently along the paths of the garden of delight. She almost expected him to stoop then and there and wrap her in his strong arms and kiss her.

He did no such thing. He made her a very proper bow, sweeping off his smart velvet bonnet, and then straightened and looked at her almost apprehensively. 'Perhaps, my lady,' he said, 'while I eat, you could explain to me the danger you face.'

She took a step back, astonished. He sounded cool, restrained, proper, and not in the least like a lover. She felt rebuked. 'Of course,' she said, putting her hand to her cheek. She was flushed: blood hung beneath her white skin, a mark of shame. 'I will tell you all I can.'

They went towards the door and he bowed again to her, indicating that she should pass through it before him. So correct, so calm. Could he not sense the excitement that raced through her just to see him standing by her? Was he immune to her? Why had he returned, if he did not desire her? Had she been mistaken?

All through the remainder of that day she sought an answer to her questions and found none. Geoffrey Lymington behaved as though he were a hired mercenary captain: he toured the manor to discover how it might best be defended, examined and tested the available stock of weapons, encouraged the men. But to her he was as proper as a monk, not showing by look or touch what he felt for her. Or did not feel.

But his face, his face, when he put back his cloak and revealed himself: spellbound, elevated, glowing. He must care for her. She did not understand why he would not show his feelings, but perhaps he had his reasons. If only they had more time, time to fall in love as men and women had always done.

If only. But they had no time. Before the early dark had closed down upon the countryside with frost and sleet one of the de Verney tenants arrived at the manor, terrified, bearing the news that Sir Ralph Aycliffe was risen in arms and would doubtless descend upon them the very next day.

When the man had gone Rosamund sat very still in the lord's chair in the great hall, trying to prevent her hands from twisting before her and revealing her fear. Hugo stood beside her, looking at the tall figure of Master Lymington as though he alone carried the hope of safety. There was a long silence.

'So,' Rosamund said at last, 'we will not have to wait long, then.'

Master Lymington pushed his right hand wearily through his thatch of shining hair, then rubbed his scabbed brow. He was pale and there were long blue streaks under his eyes. 'Well, my lady,' he said with a sigh, 'I believe that we have done all we can. There is no time to build defences here, no time at all. We shall have to face them with what we have. I know your men know what to do and that they will all do their best.' He glanced around the hall and the remnants of Lionel's household watched him eagerly, nodding. None of them had murmured at taking instruction from a man who could barely be five and twenty. They were all only too pleased to have a soldier of any sort come among them. 'As for me,' said Master Lymington, 'I did not sleep last night, and I am dog-weary. Show me a place where I can lay my head, and I will sleep till the morning and be better for it.'

'Sleep?' repeated Rosamund wretchedly. It was barely six of the clock and she had hoped for his company for a good while yet. Then she registered the strain and fatigue on his white face and shook her head at her own thoughtlessness. 'Of course,' she said, 'of course. I am very sorry not to have thought of it before. A room is prepared for you, Master Lymington.' *Geoffrey*, said her desire. *Geoffrey*. 'Shall I show you there?'

'You are very kind,' he said, and heaved himself to his feet to follow her from the hall and through the corridors to the best guest chamber.

'By the Rood,' he said, looking about him with big eyes, 'here's splendour! I have never had such a fine chamber to myself in my life. I am more used to sleeping at the foot of my lord's bed, or on a pallet in the hall. I shall hardly know what to do with myself.'

'I hope you will be comfortable,' Rosamund said. She wanted now to tell him that she thought he was beautiful, that she desired him, that she had dreamed of him, that he had saved her from the terrors of her own imagination. But she did not know how. Instead she said softly, 'Master Lymington, thank you for coming to help me. I am more grateful than I can say.'

Suddenly his eyes glowed at her. He came forward and caught her hand in his, stooping over it and setting his lips to the tips of her fingers, as chaste a kiss as could be imagined. 'My lady,' he murmured, and just for a second he set the back of her hand to his cheek. She had barely time to feel the velvety stubble beneath her fingers before he had pressed them again to his lips and lowered them, looking into her eyes. 'Good night,' he said softly.

She was dismissed, there could be no mistaking it. She ached to take him in her arms, but his correctness infected her and she merely dropped him a little curtsey and turned away.

Later, in her cold bed, she wept. Margery hung over her, little hands clinging to her shoulders, whispering into her ear. 'My lady, my lady, don't weep. If he doesn't fancy you, why in Heaven's name did he come?'

'But what can I do?' Rosamund wept. 'What can I do? Tomorrow Sir Ralph will come and we will all be killed. There is only tonight.'

'Go to him, then,' suggested Margery.

Rosamund suddenly became very still in her arms. She turned and looked up into Margery's face, her eyes wide and dark in the light of the candles. 'Go to him?' she repeated hesitantly.

'Go to him! Go to his chamber! My lady, it is the middle of the night and you have not slept. What man would resist you if you went to him? He will fall at your feet, see if he does not. Go!'

She went, wrapped in a robe of thick wool the colour of curded cream, carrying a candle shielded in her hand, her naked feet silent on the floorboards. Her heavy chestnut-coloured hair was spread over her shoulders like a cloak. It was cold in the corridors of the house, but it was not the cold that made her shiver. She stood outside the closed door of the guest-chamber for some time, listening to the pounding of her heart, wondering if she dared set her fingers to the latch. He would be asleep, his white eyelids lowered over his brilliant eyes, his lips softened with slumber. Rosamund stared into the blue heart of the crocus flame of the candle, her pupils contracting to pinpoints. Behind her, in the shadows of the hall, the striking clock sounded midnight.

The chimes seemed to go on forever. When they had died away into muffled echoes and then into silence Rosamund set her fingers to the latch and lifted it noiselessly, stalking step by delicate step into the chamber where her heart's desire lay.

The candle cast a glowing pool of light around her, but the room was not entirely dark. The banked-down fire burned with a warm, ruddy light, and through the half-closed shutters a pale winter moon was peering. Red and blue light mingled on the white planks of the floor and cast a confusion of coloured shadows onto the damask curtains which hung the great bed. She seemed now to have passed beyond fear. She walked steadily and in silence to stand beside the pillow and she lowered the candle and placed it soundlessly on the little table by the bed. The light shivered and then burned up with a clear flame, driving back the darkness within the heavy curtains.

He was fast asleep, turned away from her and almost invisible beneath the heavy covers of the bed. She could see his glossy hair and his left hand spread out upon the white pillow. It was a big hand, long-fingered, with strong flat knuckles and blue veins pencilled between fingers and wrist. His other hand and arm were thrust beneath the pillow like a sleeping child's. His slow steady breathing whispered in and out, lifting and lowering the covers as his lungs filled and emptied.

She stood for some time watching him. Her stomach wrung with helpless, empty desire. She longed to hold him, to run her fingers through that heavy mop of hair, to feel his long-fingered hands touching her in return. It seemed almost impossible that he should continue to sleep while waves of emotion flowed from her towards him, but he did not stir. Rosamund imagined herself waking him. He would roll over in the bed and look up at her with wide, sleepy, astonished eyes, then whisper her name and hold out his hands to her. She saw herself sinking into his arms, her face turned up to receive his eager kisses, her eyes closing in rapture.

Under her steady gaze the young squire lay still. He was dreaming. His breath faltered and he muttered to himself, then let out a heavy sigh. The long fingers on the pillow tensed, gripping at the smooth linen, and then relaxed. Rosamund let out a long breath of decision and slowly stretched out one hand to touch his shoulder.

For a moment he did not move or seem to wake. Then, all at once, he was up from the bed, naked in the candlelight, moving as swiftly and fluidly as a pouncing cat. Something flashed and then strong hands gripped Rosamund's shoulders and dragged them back and she gasped in shock as a sharp point pricked her throat.

For a moment she felt nothing but astonished fear. Then she realised that the brightness at her throat was Geoffrey Lymington's dagger. Then, even as the knowledge filled her brain with cold coiling dread, he released her, pushing her away from him, pulling the naked blade from her throat with an exclamation of horror. She staggered then drew herself upright, clutching the post at the foot of the bed and staring into his face.

He was quite white and the pupils of his eyes were wide and black, so wide that the green iris was no more than a glittering ring. 'Holy Jesu!' he hissed, with the fury of fear. 'God's death, my lady, do you not know better than to creep up on a soldier? I could have hurt you!'

Rosamund was too frightened to reply. She stood shaking her head, breathing raggedly. His face changed, filling with remorse. 'I am sorry,' he said, a little more calmly now. 'I am so sorry, my lady. The room – the place – strange to me – I – '

Still she could not gather her wits sufficiently to reply. She put her hand to her throat, feeling the place where the dagger had touched her skin. A sting of pain made her wince and she drew her hand away and stared in disbelief at a single bead of bright blood, like a ruby.

'I have hurt you! My lady, in the Virgin's name, you know I – '

He fell silent. She lifted her eyes to look at him and for the first time registered his nakedness. Her eyes flashed up and down his body, in one glance seeing all of his beauty, hesitating infinitesimally as they rested on the dark arrowhead of curling hair in his groin where his penis hung softly over the dangling pouch of his testicles. She looked back at his face. Her breathing slowed and very slowly her hand clenched into a fist. Geoffrey stood for a moment puzzled and staring, then he took a quick shocked breath and grabbed for the cover of the bed. He pulled the glossy fabric across him to hide his groin and flushed scarlet as he did so.

Still his torso was naked and Rosamund felt desire begin to return, stalking into her as her eyes passed slowly over his bare broad shoulders, gracefully clothed with strong muscle, the lifting cage of his lean ribs, his taut, ridged abdomen. The flat plane of his diaphragm below his ribs rose and fell, catching the light as he breathed. Her throat tightened and a shiver ran between her shoulder-blades, chilling her with icy yearning. But what could she say to him? She gazed, and was silent.

Geoffrey caught his lower lip between his teeth, shifting his feet awkwardly on the bare floorboards. 'My lady,' he said at last, 'why are you here? What is the matter? Are they coming?'

With a question to answer she could speak. 'No,' she said. 'No, there is no danger.'

'So,' he insisted, 'why are you here?'

His arched brows were drawn down tightly over his glittering eyes. He frowned as if he could not believe why any lady should come all alone to a gentleman's room. Surely, surely to God, he must want her? Why was he making her ask? Rosamund had not considered the possibility that explanations might be necessary. She had not thought of what she could say. In her imagination he had opened his arms to her wordlessly and their kisses were their eloquence.

He was still looking at her in helpless confusion, he really wanted an answer. She sought her vocabulary and found no inspiration. 'I wanted,' she began, hesitated, and then blurted out, 'I wanted you to swive me.'

The moment the word was past her lips she knew it was wrong: crude, coarse, inappropriate. She clamped her hand at once across her offending mouth as if her fingers could snatch the word back out of the air, but it was too late. The damage was done. She gazed at Geoffrey over her smothering hand, appalled.

His face changed at once. The nervousness and apprehension left it and it hardened, becoming cold and severe. He set his jaw and his nostrils flared as if he winded some unpleasant odour. There was no hint of tenderness left in his expression. He flung back his head and laughed, a cold, unpleasant laugh. 'Is that all?' he asked the rafters. 'Is that all you want?' He flung aside the bedcover and walked naked towards her, smiling bitterly. 'My Lady de Verney, as I have said, I am your most humble and obedient servant.'

Rosamund took a step back, afraid of his sudden chilly energy. Not even his splendid nakedness attracted her now. She opened her mouth to explain that she had not meant it, not that word, that she had meant – But before the first sound escaped her he pounced, catching her by

65

her arms and pulling her towards him. She gasped and he caught hold of the fronts of her robe and made as if he would tug it open. 'No!' Rosamund cried, not understanding his sudden violence, and she caught the robe from his hands and tore herself away.

'Come, come, my lady,' he said through his teeth, 'don't be coy. That won't get you what you *want*.' And he reached out again and seized the creamy wool and dragged it apart to reveal Rosamund's full white breasts.

She hung from his hands, trembling, her eyes tightly shut. He stared down at her naked flesh, his lips parted, breathing shallowly. Before his eyes her coral nipples erected, stiff with cold and shame. 'Christ Jesu,' he whispered, as if the treasures of the Orient were suddenly poured into his hands. He was still for so long that at last Rosamund opened her eyes, risking a glance at him. His chest was rising and falling with his breathing and in his loins, in the dark triangle of his groin, his phallus was rearing into proud, eager life. Rosamund watched, fascinated, as the pillar of flesh lifted and grew and swelled, the pale skin darkening with the rush of blood and drawing back and back from the purpling tip. It was beautiful. Even in her fear she yearned for it.

'Please,' she whispered, licking her dry lips with the tip of her tongue. 'Geoffrey, please.'

His eyes lifted to her face and he seemed suddenly furious. 'Please?' he repeated mockingly. 'Please? Oh, forgive me, my lady, if I am slow to obey you!'

'No,' she protested, 'I didn't mean – ' But he dragged her towards him, pushing the sleeves of her gown fiercely down her white arms so that they were pinned behind her, her naked breasts jutting lustfully forward. He laughed and put one big hand over her breast, trapping the hard nipple beneath his palm and chafing it roughly. 'No,' Rosamund tried again, writhing, 'no, please – '

'It is too late to change your mind,' he hissed into her face, and then his mouth descended on hers. His lips should have been soft, but they delivered his kiss with

66

such controlled ferocity that they might have been made of steel. She gasped as his hot tongue probed her mouth, thrusting without compunction between her lips. The plush roughness of his three days' beard scrubbed at her tender cheek, hurting her and stinging her with pleasure. She gave one desperate heave, trying to free herself from his iron grip, and then moaned and submitted, hanging limply in his grasp as he consumed her with his hungry mouth and crushed her aching breast beneath his hand.

He tugged her roughly to the bed and flung her onto it. Before she could find her balance and push herself up he hurled himself on her, pinning her down with his strong, lean body. One hand caught at her thigh, pulling it to one side, opening her to his assault. She whimpered, 'No,' and tried to drag herself away, but he drove his hips between her open thighs and caught at her wrists, pulling them above her head. She tried to pull free, tried again, but he was too strong for her. She gave a little whimper of desperation and he smiled and held her helpless.

There was a long moment of stillness. Rosamund lay gasping, staring up into Geoffrey's bright, fierce eyes, and as her breath heaved in and out so her breasts lifted and fell, rubbing her tight nipples against the hard plane of his chest. Between her legs his swollen penis waited, hard and ready, nudging against the moist lips of her sex.

He took one hand from her wrists, holding her securely with the other. His hand moved down to her body and cupped one full breast, weighing and approving it. He caught the dark tip between finger and thumb and squeezed experimentally. Rosamund winced and turned her head aside, closing her eyes as cold tendrils of sensation radiated from the little point of flesh. He squeezed again, watching her reaction, and then his hand continued unhurriedly down her body, stroking the soft swell of her belly, and his long agile fingers began to explore the dark curls of hair that clothed her pubis. She gave a little cry, not knowing herself whether she was petrified with fear or with lust.

His fingers slipped between her thighs and gently, softly, traced the lips of her wet, swollen sex. A long sigh escaped Rosamund's loosened lips and the muscles of her vagina clenched tight with sudden want. Her head fell back, exposing her long white throat. Now his weight above her was not frightening but wondrous, his strong hands were tools of her delight, she lay powerless and desperate and aching for him.

'You are wet,' he murmured. His voice was thick with lust. 'Wet as a river. You are ready for me.'

And he took her. He placed the hot swollen head of his cock precisely between the moist, eager lips. Then he reached up and caught hold of her white wrists and pulled her arms wide apart, holding them there like one crucified so that her breasts were lifted high and offered to his gaze. He stared down into her face as his tight flanks hollowed and he thrust slow and firm and pushed the whole length of his stiff, rampant penis into her snug, aching tunnel.

Rosamund's eyes opened wide and her lips parted and she breathed in great gasps as if she was smothering. He was penetrating her, possessing her, and it was bliss such as she had never imagined. She could not move, her wrists were pinioned by his strong hands and her body was trapped beneath his delicious male weight, and there was nothing but ecstasy.

'You wanted me to swive you,' he hissed, withdrawing from her and thrusting again, harder this time. The thick shaft slid back into her all at once, making her grunt with shock and pleasure. 'You wanted to be swived, my *lady*.' Again he thrust and filled her, and this time a moan escaped her shaking lips. Even the bitterness of his words could not detract from her pleasure. 'Your wish is my command. I will swive you until you beg for mercy.' And he began a steady, driving rhythm, breathing in hot pants as he pushed himself in and out of her. Sensation pooled in her loins and began to spread, cold between her shoulders and on the points of her breasts, hot on her throat and in her belly. Her body juddered as he rammed her. The hard, hairy base of his penis rubbed against her clitoris and it swelled and flushed, and as the stimulus went on and on so she began to groan in time with his movements. Her eyes were still open, gazing up at his face. He was frowning, concentrating on the approaching moment, his eyes closed tightly and his lips drawn back from his teeth. He looked beautiful and remote and angry. Her lips were dry with her panting and she was crying out now with urgency, trying to lift her round hips to accept his thrusts, gasping as he shafted her remorselessly. Every time he withdrew from her she whimpered with grief, then cried out in joy and triumph as his thick rod filled her again.

'Oh,' she cried, writhing under his restraining hands, 'oh, oh, Jesu have mercy.'

'Only I can have mercy on you,' he hissed, never slackening the pace of his urgent movements. 'And I will not, my *lady*, I will not spare you, I will swive you until I see you die beneath me.' He thrust harder still, more sharply, and she groaned with the pleasure and the pain. 'Do you feel me?' he demanded. 'Do you?'

'I feel you,' she moaned, her head thrashing from side to side. The sensation was growing, mounting within her in a crescent wave of bliss. 'My lord, my lord, I feel you, oh God in Heaven, I feel you.' Her hips bucked beneath him as if she would draw him into the very centre of her. Hot red pleasure possessed her and she writhed as her whole body succumbed to the throes of orgasm. 'Oh God, oh, oh – '

Her eyes rolled back and a long, wavering cry of ecstasy hung on her lips. Geoffrey made a noise like a beast in pain and gave one last, convulsive thrust, forcing himself up into the very heart of her. He let go of her wrists and fell on her, his heaving chest crushing her breasts, his hot breath scalding the hollow of her shoulder. They lay together very still, breathing in quick shallow gasps, sweat shining on their exhausted limbs.

Then, suddenly, Geoffrey withdrew and pulled away, sitting upright on the bed with his back turned to her. She lifted her head and made a little sound of protest, narrowing her eyes to peer through the mist of pleasure that hazed them. His back was beautiful, tapering from broad shoulders to narrow waist, the deep furrow of his spine like a line drawn in snow. His head was bowed. She said softly, 'Geoffrey?'

He did not lift his head. 'And do you welcome all guests to de Verney manor so warmly?' he asked, and his voice was thin and cold.

She was still with shock. Then, without a word, she slipped from the high bed to the floor. Her legs were shaky, but she stood firm as she pulled her gown back around herself. After a moment he lifted his head and looked at her, a wary, puzzled look.

'You take me for a whore,' Rosamund said evenly. He flinched, but he did not deny it. She felt very weary and old, as if all her illusions had been stripped from her with her modesty. Soon she would weep: but not before him. 'You are mistaken,' she said, and her voice sounded tired. 'I expressed myself badly. A whore would have had more subtlety, do you not think?'

He did not speak, only frowned. Rosamund drew a long, deep breath and said, 'Sir, I swear to you that no man has known me before except my husband.' Then she turned and went towards the door. She felt quite empty. She had known physical rapture, but his coldness had turned it to bitterness. She suddenly hoped that she would die on the morrow, rather than live with memories so blighted.

Before she reached the door his footsteps were behind her, quick and quiet. He caught her shoulders in his hands, holding her back, and turned her to face him. She allowed it, and stood still with her eyes closed and her heart aching. From behind the screen of her closed lids she heard his voice, hesitant, trembling a little. 'My lady,

70

I – ' He broke off. 'Tell me your name,' he said, and his voice shook.

She opened her eyes and looked into his face. He looked like a boy, young and defenceless, as if she had hurt him rather than he her. His beauty robbed her of words. She clenched her hand before her breast and made herself speak. 'Rosamund,' she whispered.

'Rosamund,' he breathed. He lifted one shaking hand and touched her cheek, then laid his fingers briefly to the tiny scab on her white neck where his dagger had touched her. His face contracted in a spasm of regret and shame. 'I am so sorry,' he said, soft as a breath, his eyes lowered. 'I have done everything wrong.' He lifted his eyes to hers. They were glittering and bright in the faint light of the candle, of the smouldering fire and the winter moon. 'I, I wanted you so much. You know I did, we both felt it. But I thought you were a virtuous lady. I came back to help you, not to lie with you. It would have been wrong to suggest anything . . .' He shook his head, gazing into her face with transparent earnestness. 'It was so difficult,' he went on uncertainly. 'I made myself cold. I didn't want to shock you, to shame you. And then, then, to hear you say that, that word – I thought I had been mistaken in you. I thought you had made a fool of me. I was angry.' He looked once more into her eyes, and then his head fell. 'I'm sorry,' he repeated. 'I don't expect you to forgive me.'

Her anger melted at the sight of his contrition. She managed a wan smile. 'It's not all your fault,' she offered. 'I surprised you; and then I used the wrong word, did I not?'

He nodded, still looking into her eyes. She was very conscious of his closeness, of the warmth emanating from his naked skin. 'But I was angry,' he said. 'I was so rough with you. I must have hurt you. And I meant to be chivalrous!' He gave a little bitter laugh and shook his head. '*A verray parfit gentil knight*,' he quoted ironically. 'You may be an apprentice in the art of love, my lady, but I am not. I should have known better.'

Rosamund lowered her head. He sounded as if all was lost. 'Well,' she said at last, 'you did not hurt me. I do forgive you, Master Lymington.'

'Geoffrey,' he said softly. 'Geoffrey, my lady. You used my name before, don't stop.' His voice was suddenly warm, caressing and tender, and Rosamund felt a tiny glow of hope warming her heart. She looked up into his face and her stomach curled and softened as if the brightness of his eyes were melting her like warm honey. He lifted his hand to her cheek again, a touch of feathery lightness. 'Don't go,' he whispered. 'Don't go yet.'

She leaned her cheek into his palm, closing her eyes and letting out her breath in a soft sigh of bliss. For a moment he stroked her white skin with his strong fingers. Then he cupped her chin in his hand and turned it towards him. She opened her eyes and looked at his beautiful face hanging above her, gazing down at her, and an overwhelming sense of peace and contentment possessed her as she realised that he was about to kiss her and that his eyes were glowing with desire. She parted her lips and stretched her long throat up and he lowered his head and placed his mouth on hers, gently, so gently.

Her dream was true. His lips were softer than rose petals, sweeter than wine, and his strong searching tongue was smooth as cream. The hot, dark pleasure that had consumed her as he took her retreated, shrinking into insignificance beneath the delicate, sensual rapture of their kiss. She sighed with bliss and opened herself to him, savouring the exquisite sensation as he explored her mouth, tasting the inside of her soft lips, inviting her hesitant tongue to twine around his, stabbing deeply into her throat so that she gasped. She lifted her hands and placed them around his back, sweeping them across his silken skin, feeling the hard bone and the strong muscle beneath it, the points of his shoulders, the delicious hollow of his spine. Her robe fell open and their naked bodies pressed together, breast to breast. He wrapped his arms around her, his big, strong hands pressing between her shoulders and cupping the swell of her buttocks, holding her close.

They kissed until she lost all sense of time, until her head was spinning and her knees were weak with ecstasy. At some point he lifted his mouth from hers and kissed her closed eyelids, her cheeks, the point of her jaw. Her head fell back and his lips fastened to the white column of her neck. She felt his teeth then, biting into her soft flesh as he would bite into an apple, and a feverish clutch of pleasure made her body jerk against his. He set his teeth into her neck, lashing her skin with his tongue until she cried out in sweet pain. Then he released her and kissed the dark mark and stooped to catch her behind the knees and around her shoulders and he lifted her into his arms. She lay limp and unprotesting, her heavy hair trailing down and sweeping against his thighs as he carried her towards the rug of white sheepskin that lay before the glowing fire.

He laid her down on the soft white wool and crouched over her, his strong lean thighs straddling her legs. He leant forward so that he could kiss her again and as he kissed her he ran his hands down her shoulders to the swell of her full breasts. His fingers traced the outside of her breast, the smooth heavy curve up to the nipple, and then he held the white globes in his hands, squeezing them, kneading them. Rosamund let out a sigh of pleasure and arched her back, inviting him to caress her more strongly. For answer he moved a little further down and kissed her throat, her collar-bone, her breast-bone, so that she whimpered with anticipation. Then he took her breasts in his hands and lowered his lips to her nipples, suckling each in turn, drawing out the darkening tips into stiff buds of sensation, and Rosamund's sighs became moans of delight. For long moments he worshipped her swollen, sensitive breasts, lapping at them, rubbing the taut nipples with his thumb, while her head turned from side to side in helpless bliss. Then he moved again, lifting himself lightly above her. She

felt his hand on the tender skin of her flank and automatically she parted her legs, offering herself to him.

'Beautiful,' he whispered, and his breath stirred the
soft curls of her mound. She drew in a sharp breath,
astonished and disbelieving. Then he placed the palms
of his hands on the inner surface of her white thighs and
gently, firmly, pushed them apart. She spread her legs
wide, knowing that his glittering eyes were devouring
the sight of her open sex. She was slippery and shining
with desire, and between the moist lips the pale pearl of
her clitoris was engorged and exposed, protruding from
its hood of flesh, begging for his touch.

His hands moved again, encircling the soft mound,
and his long fingers very gently spread the damp folds
of flesh apart. Rosamund shivered and her stomach
jerked, forcing out gasps of need. Geoffrey leant forward
and parted his lips and placed his warm mouth over her
sex. She whimpered as his breath sighed against her
skin. Then, very delicately, his tongue lapped at her,
running in one movement from the bottom to the top of
her labia, making her shake with the promise of pleasure.
He began to lick at her, the point of his strong tongue
worming its way through the whorls of flesh. She
moaned and shifted her hips, trying to make him lick
her at her epicentre, at the place where she ached and
yearned for him. But he teased her, concentrating on the
lips of her sex. After a moment he caught hold of her
thighs and held her still while he thrust his tongue up
inside her, as far into her as he could, making it move
within her like a tiny penis.

'Oh,' Rosamund whispered, 'please, my lord, please.'
She tried to move so that his tongue would caress her
where she most desired, but he held her firmly, still
thrusting inside her. She relaxed and lay limp, accepting
what he did to her, and by subtle degrees her pleasure
grew.

Then, suddenly, he had stopped. She lifted her head
and made a little noise of protest. He was kneeling over
her, his mouth glistening with her juices. Quickly he

kissed her and she tasted herself on his lips and tongue, salt and sweet, with a musky tang of woman. He took her hands in his and placed her palms on her breasts. 'Stroke yourself,' he whispered. 'Touch yourself, sweetheart.' And he was gone, sliding back towards her spread thighs. She hesitated, then gingerly ran her hands over her breasts, flickering her nails over her turgid nipples. Quick jets of pleasure ran through her, flashing like lightning through her spine. She gasped and caught her lip in her teeth.

He kissed her belly, kissed the soft fleece of her mound. Then he lay again between her legs, and this time he did not tease her. His dexterous tongue began to lap moistly against her swollen pearl of pleasure, flicking against it, rubbing at it. She cried out and her searching fingers involuntarily seized her hard nipples, pinching them until they ached and stung with sharp delicious pain. He continued to lick at her clitoris and she moaned deep in her throat as beneath his working tongue his strong fingers began to search the damp folds, probing and exploring. His hand slipped below the entrance to her vagina, drawing moisture back to the dark, secret place behind, spreading her juices there until she was slippery and tender. His thick thumb slipped into her sex and began to move in and out. Her gasps and moans instantly adjusted to match the rhythm of his thrusts and her hips began to lift and lower as if waves were rocking her. The pleasure built and built within her: her cries became sharper and more urgent. Then she let out a squeal of shock as his forefinger slid along the juicy furrow between her buttocks and found her tight, puckered hole and began to penetrate her there. For a moment she tensed against him. But then his hot tongue lashed against the quivering stem of her clitoris and her cry of protest became a groan of delight. He drew in the little shaft of flesh between his lips, working at it mercilessly as he pushed his finger and thumb into her moist orifices. She felt shame and embarrassment that he could touch her in that shameful spot, but the rich, dark, heavy

75

pleasure that it gave her was undeniable. Her crisis was approaching, swelling up from her deliciously filled sex and anus, glowing white-hot in the shivering bud of her clitoris, tipped with icy delight in the tormented peaks of her breasts. Rosamund flung back her head and cried out and her body arched and stiffened and Geoffrey held her there, the tip of his tongue just flickering against her, his finger and thumb squeezing gently within her, keeping her balanced on the fulcrum of ecstasy so that her rigid body quaked and shook for long, convulsive seconds.

At last he released her and kneeled upright, drawing her into his arms. She lay shuddering, her eyes wide and dark with shock, looking up at him as if he were a sorcerer. He smiled down into her face and said nothing. The warmth of the fire glowed on their naked flanks, casting a ruddy flush over pale skin.

'What did you *do* to me?' she whispered at last. 'You touched me – Holy Jesu, it must be wicked to touch a woman there!'

Geoffrey chuckled gently. 'Sweetheart,' he said softly, 'last night I saw a friend of mine take a woman there, and she seemed to get nothing but pleasure from it.'

'Take her?' Rosamund repeated in disbelief. 'In her, her fundament?'

'He put his cock in her arse and swived her there,' Geoffrey said with relish, grinning as Rosamund turned her head aside in confusion at his coarseness. 'Shall I do that to you, Rosamund?'

'No!' Rosamund exclaimed, putting her palms against his chest as if she would push him away. 'No, never!' For a moment she was stiff with tension; then the memory of pleasure softened her limbs. She looked up at his knowing, teasing face and felt suddenly naive and unsophisticated. 'You have had so many women,' she whispered sadly. 'Have you not, Geoffrey?'

'Many times many,' he agreed, still looking down at her with a smile.

'I am sure I must seem boring to you,' she said, closing

her eyes. She remembered her description of Edmund Bigod. 'Insipid,' she suggested.

'Rosamund,' Geoffrey said softly. Reluctantly she opened her eyes and looked into his face. He had ceased to smile. 'My lady, believe me. I have never in my life lain with a woman as lovely as you. I have never in my life desired a woman as much as I desired you, the moment I saw you.' He traced his fingers down her nose. 'You remember,' he said, 'how you touched me, and you felt I was hard already. I longed for you so much, just looking at your face.'

Rosamund reached up impulsively and put her arms around his neck, hugging him close to her. They kissed, a long, sensuous kiss. His mouth tasted of her sex. The movement of his tongue between her lips made her bowels coil and writhe again with desire for him. Very hesitantly she put her hand on his thigh and began to slide it upwards towards his loins. She expected to find his phallus there soft and weary, since it had worked so hard earlier. Instead she let out a little gasp of surprise and pleasure as her fingers touched a hot, iron-hard length of flesh, taut and throbbing with eagerness. Her lips were suddenly dry and she ran her tongue around them to moisten them, swallowed hard, and looked down.

Her fingers barely met around the dark, straining shaft. She moved her hand experimentally, gently drawing the satiny skin up and down. Geoffrey took a quick, deep breath and let it out in a long hiss of pleasure. Rosamund delicately trailed her fingertips over the tight, close-drawn pouch of his balls, feeling how the skin was tense and the heavy stones swollen with seed. She explored a little further back and touched that strange place behind the soft sac where the skin was surprisingly smooth and taut and hairless. Curiosity tempted her to probe further, but shame prevented her. She returned her hand to his magnificent, jutting phallus and slowly stroked it up and down, imitating the movement of a woman's sex around it and listening to his breathing shake. The tip of his cock swelled still further, becoming a broad, glistening dome, and a single clear tear appeared in the tiny slit. She ran her thumb over it, smearing the fluid over the purple glans.

Geoffrey shivered. 'My lady,' he said thickly, running his hands over her white shoulders, 'I would have you again.'

She looked up at him eagerly. Her loins felt hollow with need. 'Oh, yes,' she breathed, and began to lie back again on the soft fleece.

'No,' he said, 'no, sweetheart, before I took you. Now we should give pleasure to each other.' He drew her back up and kissed her, then knelt upright on the rug, his proud erect cock thrusting upwards from his groin. 'Come,' he said, 'kneel over me. Take me as you will.'

Rosamund had never imagined that there might be more than one way of doing the deed, and for a moment she stared in incomprehension. Geoffrey smiled and gently tugged her towards him, spreading her thighs so that she straddled him, her wet sex hovering open and inviting over his tumescent penis. He put his hands on her breasts, rubbing at the dark nipples. 'Come,' he whispered.

The head of his cock was hot and expectant between the parted lips of her sex. The sensation was so strange, so piquant: she was in control, and yet what she controlled was the possession of herself. She hung above him for a moment, relishing the tension that filled them both, and then she began to sink down upon him.

His long, thick shaft slid easily between her silken walls. She lowered herself slowly, inch by inch, savouring each moment as she felt herself penetrated, opened, filled. Then he was fully inside her and her swollen clitoris rubbed against his body. She moaned with pleasure and her eyes closed. Her hips moved in little circles, stimulating herself against him until she thought she would die of ecstasy then and there. She lifted herself up again and sank down again, again, again, writhing with pleasure as she impaled herself upon his hot, throbbing cock.

Gradually, as her rapture grew, she lost control. Her head rolled from side to side and she moved in jerks. Geoffrey released her breasts and instead took hold of her full white haunches, gripping the rich orbs in his strong hands and wresting supremacy from her. Now he lifted her up and down on his eager penis, tautening and thrusting with his firm buttocks as he lowered her, shoving himself up into her as she groaned and shuddered. She leant back, resting her hands on the floor, her back and her white throat arched and her breasts jutting wantonly towards the rafters. He reached eagerly forward with his lips to suck at her stiffened nipples and as she felt his mouth on her her sensitised body lurched instantly into orgasm. She spasmed around him, her body heaving, her inner muscles clutching frantically at his body as it slid in and out. His face tensed with ecstasy. He drove himself into her, ramming furiously upwards, gasping her name on each thrust, until he cried out and pulled her soft body close to his and shook as he spent himself inside her, rigid with tension as his seed pumped from him.

She pushed closer to him, hiding her head in his shoulder. Their arms were wrapped around each other, around shoulder and waist. Rosamund's hand stirred faintly in Geoffrey's thick, shining mop of hair. Their hearts pounded, gradually slowing as the waves of pleasure receded.

Beneath them the hall clock coughed and chimed, a single melancholy stroke. Rosamund turned her head on Geoffrey's shoulder. One hour: only one hour. Tears prickled at her closed eyelids. She clutched his bare skin more tightly, feeling his hands squeezing her in answer.

'I must go,' she whispered.

'Don't go. Stay here with me.'

'I must go. What would they think? And you must sleep, you are tired.'

'I would waken all night to give you pleasure.'

79

'No, I must go.' She drew back slowly, fighting tears. The sensation of loss as his body slipped out of hers was overwhelming. He clung to her, pulling her close, blindly seeking her lips with his.

'One day,' he whispered, 'one day I will lie with you in the morning, and at noon, and in the afternoon, and in the evening, and all through the night. I shall have you at Matins and Prime and Terce and Sext. We shall have a Holy Office of wantonness.'

She wanted to believe him, but she knew that when the dawn broke it would signal the approach of Sir Ralph, coming to take the manor by force and punish her for her insult to him. Against his power they would be helpless, although Geoffrey were braver than a lion at bay. She could not make him promises knowing that the morning might bring them suffering and death. She pulled away from him and got to her feet, catching up her robe and drawing it on. He knelt on the rug, looking up at her, the firelight illuminating the fine bones of his face with red and gold.

'Thank you,' she said softly. She reached out and touched her fingers to the scab on his brow, the bruise on his cheekbone, smiling sadly.

'I am sorry about the first time,' he said. Perhaps he, too, felt their doom approaching, for he spoke no more words of love or desire.

She shook her head. 'That gave me pleasure too,' she told him, and as she looked back she realised how true that was. The dark consuming passion of his violence had set her blood burning: a different pleasure to the second, as different as the squeal of a trumpet is different to the soft music of a flute; but still music.

She went to the door and he did not pursue her. The latch resisted her hand, as if it too wanted her to stay, but she forced it and at last it let her go. The door opened and she stepped out into the cold of the corridor.

She turned back to take a last look at him, naked and beautiful in the firelight. 'Good night,' she whispered.

'Good night,' he replied, soft as a breath.

She closed the door and went away. A little way down the corridor she stopped and looked out of the mullioned window onto the dark garden. The moon's pale face was hidden behind a swathe of thick cloud, and countless small flakes of snow were spiralling down from the blank sky.

Chapter Four

*I*t was still snowing, small hard flakes from a sky the colour of soiled linen, when Geoffrey and the people of de Verney manor went out to resist the attack of Sir Ralph Aycliffe and his men. The snow made Geoffrey despondent. He had hoped that the manor's people could fire on Aycliffe from a distance and make him think twice about a direct assault, but the visibility was appalling. The attackers would be upon them before they could nock an arrow to the string.

He kept a cheerful face, providing a constant stream of encouragement and banter, but behind the soldier's grin he was far away. He was kneeling still before the fire in the guest chamber, the sheepskin beneath him as soft as a cloud, all of his being centred in his penis where it lay buried and throbbing within the clinging warmth of Rosamund's arching body. He had had passions for women before, but never like this. He was obsessed. He hardly knew her, but he worshipped her. Geoffrey loved his life, but he was ready to lay it down for Rosamund de Verney, without reservation and without regret.

Did she love him in return? He knew that she desired him. What else could have brought her to his chamber? The mad folly of that action still stunned him with amazement. A lady, a widow of less than a week, coming in the night to the bed of a man she had known for a handful of hours, offering herself.

But it did not mean that she loved him. She knew that this day would bring disaster. Perhaps it was a last fling, her only chance to discover what marriage to a dotard had hidden from her. Perhaps any man would have sufficed, and if Geoffrey had not arrived it would have been one of her servants: the tall young man with the limp, one of the farm hands, any man at all to show her the way of lust before –

'No,' Geoffrey muttered to himself, shaking his head. Then some sixth sense jerked him upright, staring wide-eyed into the falling snow, his nostrils flaring as he settled his helmet more securely. 'Arrows on the string,' he said quickly, and around him the men jumped and began to obey. 'They're coming.'

They stood ready, bows taut, crossbows lifted, the manor's one dilapidated gun primed and ready to fire. They heard riders approaching, but could not tell from where. Then, suddenly, dark shapes loomed out of the snow, shouting war cries and waving swords and axes that shone dully in the grey light. A volley of missiles met them and some shrieked and fell, but before the de Verney men could reload the rest of Aycliffe's men were upon them.

In minutes the attackers were pounding against the gates of the manor courtyard and clambering up onto the wall itself. The manor's people were speared upon the wall as they tried to keep them from entering. Geoffrey fought like a demon, shutting his mind to the death around him. He saw the leader of the attackers, a big man on a strong war horse, and breathed, 'Aycliffe!' If he could kill him, then the attack would dissolve. He grabbed a bow from the limp hand of one of the dead defenders and lifted it, drawing back the string to his ear.

A shout made him turn. The flimsy gates were open and the attackers were pouring through them. Geoffrey shouted orders, his voice cracked with urgency, not

knowing if any de Verney man heard him. He saw
Aycliffe himself rear his horse and turn it, driving the
great beast towards the gates.

Geoffrey dropped from the wall and plunged desperately towards the house, slashing with his sword, duck-
ing as blows were aimed at him. Aycliffe was before him
wrestling with his horse: the massive iron-shod hooves
had slipped on the snow and gravel and the stallion was
squealing as it fought to stay upright. Geoffrey grinned
savagely and hurled himself at Aycliffe, catching hold of
the man's armoured leg and pulling with all his strength.
The metal-clad figure turned, shouting in protest and
brandishing its heavy mace, but it was already off
balance and toppling from the war-saddle towards the
churned filthy snow.

With a wild yell Geoffrey flung Aycliffe to the ground
and stamped hard on his right wrist. The struggling
knight shrieked and let go of his mace. Suddenly the
prospect of victory glowed before Geoffrey as brightly
as a jewel. He would kill the villain who threatened
Rosamund and then she would love him. Panting with
urgency he kicked at the knight's helmet as he tried to
rise. Aycliffe grunted and slumped back. The helmet
came loose and the second kick dislodged it. Geoffrey
bared his teeth and lifted his sword.

Then there were hands on his arms, pulling him
backwards, wresting his sword from him. The dream of
victory evaporated and as they dragged him down all he
felt was the desolation of failure.

'No!' Rosamund shouted, pushing herself away from the
window. Margery and Hugo tried to catch her and hold
her back, but in seconds she had forced open the door
and was running across the snowy gravel, her heavy
skirt clutched in both hands, calling out Geoffrey's name.
One of Sir Ralph's men had his sword drawn back, ready
to thrust, and without a thought she flung herself on
Geoffrey's limp body, staring upwards with wild eyes,
daring the soldier to run her through.

The man hesitated, uncertain. Rosamund waited to feel the bitter steel in her belly or her ribs, letting out her life. Then behind her a harsh voice said, 'Wait.'

The cold fear of death was replaced by a deeper chill. It took every ounce of Rosamund's courage to turn and look up into the black eyes which she knew awaited her.

Sir Ralph had got to his feet. He was helmetless, and there was a livid bruise on his brow where Geoffrey's kick had landed. He looked at Rosamund for a moment, his dark face cold and remote. Then he said to someone beyond her, 'Call a halt. We have the lady of the manor.'

Hands seized Rosamund by the arms and the scarf around her hair and pulled her upright. She closed her eyes briefly, then opened them to stare hopelessly down at the silent figure of her lover. The wound on his forehead had opened again and dark blood trickled swiftly down through his glossy hair to stain the muddy snow. The blood was flowing: he was alive. The knowledge refreshed her courage. She lifted her head and glared into Sir Ralph's black eyes. 'How dare you,' she hissed. 'How dare you come here with armed force against us.'

'My Lady de Verney,' said Aycliffe, in his gravelly, bitter voice. 'I dare because your husband is dead together with his protector the Duke of York, and there is nobody to say me nay.' He looked down at Geoffrey's still figure, took a step forward and spurned it with his toe. Rosamund stiffened against the hands that held her and Sir Ralph looked up at her, narrowing his eyes with curiosity and pleasure. 'None, that is, except this young cockerel,' he said. 'Is this your wifely virtue, Lady de Verney? A widow for less than a week, and already you have found yourself a lusty young squire for your bed?'

Hot blood stained Rosamund's cheeks, despite the lashing of the snow. 'No,' she protested, somewhat uncertainly. 'Master Lymington is – my cousin.'

'Your *cousin*?' repeated Sir Ralph, smiling openly in disbelief. 'I thought you had no family, Lady de Verney.' Suddenly he strode towards her. She flinched, but his men held her firmly. He caught hold of the woollen scarf that hid her hair and with a jerk pulled it from her, then seized her chin and tilted up her face. She shuddered at the touch of his hands and her stomach clenched with shame.

Sir Ralph's black eyes rested on the mark of Geoffrey's teeth and tongue that bloomed darkly on Rosamund's white throat. He said again, 'Your cousin, my lady?' and then he released her face so roughly that she gasped.

'You villain.' Rosamund struggled uselessly against the strong hands of Sir Ralph's soldiers. 'You have no right.'

'Right?' Aycliffe sounded as if he were laughing. 'Who cares for right? Lady de Verney, I have the power.' Before she could speak again he turned from her, raising his arm to summon his men to him. 'The manor is ours,' he called. 'Some of you go inside. No looting, the place is mine now. You know what you seek.'

'And its people, my lord?' called a harsh voice.

'As you wish,' said Sir Ralph carelessly. The men growled and went at a run towards the door of the manor. Rosamund twisted to watch them go, hardly able to believe how her whole life was collapsing around her ears. Margery and Hugo were inside: she wished desperately that they had run away, fled, escaped.

'Someone find a horse for Lady de Verney,' said Sir Ralph. 'Tie her feet to the stirrups. Ned, give her your cloak, we don't want her freezing on the way.'

'What about this knave?' said a sergeant, showing black broken teeth as he stirred Geoffrey's unmoving body with his foot. 'Shall I, my lord?'

His sword hung above Geoffrey's naked throat. Rosamund stood silent, stifled with horror, waiting for the order that would end her lover's life. Nothing happened: the sword wavered. She lifted her eyes hesitantly to Sir Ralph's face. When he saw how much Geoffrey meant to her, surely he would begin his revenge upon her by killing him?

But Sir Ralph was smiling. 'No, no, Mak,' he said,

almost jovially. 'This young blood will be more useful to us alive than dead. Sling him over a horse, bring him too.' He grinned like a wolf into Rosamund's face, then turned away.

The room where they thrust Rosamund and left her was in the curtain-wall of Sir Ralph's castle, a superannuated guardroom. It was small, high-ceilinged, with cold, damp walls of naked stone. A meagre fire glowed in the grate. In one of the walls there was a stone bench, and when the sergeant had gone away and left her alone she sank down upon it and hid her face in her hands and abandoned herself to tears.

The journey to Murthrum Castle had in itself been a nightmare of cold and discomfort as her ill-tempered mount struggled through the thickening snow. But she had not suffered as much as might be expected, for her brain was still numb with the horror of what she had seen before they took her from her home. Aycliffe's men had burst into the house and she had heard Margery screaming. At the sound Matthew, who was standing meekly enough among Sir Ralph's prisoners, seemed to go half mad: he raged and broke free of the cordon of men around him and flung himself towards the door of the manor. One of Aycliffe's men had dashed after him. The man overtook him on the very threshold and transfixed him on the point of a heavy pike. Matthew howled with agony and fell and writhed briefly in the bloody snow. Another of the soldiers appeared in the door pulling Margery by the hair. They laughed to see her shriek and struggle, and before Rosamund's eyes they forced her down over Matthew's twitching body and dragged open her bodice and flung up her skirt.

Rosamund shook her head, trying to drive the images from her fevered mind, but she could not quell her memory. Again and again it showed her Margery screaming and writhing in the soldiers' hands, her naked breasts shuddering. The sergeant, Mak, had grinned and tugged at his points, released his stiff, scarlet cock, and fallen onto Margery's heaving body like a beast onto its prey.

At least she had not actually seen them kill Margery. Perhaps they had let her live, once they had had their sport with her. Rosamund wanted to look forward to a day when all of this nightmare would be undone and she would live again at De Verney Manor. But it was impossible to imagine.

Suddenly the door opened, letting in a freezing wind and a puff of snow. Rosamund started and sat up, dashing her hand across her face to hide the traces of her tears. A young man entered and she frowned in puzzlement, for he did not look anything like the stark, rough soldiers that Sir Ralph had brought with him to attack the manor. He was slender and smooth-skinned, almost effete in appearance, with blond hair combed down to his shoulders and wide, baby-blue eyes. His clothes looked expensive, and the dagger in a sheath at his narrow waist had a silver hilt.

'Come with me,' the youth said without preamble. Rosamund thought of refusing, but it would be ignominious to be dragged. She got to her feet, stifling a shiver, and went obediently to the door.

She followed the young man through the door onto the drifted cobbles of the castle's narrow court. Cold air swirled around her and she shut her eyes briefly and wrapped her arms tightly across her breast.

Ahead of them the castle keep loomed like a mountain through the snow. It was an ancient building, square and high, made of wet, black stone that was green with moss wherever the sun did not fall. An open stone stair led up to the entrance to the keep, a broad round-headed arch. The door was made of heavy oak, strengthened with curling scroll-work in black iron. It was dour and threatening and exuded a sense of evil that was almost tangible.

'Go on,' said the young man as Rosamund hesitated at the foot of the stair. She wondered suddenly if she could break free and run. She lifted her eyes to the curtain-wall and saw standing on it Sir Ralph's soldiers, grinning at her and making lewd gestures. Rosamund closed her eyes in despair. When she opened them the youth was smiling unpleasantly at her, showing white, perfect teeth. His hand was resting on the ornamented hilt of his dagger. 'Do I have to insist?' he enquired.

Rosamund took a long breath and began to climb the steep, uneven stone stairs, holding up her heavy skirt in her cold hands. As they reached the top the door swung silently open. The young man took her by the arm and led her through into a curtained passageway, dark and smelling of old fabrics. They walked a little way forward, then the young man reached out and drew back one of the curtains. Light poured through, making Rosamund blink, and the youth put his hand in the small of her back and propelled her through the opening into the Great Hall.

Inside the hall she stood gazing around her in astonishment. The castle might be old, but the hall held every luxury. The high raftered ceiling was painted in geometrical patterns in clear colours. Tapestries bright with scenes of the chase covered the cold stone walls. A great fire burned in a fireplace with a high-pointed arch, and even the floor was laid with coloured tiles and strewn with the skins of animals –

Her gaze froze and she took a step back, gasping with shock. In the centre of the hall, where the high table should be, a tall chair had been placed. It was carved and padded with silk damask and in it half-lay Sir Ralph, dressed in a long, loose robe of dark-blue velvet embroidered with gold. The robe was open, showing his broad chest and the muscled ridges of his belly. He lay with his legs spread, and between them a girl was kneeling, naked, her hands tightly bound behind her, her head rising and falling as she serviced Sir Ralph with her lips.

'Jesu have mercy,' Rosamund breathed. She turned as if she would run from the hall, but the young man was standing behind her, smiling coldly into her appalled face. The blade of his dagger gleamed. 'Going some-where?' he asked. 'I think not. Turn around, my lady.'

He gestured with the dagger. Rosamund fixed her eyes on the bright blade, wondering if he meant what he said. The edges of the dagger were blue with sharpness. She licked her lips and tried to swallow in a suddenly dry throat. How could she turn and look again at that scene of lechery? She trembled and her empty stomach churned.

'Are you deaf?' asked the young man unpleasantly, and Rosamund tensed herself and turned.

She meant to stand with her eyes closed, but as she looked back across the hall she saw that Sir Ralph had provided himself with entertainment while the girl pleasured him. Before his chair was placed a wooden frame like a rack, and on it another lovely girl was tied, naked and spreadeagled. She was slender and fiery-haired and she was struggling against the harsh ropes that bound her wrists and her ankles. The rack was arched so that the girl's hips were forced upwards and her pubis lifted towards the rafters, her sex open and unprotected. Rosamund stared in amazement and horror, wondering what the girl had done to be so punished.

Sir Ralph made a sound and Rosamund glanced involuntarily towards him. He was gesturing with one hand towards the girl on the rack. At his command another girl came forward, also naked, and knelt before Sir Ralph. She had long blonde hair the colour of moonlight. She held out her hands towards her lord as if for his approval. Upon them lay an object made of glistening wood. Rosamund's sex clenched as she saw it, for it was a phallus, long and thick, bulbous at the tip and swelling at the base into a semblance of testes. Sir Ralph nodded and the girl got to her feet and went towards the rack.

The bound girl saw her coming and moaned, throwing her head from side to side. Her shoulders lifted and fell uselessly, making the hard tips of her breasts shiver. The blonde girl clambered up onto the rack and felt within the redhead's proffered mound. Then without warning she thrust the massive wooden shaft deep into the soft flesh, withdrew it gleaming with juice, and drove it in again. The bound girl cried out, straining against her bonds. It might have been a cry of pain, but Rosamund heard the overtones of desperate pleasure in it. Her eyes flickered from the wooden phallus as it slid in and out of the flushed pouting sex to the girl's face: her eyes were closed and her mouth open in a soft triangle of ecstasy. The blonde girl moved the phallus faster and faster, drawing it quickly out almost to the tip and then thrusting it back in with all her force, and the redhead began to cry out rhythmically, lifting and lowering her slender hips in time with the thrusts.

This display had its effect on Sir Ralph. He watched for a few moments impassively, his black eyes quite cold. Then, gradually, his lips drew away from his teeth in a snarl of mounting pleasure. He lifted his big hands from the arms of the chair and seized the girl servicing him by the hair. She let out a little stifled cry and her bound hands opened and closed spasmodically behind her naked back. Sir Ralph began to jerk his hips up towards her face, thrusting himself into her mouth as if it were her sex. The girl cried out again and tried to draw back, but he was holding her tightly. His thick, glistening cock drove deeply into her tender mouth. The girl on the rack was twisting against her bonds as the thick wooden phallus drove her closer and closer to orgasm. At last she screamed out and her body stiffened and twitched, and as if this were his cue Sir Ralph gave a great cry and thrust his cock hard into the mouth of the hapless girl before him, his hands gripping her hair like claws.

For a moment there was stillness. Rosamund stood very still, shaking. She was trying not to imagine how it would feel to have a man's member in her mouth, a hard pillar of flesh moving between her lips. Despite her fear and revulsion her belly was warm and melting with wantonness and she shut her eyes and chastised herself.

Was she going to allow this man to arouse her, when he had taken her captive from her home? Somewhere within the walls of the castle Geoffrey was a prisoner. He had given up so much for her. His suffering was her responsibility. How could she treat Sir Ralph with anything but contempt?

Sir Ralph pushed the girl away from him. She staggered up, her head bowed, a dribble of white seed trickling from her slack lips. Sir Ralph lifted himself in his chair, pulling his gorgeous robe closed, and waved his hand. More people came forward and released the redheaded girl from the rack and cleared all away. The young man took Rosamund her by the arm and led her forward to stand before Sir Ralph.

'Lady de Verney,' said Sir Ralph, smiling very slightly.

'You are a vicious brute,' Rosamund said, throwing her head back and setting her jaw. 'Release me at once. And where is – '

She only hesitated infinitesimally, but it was enough for Sir Ralph. He threw back his grizzled head and laughed. 'Where is your *cousin*?' he mocked her.

'Where is Master Lymington?' demanded Rosamund, regaining her composure. 'He was wounded. Has he been cared for?'

'Lady de Verney,' said Sir Ralph, leaning his chin on his steepled fingers, 'I do not believe that I like the tone of your voice. You are in no position to adopt such a manner with me. I hold your life and honour in my hands.'

'Kill me then.' Rosamund flung up her hands in a violent gesture of anger and despair. 'You have stolen my property and killed my people. Why stop there?'

If she meant to shock him into better behaviour, she failed. He leant back a little in his tall chair. 'It may come to that,' he said with a cold smile. 'But for the time being, my lady, I mean to take my revenge on you for your behaviour to me all those years ago. I intend to humiliate you, my lady. And in addition, I intend to take more from you than your husband's lands.' He lifted his hand and from behind him a man came forward with a little portable desk which he set by Sir Ralph's chair. It was strewn with papers. Rosamund stared, astonished.

'Here,' said Sir Ralph slowly, 'I have your husband's will.' He reached out and lifted one of the papers and held it towards her. His impenetrable eyes gleamed oddly. For a moment Rosamund could not tear her eyes from him. Then she looked at the paper.

He did not lie, it was Lionel's will. It was stained with scarlet. 'Holy Virgin,' Rosamund breathed, 'whose blood is on it?'

Sir Ralph shrugged. 'One of your people, I imagine,' he said in an offhand voice. Rosamund breathed raggedly, thinking of Hugo waiting with his crossbow within the manor, trying to protect Lionel's legacy from the villains who came against it. She closed her eyes and for a moment hardly heard Sir Ralph's voice as he continued to speak. 'I see that your husband has generously left everything he possessed to you. A touching display of confidence, I feel. I wonder if he would have done the same if he had known that within a week of his death you would be coupling with some hitherto unsuspected cousin: coupling with such vigour that he has left his mark upon your skin, like a rutting beast.' She flung up her head, her cheeks stinging with anger and shame, and Sir Ralph bared his teeth in a feral grin. 'However,' he said, 'everything is yours. And it will make things very much easier for me if you concede that everything shall be mine. So, my lady, I will present you with this paper. It is a deed of assign. In it you give everything you possess to me: your own dowry lands and those that have come from your dead husband.' He lifted another paper. 'Sign,' he said simply.

Rosamund shook her head slowly from side to side, unable to believe what he demanded of her. Did he really expect her to give him everything? Give it to him, without a struggle? His gall left her speechless.

'Sign,' said Sir Ralph again, pushing the paper towards her. 'There are witnesses aplenty here. Sign.'

93

Her voice was hers again. 'Are you mad as well as wicked?' she exclaimed. 'In God's name, why should I sign? Hold de Verney manor while you can, you brigand. I will not lift my hand to make it easier for you!' She was shaking with anger. He wanted not just Lionel's lands, but the lands that she had brought with her to her marriage. She was the last of her family and they should be hers. 'I will sign *nothing*,' she hissed, squaring her shoulders and lifting her head. 'Nothing.'

Sir Ralph smiled at her and rested his chin in his hand. 'It would have disappointed me,' he said, 'if your spirit had not matched your beauty, Lady de Verney. It will be so much more of a challenge to break you. Before I am done with you, you will be my slave.'

'I would rather die,' Rosamund said proudly. But although she spoke boldly she knew that Sir Ralph's unfathomable black eyes were working upon her, filling her against her will with fear and a slim spiralling flame of erotic excitement. What could he intend for her? Of what would her humiliation consist? For a moment she saw herself naked and bound, kneeling at his feet while he held her head in his strong hands and thrust his erect penis into her mouth. Her head spun with a confusion of lust and hatred. At last hatred prevailed. Let him try, she thought viciously to herself. I have sharp teeth: he will find out to his cost.

'Lady de Verney,' said Sir Ralph, 'if you do not sign this paper, you will most assuredly die. Though perhaps not in the way you mean.' He dipped a quill in a little silver inkwell and held it towards her. His dark face was smiling very slightly, enjoying her fear and discomfiture. 'Sign,' he said again.

'I will not,' said Rosamund.

'Very well.' Sir Ralph sat back in his chair and gestured to a couple of the young men who stood a little behind him. They hurried forward. Like the youth who had taken her from her prison, they were well dressed and fair-featured, finely built specimens of slender manhood. 'Strip her,' Sir Ralph commanded.

Rosamund gasped in fear and shame. She turned to flee, but before she had taken a step strong hands were on her, holding her though she struggled, swinging her back by force to face Sir Ralph's gloating smile. 'No,' she breathed. 'No, no.'

'Sign,' whispered Sir Ralph. Rosamund set her teeth in desperation and shook her head. Sir Ralph lifted his hands in a helpless shrug and behind Rosamund a sharp *snick* of blade on cord revealed that one of the youths was cutting through the laces of her gown. For a few moments she writhed against their restraining hands as the woollen gown loosened and began to slip to her feet. Then she realised the hopelessness of struggle and thought that perhaps Sir Ralph wanted to see her distressed, and she made herself stand still. The gown slipped down her thighs and the young men coaxed the tight sleeves from her arms. All was not lost: beneath the overgown was an undergown of golden silk, closely fitted to her arms and upper body. She closed her eyes, trying to pretend that she was alone, that there were no greedy faces staring avidly as her clothes were removed from her.

She stood now in the silk undergown, her eyes tight shut. The youths made no more move to strip her. After a second she could not bear not knowing what was to be done to her, and she opened her eyes. She started with shock, for Sir Ralph was standing before her, holding the gleaming blade of a dagger before her face. She tried to pull away, but hands held her still.

'Such beautiful silk,' said Sir Ralph. 'Such a pity.' And he moved the point of the dagger towards her. She could not prevent herself from flinching, but he did not touch the sharp blade to her skin. Instead he set it to the front of the undergown, nicked the glossy silk, then took hold of the fabric with both hands and pulled hard. The undergown ripped as far as her waist, revealing her tight boned stays, her white shift, the swell of her generous breasts. She shut her eyes in impotent fear, knowing that her fast uneven breathing was making her breasts lift and lower above the edge of her shift. She heard Sir Ralph draw in a long, hissing breath, and her head fell in desperate shame. She knew that she should be half dead now from injured modesty, fainting, helpless: but in fact her whole body was tense and sensitised with wanton desire. Already the points of her breasts were hard, chafing against the tight confines of her stays. Before last night she would not have understood the sensations that now gripped her, but Geoffrey had shown her the way of her desire. He had held her down and swived her, he had kissed her and drawn her into blissful death with the delicious lapping of his tongue, he had lifted and lowered her on the straining shaft of his flesh, and she had known delight. Now, against her will, her body craved to explore the darker shores of lust.

'I remember these breasts,' Sir Ralph said softly. 'I remember that I touched them before, and they swelled under my hand.' He reached out and with both hands lifted Rosamund's white globes from the stays, exposing her taut nipples. She shuddered and turned her head aside. Sir Ralph looked narrowly at her as if trying to decide whether her reaction was one of pleasure or horror. He reached out, his eyes still fixed upon her face, and took one long nipple between finger and thumb, squeezing at it gently. Rosamund's head fell back, exposing her long white throat, and she let out a hopeless cry. Hopeless, because she wanted to feel nothing, or to feel only shame. But in fact as he touched her she felt sharp, abandoned pleasure.

Sir Ralph stepped back. 'Strip her,' he said again. The young men hurried to obey him. They unlaced the stays and drew them away so that Rosamund stood only in her flimsy shift, then lifted the hem of the shift above her head.

As they were about to pull it off Sir Ralph said 'Stop.' Rosamund stood with her arms raised, trapped by the folds of linen, her head concealed, unable to see, helpless. One of the young men was holding up her hands, gripping firmly at her white wrists. She gave a little whimper as she realised how she must appear, stark naked above her gartered stockings, her body exposed for Sir Ralph to examine, a mere naked torso, her face concealed by her bunched-up shift. She tried to struggle, but the hands on her wrists were strong. Unable to help herself, she breathed in irregular pants: the tips of her breasts were tight and aching with shame and need.

Suddenly, without warning, she felt strong fingers worming their way into the dark curls of her pubic hair. She cried out and clamped her thighs tightly together, but to no avail. The fingers inched their way between her legs, exploring the soft lips of her sex. She knew they were Sir Ralph's fingers; every part of her remembered how he had touched her before in the garden. She tensed her body, resisting him. Then he slipped one finger deep into the well of her womanhood, stirring the sweet juices, and with his broad thumb he rubbed quickly at her little stiff peak of delight.

'Jesu save me,' Rosamund cried. She jerked her hips away from the exploring hand, but she was unable to conceal the undulating pulse of pleasure that had convulsed her naked body. As quickly as it had come the hand withdrew and she cried out again, a cry that should have been of relief, but was of disappointment.

For a moment there was silence. Then the young man behind her drew off her shift, leaving her naked but for her stockings. She looked into Sir Ralph's cold eyes and blood burned in her cheeks.

'Well, my lady,' said Sir Ralph gently. 'I see that marriage to an old husband must have left you more frustrated that one could imagine. My pathetic attempts at shaming you have been fruitless so far, eh?' He was smiling, but she thought from the tightness of his mouth that he was angry. 'I am going to have to try harder if I am to distress you. My intention is not to give you pleasure.' He seemed unmoved by her white body, heaving before him as her breath shuddered in and out. 'My intention is that you should suffer.' He turned

97

sharply from her, signalling to one of his minions. 'Fetch Procrustes' bed,' he commanded, and then he sank back into his chair, his dark eyes fixed on Rosamund's face.

Procrustes' bed? Rosamund shivered as she remembered the story. Procrustes had forced his guests to lie on his bed and he had insisted that they fit it exactly. Those who were too tall had had their limbs lopped, those too short had been stretched, to fit the exact length and width of his infernal contraption. What in God's name did Aycliffe have in mind for her?

Sir Ralph smiled as if he read her fear. 'Sign,' he said lazily, gesturing with his hand at the table spread with papers.

'Never,' Rosamund whispered. She meant to resist him while breath was in her. But behind her stubbornness lay gnawing lust. Poor Margery had said that Sir Ralph was built like a pagan god. She had not seen enough of him, as he swived the slave-girl's mouth, to make her own judgement: but if it were true? Would he take her with his massive thick member, possess her and penetrate her and make her his? The sensation of delirious release that had gripped her when Geoffrey held her down filled her now, softening her limbs and making her tremble with anxious desire. She looked down at the floor, trying to hide the excitement that filled her and made her cheeks and throat flush red with shame. She would have given much to be unmoved, but she was powerless against her own desperate wantonness. It would be her pleasure to resist Sir Ralph until death, if it meant that he would continue to torment her so deliciously.

The grinding sound of wood dragged over stone made her start and jerk around, one hand automatically lifting to cover her breasts, the other shielding her triangle. She saw Sir Ralph's men pulling a thing that made her stretch her eyes, a strange object of wood and leather and padded velvet, something like a table in its appearance. It looked quite new, and she shrank from it.

'Admire it, my lady,' said Sir Ralph softly. 'It was

made with you in mind. In a moment I shall have you fastened to it, and then you will truly be at my mercy.'

Now Rosamund felt afraid. The threat of torture made her shiver and step back. She felt helpless and exposed in her nakedness.

'You are afraid,' whispered Sir Ralph, leaning forward a little in his chair. 'Are you not?'

She lifted her eyes to his, knowing as she did so that they would be filled with mute appeal. He smiled with deliberate satisfaction. 'Good,' he said. He lifted his head quickly and made another commanding gesture with his hand. 'Take her,' he ordered. 'Bind her to it.'

They laid hands on her and she struggled feverishly, trying to resist them. It was useless. They pulled her across the room and someone came and cast soft ropes around her white wrists. They pulled her to the terrible thing that Sir Ralph had called Procrustes' bed and began to fasten her to it. She moaned and heaved, fighting against them with every ounce of her strength, but to no avail. As they wrestled her down Sir Ralph sat back in his chair, watching her, listening to her desperate gasps of effort with a cold, contented smile.

It did not take them long to bind her. Presently they drew back, laughing behind their hands at the spectacle she presented, and Rosamund closed her eyes, real shame filling her for the first time. She was face down on the strange table, her buttocks thrust lewdly upwards, her legs bent and separated so that her backside and her sex were open and vulnerable. Her body was supported upon a velvet pad from her hipbones to her ribs: then the velvet ended and her breasts hung down into empty space. Her arms were lifted, dragged apart, her wrists fastened securely to the posts of the machine. Her hair began to come loose and fall in heavy strands around her face.

'Blindfold her,' said Sir Ralph softly.

'No,' Rosamund gasped. 'No, please.' As long as she could see she felt that some vestige of control remained to her, the ability at least to accept or reject what was being done to her.

Sir Ralph heaved himself up from his chair and came to stand before her. She could see the heavy, opulent skirts of his velvet robe. He said in a gentle, almost caressing voice, 'And if I tell them to stop, will you agree to sign?'

Rosamund lifted her head with an effort, feeling muscles in her neck and shoulders straining. His face was cold and unreadable and showed no vestige of mercy. 'And if I signed,' she retorted, 'would you release me?'

He laughed and shook his head admiringly. 'Probably not,' he agreed, 'probably not, my lady. Vengeance is sweet. I cannot tell you what pleasure I obtain from seeing you exposed before me so shamefully.' He put his hand on her face. She pulled her head away, disgusted, but he only laughed. His hand ran down her neck, across her naked shoulder, down the furrow of her spine to the proud swell of her buttocks. She gasped in protest as his hand parted her cheeks and one finger stroked experimentally down her dark, forbidden cleft. She jerked against her bonds, trying to escape his probing hands, but she could not move.

'You have the body of a goddess,' said Sir Ralph softly. 'How I shall enjoy abusing it. Tell me, my Lady de Verney, what is your greatest fear?'

'Only a fool would tell you,' Rosamund said fiercely, trying again to pull away from him.

'True,' said Sir Ralph with a chuckle, 'true.' He retreated from her a little way, moving out of her line of sight. His voice said again, 'The blindfold.'

One of the women came up and tied a thick dark bandage tightly over Rosamund's eyes, shutting out the light. She turned her head from side to side in protest, feeling suddenly hideously vulnerable. She could not prepare herself, she would have no warning of what they might do to her. The darkness was unremitting, all-enfolding.

Sir Ralph's voice spoke from just beside her head. 'Now, my lady,' he said, 'you will do as you are bid, or you will suffer for it.'

She felt hands in her hair, pulling her head back and back until her mouth opened involuntarily to relieve the tension of her neck. 'Good,' said Sir Ralph's voice. The hands were not his, they were too slender. 'Now, prepare yourself.'

It was clear what they meant to do. Rosamund wrenched her head free from the hands that held it and said furiously, 'If anyone tries it, I will bite, I swear it, I swear it.'

And then she shrieked in pain and shock, for with a whistle and a crack something narrow and flexible had lashed across her naked buttocks, searing them with astonishing, stinging sensation. She strained against her bonds, then screamed again as the lash struck her a second time. Her head fell forward, hot tears springing to her eyes. It was a fit punishment for her. Had she not taken out her frustration and shame on Margery, beating her for no reason? She lay limp, accepting the sharp pain as the lash rose and fell again.

'Now,' said Sir Ralph's gravelly voice by her ear, 'no more of biting, if you please, my lady.'

Once again there were hands in her hair, tugging back her head. She did not resist. The hands drew back her head until her throat was straining and taut and her lips were parted. Rosamund knew what awaited her. Her lips tingled and stung as if the pain from her lashed buttocks had settled there, as if bees had driven their little barbs into her swollen mouth. Suddenly she wished that she had known last night what she knew now. She would have taken Geoffrey in her mouth, worshipped him, caressed his straining body with her tongue, gasped with pleasure as she swallowed the gift of his seed. He had pleased her so much, and she had given him nothing in return.

Something was touching her trembling lips, something hot and smooth, silken and glossy. It smelt of musk and man. With a shudder Rosamund realised that she did not know which of Sir Ralph's creatures was about to take the maidenhead of her mouth. She moaned as the glossy, bulbous knob pushed its way between her lips and began to slide into her mouth, filling her. *Geoffrey*, she thought, imagining herself lying above him, kissing the smooth plane of his chest, flickering her tongue against his nipples, sliding down his body to draw his hard swollen penis in between her lips. She remembered his smell, delicious, subtle, leather and metal and horse and a tang of sharp sweat and beneath it all the perfume of his strong body. She moaned, lost in her fantasy, as the hot shaft in her mouth began to slide to and fro and the hands in her hair held her head still.

She would not have believed that lips were so sensitive, but the sensation as the stranger's penis swived her open mouth was blissful, almost as if her sex were being stimulated. She shuddered and gasped and the hot ache of the stripes on her buttocks began to ease into a warm, sensual glow, melting her with the promise of delight. She abandoned herself to the feelings that gripped her, painting her own images upon the black bandage that bound her eyes.

Without warning, the thick quivering penis withdrew from her mouth. She gave a little surprised cry and hung there, her lips parted, her head turning blindly from side to side as if it sought something. There was movement in front of her and then another cock was offered up to her mouth, thrust between her parted lips, and began to push itself deep, reaching to the back of her throat, almost making her gag as it shafted in and out. It was shorter and thicker than the last one and stretched her lips wide. She lost her grip on the fantasy that protected her and as reality intruded she began to complain and struggle, turning her head from side to side against the restraining hands.

Sir Ralph's voice hissed in her ear. 'If you resist, you will be punished. Suck, my lady: suck him.' The cock in her mouth thrust deeper as if her struggles only aroused its owner. Rosamund could hear the man grunting and gasping as he violated her mouth. She moaned in desperate resistance and tried again to pull free, to close her mouth, anything to free herself of the invading pole of flesh. The hands in her hair tugged back her head brutally, jerking her stretched throat, and she cried out.

Then, again without warning, the thick shaft withdrew and the hands released her. Her head fell forward and she moaned with relief at the unexpected freedom. She felt Sir Ralph's breathing stirring against her ear and he muttered something. She lay helpless, waiting.

Out of the darkness of the blindfold shot sudden sparks of pleasure as hands touched her naked breasts. They squeezed the dangling orbs, rubbing down their fullness towards the taut nipples that stiffened as they were kissed by the empty air. Rosamund gasped as clever fingers began to stimulate those coral peaks, drawing them out further, teasing and scratching them until she shuddered afresh with dark bliss. Moaning, she let her shoulders fall forward, dropping her swelling breasts into the stroking hands.

Then, between her legs, fingers probing the moist receptive tunnel of her sex. She cried out and writhed, trying to pull away, trying to stimulate her tender aching lips against the gentle stimulus of the invading finger. A low laugh, stirring the crisp fur around her vulva. And then gentle wet warmth as a strong, blunt tongue began to explore there. She gasped as the silken roughness dug a little way into her tunnel, tasting her, and then began to move back, fondling the taut tender membrane between her vagina and her anus.

Geoffrey, Geoffrey, she whispered behind the blindfold. He had licked her, touched her, shown her that no pleasure is forbidden: but even he had not done this. The firm blunt tip of the questing tongue was nudging now directly into her secret cleft, worming its way between her cheeks, prodding determinedly at her tight sphincter. She groaned with shame and delight as it opened her, creeping inside her, rimming the entrance to

103

her virgin passage. She imagined Geoffrey's beautiful face buried between the swelling mounds of her buttocks, his mouth open as he lapped and stroked and thrust with his strong tongue, filling her with unexpected, shameful pleasure.

Suddenly there was nothing. She hung helpless in her bonds, her breasts and sex aching, the tender hole of her anus quivering with anxiety and expectation, and she was touched by – nothing. She tried to keep her breathing steady. Her whole body was tingling with arousal, longing to be tumbled over the precipice of ecstasy into the infinite fall towards orgasm. More than anything in the world she wished to have Geoffrey with her, sliding the thick length of his wonderful cock into her body and stroking it in and out until she came.

'Well?' said Sir Ralph's voice. He must have got up, for the voice came from behind her.

'Very tight, my lord.' It was a woman's voice and Rosamund tensed with sudden horror. Had it been a woman, then, touching her there, tonguing her? Had those been women's hands on her breasts? She turned her head aimlessly from side to side as if she might escape the blindfold and be able to see her tormentors. 'I would wager that no one has ever had her there.'

As Rosamund realised what this meant and tensed against her bonds she sensed Sir Ralph kneeling down by her face. She pulled her head away from him, but his hand took hold of her chin and turned it back. She could feel him studying her, her flushed cheeks, her swollen, softened lips, and her whole body seemed to melt with shame and lust. 'So,' hissed his voice in her ear. 'So your magnificent young lover did not choose to take the maidenhead of your arse, Lady de Verney.'

She could not reply. Her breasts swung as her breath heaved in and out. Sir Ralph laughed in her ear. 'So orthodox, all these young stallions,' he said. 'They think a tall body and a big cock is enough to satisfy any woman. They do not understand ladies of your nature, do they, Lady de Verney? They do not realise that some women are so wanton that they can gain pleasure from anything, no matter how lewd or shameful.'

His hand left her face and ran down her hot neck onto her bosom. He cupped her dangling breasts, then pinched the erect nipples so hard that Rosamund cried out in sharp pleasure and pain. Aycliffe laughed and pinched again and again until Rosamund's whole body was jerking and heaving with the torment of his fierce caresses. Then his hands left her breasts and caught her by the hair, pulling back her aching head. 'Put out your tongue, my lady,' he ordered.

Rosamund tried to shake her head against his restraining hands. 'No,' she moaned, determined to disobey him while she could, 'no, no.'

At once the lash fell again across her tender buttocks, pain leaping through her from her toes to her finger-ends. She screamed and twitched, but he held her firmly. The pain seemed to bury itself in her gaping, open sex, filling her with a maddening, burning itch of lust. 'Again,' he commanded, and again the blow fell and she writhed with delicious agony.

'Now,' said Sir Ralph, 'my lady, lick me. Worship me. And it will be as well for you to be generous with your spittle.' Suddenly the huge hot head of a massive cock was pushed roughly against her lips. 'Open,' growled Sir Ralph, tugging at her hair.

With a moan of agonised defeat Rosamund opened her lips. At once he thrust strongly into her mouth and as he did so she knew that Margery had not lied. His cock was so thick that it hurt her to suck on it, but the stretching of her jaw only filled her further with lust. She groaned and made her tongue obey her, circling the huge smooth dome at the tip of Aycliffe's massive shaft. As she did so she felt again the tongue between the cheeks of her arse, moistening her, opening her little by little.

'Enough,' grunted Sir Ralph, suddenly withdrawing. Rosamund's head fell forward and she waited, barely breathing, for what she knew would come. A sturdy body moved between her open thighs and hands gripped at her buttocks, spreading the full cheeks wide apart. Then she felt the determined, steady prodding of a rampant penis, eager and swollen, pushing again and again into the tight, resistant hole of her anus. She wanted to cry out, to protest, to beg for mercy, but she knew that no mercy would be granted. Her tormentor wanted to break her, to make her beg: she would not give him the satisfaction.

He continued to thrust at her and she began to breathe in gasps, afraid of the pain. If only she had let Geoffrey do this to her! But she had refused him, and now Sir Ralph was robbing her of the only virginity that she might have offered to her lover. As the broad hot head began to enter her she shut her eyes behind the blindfold and imagined that in truth it was Geoffrey and not Sir Ralph who stood behind her, easing his stiff, swollen cock into her forbidden passage. She tried to relax, to accept this degradation, and suddenly the head of Sir Ralph's cock had passed her sphincter and the whole of him was sliding up inside her, penetrating her to the hilt. She could feel the tight, hairy purse of his balls nestling against her sex.

Then, against all her intent, she felt pleasure, hot dark pleasure, edged with the fire of pain. It was far from the blissful, soaring ecstasy that she had experienced in Geoffrey's arms, but even so she whimpered within its consuming grasp. Behind her Aycliffe grunted and began to thrust and withdraw from her, driving himself mercilessly into her virgin anus, ruthlessly taking his pleasure from her. As she jolted with his lunges, groaning at each surge of his hot cock deep inside her, she felt hands touching her, stroking her, running over her flanks, her belly, her dangling breasts, her aching, turgid nipples, and her groans turned to pants. Fingers tangled themselves in her hair, lifting her head, and she opened her mouth eagerly and reached forward blindly, welcoming the thrust of another avid penis between her trembling lips. She moaned as the iron-hard shaft drove into her throat and she fought her bonds to heave her quivering buttocks up towards Sir Ralph, offering herself to his ferocious thrusts. His dangling balls slammed again and again against the swollen lips of her sex and her clitoris stiffened and stood forward from its hood of flesh, desperately seeking her release.

Sir Ralph was plunging into her now with all his strength, his big hands gripping at her white haunches, holding her still to receive his thrusts. He was grunting like a beast at each lunge, and his balls as they beat against her were taut and pulsing. Rosamund sucked feverishly at the swollen glans that filled her mouth and rubbed her breasts against the hands that caressed them, urgently driving herself towards climax.

But before she could bring herself to the peak of pleasure Aycliffe roared like a bull and rammed himself deep inside her, his penis twitching and jerking as it spurted frantically into her forbidden passage. Then, suddenly and roughly, he withdrew, and as he did so all the other hands and cocks also drew away, leaving Rosamund suspended in her bonds, trembling and shaking on the point of orgasm, whimpering with her desperate need.

'Well, my lady,' said Sir Ralph's voice from by her head. He was panting. 'Well, now, what a condition I find you in.' At some unseen signal fingers touched her between her legs, making her writhe and cry out. 'Alas,' whispered Aycliffe, 'you sound almost as if you are in pain. What can it mean?'

Rosamund's head rolled from side to side in desperation. She could not, would not beg. She refused to abase herself before him. And yet the need, the desperate wanting, the hollowness and aching of her unbearably stimulated sex: she felt that if she were not allowed to climax she might go mad.

'Release her,' said Sir Ralph's voice suddenly, and she gasped as quick hands unfastened her, slackening her bonds, drawing the blindfold from her eyes. She blinked and closed her eyes against the light as they lifted her from Procrustes' bed. Straining against the clinging hands, she felt herself lowered into an upright position, and when she opened her eyes found herself seated in Sir Ralph's own chair.

He was standing before her, his robe drawn closed. She still had not seen the magnificent shaft that had so mercilessly driven its way inside her. The coldness of his black eyes made her shiver and gasp, suddenly hideously conscious of her nakedness, of the way that the lips of her sex were flushed and swollen, protruding from her mound, asking to be touched. She wished that she could hide herself, but she wished also for a man, for a man's hard cock to take her. She wanted to think of Geoffrey, but while Sir Ralph fastened his cold black eyes upon her she could not.

The red-haired girl came up beside Sir Ralph and knelt to him, offering her hands upwards. Upon them lay the wooden phallus. Sir Ralph lifted it from the girl's palms and drew it gently below his nose, his wide nostrils flaring as he drew in the scent of the girl's drying juices from the glistening wood. Rosamund wrapped her arms across her breasts and drew up her knees into her chest, trying to hide her nakedness from his chilly stare.

'Do not cover yourself,' Sir Ralph commanded, and as he spoke two more of the men came forward and caught Rosamund's legs at the knee, pulling them wide so that her thighs were spread apart, revealing the moist mound of her sex to Aycliffe's piercing eyes. He smiled coldly and came towards her and she pulled back into the chair, trembling, hating him and desiring him.

'Here,' he said bluntly, holding the phallus towards her, 'if you want pleasure, my lady, you must give it to yourself.'

For a moment Rosamund stared at him as if she did not understand. Was he asking her to pleasure herself here, in front of all these people, before their hungry eyes, touch herself, make herself cry out? How could he?

He was laughing at her shuddering frustration. 'You want to,' he said, throwing back his head in pleasure to see her degradation. 'You want to, you whore.' And he stepped forward and with one practised hand he thrust the head of the phallus into her aching, empty vagina.

She cried out and arched her back, automatically thrusting her hips towards the invading shaft, eager to take more of it within her yearning flesh. Aycliffe laughed again and seized her hand and laid the thick base of the phallus within it, then stepped back, still laughing. 'Go on,' he encouraged her, 'go on.'

The thick head of the wooden penis was lodged tightly between the throbbing lips of her sex. He wanted her to pleasure herself, to humiliate herself before them, and she would have liked to anger him by resisting, by drawing the phallus away from her and flinging it across the room and spitting in his face. But she could not, she could not. Her right hand held the thick base of the phallus and her right arm was pressed tightly across her body, cradling her breast. Now she closed her eyes and put her left hand to her pubis, pressing her breasts together, the erect darkened nipples chafing against the skin of her arms.

Geoffrey, pressing his lips against hers, drawing her gently down upon him as he knelt by the fire. Wrapping his strong arms around her back, caressing her shoulders and the swell of her buttocks. Geoffrey lying above her, his weight pressing her down, his face taut and enraptured, eyes shut tightly as he pinned her to the sheets and thrust deeply inside her. She remembered how it had felt to be poised above him, about to impale herself, and in her mind she sank down upon him, feeling that wonderful fullness as the whole length of him slid up inside her. She pushed at the base of the phallus and it began to move, burying itself within her. When it was deeply imbedded she hesitated, then very, very gently touched the little hard stem of her clitoris. Her belly and thighs quaked with desperate pleasure and she quickly withdrew the slick phallus and drove it back within her, shuddering as she rubbed and rubbed at the quivering bud of her clitoris, driving herself to an orgasm of such ferocious intensity that her rolling head would have beaten against the wooden back of the chair if one of Sir Ralph's men had not caught it between his hands and held it still while she cried out and quaked and sparks flashed behind her eyes, brighter than the flame at the heart of a forge.

There was silence. She sat with her eyes closed, trembling, panting, clutching with her inner muscles at the smooth wood that filled her. Presently the fever of her climax began to slip away and she opened her eyes, realising where she was, what she had done. Her right hand was still holding the phallus, its long, thick shaft thrust up into the very heart of her. Standing above her was Sir Ralph, his normally cold eyes flickering red with a tiny flame of anger.

'Well, my lady,' he breathed, looking down at her glistening, shuddering body. 'If I hoped to shame you, I have failed, it seems.' He reached down with his right hand and seized the phallus, withdrawing it from her with a suddenness that made her gasp. Its dark shaft gleamed milky white with her pearly juices. He looked at it, and then at her, and his face revealed such contained rage that she shrank back into the chair, afraid that he would strike her.

For a long moment he stood over her, staring down into her face. Then he turned away, flinging up one hand in what seemed like disgust. 'Take her away,' he snapped, and his people leapt to obey him.

Chapter Five

Ice-cold water, striking the face like a blow, dragging consciousness from the darkness in which it had taken refuge. Geoffrey moaned and lifted his head. Water dripped from his hair, trickled down his cheeks, down the cords of his throat. His head ached and he was desperately thirsty. Automatically his tongue licked around his lips, trying to catch the trickles of water. And something was amiss with his body: he was giving his hands orders to move, to wipe water from his hair into his parched mouth, but –

With a start his eyes opened and he jerked furiously, realising that he was bound. He twisted his head from side to side, staring about him in shock and anger. As he looked about him memory returned. He had had Aycliffe at his mercy, but then the soldiers had come and dragged him down and pain had exploded in his skull, followed by darkness like despair and death.

So this was Aycliffe's hall. He looked up at the high painted rafters, trying to control his breathing. He was bound hand and foot, fastened upright to a sort of vertical frame, clad only in hose and his thin linen shirt. Fear began to grip at his belly, making his bowels clench as he thought of torture. There was some play in the cords that held his wrists and he twisted around, looking over his shoulder. Behind him there was a great fire, casting warmth and glowing light onto him. He thought briefly of Rosamund, then pushed the thought aside. It was too painful: it would make him weak.

Movement in front of him. He snapped around again, breathing fast, expecting horrors. From the curtained passage at the end of the hall approached a single, slight figure, a girl, as fair-faced as an elf, with fine pale-gold hair hanging around her face like a sheet of gauze. She was dressed in a thin silk gown of pearly white, loose and unbound, so fine that it showed through its diaphanous folds the dark shapes of her nipples. In one slender hand she carried a glass jug full of water. She was beautiful, but Geoffrey's eyes fixed not on her face, but on the water.

'You are thirsty,' she said in a soft musical voice, coming to stand before him.

He tried to speak, but his dry lips would only croak. The girl smiled at him, a smile of bewitching sweetness, and lifted the jug of water. He leant forward eagerly and the girl smiled into his eyes and began to pour the water from the lip of the jug in a thin stream, letting it fall wasted to the floor. It was beyond his reach, no matter how much he strained. For a moment he gasped with desperation; then he pulled fiercely back, folding his cracked lips into a stern line and glaring at the girl with bitter anger.

Now the girl's smile looked demonic. She stopped pouring the water onto the floor and instead lifted the jug to her own lips. She took a mouthful of the water and then came close to Geoffrey, lifting her face towards him, offering him her mouth with its burden of sweetness. He gazed at her in disbelief, trembling, and after a moment turned his head aside, refusing her. She parted her lips and the clear water began to trickle from them, running down her chin, dampening the top of her gown so that it clung transparently to her opalescent flesh.

'Drink,' she whispered. 'Drink from my lips.' She took another mouthful of water and again stood with her head tilted back, offering herself. Her lips looked moist and cool, irresistible. Geoffrey gave a little moan of defeat and lowered his head, reaching out to place his lips on hers. She opened her mouth and he slipped his tongue eagerly inside it, tasting the coolness of the water and the warmth of her body, gasping with sudden bliss. When the water was gone he drew back, and the girl looked up at him with eyes that sparkled like chips of a winter sky and again filled her mouth from the jug.

Again and again he drank from her lips. Water spilled between them, wetting the naked skin of his throat, soaking her thin gown until it was almost invisible. Her nipples stood up tightly beneath the translucent silk, stimulated by the coolness of the liquid. She began to resist him as he tried to sip the water, closing her lips, barring the way with her tongue, forcing him to thrust into her mouth deeply, lasciviously, as if he loved her. Her body pressed against his and the hard points of her nipples rubbed against his chest. The slaking of his thirst freed him to feel lust, and against his wish he felt it. The damp silk gown brushed against him, rough and tormenting, and a familiar warmth began to grow in his loins. He kissed the girl harder and harder, out of desire now rather than thirst, and her eager tongue responded, pushing between his lips into the warm cavern of his mouth. Her slender hand touched the hard edge of his hipbone, traced down the hollow of his loins to cup the soft weight of his testicles, and he shuddered. His thin woollen hose were no protection against the gentle insistence of her exploring hand. He knew that this, too, was torture, that he should be unmoved, but he could not resist. His penis grew and swelled and the girl deftly unfastened his points and reached inside and wrapped her cool hand around his stiffening shaft. She began to rub steadily as their tongues twisted and coiled within their wide-open mouths.

After a few moments she pulled away, reaching up to stroke his face with her slender hand. He stared at her, panting, dreading what might follow. She stooped and set the jug to the ground and then knelt at his feet, looking up at him, licking her lips with a lascivious smile.

At the suggestion of what she might do to him Geoffrey's erect penis jerked eagerly upwards, seeking the haven of those moist lips. The girl pushed down his hose, baring his genitals and buttocks, and kissed the inside of his thigh, where the skin was tender and hairless. Then she ran her cool tongue up the smooth delicate skin towards the warm pouch of his balls. He moaned and closed his eyes. Her tongue traced the full length of his phallus, trickling cool saliva along the hot shaft, and then her lips opened to admit him, deftly fitting themselves around the aching glans while her quick tongue flickered at the little membrane beneath the head, making him gasp. She took him into her mouth and began to service him with determined skill, moving her head fast and gripping him tightly with her clever lips. Her hands tugged at his taut buttocks, encouraging him to thrust himself into the warm haven of her mouth. Hot pleasure filled him; sparks coruscated behind his closed eyes. He jerked his hips towards the girl's working mouth, letting out little guttural cries, his hands clenching into tight fists on the cords that tied him to the frame.

She was skilled, and within moments he was on the verge of climax, his balls taut and his cock straining and quivering as the hot seed readied itself. He gasped in disbelief and delight as he felt himself enter the final moments, the point of no return, where three urgent jerking lunges would bring him to shuddering release. He cried out as he thrust once, twice –

And then the clever lips resisted him, clamping onto the shining, twitching head of his cock with painful tightness, pinching at the tip so that Geoffrey gave a wordless animal cry of helpless frustration and writhed within his bonds, heaving his hips despairingly as he felt the promise of ecstasy fade, forbidden.

For a few moments he stood with his eyes tightly shut,

114

panting with misery and disappointment. His thick, proud phallus stood out before him, swollen and aching, weeping clear tears of need. He felt defeated and ashamed. She had made game of him, teased him and goaded him and left him gasping. He tried to will his erection away, but it refused to obey him.

At last he lifted his head and opened his eyes, meaning to say something cutting and superior to his tormentor. But the words choked themselves in his throat, for before him stood Rosamund de Verney. He tensed with a conflict of emotions: eager, desperate relief to see her unharmed, sudden quick love and desire, and over all a sense of utter shame that she should see him so degraded. She was wrapped from head to foot in a dark, thick cloak, her chestnut-coloured hair loose upon her shoulders, and her great dark eyes were fixed upon his. He thought that they were full of horror and reproach, and his cheeks flushed scarlet with guilt.

'You see, my lady,' said a deep, harsh voice, 'that all men are alike.'

Geoffrey's eyes jerked from Rosamund's lovely face to the man who had spoken. A big man, not tall, but strong, dressed in silk and velvet: dark greying hair, with a hard, determined, handsome face and thin sensual lips. He did not recognise the face, but it could be nobody but Sir Ralph Aycliffe. There was a dark bruise on his high forehead and Geoffrey felt a sudden surge of satisfaction to see his own handiwork. Anger possessed him, and with a sense of relief he felt his erection begin to deflate. His hands made fists and he said through his teeth, 'I had you down, you bastard.'

'So you did,' agreed Sir Ralph coldly. 'I will not forget it.'

'Rosamund,' Geoffrey gasped, twisting against the cruel cords, 'my lady, are you well? Forgive me, I didn't mean –'

'My Lady de Verney,' said Sir Ralph, and Geoffrey stopped speaking as he saw how Rosamund turned very slowly to look into the knight's face. She looked controlled, not herself. Once Geoffrey had seen a magician at a feast putting people into trances and making them do ridiculous things: undoubtedly witchcraft, but harmless enough. The same witchcraft was at work here, but turned to cruelty and lust. Rosamund's dark eyes looked like mirrors, glazed and reflective.

'My lady,' Sir Ralph went on, 'here is your – *cousin*.' Geoffrey's face twisted with desperate tenderness as he realised how Rosamund had tried to conceal their relationship. 'You wanted to know he was unharmed. You see that he is so recovered in body that he is able to enjoy the attentions of one of my servants.' Rosamund's eyes turned once towards Geoffrey, but before he could excuse himself they had left him, fixing again on Sir Ralph's face. 'If he dies,' said Sir Ralph, 'you know that it is your doing. Sign the paper, or he will suffer.'

'You bastard!' Geoffrey shouted, lunging against the bonds that held him with such force that the whole frame creaked. 'You bastard, don't threaten her!' Rosamund's face was turned again towards him, white and strained, and he spoke earnestly into her cavernous eyes. 'My lady, don't do anything because of me. Don't let him torment you with me. Please, my lady, forget me.'

'Very chivalrous,' sneered Sir Ralph. He gestured with his hand and the blonde girl appeared from behind him and came towards Geoffrey. Now in her hand she carried a knife, a long-bladed dagger with a sharp, keen point. Geoffrey stiffened as she came and stood close beside him and laid the blade against his cheek. It felt both cold and hot, stinging with sharpness. He closed his eyes and swallowed.

'Sign,' repeated Sir Ralph. Geoffrey's eyes snapped open and he opened his mouth to speak again, to warn Rosamund that there was no point in giving way to threats. But as he drew in breath the girl moved the point of the dagger, sliding it around under his jaw and lifting it so that he had to strain upwards to escape the deadly point. He fell silent, his breath shuddering, feeling the blade beginning to prick the tender underside

116

of his chin. But he kept his eyes open, watching Rosamund, trying to signal with his look that she should not give in.

At last her peony lips parted. She said almost inaudibly, 'No. I will not.'

'Must I prove that I mean what I say?' asked Aycliffe angrily. 'Whom shall I cause to suffer, my lady?' He signalled with his hand and snapped to the girl, 'I want him naked.'

The blonde bowed her head obediently and began to cut at Geoffrey's shirt and hose with the dagger, stripping them from him. She was in a hurry and it made her careless. As she slit one of his sleeves and pulled it back the sharp blade of the knife nicked the white flesh beneath the linen. Geoffrey flinched as blood began to well from the cut and trickle down his raised arm towards the hollow of his shoulder.

Death seemed inevitable. Perhaps if he could draw Aycliffe's anger upon himself he might give Rosamund a chance to escape. It might make things worse for him, but what matter? He hauled against his bonds and said furiously, 'Aycliffe, you are no knight. You are a treacherous villain.'

'Treacherous?' repeated Sir Ralph, quite unmoved. 'To whom? I think not.' He came and stood a little way in front of Geoffrey, examining his naked body with cool black eyes. 'A fine specimen,' he said. Geoffrey's head pounded with impotent rage. Sir Ralph looked over his shoulder and smiled at Rosamund's white, silent face. 'I see why you picked on this one,' he said almost conversationally. 'A very splendid body. And so well equipped.' He reached out with one hand and to Geoffrey's unspeakable horror took hold of his softened penis and began gently to rub at it.

'Jesu,' spluttered Geoffrey, trying desperately to pull away, 'take your hands off me, you filthy sodomite.'

Aycliffe tugged gently at Geoffrey's limp phallus for a moment. Then he smiled and drew back, saying, 'For now.'

Geoffrey sighed with relief, but Sir Ralph had barely begun. He snapped his fingers and from the curtains at the end of the hall two more women appeared, also young and lovely, one red haired, one dark. Both of them were dressed as the blonde girl had been, in flimsy silk that barely hid their beautiful bodies. They stood before Sir Ralph, silently awaiting his command. 'Here,' he said, gesturing at Geoffrey's naked body with one casual hand. 'Please him. I want him hard as a rock.'

At once the girls began to work on him, rubbing their bodies against him, caressing him with hands and lips and tongues. He shut his eyes, trying to will away the sensations, trying to prevent his quivering penis from swelling and rising as the girls tormented it with delight. For a little while it seemed that he would be successful: his phallus hung unmoving between his thighs, thick and soft. Then Sir Ralph said sharply, 'See your mistress, Master Lymington.'

Geoffrey's eyes opened of themselves. He saw Rosamund before him and his lips gaped open in wonder and horror. The thick cloak lay behind her on the floor: Sir Ralph was holding her wrists behind her back. Her head was tilted back to reveal her long white throat, her dark eyes were fixed on Geoffrey's face with mute, beseeching entreaty, and her body –

She was clad in a vile garment, black, soft and glistening like leather. It clung to her waist, pulling it in tightly. Above the waist her breasts were exposed and forced upwards by the tight-laced garment, and Sir Ralph held her wrists and dragged back her shoulders, thrusting her upper body forward, offering the soft white mounds to Geoffrey's astonished gaze. Below her waist the – thing – was snugly fitted to the hip-bones, then abruptly ceased, revealing the splendour of her white buttocks and the swell of her pubis beneath its cushion of dark fur.

Geoffrey had seen such things before in the low taverns of Southwark where he and his friends were wont to go for a little salacious entertainment when their

118

time permitted, but he had never dreamed that anyone might compel a lady to demean herself so. It was terrible to see the woman he loved dressed like a whore, but his body did not share his mind's disgust. Instantly and of itself his penis began to jerk upwards and at once one of the girls fastened her lips upon it, licking and sucking. Another thrust up her face between his spread legs to suckle at the dangling weight of his balls, while the third knelt behind him, slithering her soft agile tongue deep into his anus. He writhed and gasped with helpless ecstasy, and Sir Ralph's command was obeyed: he was hard as a rock. The girl with his penis in her mouth gave a little moan of satisfaction and flickered her tongue over the swollen knob, encouraging the turgid shaft to swell still further.

'Now,' said Sir Ralph with a vicious grin, 'keep him there. You, Master Lymington, shall see how much this mistress of yours is enslaved to me.'

He released Rosamund and stood a little back from her. At once she lowered her head and covered herself as best as she could with her hands, the picture of feminine modesty. Sir Ralph smiled mockingly, then snapped his fingers again, and from the curtain came forward a pair of young men. They were tall and well muscled, clad in leather breeches and doublets of black leather without sleeves, so that their strong arms were bare and glistening. One of them carried a whip, a long-lashed whip with a thick handle of doubled and plaited leather. Geoffrey felt his stomach close and heave with horror and fear. 'Rosamund,' he whispered.

She lifted her head and looked at him. Her lips were parted and trembling and her eyes were so soft and gentle that his heart wrung with helpless love. What did it matter that Aycliffe had dressed her like the most vicious type of whore? He hated her and sought revenge on her for her insult to him. This was his vengeance. Geoffrey suddenly felt such a surge of pity and sorrow that he thought his heart would break. Rosamund opened her lips as if she would speak, but before a word could escape her Sir Ralph snapped, 'Remember what I told you, my lady.'

Rosamund looked as though she were on the edge of tears. Geoffrey tried to pull his aching penis out of the warm, welcoming mouth of the girl who sucked at it. 'What have you done, you son of a whore?' he demanded angrily. 'Have you said you will hurt her if she speaks to me? What have you threatened her with, you bastard?'

Sir Ralph ignored him. He took the whip from the young man, running its thick handle thoughtfully between his fingers. Then he said, 'Suck her breasts, both of you.'

'No!' It was Rosamund's voice and Geoffrey gasped with shock. He had almost believed that her sufferings had robbed her of the power of speech. 'No,' she cried again, her low sweet voice taut with urgency. 'I beg you.'

'I warned you,' said Sir Ralph, and he signalled to the girls who clustered around Geoffrey's loins, dangling like great leeches from his swollen flesh. The girl who was sucking at his testicles reached up and took hold of the taut, upraised sac and twisted it sharply. Geoffrey arched his back, unable to contain a howl of pain. Then he whimpered, his eyes tight shut as the girl who had just tormented him returned to her gentle sucking, soothing away the hurt, and the one with his penis in her mouth flickered her tongue over him ever more eagerly, restoring his stunned phallus to its previous iron hardness.

After a moment Geoffrey felt in control of himself again. He wished that he could keep his eyes closed, but it would be cowardly. He swallowed hard and lifted his head and looked.

Rosamund was standing very still, her face pale and tense. On either side of her the young men stood, and as if the opening of Geoffrey's eyes was a signal they stooped their heads and began to lick at the dark peaks of Rosamund's full breasts. She shivered and closed her eyes. The flesh of the areolae began to swell and the nipples erected, the colour of rose-hips, hard eager points of pleasure. Each young man took the breast he worshipped in his hand, squeezing it as he suckled and lapped at the distended tip. Rosamund's head fell back and her red lips parted and a little smothered moan escaped her.

Geoffrey drew in a shallow breath of horror. That should have been a moan of despair and shame: but he had heard Rosamund cry out as he took her, he had heard her moan and pant as his body filled her, and he knew that the sound she had just made was one of pleasure. She was enjoying what Aycliffe's minions were doing to her! How could she?

His reaction had not escaped Sir Ralph. The older man smiled, a smile of cold, bitter triumph. Then he went to Rosamund, reached down and laid his hand on her white thigh. He pulled her a little towards him so that her mound was thrust forward, the pink lips just showing through the dark curls of her pubic hair. Geoffrey shuddered with disbelief and vile, shameful arousal: dark rods of pleasure beat at him as the three girls continued to lick and suck his genitals. Very slowly Sir Ralph pushed the handle of the whip between Rosamund's parted thighs, dipping the hard knob at the end of the shaft into the wetness of her sex and then withdrawing it to stroke and stroke at the little pearl of flesh that stood up just below her triangle, hard and aroused already. Rosamund's back arched and she would have fallen if Sir Ralph had not caught her around her shoulders with his strong arm. She lay where he held her, letting out little helpless moans of pleasure as the two young men squeezed and fondled her breasts, sucking earnestly at her swollen nipples, and Sir Ralph gently, persistently masturbated her with the handle of the whip.

'Oh, Christ,' Geoffrey groaned. He felt almost sick to see Rosamund respond to Aycliffe as if he were her lover, but he could not draw his eyes away. His aching testicles were tensing again, eager to shoot hot sperm between the working lips of the girl who was worshipping his penis with her mouth. His buttocks clenched spasmodically, trapping the probing tongue of the girl behind him, and she lubriciously quivered the warm point in his trembling anus. He was going to come, here in Sir Ralph's hall, unable to control his shameful lust at the sight of Aycliffe rubbing Rosamund's sex with the whip so that she moaned and jerked with ecstasy. There was nothing he could do. He began to pant regularly, thrusting himself eagerly into the warm mouth that surrounded his straining penis, feeling the pleasure rising and rising in waves within him, avidly watching as Rosamund's beautiful body shimmered with the rhythm of Aycliffe's caresses. Her sex was tilted upwards and the thick shaft of the whip slid smoothly between the jutting, engorged lips, vanished briefly into the warm dark tunnel of her desire, emerged glistening to stroke again and again at the delicate pink pearl of flesh, making his mistress sigh and heave with delight. Those moist folds of flesh had encircled his hungry cock, drawn him within them, given him the greatest pleasure he had ever taken in a woman's body.

And then, once again, the sensation abruptly ceased, pleasure evaporating into the scalding steam of pain as one of the girls twisted at his tender, swollen sac. Geoffrey cried out helplessly and writhed in his bonds, his whole body tight and arching with agony. The girls pulled away from him, laughing, as the sharpness of the pain resolved itself into a dull ache compounded by the terrible tenseness of his full balls.

He struggled uselessly, making the frame jerk and sway. Sir Ralph was standing beside Rosamund, still holding her up with one hand around her slender leather-girded waist. She was shaking as she stood and her hands were covering her face. Aycliffe had ceased to stimulate her and now he was holding the whip delicately between finger and thumb. As Geoffrey watched he passed the stiff plaited leather beneath his nose and then extended his long pointed tongue and began to lick at it, tasting the pearly juices that gleamed in the grooves.

'The Devil take you,' Geoffrey raged. 'Let me go, let me fight you for her. As God is my witness, I will fight you naked, my bare hands against your sword.'

'For this whore?' asked Sir Ralph, licking his lips and looking at Rosamund almost as if he were puzzled. 'Why should you want her?'

'You are afraid,' Geoffrey hissed. 'I overcame you before and now you fear me. You are a coward.' He felt no fear, only a ferocious, exalted excitement. He felt like a Crusader fighting for God. 'Let me fight you,' he repeated eagerly. If Aycliffe accepted it would be a Heaven of pleasure for Geoffrey to do justice on him with his bare hands.

Aycliffe's face was suddenly still and cold. His dark heavy brows drew down into a solid bar of anger over his gleaming eyes. He was still, staring. Geoffrey jerked again at the bonds around his wrists and drew his lips back from his teeth and he and Aycliffe stared at each other like dogs bristling and snarling before a fight. 'Coward,' he said again, and spat on the floor.

'Master Lymington,' said Sir Ralph very softly, 'if I did not have more important things to do, you would soon learn the folly of calling me coward. But as it is, my quarrel with you takes second place to my plans for the Lady de Verney.'

He seized Rosamund's hand and she started and gasped as he forced the whip into it, folding her white fingers closed around the moist handle. 'Now, Lady de Verney,' he said thinly, 'I will take particular pleasure in punishing you and your high-spoken gallant at the same time. Whip him, my lady.'

Geoffrey frowned in disbelief, feeling his angry exaltation beginning to desert him. What new refinement of torture was this? Aycliffe would have overreached himself, for he could not believe that Rosamund would hurt him.

Lady de Verney clearly felt the same way. She shrank

123

from Sir Ralph, the whip drooping from her limp fingers, her face white with horror. She shook her head.

Sir Ralph smiled. 'My lady,' he said softly, 'you have forgotten your promise. You have forgotten that I have the power to insist.' He jerked his head and the blonde girl jumped to her feet, breathless soft giggles of eagerness stirring her breasts beneath her thin silk gown. She had the knife still and she set it quickly to Geoffrey's cheek, laying it against the high cheekbone where the bruise he had taken at Sandal was beginning to heal.

'I will see you lay the lash to his flesh, my lady,' said Sir Ralph, 'or you will see him hurt.'

Geoffrey closed his eyes, fighting fear. The blade of the knife stung him with the premonition of pain. Shivers of sensation, like cold quivering fingers, ran down his arms and nestled between his shoulder blades, physical manifestations of dread. And yet his poor desperate penis was still hard and erect, aroused so many times that it could not now relax but must remain at attention, stiff and eager, preparing to die in the breach.

The blade of the knife moved and his breath hissed through his teeth. He made himself stand still, feeling sharp hot pain and then the swift trickling of warm blood. He heard Rosamund whimper and cry out, 'No, no, I beg you!'

'Oh, come, my lady,' said Sir Ralph. Geoffrey opened his eyes and glared at the grinning knight with hatred burning inside him like a core of flame. 'Come, that is nothing; he might cut himself thus shaving. But if you do not like it, my lady,' Aycliffe's voice changed, becoming hard and vicious, 'then you must beat him!'

'No.' Rosamund suddenly flung the whip aside and leapt towards Geoffrey, holding out her hands to him. The young leather-clad men seized her and held her back and she fought them, weeping and struggling. 'Geoffrey,' she called to him, 'Geoffrey, I'm sorry, forgive me, I beg you.'

He meant to tell her that he loved her, that he understood that none of this was her fault. But then the blonde girl moved her hand in a quick silent flash of blue steel and Geoffrey stiffened and stood motionless, breathing shallowly through parted lips, unable even to close his eyes, filled with quivering, shaking horror. The knife was poised beneath his testicles, balanced against the delicate skin.

Rosamund, too, was frozen with fear. Sir Ralph stood for a moment with his arms folded, enjoying the scene, then he reached down and lifted the fallen whip. 'Now, my lady,' he said with relish, 'beat him. And do a proper job of it, unless you would see him gelded.'

There was a little moment of stillness. Then Rosamund let out a sob and snatched the whip and moved towards Geoffrey, tears gleaming on her cheeks. The knife withdrew and Geoffrey closed his eyes and gasped with relief. Then relief turned to pain as the lash cut across his back. He snarled and twisted and gritted his teeth, determined not to cry out.

The whip rose and fell four times. Each time he stiffened, clamping his teeth together against the cry of shock and pain. Then nothing, and he opened his tight-shut eyes to see Rosamund kneeling on the ground at his feet, her naked buttocks thrust obscenely out behind her, her face sunk in her hands, weeping. 'No more,' she whimpered, 'I beg you, no more.'

'You dog,' Geoffrey hissed as Sir Ralph walked slowly over to stand above the shuddering body of Rosamund. 'You piece of filth. If you want to hurt me, do it yourself! Don't torture her.'

'Your pain, I assure you, is entirely secondary to hers,' said Sir Ralph, barely sparing him a glance.

'Let her go, you devil!' Geoffrey tried to control his voice, but he could hear that panic and pain and despair were beginning to creep into it. 'Kill me, if you must.'

Sir Ralph lifted his head, looking for a moment interested. 'I don't understand why you should care so much for a whore,' he commented.

'Don't call her a whore!' Geoffrey raged.

'But she is a whore,' Sir Ralph insisted. 'Only a whore

would allow the man who had just caused her to whip her lover to give her pleasure. And, if you watch, you will see that this is just what Lady de Verney will permit me to do.'

Geoffrey had no answer. He stood trembling, looking down at Rosamund's slumped, shaking body. She turned under his eyes and looked up at Sir Ralph and once again her face wore that strange, glazed expression, an expression of resignation, of hopelessness, of transparent slavery.

'Rosamund,' Geoffrey whispered, 'don't let him.'

Her eyes turned to him, filling with tears. 'Don't,' he said again, pleading. 'Resist him. Rosamund. Please.'

Now Sir Ralph's two young henchmen brought forward a wooden bench, hip-high and padded with dark velvet. They caught Rosamund by her shoulders and began to lift her. She struggled and Geoffrey caught a quick breath of tormented relief to see her fight them. Then they had her in their hands and were laying her upon the prickling velvet. They shackled her white wrists above her head: the lifting of her arms caused her heavy breasts to tauten, emerging almost completely from the vile leather corset around her waist. Her hips were placed at the very edge of the bench, pointing directly towards Geoffrey, and her ankles were secured to the edges of the frame so that her knees were raised. The two young men took hold of a knee each and pulled them wide apart, tautening the muscles of her thighs, exposing the glistening flesh between them. Rosamund moaned and her head rolled from side to side in what might have been helpless protest or delicious anticipation.

'See,' said Sir Ralph very softly, 'see how she is enslaved to me.' He came and stood by Rosamund's white hips and reached between her open, quivering thighs, placing his hands on either side of her sex so that the dark fur and the moist pink lips were framed by his strong fingers. Then he pressed down gently and pulled his hands apart and her tender flesh opened, the lips parting, revealing the taut stem of her clitoris and the dark entrance to her vagina. 'Such a beautiful, tender little cunny,' said Sir Ralph. 'I touched it once years ago and it shuddered with pleasure. Imagine how much more she will appreciate me, now you have shown her what men are good for.' And with the greatest delicacy and deliberation he placed one broad finger on the little erect pearl and moved it and Rosamund let out a long, breathy whimper of agonised pleasure.

Geoffrey could not close his eyes, he could not turn away. Greed and horror and lust made him watch as Sir Ralph stimulated Rosamund very gently with his finger, making her gasp and moan, proving beyond all doubt that she was faithless, lewd, a harlot beyond redemption. Once Sir Ralph drew his finger back a little, tormenting her with the lightness of his touch, and she lifted her round hips and pushed them upwards, rubbing herself against Sir Ralph's hand, as lascivious as a cat.

'Whore,' Geoffrey whispered, tears of despair stinging his eyes. 'Whore.'

Sir Ralph dropped to his knees and began to lap with his strong pointed tongue at the soft whorls of Rosamund's secret flesh. She moaned more loudly and her body writhed. The two young men stooped again to worship her breasts, licking with hot wet mouths at her taut nipples, and her cries became pants. Geoffrey stared, riveted, feeling his penis thicken and swell, aching to bury itself in that warm welcoming tunnel. One of the girls knelt beside him and began to service him with her mouth, delicate caresses that drew him to the peak of hardness and then kept him there, shuddering with arousal.

Rosamund cried out and shook beneath Sir Ralph's tormenting caresses. He licked her with lustful skill, bringing her to the very edge of climax. She twisted and heaved, trying to rub herself against his face, but he drew back, laughing, and turned to look at Geoffrey. 'Proof,' he said, reaching out with his hand and stroking

Rosamund's weeping flesh so that she jerked. 'What more proof do you need?'

The young men were still teasing the tips of Rosamund's breasts with their tongues. She moaned and whimpered, her head rolling, whispering, 'Please.'

Geoffrey wanted to shut his eyes in shame and despair to hear her so degraded, but some vile lust prevented him. He winced as the red-headed girl crouched behind him and began again to stimulate the tender skin of his dark cleft with her tongue. Sharp pleasure tightened in his balls and his rearing cock jerked in the blonde girl's mouth.

'I shall have pity,' said Sir Ralph mockingly. 'You may complete her enjoyment, Master Lymington.' He reached out again for Rosamund's sex. 'Let us ensure that she is ready to receive your homage.'

He thrust two fingers between the lips of Rosamund's vulva, making her shudder and moan, then withdrew them shining with moisture. For the first time he opened his garments, exposing his massive, stiff penis, and he began to rub Rosamund's juices onto the hard gleaming shaft. He did this again and again until she was whimpering and writhing with each touch and his thick rod of flesh and its purple head were glossy and slick with creamy dampness. Then he stood back and gestured with his hand.

The girl before Geoffrey drew back, leaving his aching, engorged penis hanging in the empty air, twitching with a life of its own. The girl behind him continued to lick at his cleft, pushing her tongue into the tight hole of his anus. The young men raised themselves and picked up the bench with its burden of shackled woman and carried it closer and closer to Geoffrey's straining body.

Rosamund lifted her head as she felt the movement. They set her down before him, so close to him that the swollen head of his cock was just pressing against her tender sex. She strained upwards towards him, her back arching, her breasts thrust forward by the bonds that fastened her arms above her head. 'Geoffrey,' she whispered, 'Geoffrey, please. Have mercy on me.'

He wanted to refuse her, to forbid her the pleasure that his body could give, but he could not. With a growl of agony and delight he thrust forward with his hips. Her soft flesh parted for him and the consuming bliss of penetration surrounded his swollen shaft as it drove deeply into her shuddering body. He filled her to the hilt and then stood still, the tense sac of his balls resting against her soft buttocks, savouring the delicious, clinging warmth. Her eyes were wide open, staring into his in astonished, unbelieving ecstasy.

'Geoffrey,' she whispered again, 'oh God, Geoffrey.'

He knew what she wanted, what she needed. He needed it too: he needed to push himself into her again and again, possessing her, driving her to delirious climax as he took his pleasure from her. He was about to withdraw and thrust again when he stopped, shivering, his back and shoulders taut with fear.

He could feel something, something hard and hot pressing between his buttocks. His secret crevice was wet and slippery with the redhead's saliva and the hard hot thing was sliding on the dampness, seeking the puckered entrance, pushing against it. He stood very still, not wanting to believe it.

Aycliffe's voice hissed in his ear. 'Yesterday,' he said softly, 'I took the virginity of your mistress's arse, Master Lymington. I shed my seed in her bowels. And today I will take yours. If you are a virgin, that is. I know what men say about the trials of a pageboy's life. Did your master ever enjoy himself with you, Master Lymington?'

'Oh God,' Geoffrey moaned. But he could not pull away, for his stiff cock was buried deep in Rosamund's body, wedging him in one place. The only way he could move was backwards: backwards onto the great thick cock that waited to pierce him.

Rosamund whimpered and shifted her hips, looking up at him with entreaty in her dark eyes. 'Geoffrey,' she whispered, 'please do it. Please, please.'

A terrible conflict of fear and desire raged through Geoffrey, making him shut his eyes and sob. There were strong hands on his hips, holding his muscular haunches, preparing him: and now the massive knob behind him was beginning to advance, forcing its way into him, opening his tight sphincter. He cried out in horror and shame, knowing that he was violated, desecrated, deflowered. He expected searing pain. But once the initial thrust was past there was no pain, only a strange, hot sense of fullness, of delicious, clinging tightness, the bitter mirror image of the pleasure he felt in sheathing himself within Rosamund's willing body.

'Take her,' hissed the voice in his ear, 'pleasure her.'

'Geoffrey,' Rosamund moaned.

And with a desperate cry of agony and delight Geoffrey drew back from Rosamund, and as he did so he impaled himself on the hot thickness of Sir Ralph's rigid shaft. He writhed once and then began to move regularly, pushing himself into Rosamund over and over, penetrated and possessed as he possessed her. Unimaginable sensations flooded over him, all the red bliss of coupling mutated and multiplied tenfold by the dark viscid pleasure that surged through him as Sir Ralph's cock slid smoothly in and out of his anus. He was lost, drowned in bliss, hardly aware of the fact that Rosamund was crying out and shaking as his eager movements drove her over the edge of ecstasy. Her warm flesh spasmed around him, gripping him as though with satin fists.

Then, suddenly, he felt himself slipping out of her, cold air kissing the sensitive tip of his cock. He gasped and opened his eyes and saw that the bench with Rosamund upon it was being drawn away so that she was out of his reach. She was slumped and panting, her breasts heaving, her thighs obscenely parted, white juices beading the scarlet flesh of her sex. Geoffrey strained towards her, feeling bliss recede.

Then he felt again the smooth intrusion of Sir Ralph's

shaft, sliding deeply into him. The experience was sharper now, sudden, unmixed with any other sensation. Geoffrey gasped in protest, not wanting to believe that he could obtain pleasure from this alone. He tried to pull away, but Sir Ralph's hands were firm and hard on his haunches, holding him still to receive his surging thrusts.

'No,' Geoffrey groaned, feeling his discharge beginning to tremble between his legs, shivering along the length of his rigid cock. 'Oh God, no.'

And then the blonde girl was on her knees again before him, reaching out with one slender hand to grip at the base of his penis. He shuddered, expecting to feel her lips, but she did not reach for him, only tilted his quivering cock downwards, pointing it towards her mouth. She licked her lips expectantly, but did nothing that might push him into climax. She sat back on her haunches, waiting, her red lips parted, and Geoffrey moaned and jerked helplessly as Sir Ralph swived him.

He fought the sensation, clenching his fists, clenching his buttocks, trying to resist. But it was hopeless. His head fell back and the muscles of his loins and his flat belly tensed and shook. Sir Ralph drove himself deep, snarling as he climaxed, and Geoffrey let out a long, agonised cry. His cock began to twitch with desperate urgency as the hot seed pumped up his taut, hard shaft and spurted time after time into the empty air. The girl moaned with pleasure and opened her mouth to receive the glutinous gift. He had been waiting so long that now the crisis was almost unbearable: for long moments his penis jumped and heaved, forcing out his thick come in trailing, milky jets.

Sir Ralph withdrew swiftly from Geoffrey's shuddering body. The young squire cried out once, a desperate, hopeless moan, like a coursed-down stag. Then he slumped and hung in his bonds, his head lolling, limp and senseless. Aycliffe set his hand on the taut, muscular plane of one buttock and ran it slowly, experimentally up to the shoulder-blade. There was no reaction. Sir

Ralph smiled coldly, digging his strong fingers into Geoffrey's thick glossy hair. Then he flung back his head and began to laugh, softly at first, then louder and louder, crowing with satisfaction and triumph.

Chapter Six

They took Rosamund away, limp and shivering, and left her in a small bedchamber. The door was bolted fast and there were bars over the narrow window. Outside more snow was falling. She clung to the bars and stared out into the encroaching darkness and the strange livid glow of a snow-covered landscape, her face blank.

Presently she began to revive. She tore at the vile corset that clutched her pale flesh so lubriciously and flung it to the floor, spurning it with her foot. A loose, soft woollen robe had been left on the bed and she drew it on and sat down on the bare floor by the little fire, staring into the flames.

She chewed at her lip, her face twitching in regret and shame as she thought of Geoffrey's suffering at Aycliffe's hands. She had not realised, she had not understood, when he entered her, that Sir Ralph intended to torment him thus. And she had begged him to take her!

Rosamund hid her face in her hands and began to weep, slow shuddering sobs of the deepest agony. She could not help but picture Geoffrey's face as he writhed, impaled upon Sir Ralph's surging cock, tortured by his own pleasure as by the rack and hot irons. Even if they lived, he would surely never, never forgive her for being the cause of his dishonour.

The light seeped from the sky. There was no candle in the room and the fire was fading. It was cold, and Rosamund began to shiver. She looked up at the narrow window and saw a sliver of tattered moon high above her, flying through the yellow clouds of snow. It was so pitiless and cold that she could not watch it. She clasped her hands together and lowered her head, praying aloud in a desperate undertone.

'Holy Virgin,' she began, and then her voice faltered. How would the immaculate mother of God understand the sins that she had committed today? She laid her head in her hands for a moment, and then inspiration came to her.

'Mary,' she whispered, 'Holy Magdalen, see me and have mercy. Forgive me my sins, blessed Magdalen, you will understand them. You will understand that the body can do what the heart would never consent to. Forgive me, Saint Mary, and look down on my beloved, on Geoffrey, and bring him comfort.'

Her prayer brought her a little solace. She sighed, then got up. There seemed nothing else that she could do, and so she crawled into the high bed and laid her head on the pillow. The bed was luxurious, with smooth linen sheets and thick, heavy blankets, and within moments she was cocooned in blissful warmth. Exhaustion and misery drove her almost instantly into the shielding arms of sleep.

She woke in the morning reluctantly, unwilling to return to the horror that her life had become. A plainly dressed man came to the room and made up the fire, brought her food and the wherewithal to wash herself. He left her alone at once and she stood by the fire contemplating the broad basin of steaming water, the linen towels, the little pot of liquid soap perfumed with jasmine.

Presently she shook off the robe and began to wash herself, rubbing the delicate soap over her white skin and rinsing it off with the water. Her body showed no signs of the abuse it had suffered yesterday: her skin was clear and smooth as the snow upon the window-ledge. She rubbed gently between the cheeks of her bottom, feeling a strange, stinging tingle of memory as she pictured what Sir Ralph had done to her.

Sir Ralph. She hated him, loathed and despised him. For him to seek vengeance on her was understandable, though unchivalrous. But to use her lover as the instrument of his revenge was contemptible. And yet she knew that Aycliffe had tapped some deep urge within her, something that Geoffrey's roughness had only begun to explore.

If he had sought to abuse only her, she would have welcomed the struggle. The more extreme the trials he conceived for her, the more it would be her victory to accept them without shame. But she had not dreamed that he would use Geoffrey against her, and she did not know if she could bear it.

She made herself eat a little of the food, though her stomach closed at it. Time after time, with increasing hopelessness, she thought of Geoffrey. He had come to her of his own free will to help her and he had shown her a Heaven of pleasure, and she had repaid him with torture and shame.

Outside the room she heard the heavy tread of booted feet and she jumped up from the bed, hastening to stand by the window and wrapping the woollen robe closely around her naked body. Her bowels twisted with sudden fear.

The door opened and Sir Ralph entered, one of his young henchmen close behind him. He looked determined and yet somehow wary, as if he were not now so certain of victory. Rosamund set her jaw and folded her lips tightly together, challenging him with her gaze.

For a moment Sir Ralph looked at her in silence. Then he said slowly, 'I begin to believe that I was mistaken in you, Lady de Verney.' Rosamund did not reply, but turned her head away scornfully. 'I thought that you were a virtuous lady. Now I believe that you have the instincts of a whore.'

135

'A type of woman I am sure you know well,' retorted Rosamund. 'But you are wrong.'

'Why then do you enjoy everything I do to you?' demanded Sir Ralph, and real anger and frustration appeared for a moment from behind his urbane mask. 'A virtuous lady would have died of shame two days since, and you seem to feel nothing but pleasure! What must I do to make you ashamed?'

Rosamund scowled at him and did not reply. He jerked his head abruptly and the young man silently left the room, closing the door behind him. 'All those years ago,' said Sir Ralph softly, 'when I came upon you in the garden, were you truly resisting me? Or did you really want me?'

'I have never wanted you,' Rosamund said through her teeth. 'I loathe and despise you. I wish you were dead.'

'Do you so?' exclaimed Sir Ralph, his eyes kindling with fury. He crossed the room in two strides and caught hold of Rosamund's wrist, pulling her towards him. She stared into his face, shaking with fear and hatred, and his hot eyes burned her. 'Do you? Hate me all you wish. It will make this even more pleasant for me.' He reached for her other wrist. She pulled her hand away from him, but he was too quick for her. His grip was stronger than a vice. Baring his teeth with effort he forced her hands back and down, behind her, so that he stood so close to her that their bodies were almost touching. Rosamund gasped and tried to pull free, but it was useless.

'Now,' said Aycliffe softly, 'now I am going to take from you what I wanted to take in the garden, my lady, whether you hate me or not.'

And without another word he wrestled her wrists above her head and slammed her against the stone wall of the little chamber, almost knocking the breath from her. Rosamund closed her eyes and wrenched at her hands, thrusting her body forward to try to keep him at a distance. It was like fighting the wall itself. Sir Ralph smiled and breathed faster and lowered his mouth towards hers. She turned her head from side to side, trying to escape him, but after a few seconds he trapped her and pinned her lips beneath his. His strong tongue pushed at her mouth. For the space of twenty heartbeats she resisted him. Then it was as if a great fist had clamped around her belly, wrenching her guts with a brutal contraction of lust. His hard body pressing against her spurred her to struggle and writhe with loathing and desire, and her lips parted of themselves to allow him to enter her mouth with his hot tongue. She did not return his kiss, she did not move in response to him, but as he kissed her, as his tongue twisted within her mouth and seemed to thrust into her very throat, she had to strive to restrain a hoarse moan of lecherous enjoyment. The skin of her breasts tensed and her sex closed in on itself, gripping an invisible phallus, clenching with desire.

'If I had not lifted my mouth,' hissed Sir Ralph, 'you would have been mine then. I would have had you. I felt your pretty little cunny and you were ready for me. Did that aged husband of yours know he had married a whore?'

'Don't call me a whore,' Rosamund replied furiously, tugging at her pinioned hands. Sir Ralph laughed and released her wrists and she battered her fists against his broad shoulders, wanting to hurt him. He laughed again and ignored her blows, and now his hands were free to seize the front of the robe and pull it open, baring her breasts to his hot eager gaze.

'No,' Rosamund moaned, arching her back in protest. Sir Ralph stared into her face for a moment, and then again placed his mouth firmly on hers and began to thrust his hot tongue between her lips. As he kissed her his big hands went to her naked breasts and he began to flicker his thumbs against her nipples, coaxing them into fullness. Rosamund gasped as sharp splinters of pleasure radiated from her swelling breasts, sending a flood of warmth through her loins. Suddenly she felt revulsion at her own response and she fought against it by fighting against the man who aroused her, twisting her hands into his thick greying hair and digging her nails hard into the back of his neck.

Sir Ralph tore his mouth from hers, growling with pain. 'Bitch,' he snarled, and again caught hold of her wrists. He held them firmly in one hand and with the other he unfastened the narrow leather belt that confined the waist of his woollen doublet. He twisted it around Rosamund's wrists, binding them securely together, and then he drew back a little and smiled into her furious face.

'Now,' he said, 'I am going to have you, my lady.'

Rosamund closed her eyes, not wanting him to see the urgent lust that was consuming her. She had fought him, he had defeated her, and now she longed to feel him inside her, but she could not admit even to herself that she wanted him. So she shook her head, protesting dumbly and struggling against his restraining hands.

Sir Ralph put his hands to his doublet, pulling it open, quickly unlacing his points. His cock sprang free, massively erect, scarlet with the hot blood that stiffened it. He tugged at Rosamund's bound hands until her arms were around him, holding him close in her embrace as if she loved him.

'Fight me now,' he whispered, and he moved his body against hers, slowly and lasciviously. His thick, hot penis pressed against the naked skin of her belly and she bit her lip to hide her yearning. Sir Ralph put his hands on her breasts, ran them down her body to her hip-bones, then further down, onto her soft thighs. With a jerk and a grunt he forced one knee between her tight-pressed legs, forcing them open. Cool air kissed the delicate flesh of Rosamund's sex as it gaped hungrily, eager as a starving man for food. She gasped and turned her head away and the skin of her loins and belly fluttered with irrepressible excitement.

'Did that young gallant swive you well?' hissed Sir Ralph in her ear. 'He was well weaponed. Did he serve you well in the combat? Did he fill you, my lady, as I will?' And then he stooped a little and caught hold of

Rosamund's thighs, lifting her bodily, pulling her legs apart. She caught her breath in shock and sudden helplessness as he lifted her feet from the floor. Sir Ralph's hands clutched at her white buttocks and she felt the great shining knob of his swollen cock prodding between the lips of her sex, seeking entrance. For a moment she thought she would die of anticipation as he found the moist gateway and lodged himself there: then he took a securer hold and drew back his lips from his teeth and drove steadily into her.

Rosamund could not keep in a long sigh of ecstasy as she felt his huge cock entering her. The wall was hard against her back and her tied wrists prevented her from clutching at Sir Ralph's shoulders with her hands, from trying to pull him deeper inside her. She was at his mercy, impaled and powerless and already shivering with pleasure.

Even in his anger, Geoffrey had been gentle compared with the way that Sir Ralph took her now. He pounded into her as a smith's hammer pounds the anvil, tupped her as the ram tups the ewe, battered her with the ram of his flesh as if he laid siege to a mighty castle. With every stroke his thick, hard body rubbed against her sex, stimulating the eager bead of her clitoris, and her taut swollen nipples rubbed deliciously against the rough wool of his doublet. She wrapped her legs around him, linking her ankles above his working buttocks. His strong hands clutched ferociously at her soft white haunches and her naked breasts juddered with the rhythm of his lunges as he shafted her. Her sighs turned to gasps, her gasps to pants, her pants to moans of delight, and still he swived her, the swollen shaft of his eager cock sliding out of her to the tip and then lunging back into her with incredible force.

Rosamund felt her crisis approaching as if she were being dragged in chains to the edge of a dizzy cliff. Her eyes were open and staring, but instead of Sir Ralph's face, flushed with lust and grim with determination, she saw red darkness, sparkling with points of vivid white.

Faintly, as if from another life, she heard her own voice, not moaning now but grunting wordlessly like a beast as the senseless animal pleasure increased within her. Then he flung her from the cliff of climax and she plunged into emptiness, spiralling downwards and screaming as she fell, her whole body convulsed with brutal spasms of violent joy. She hung then limply in his arms, shuddering and twitching as he continued to thrust furiously into her, driving himself to his own desperate, barbarous release. At last he forced himself into her and as his massive cock pulsed within her quivering body he snarled like a beast and sank his teeth into the white skin of her shoulder.

It was over. He pulled abruptly out of her, gasping as his stripped, softened cock met the cold air of the room, and dropped her slackening thighs. She staggered, only her tied wrists keeping her upright. With a snarl of impatience he reached behind him and tugged at the belt, releasing her, and as her bonds fell to the ground she slumped against the wall, her tingling hands flat against the cold stone, her breathing shaking her.

'Admit it,' he hissed, leaning towards her. 'Admit it: you took more pleasure in *that* than in anything your fine young gallant has done for you. Admit it.'

'Why,' whispered Rosamund, pulling sense back from her dark haze of erotic exhaustion, 'why, are you afraid that he bettered you? Well, he did. You are strong, but he is subtle. You will never understand what he did to me.'

For a moment Aycliffe stared at her as if he did not understand what she had said. Then he swung away from her, grimacing with rage, stuffing his softening penis back within his clothes. He went to the door and yanked it open, yelling for his servant.

Sir Ralph snatched the paper from the young man's hands. 'Sign,' he demanded, stalking towards her, the deed clutched in his trembling fist. 'Sign, and be damned to you, you bitch. Sign it.'

'You have not earned it,' Rosamund taunted him,

smiling with a sense of sudden, delirious power. 'You have not deserved it.'

'Sign it!' Without warning Aycliffe's hand lashed out, striking her cheek so hard that she staggered and fell to the ground, crying out with pain. 'Sign it,' he grated, standing above her with the paper in his hand. 'Or there will be worse.'

'No,' Rosamund whispered, shaking her head to try and clear it. 'No, never.'

Sir Ralph dropped to his knees beside her, thrusting the crumpled paper into her face. 'Sign it,' he repeated, his voice soft as a breath and livid with rage, 'or you will see your *subtle* young lover sliced limb from limb.'

The breath sighed from Rosamund's lungs. She swallowed hard, trying to control herself, wondering how she might gain advantage even from this threat. Inspiration came to her. 'How do I know he is alive?' she demanded. 'He was hurt, and you abused him so. How do I know you have not already killed him?'

'You will not take that chance,' Aycliffe spat into her face. 'Sign, or he dies.'

'Prove that he lives,' Rosamund retorted, clenching her fists.

Sir Ralph's face writhed with fury and he got to his feet. 'Very well,' he said, throwing up one hand as if he did not care. 'Very well. I need not fear any interludes of mutual adoration.' He reached down and pulled her roughly to her feet. 'But I will not take any risks,' he hissed, and thrust her into the hands of his henchman. 'Bind her,' he commanded.

The young man forced her through dank corridors beneath the great hall. Her hands were locked behind her back with metal cuffs, making her shoulders ache. Sir Ralph walked a little way behind them, smiling coldly.

At a narrow, barred door the young henchman handed her over to a jailer, a balding greasy man in a leather apron who leered stupidly over her scantily clad body until Sir Ralph shouted at him and cuffed him around the head. The jailer flinched from his master's anger, but did not stop looking at Rosamund with his dim eyes glazed with lust.

They proceeded down a narrow, dripping corridor to a small, barred door. 'There,' said Aycliffe, gesturing at the bars. 'You may see him.'

Rosamund swallowed, then advanced towards the grim doorway. She looked through the bars, blinked at the dimness of the light, and stepped closer, peering.

There was Geoffrey, seated in a little dank cell beneath a meagre barred window. He was chained to the wet stone wall by one ankle and heavy manacles weighed down his wrists. He sat on a little straw-covered shelf in the stone, his face turned up to the window, his bright eyes open and full of such wretchedness and desperate yearning that Rosamund's heart lurched and wrung with misery. He was clad in rags, tattered hose and a rough shirt, and above the coarse clothes his beautiful face glowed in the light of the narrow window like a jewel flung into the mire.

'You see he is alive,' said Sir Ralph softly. 'And if he lives, he can die.'

'Let me speak to him,' Rosamund begged, turning to look up into Aycliffe's black eyes. 'Let me. If you do not, I swear I will never sign the paper.'

There was a silence. Aycliffe looked at the jailer, but the fool only sniggered. After a moment of calculation Sir Ralph said slowly, 'Any man would hate you after yesterday. Yes, you may speak to him. Speak, and be damned to you. I hope he spits in your face.' He stooped until his face was level with the jailer's. 'One word of affection,' he said through his teeth, 'one sigh, and you separate them and call me back. Do you understand me?'

The jailer's glabrous face twisted into a conspiratorial sneer and he grunted. Sir Ralph looked hard at him, then at Rosamund: then he turned and stalked back along the dank, cheerless corridor.

'Soft,' the jailer grunted, reaching out to stroke one filthy hand down Rosamund's arm. 'Pretty.'

She flinched away from him, revolted, and said in a low, urgent voice, 'Your master ordered you to let me in.'

The jailer's face changed, shadowed with sudden fear. He turned to the door and drew from his belt a heavy iron ring laden with great keys and began to sort through them with maddening slowness, muttering to himself as he did so. At last the key turned in the lock with a screech and the door sprang open. The jailer bent in a hideous parody of a bow, gesturing that Rosamund should enter the cell.

Slowly she stepped across the threshold, shivering with sorrow and trepidation. Geoffrey had turned away from the door. He was sitting now with one arm resting against the wall and his forehead buried against it, hiding his face. Rosamund realised with a shock of wretchedness that he must have heard her voice, and that he had turned away to conceal himself from her.

Behind her the door swung shut with a crash. She started and glanced behind her and the quick movement made one shoulder of the robe she wore slip down her white arm. Above the elbow it stopped, held by her bound wrists. She could not lift it and she closed her eyes for a moment in frustration. It would look as though she were trying to tempt him, to seduce him, when nothing was further from her mind.

Still he had not raised his head. Rosamund took a couple of unsteady steps towards him, sobs beginning to shake in the pit of her stomach. When she spoke her voice was thick with unshed tears. 'Geoffrey,' she whispered, 'please look at me.'

He said nothing, but put his elbows on his knees and buried his face in his hands. The chains on his wrists clanked mournfully as they swung to and fro. Rosamund watched his broad shoulders rising and falling as he breathed and the cold of the cell seemed suddenly to

143

pierce her to the heart, making her shiver with hopelessness. 'Geoffrey,' she whispered, 'in God's name.'

At this he lifted his head very slowly and rested his gaze on her. His face was quite white above the shaded softness of stubble, its smoothness marred by the scar above his brow and the little dark scab where the blonde girl's knife had cut his cheekbone. His eyes burned like coals beneath his fiercely contracted brows. His face was as perfect and as pitiless as the stoop of a hawk. 'God's name?' he repeated softly, and his voice too was livid with anger. 'How dare you? You are Aycliffe's whore!'

His head fell again. Rosamund shook her head, but he could not see her. She came a step closer to him, her shoulders jerking as she tried to show him her helplessness. 'Geoffrey,' she said urgently, 'look, look at me. I am bound, do you see? I am a prisoner, like you. I hate him, I detest him, I swear it. Look at my face! He struck me to the ground.'

Geoffrey's head jerked up and he stared wide-eyed at the bruise on Rosamund's pale cheek. Then he began to shake his head, the gesture growing more and more violent as if he wanted to deny himself any softness. 'You probably enjoyed it,' he said through his teeth. 'You enjoyed everything else he did to you. If you hate him, why did I see you writhe like a cat when he touched you?'

'I – I can't explain,' Rosamund said. She came a little closer to Geoffrey, gazing into his hostile eyes, trying to make him understand. 'Geoffrey, you ought to believe me. It was the same for you.'

'It was not!' The denial sprang to his lips at once and he turned from her and made his hand into a fist and struck it against the stone wall. His chains creaked and jingled. 'It was not!'

'It was,' she persisted. 'Did you desire those women, then, when they – used their mouths on you? Is that why I heard you cry out with pleasure?' He closed his eyes and leant his forehead on his clenched fist, shuddering.

144

'My God,' Rosamund cried, 'even when Sir Ralph had you, even then, that gave you pleasure, I swear it!'

'No!' Geoffrey shouted, springing to his feet, his hands stretched towards her as if they would strike her or squeeze her white throat. 'No, it did not! I'll kill you if you say it!'

Tears sprang to Rosamund's eyes and trickled down her bruised cheeks. 'It did,' she whispered. 'I saw you, I heard you. He made you . . .' She struggled to find words, her face twisting with misery and shame. 'He made you spill yourself.' She wanted to conceal her face to hide her tears, but her hands were bound. Instead she lowered her head, letting her heavy hair fall forward like curtains to shield her from his furious eyes.

There was a long, taut silence, broken by Rosamund's stifled sobs. Then she heard the chains shift and the sound of Geoffrey sitting back down on the stone bench. The silence stretched on. At last his voice said in a smothered whisper, 'It is true. God help me. What sort of beast am I?'

Rosamund flung back her hair and saw him staring at the floor, his strong fingers digging into his thick hair, his face tormented. She fell to her knees at his feet, longing to take his battered face in her hands, to caress it and bathe it with her tears. 'Geoffrey,' she whispered, 'I didn't mean to hurt you. I only wanted you to understand: the mind can hate but the body can still enjoy. For you and for me it is the same.'

'I'm sorry,' Geoffrey whispered. 'I'm sorry. I couldn't bear it, I couldn't bear to see him using you.' He lifted his face and she saw that it was streaked with tears. She whimpered and pressed her cheek against his, tasting the salt of his tears as she kissed his cheekbone, his stubbled jaw, rubbing herself against him with desperate love.

'I've failed you,' Geoffrey whispered. 'I came to save you and I have done nothing, nothing but give you more pain.'

145

'No,' she murmured, aching to embrace him. 'Geoffrey, no.'

He could not put his chained arms around her, but he held her between his hands and buried his head in her naked shoulder, breathing unevenly as he regained control of himself. When he lifted his head his pale face was bright with love. She looked into his eyes, the shifting dazzle of sunshine in a forest, and suddenly all her hurts were soothed, her sins forgiven her, her sorrow comforted. She turned her face up to his and he whispered, 'Rosamund,' and softly, softly set his lips on hers.

Ethereal bliss, love distilled into rapture, perfection of sensation. Their mouths opened to each other, lips and tongues moving, touching, exchanging gentle grazes of sublime desire. For a little while Rosamund kept her eyes open so that they could feast on the beauty of his spellbound face. Then the ecstasy overcame her and her eyelids slid shut as if they were very heavy and she let her head fall back, offering her parted lips and her white naked throat to his caressing mouth and his strong sensitive hands.

Presently something broke the spell. He drew back, his hands still lingering on her face, looking towards the closed door of the cell like a hunted beast. 'That bastard,' he hissed, 'that son of a whore, I bet he is watching us.' He shivered, then looked back at Rosamund. 'He said to you, "Sign". What did he mean?'

Rosamund took a deep breath. 'He has a deed of assign of all my possessions. He wants me to sign them over to him so that he may enjoy them without difficulty.' Geoffrey's face showed his disdain. 'Geoffrey,' Rosamund said softly, 'he says that unless I sign, he will kill you.'

At this Geoffrey's expression changed, becoming tense and earnest. 'Listen to me,' he said, fast and soft. 'Listen. As long as there is something he wants from you he will keep you alive. You, and maybe me too, though that doesn't matter.' She began to protest, but he laid his finger on her lip to silence her. 'The moment you sign

146

that, that thing, your life is worthless and so is mine. If it pleases him then to kill us both nothing can stop him. You must refuse. Do you understand me? You must refuse.'

'Oh, may God forgive me,' Rosamund moaned, 'You came to help me, and this is your reward.'

Geoffrey caught her face in his hands and looked into her eyes. Suddenly, unexpectedly, he smiled, his eyes glittering beneath the brown brows that swept upward like a kestrel's wing. 'Rosamund,' he whispered, 'my lady, I have no regrets. Even if my death comes of it I will not regret that I came to you.' He looked as he had done when he revealed himself to her: transfigured, ecstatic, enraptured. His beautiful lips moved, speaking almost soundlessly. 'I have had my reward, my lady. I spent a night in your arms.'

Tears welled again in Rosamund's eyes as he lowered his lips to hers. Her eager love filled her, tugging at her, tormenting her. She kissed him, his cheeks, his lips, his closed eyelids, his throat. As she moved against him her loose robe shifted, then fell from her other shoulder, baring her white breasts. She drew a quick breath and sat back, intending that Geoffrey restore her to modesty.

He looked at her naked shoulders, breathing quickly. Her heart leapt as she sensed his sudden, urgent arousal. After a moment their eyes met and Geoffrey said softly, 'Do you remember when you first looked at me?'

'I remember,' Rosamund whispered. Her lips were dry.

'I looked down at you,' Geoffrey said, 'and I could see your – breasts lifting under your gown, and suddenly I imagined you like this, with your shoulders naked and your breasts bare, like this, and you were leaning forward and you were going to – take me in your mouth. That's what I imagined. That's why I was hard when you touched me.'

There was a long, shivering silence. Rosamund's nipples swelled, jutting proudly forward, and her breasts ached for Geoffrey's hands. Beneath his hose she could see the outline of his penis growing, thickening and lengthening as she watched. She longed to feel him, to taste him. She licked her dry lips and swallowed. 'Let me do it to you now,' she whispered at last.

Geoffrey's eyes flickered to the door. 'He's watching,' he muttered.

'I don't care.' Rosamund leant forward, soundlessly cursing her bound hands, and set her lips to the rough wool of Geoffrey's hose. Beneath the fabric his phallus moved, jerking eagerly towards her lips. It was hot and hard and she could smell its subtle, musky scent. 'Let him watch,' Rosamund breathed. 'Let him see what he does not understand. Geoffrey, let me.'

For a moment Geoffrey did not move. Then with a gasp he tore with his chained hands at the fastenings of his ragged clothes. The shirt and hose parted to reveal his flat naked belly, taut with muscle, and the line of dark hair that led down from his navel to the curling arrowhead of his groin. He shifted his hips and the movement released his pinioned phallus; it sprang out from its cage of wool, already thick and hard.

Rosamund sighed with delight and reached forward, opening her soft lips, drawing in his scent with voluptuous rapture. She brushed her cheek against the hot rod of flesh, marvelling at the way it continued to swell and thicken as she touched it. Then she extended her tongue and very gently began to trace the length of his magnificent shaft, feeling the ridged, protruding veins, the smooth swell of the tumescent glans, the tiny opening at the tip. She probed gently into the little eye, hearing Geoffrey gasp, feeling him shiver with response.

It was so beautiful, so strong, so masculine. She knew that he would want her to take it in her mouth, but she had not explored him enough. She wanted to familiarise herself with every inch of him, to know him intimately, to show her love to every part of him. Lowering her head a little, she brushed her nose against the taut, hairy sac of his testicles, then caressed them with her lips, drawing one heavy stone into her mouth, then the other.

He groaned and opened his thighs wider, leaning back against the stone, and she probed with her warm tongue deep between his legs, exploring the delicious smoothness of sensitive membrane between scrotum and anus, breathing in his secret scent.

Her breasts ached with longing and between her legs she felt warm and hollow, liquid with need. She knelt on the hard floor and gently lifted and lowered herself upon her heels, providing a gentle, warming stimulation, unable to resist a whimper of pleasure as the soft wool of her robe brushed against her stiff clitoris. The skin of her breasts rubbed against Geoffrey's thighs as she stooped over him.

'Rosamund,' he whispered, and he set his hands on either side of her head, steadying her. He wanted her to take him in her mouth, and now she was ready, ready to worship him with lips and tongue. She opened her mouth and leant towards him and his eager, rearing phallus jerked towards her, twitching with desire. Very gently she placed her lips around the velvety glans, feeling its miraculous combination of feather-softness and rigid, uncompromising hardness. She moaned with delight and allowed her lips to close on the shaft and glide downwards, taking him in as far, as far as she could, feeling him probe to the very back of her willing throat.

The pleasure was intense, exquisite. She let her lips slip up and down his straining shaft, making it glisten with the trickles of her saliva. As she moved her head she teased with her agile tongue at the tiny membrane at the base of the swollen glans, sensing how when she touched him there he shuddered and tensed with ecstasy. She wished that she could watch his face as she drew him closer and closer towards his climax, but then she would not be able to feel this bliss, this haze of delight as she took him in her mouth, experiencing his pleasure with such intensity, such immediacy, that it was as if she shared his body.

Geoffrey groaned and his hips moved, thrusting up

towards her face. Rosamund gave a gasp of astonished rapture as his hands tightened in her hair and he began to push himself into her mouth, taking control over his own pleasure. He was ravishing her, possessing her, and it was bliss. His movements strengthened, he thrust himself between her lips faster, deeper. Inside her mouth the silken, quivering head of his cock swelled further, preparing for his climax, and the blood began to pulse and twitch in the throbbing shaft. His hands in her hair were like claws and as his hips began to jerk uncontrollably Geoffrey cried out helplessly, 'Oh God, God.' The sound of his orgasm drove Rosamund to such a fever of delight that her body too began to heave. As his cock surged and spurted deep in her mouth she moaned and tumbled into the throes of a strange, piercing, unfocused climax, an orgasm that grew from the salty taste of Geoffrey's hot seed in her mouth and throat and the frantic clasping and unclasping of her pinioned hands as much as from her juddering breasts and her empty, aching sex. The pleasure went on and on, a long plateau of delirium, refreshed by every jerk of Geoffrey's spasming penis between her swollen lips.

At last Geoffrey's cock ceased its twitching and lay in her mouth, still splendid in its length and thickness, but beginning to soften. His hands stroked aimlessly at the tangled mass of Rosamund's chestnut hair. She licked him very gently, coaxing the last remnants of his seed from him, making him shiver and moan. He took her face in his hands and lifted it from his naked belly, turning her lips up to his and kissing her, exploring with his tongue the warm softness that had received his liquid gift.

'Rosamund,' he whispered at last, 'I love you.'

'Oh, Geoffrey.' She closed her eyes and pressed her face against his strong throat. 'I love you, my lord, I love you.'

Suddenly the door swung open with a crash. Rosamund gasped with shock and turned in Geoffrey's hands to see Sir Ralph striding towards her, his face dark with fury. The jailer was hobbling behind him, snorting with fear. Sir Ralph snarled wordlessly and reached down to seize Rosamund by one arm and drag her away from Geoffrey's love and his strong hands and his soft lips. She cried out with protest and Geoffrey roared and leapt to his feet, springing at Sir Ralph like a tiger, his hands outstretched. Aycliffe flung up one hand to ward Geoffrey off, pulling back to a safe distance and dragging Rosamund with him. Geoffrey flung himself after Sir Ralph as he retreated and got one manacled hand on his arm. 'Got you,' he snarled, 'you bastard, I'll kill you!'

Sir Ralph wrestled against Geoffrey's fevered grip, his face twisting with anger, not with fear. For a moment they stood poised, balanced against each other. Then the little jailer slipped past his master and pulled the heavy ring of keys from his belt, held it by one key and whirled it through the air to strike Geoffrey on the back of the neck. He grunted and pitched forward onto his face, sprawled senseless at Rosamund's feet.

She called his name and tried to throw herself down beside him, but Sir Ralph gripped her arm and held her up. 'You villain,' he said to the jailer, 'you did not call me. Were you handling yourself as you watched them? You will suffer for this.'

The jailer drew back, moaning and protesting with fear, and Sir Ralph turned on Rosamund with ferocious venom. 'Enough time,' he spat, 'for you to pleasure him with your mouth, you whore!'

'You do not know what pleasure is,' Rosamund flung back at him, her eyes snapping with rage. 'You have no idea.' She pulled again at his restraining arm, desperate to kneel beside Geoffrey and kiss his stunned face.

'You love him?' demanded Sir Ralph, shaking her. 'You love him? Good!' He thrust her suddenly into the jailer's hands. She flinched and shuddered to feel his greasy fingers beginning to paw at her naked skin. Sir Ralph dropped to one knee beside Geoffrey's unmoving body and caught hold of his head by the hair. He wrenched it back, turning it to expose the white, vulner-

151

able throat. Geoffrey's eyes were closed, his lips parted, beautiful as in sleep. 'Swear you will sign,' Sir Ralph hissed, 'or you will see him die now, my Lady de Verney.' He drew his dagger and set the point to the hollow of Geoffrey's throat. 'Feel how the blood beats here,' he said softly, grinning into Rosamund's horrified face. 'Feel the life. Shall I let it out, my lady? Shall I stain your pretty feet with his blood?'

'No.' Rosamund could not bear it. She knew that what Geoffrey had said was true, that the moment she succumbed their lives would be worthless, but she could not bear it that he should be killed before her, his skin split like a ripe fruit and his blood spilling. 'No,' she repeated, pulling against the jailer's hands. 'Don't, don't hurt him.'

Sir Ralph did not move; the blade lay still at Geoffrey's throat. 'Swear,' he said.

He wanted her to enunciate her own defeat. Rosamund fastened her eyes on Geoffrey's face, drowned in unconsciousness. Her love welled up within her until she thought her heart would break. She said through her tears, 'I swear. I will sign.'

Sir Ralph's face glowed with triumph. He got to his feet. Rosamund closed her eyes with relief as she saw the sharp steel drawn away from Geoffrey's throat. Aycliffe caught her arm again, pulling her from the jailer's grasping hands. He looked into her face, his black eyes shining. 'At last,' he said, 'I have broken you.'

Her strength had deserted her. She let him tow her unresisting to the door, craning her head back over her shoulder to gain one last glimpse of Geoffrey as he lay like one already dead.

Goodbye, my love, she whispered soundlessly. *Goodbye.*

Chapter Seven

*A*ycliffe thrust a pen into Rosamund's hand. 'Sign,' he said coldly.

Rosamund set her jaw and squared her shoulders. 'On one condition.'

'Condition?' Sir Ralph sounded as though he did not believe what he had heard. 'Who are you to lay down conditions? Sign it, or he dies!'

She laid down the pen and caught hold of his arm. He frowned in astonishment. She had never voluntarily touched him before. 'Listen to me,' she said earnestly. 'We agreed: his life for my signature. My condition now is that you release him. Let him go free. What good is he to you?'

Sir Ralph stared into her face. His black eyes narrowed into mere glittering slits. 'And if I do,' he asked, 'what then?'

Rosamund licked her lips, trying not to show that she was shaking with fear. 'I will do anything you want,' she said. 'I promise. I will be yours to command.'

'You are mine to command now.'

'I mean I will submit to you,' she said, feeling herself degraded and humiliated by the very offer. 'I will not resist you any more. Unless – you want it.'

There was a long silence. Sir Ralph's eyes were as

unreadable as chips of glass. Rosamund looked into his face, breathing fast, feeling as if she had played her last card.

At last he said, 'Very well. Why not? I enjoy your body, and he is no good to me. As you wish. I shall free him, if you sign.'

'Swear,' said Rosamund quickly, her hand tightening on the hard muscle of Aycliffe's arm.

'I swear,' he said evenly.

Rosamund hesitated, then released him and lifted the pen. It took a terrible effort to move her hand, to make it form her florid, spiky signature: *R de Verney*. When it was done she got up from the chair and went to the window, gasping for air, not watching as a pair of Sir Ralph's faceless minions came forward to witness the document.

'Call the jailer,' said Sir Ralph from behind her. Rosamund put her face in her hands for a moment. She was a slave now, this man's slave, by her own gift. It was worth it, she told herself, if it bought Geoffrey his freedom. She hoped that he had the sense to run as fast and as far from Murthrum Castle as he could, and then to forget her. Or perhaps ... she fell into daydream in which she stood chained to a pillar like Andromeda and Geoffrey, armoured and helmed as gloriously as a prince, fought Sir Ralph in single combat, killed him outright with a single blow, and ran to free her, his face alight with love.

The door opened and Rosamund turned to see the little squat jailer cowering before Sir Ralph, tugging at his forelock. 'M'lord,' the little man muttered.

'Your prisoner,' said Sir Ralph. 'Go back to his cell at once. Kill him.'

'What?' Rosamund exclaimed. She hurled herself across the room, her eyes ringed with white, her mouth gaping in disbelief. Two of Sir Ralph's men caught her and held her while she bucked and writhed, struggling against them. 'You promised,' she cried hopelessly. 'You swore!'

Aycliffe smiled at her with a grim coldness that made her fall silent, wondering what horror could follow. 'Before you kill him,' he continued to the jailer, 'tell him that this lady, the Lady de Verney, has been strangled at my orders. Do you understand me?' The little man nodded. 'Repeat,' Sir Ralph snapped.

'Lady de Verney,' muttered the jailer, 'strangled at my lord's orders. Then kill the prisoner.'

Sir Ralph nodded and dismissed the jailer, then turned to face Rosamund. She stood quite motionless between the hands of his henchmen, her face whiter than a sheet of paper. She was filled with such disbelief, such horror and fear that movement and speech had deserted her. He took a step towards her and she stiffened, drawing unconsciously backward, expecting at any moment to feel his strong hands on her throat, squeezing out the life.

At last she recovered her voice from its pit of horror. 'You devil,' she whispered. 'You lying, treacherous, *wicked* devil.'

He came another step towards her and she tensed, trying not to flinch from him. He saw her fear and grinned, a grin like a hungry wolf's. 'Are you afraid of me?' he laughed. 'Now do you fear me, my lady?'

She shook her head, repeating, 'Liar. Liar.'

'I did not lie. I said I would free him. And so I am: freeing him from the toils of this mortal life. Surely you would rejoice as he ascends singing to Heaven to lie in the arms of the Virgin?'

Rosamund closed her eyes. At the thought of Geoffrey dead her spirit seemed to desert her. Life would be meaningless without him, death a blessed release. And by her death at least she could deny Sir Ralph her body, for which he had professed such eager desire. She lifted her head and breathed deeply, calming herself, then opened her eyes again. 'Kill me then,' she said evenly, 'I am ready.'

Sir Ralph smiled into her ardent eyes. 'Kill you? I never intended to kill you.' Her face changed, racked

155

with puzzlement and uncertainty. 'I am bored with you, yes, and you have served your purpose, but that does not mean I intend to kill you. A far too easy way out. I merely intended to add the spice, the piquancy of despair to your young gallant's death.'

Tears of rage and helpless frustration filled Rosamund's eyes. 'You are worse than a demon,' she whispered. 'You are the Devil himself.'

He turned away from her, not even laughing now. 'My people have expressed a – what shall I say – a desire to entertain you before I have you thrown out,' he said carelessly. 'I give you to them.' He stood before one of his young henchmen and smiled, lifting his hand to caress the young man's cheek. 'Harry,' he said in a tone almost of affection, 'she is yours. Amuse yourselves. Anything you wish.' Sir Ralph looked back over his shoulder, his cold black eyes sparkling. 'Goodbye, Lady de Verney,' he said, and he left the hall.

Geoffrey woke slowly in the chill dampness of the cell. He groaned and pushed himself to his feet, his chained hands awkwardly rubbing at the back of his neck. His head ached ferociously and a tender lump revealed where the heavy keys had struck him down.

Rosamund! He closed his eyes tightly, fighting tears. Her face as she looked up at him had been transparent with love: the touch of her lips had been Heaven. And now she was lost to him. He was certain that Aycliffe would ensure they did not speak again.

A footstep in the corridor made him frown and draw back a little against the wall. The key screeched in the lock. The door opened and the little malformed jailer entered, dropping his ring of keys to jangle at his belt. He lurched uncertainly towards Geoffrey, a long-bladed, dirty dagger clutched in his fat fist.

Geoffrey stared, his eyes wide beneath his tightened brows. The peak of his hair lifted with shock and sudden fear and his hands clenched around the chains that fastened his wrists.

The jailer stopped a little way out of his reach. 'Master says,' he began, and then hesitated. He scratched his head, his mouth lolling open. Then his face brightened. 'Master says the lady, the pretty lady . . .'

His voice died away again and his expression clouded with forgetfulness. Geoffrey prompted desperately, 'Lady de Verney? What about her? What, in God's name?'

The jailer's face suddenly cleared. 'Master had her strangled,' he said, smiling broadly and showing blackened, broken teeth.

Geoffrey staggered as if he had been struck in the face. 'What?' he whispered, struggling against the urge to fling back his head and howl his grief to the skies like an animal that has lost its mate. 'What did you say?'

'Master says, tell him Lady de Verney has been strangled. Then kill him,' the jailer said. He smiled again, contemplating his feat of memory with simple pride. Then his face changed, becoming hard and businesslike, and he came towards Geoffrey on the balls of his toes, the dagger extended before him.

'Kill me?' Geoffrey repeated. Anger filled him, driving away grief and love, lifting the hair on his head with fury like the lightning that crackles around the prow of a ship. 'By Christ, no!'

The jailer lunged at him with the dagger. Geoffrey sidestepped and with one swift motion caught the little man around his neck with the chains that bound his wrists. The jailer made a croaking noise and plucked at the chains with his hands. The dagger fell to the floor. Geoffrey snarled silently, the muscles on his arms bunching as he tugged. The jailer thrashed and struggled, his hands clawing at Geoffrey's face and hair, his feet drumming as the chains cut off his breath.

Presently the struggles ceased. Geoffrey held the body still for a few more minutes, until he was certain that life was gone. Then he stepped back, letting it crumple with a crash to the stone floor of the cell. He was panting and sweat was running down his face and throat.

157

Moving quickly, he tugged at the jailer's ring of keys and riffled through it, freeing first his hands and then his shackled leg. His wrists and ankles were bleeding where the manacles had rubbed through the skin. He fastened the chains to the man's body, hoping that it might briefly fool anyone looking into the cell. The dagger had slipped into the shadows beneath the stone bench, but he knelt and fished it out and stuck it into his waistband, glad to have a weapon.

There was nothing more to be done. Geoffrey stood in the middle of the cell, suddenly irresolute. Every part of him wailed with silent grief and cried for vengeance, for Aycliffe's blood on the dagger's blade to pay for Rosamund's death. But he knew that he had no chance of getting close enough to Sir Ralph to wound him, far less to kill him. It would be hard enough to escape from the castle with his skin. Better to flee, to accept the ignominy and come back one day with the strength to repay old scores.

He drew the dagger and held it up by the blade in the light that trickled from the little barred window. It glowed, a little cross of dirty metal.

'By this cross I swear,' Geoffrey said softly. 'I swear by Our Redeemer who died for us, I will not rest until I have avenged my lady's death. I swear that I will not lie with any woman until the devil Aycliffe is dead.' The cross blurred before his eyes as they filled with tears. He bowed his head, blinking away the signs of grief, and returned the dagger to his waist. Then he went to the door and slipped silently through it, locked it, and flung the ring of keys back into the furthest corner of the silent cell.

For more than a week Sir Ralph's men kept Rosamund in a little room off the great hall, their toy and plaything. She did not resist them, rather she welcomed them. When they were with her she could let her body's sensations drive the grief and loss from her numb, aching brain, and afterwards she could sleep. On the nights when no man came to her she would lie awake, weeping slow, agonised tears.

The men were not as vicious as their master. Some of them even seemed to pride themselves in giving her pleasure as well as taking pleasure themselves. They worked hard to arouse her, teasing out the coral peaks of her breasts with lips and tongues and teeth, thrusting their faces close between her open thighs to lap at her sensitive flesh until she gasped and groaned with delight. If she had cared to be curious she would have wondered whether they relished the chance to be the master for once, to grant pleasure rather than having it taken from them: for they were handsome and young, and she was sure that Sir Ralph used each and all of them as his catamites when his fancy turned that way.

They were inventive, too, and relished any chance to experiment. Rosamund was novel to them. They enjoyed exploring every orifice of her opulent body, by ones and twos and even threes. Sometimes they made her kneel on all fours to take one of them into her mouth while another gripped her white buttocks and thrust himself vigorously into her sex. Sometimes they held her upright while one eased his cock into the tight velvet fist of her anus and another filled her moist vagina with his stiff eager shaft, each of them excited and aroused by the feeling of the other's hard, swollen penis working to and fro, close, yet tantalisingly separated.

Not all of them were skilled. The younger ones would take her with clumsy urgency, arousing her impatiently with hands and tongues until she was wet and whimpering with desire, then spilling themselves within her with such speed that she could not reach the peak of pleasure. But it was no hardship, for there was always another cock available, thick and throbbing, ready to drive itself deep within her and stroke in and out, in and out of the soft grasping pouch of her vulva until her body tensed and arched and she lurched into the inevitable, aching oblivion of orgasm.

Oblivion was all she sought. When she was alone she

159

would think of Geoffrey, and then she was full of pain and sorrow and desperate, bitter regret. Better to be a rutting animal, soulless and mindless, panting her way to ecstasy in a stranger's arms.

Then, after nine days and nine nights, suddenly she was alone. She slept alone, plagued by anguished dreams. In the grey dawn a rough soldier came to her. He brought her clothing, coarse linen and wool like a lower servant, and ordered her to dress and turned his back as she did so. His propriety brought an ironic smile to her lips as she thought of the number of men who had recently enjoyed her body. When she was dressed, he guided her with the point of his spear to the courtyard, to the gatehouse, and across the drawbridge into the melting snow.

And there he left her. He returned over the moat and after a few moments the drawbridge lifted. She stood for a moment in disbelief. Then she called up to the faces that she could see on the wall, 'For God's sake, where am I to go?'

'Anywhere you like,' called back a coarse voice.

'But,' Rosamund began, taking a step towards the gatehouse. The men jeered and one of them flung a handful of filth at her. She withdrew, her brows knitted with anxious misery, wrapping her coarse woollen clothing more tightly around herself to try to keep out the damp, penetrating cold.

She stood for some time beneath a holly tree by the track to the gatehouse, confused and irresolute. Where could she go? What could she do? She was not a native of Lincolnshire, and though she had lived there seven years she would have been hard put to find her way back unaided through the cobweb of ways to de Verney manor.

And she did not want to leave Murthrum Castle. It was a vile place, foul and full of wickedness, but it was the last place in which she had seen Geoffrey alive. Like a dog that lies at its dead master's feet, she could not leave.

Presently the drawbridge lowered, creaking and rattling, and the gates opened. Rosamund emerged from the sheltering tree, shivering with cold, to see who was setting forth.

It was Sir Ralph, dressed for the hunt in warm leather and wool, half a dozen of his men behind him on strong horses, hounds tumbling around their feet. Sir Ralph was laughing with one of his huntsmen, but the smile disappeared from his face as he turned and saw Rosamund. His black eyes looked like the water of a deep lake seen through a hole in the ice.

Rosamund stumbled forward, reaching up to take Sir Ralph's horse by the rein. 'Please,' she said huskily, 'please tell me where you have buried him.'

Sir Ralph's face was very still, betraying nothing. As he looked down at her his lip quivered as if he were about to snarl and bite. After a moment of silence he said in tones of the utmost contempt, '*Buried* him?' and then he threw back his head and laughed.

'Oh, God help me,' Rosamund cried, stretching up to try to catch hold of his hand, 'tell me you have given him Christian burial.'

With a growl Sir Ralph struck her hand from his arm. 'If you are still here when I return from the hunt,' he hissed, 'I shall have you whipped from the door. Or shall I set my hounds on you now?' He cracked the long whip he held and the dogs pranced up to his horse, obedient and eager. 'Shall I hunt you, Lady de Verney? They will never have had a tenderer doe to chase. How much grace shall I give you?'

Rosamund reeled backwards, her hand pressed to her mouth to hold in her agonised sobs. Sir Ralph watched her coldly, then cracked his whip again and called to the hounds: 'Tyrell! Montjoie! Beaumont! *Il est hault!*' He held out his arm, pointing with the whip at Rosamund's stumbling figure, and at last she turned and broke into a desperate run, the tears cold on her cheeks.

She did not hear Sir Ralph recall the dogs. Nor, when the hunters had passed on their way, did she see a single rider emerge from the castle gateway and steer his horse slowly down the road, carefully tracing her uneven footprints.

She did not know her way, and in a long morning's walking on the slush and ice of the roads she found no place that she recognised. The weather was grim, and even the peasants were mostly within doors. The frosted fields were deserted.

At last she came to a great road, a highway wide enough to allow three carts to run side by side. It was the Great North Road, which ran from London all the way to the wilds of Scotland. De Verney manor lay beyond it, but she could not go there.

For a while she hesitated, uncertain of what to do. There was a building close by, a long, low thatched place with outbuildings and a tall chimney releasing a plume of fragrant wood smoke to the grey sky. It had a spray of greenery hanging above the door, the sign of an inn.

It occurred to Rosamund that she was very hungry and tired. The thought of a joint of tender meat, or even a plate of porridge, glowed before her. She was penniless and she did not know how to beg, but she crossed herself and muttered 'The Lord will provide,' and went towards the inn.

The moment she went through the door she wished she had not entered. It was the sort of place at which she and Lionel would not have stopped on a long journey. Within it was dark, smoky, low-ceilinged, and it stank of grease and sour ale. There were half a dozen customers drinking and devouring dishes of cheap, smelly stew, and as Rosamund appeared in the doorway every head turned and every eye stared at her.

She would have withdrawn at once, but the warmth was so blessed after the chilly dampness of the road that her feet refused to turn. She stood by the door, feeling herself blush beneath the unwinking gaze of a dozen hostile, hungry eyes.

'What do you want?' demanded a man in a greasy

apron, presumably the landlord. He spoke with a strong local accent, like the peasants who had tilled the fields of de Verney manor. For a moment Rosamund did not realise that he was addressing her. Where was his bow, the humble touching of his forehead, his, 'Your servant, my lady?'

Then she realised how she must appear, travel-stained and weary and dressed like a dairymaid. She drew herself up and said, 'I want something to eat and drink.'

At the sound of her voice, aristocratic and Southern, the faces of the customers grew greedy and eager. 'Who's this?' asked one of them, 'Queen Margaret herself come among us?'

'Or the Lady of the Lake,' said another.

One of them jumped to his feet and came over to Rosamund. He took her familiarly by the elbow and breathed the fumes of ale into her face. 'Down on your luck, my lady?' he asked her. 'Come on, come and sit with me, I'll look after you if you make it worth my while.'

Rosamund shook off his hand in shock and disdain. 'How dare you,' she said haughtily, unable to restrain a sniff of disgust.

'How dare I?' The man was suddenly angry. He caught her arm and with a sharp tug hurled her towards the table where his friends sat, demanding, 'Come, then, Your Grace, where's the money? You want Clem here to feed you, how will you pay him?'

Shaking with fear, Rosamund clutched her cloak more tightly across her breast. 'I – I have no money,' she stammered. 'But if there is – work I can do – '

'Work? I have work for you!' shouted the first man, and the others growled in delighted agreement and got to their feet. Rosamund saw their faces fixed upon her, twisted and snarling with brutal lust, and she gave a gasp of horror and tried to flee. Before she had taken three steps the first man had caught her. She struck his face with her hand and he roared with pain and anger and twisted her arm up hard behind her back, making her cry out. Then from everywhere there were hands upon her. She screamed and fought every step of the way as they dragged her across the room, but they were many and strong.

'High and mighty bitch,' hissed the first man, abandoning her to the hands of his friends while he wrestled with his clothing. 'Think you're too good for us, do you? Hold her down on the table, lads.'

Rosamund screamed again, but the only people to hear her were those who were bent on violating her. She struggled desperately as they flung her onto a filthy table and held her down and the first man took hold of her skirts and tossed them up, revealing her white legs and the soft dark mound between them.

'That's a fair sight,' he said admiringly. 'Skin as white as a lady's.'

'No,' Rosamund moaned, feeling his filthy hands on her thighs, parting them, holding them wide open. 'Oh Jesu, no.'

'Hold her,' the man hissed. He pushed his fingers up into Rosamund's sex, so hard that she cried out. 'Sweet as a nut,' he said, and replaced the fingers with the hot, smooth head of his cock.

'No!' Rosamund cried, trying to close herself, to squeeze herself shut against him. She heaved against the restraining hands, shutting her eyes tightly so that she would not see the flushed sweating faces leaning over her.

The man snarled with triumph and began to push himself inside her. Then without warning the door opened and a voice said, 'I heard screams. What in God's name is happening here?'

The man who was about to rape Rosamund withdrew and suddenly the hands holding her were gone. She lay still for a moment, hardly believing, then quickly twisted upright, pushing down her skirts and gasping for breath.

The landlord and his customers were staring with louring anger at a single man who stood in the doorway with his sword held before him. He was a man of middle years with a good woollen gown under his heavy travelling cloak and a neatly trimmed beard. Rosamund thought for a moment that the men would jump at him and overwhelm him with their numbers, but they made no move to do so.

'Clement,' the man said to the landlord as he replaced his long sword in its sheath, 'you know better than to allow this sort of thing. My lass,' this to Rosamund, 'are you hurt?'

'No,' Rosamund stammered, sliding awkwardly down off the table and trying not to shiver as her trembling legs hit the floor. She frowned as she looked at the man's face: he seemed somehow familiar, as if she had seen him before. 'Sir,' she managed to say, 'I am most grateful to you.'

The man looked puzzled to hear her speak. Then his face contracted in a spasm of amazement and he stepped towards Rosamund, holding out his hand and asking hesitantly, 'But surely, you cannot be – Lady de Verney?'

'I am Rosamund de Verney,' Rosamund said, and as she spoke her own name the tears came and she sobbed, violent sobs that left her shuddering.

Her saviour took off his own fur lined cloak and put it around her shoulders. As he led her from the hateful inn he kept up a continuous, calming flow of talk. 'Plaseden, my lady, Walter Plaseden. I knew your husband, we did some business once, perhaps you remember my face? And I remember yours, of course, my lady, any man would. Just as well for you that I came in; that is an ill starred place you found yourself in. They know me, though, they know not to cross me. No need to tell me your tale, my lady, I have heard it, everyone in these parts has heard it. That beast Aycliffe will have much to answer for when there is justice in the land again.'

He had taken her out to his horse and lifted her gently to the saddle. He stood beside her now, looking up into her face. 'Now, my lady,' he said, 'I am your servant. Where may I take you?'

Rosamund rubbed at her eyes, trying to stop the tears.

'Master Plaseden,' she managed to say, 'I am so very grateful.' She frowned at his face, trying to think when she might have seen him before. 'I thought – ' she managed at last, 'to the father of an old friend, a friend of my husband's, who lives not far from here.'

Plaseden shook his head. 'I would go far from here, my lady, if you can. Sir Ralph has let it be known that if anyone here helps you he will mete out the same fate to them as he did to de Verney manor. There is no justice in the land. With the Duke of York dead who is there to prevent him from doing as he pleases? He has more men under arms than any other for miles around. No, my lady, I would go to friends and family elsewhere.'

'But I have none,' Rosamund murmured helplessly. 'And Lionel's people live far away, in Wales almost, and they are remote cousins. They have never met me. I would not even know how to find them.' And, she added to herself, they would not love the woman who has lost their family's inheritance to a villain and traitor.

There was a short silence. Then Plaseden said, 'Well, my lady, I am on my way to London for my business. Is there no one there you could apply to for help?'

Rosamund frowned. Then her face cleared. 'Perhaps,' she said, brightening. 'Yes, I believe there is. There is the lawyer who acted for my guardian when my marriage was arranged. He said he would always be pleased to help me if ever I needed it.'

'Can you find him again?'

'I think so.'

Plaseden smiled up at her. 'Well,' he said, 'it will be my privilege to conduct you as far as the City, my Lady de Verney, if you will accept my protection.' Rosamund's face must have shown the thought that flashed across her mind, for Plaseden held up his hands in quick denial. 'You shall travel as my daughter,' he said earnestly. 'We will find you a horse at the next decent inn, and better clothes, and by my sword, my lady, you will travel unmolested.'

Tears of gratitude sprang to Rosamund's eyes and ran

down her cheeks. 'Thank you,' she whispered. 'You have come to me like a miracle, Master Plaseden. Thank you.'

And now she stood before the fine tall building in Lincoln's Inn where Master Waldron had his chambers, gathering the nerve to enter.

She wished that Walter had been able to accompany her to the lawyer's rooms, but her trouble had put off his business for too long. He had left the City that day for Kent. But he had done so much for her. She was dressed like a respectable gentlewoman now, and beneath the high neck of her gown nestled a purse heavy with pieces of gold and silver. Walter had made her take it, he had insisted. 'You can repay me, my lady, when you have regained your lands,' he said, and kissed her on the forehead like a father. 'Good fortune to you, and God bless you.'

She had almost wept to lose him. For days she had lived shielded by his kind thoughtfulness. Now she was alone again, but at least alone with a fair sum of money to her name, and the hope of help before her.

The lawyer's clerk showed her in at once. He knocked on the panelled door. She stood behind him, smothered with memory: she had come here with her guardian to sign the marriage contract. This was the place where she had first met Lionel. She remembered how shocked she had been by his age, but how courteous he had been to her, how gentle. He had given her a necklace of pearl and garnet. It had been her favourite for years. She imagined that Sir Ralph would have given it now to one of his whores.

The door was open and Master Waldron the lawyer was coming towards her, wheezing as fat men will do. He had prospered in seven years, and now he was dressed in velvet and damask beneath his lawyer's gown and wore a heavy gold chain around his neck. 'My Lady de Verney,' he said.

'Master Waldron,' Rosamund began, 'I have come to you –'

'Please, my lady, do not ask me to help you,' said the lawyer.

Rosamund stared at him, her jaw dropping. 'What?' she whispered, unbelieving. 'What do you know of what has happened to me?'

Waldron shook his finger at her angrily. 'The Duke of York is dead,' he said with tetchy impatience, 'and rotting on York gate! Until the Earl of March comes for his inheritance it is dangerous to be an adherent of York, my lady, and everyone knows that your husband was the Duke's man till death. His name was called in the roll of traitors. I cannot risk helping you. Nor will any lawyer in London.'

'You do not even know what has happened,' Rosamund gasped, throwing up her hands in disbelief. 'Master Humphrey, my lands – '

'Stolen from you? Yes, I heard,' said the lawyer, shaking his head. 'News travels, my lady. Do you think you are the only one? These are lawless times.'

'I can pay you,' said Rosamund, fumbling at the neck of her gown.

Waldron still shook his head. 'No, my lady, I cannot help you. I cannot and I will not. I am sorry, but that is all there is to say.' He caught his clerk's eye. 'Nicholas, show the lady out.'

Rosamund tried to protest, but the clerk's hand was on her arm. Before she had taken breath the door was closed in her face and the clerk was leading her down the stairs, to the door of the building, bowing with absurd lowness as he guided her through the door and out into the street and closed the door in her face.

It was impossible. It could not be! She stood gasping, shaking with astonishment and confusion, as people pushed past her, jostling her from side to side. For a moment she stared blankly around her, watching faces as they passed. So many people, all strangers, all uncaring, intent on their own concerns.

'What shall I do?' she whispered. She returned to the door of the chambers and beat on it with her hand, but

168

the clerk opened the spyhole and snapped through it, 'My lord will not see you again,' and slammed it shut in her face.

She stepped back, her hands to her mouth, shivering. For a moment she could not think coherently. Then suddenly she felt a fool. 'What should I care?' she said to the closed door. 'There are other lawyers in London. I have money, I will find another. A fig for Master Humphrey Waldron!'

She turned from the door and began to walk confidently down the busy street. She would go to another lawyer. He might not believe her tale at once, but money would speak for her, she was confident.

The streets were narrow and she caught at her skirts, pulling them in to keep them from the mud and filth that lay in the gutters. Smells assailed her nose. She began to plan what she would do when she had regained her lands. What revenge could she take on Sir Ralph? How could she repay him for –

No, she would not think of it. If she began to think of it she would think of Geoffrey, and that way lay only grief. Rosamund folded her lips tightly together and squared her shoulders and walked on.

Suddenly someone barged into her, making her stagger and almost fall. Then something tore at her throat and she felt a quick, vicious jerk, and a lithe dark figure was fleeing away down an alley, vanishing into the shadows.

'Oh, no,' Rosamund cried, feeling at her torn gown, at the bruise on her neck where the cord of her purse had been wrenched away. 'Oh, no! Thief, thief! Stop!'

She ran a little way down into the maze of alleys, but the thief was long gone. Frantically Rosamund caught at the sleeves of passers-by, asking them what she should do, where she could find the watch, the sheriff, someone who could help her. But robbery was a daily business, and nobody was interested.

Thin cold rain began to fall. Rosamund clutched the torn bosom of her gown across her and took shelter in a doorway. As she stood waiting for the rain to pass she slowly began to realise what had happened to her. Her only hope of help had refused her, and now all the money that she possessed had been stolen from her. How had the thief known, how had he guessed? She could have sworn that the purse did not show.

She was alone in London, more helpless than she had been even on the road outside Murthrum Castle. She knew no one except the unspeakable, cowardly lawyer: no family, no friends.

Gradually the tears came. She stood in the rain with her face buried in her hands, weeping with sheer impotent misery.

After a while, as she lifted her head to draw breath for another sob, she saw a woman's gown, lifted from the mud, revealing high pattens, shoes with a thick wooden sole to keep the feet dry. Slowly she lifted her head. The owner of the gown was a young woman, about her own age, with a pretty, brazen face beneath a clean white headdress. A few tendrils of bright copper-brown hair escaped from under the white linen in fetching disarray.

'Can I help?' asked the young woman. 'What's the matter?' She had bright hazel eyes, sparkling and inquisitive.

Rosamund drew back a little, suspicious. 'I've been robbed,' she confessed at last, gulping back the tears.

'Oh, poor creature. Where are you lodging?'

Rosamund helplessly shook her head. The appalling truth of her situation hit her with fresh immediacy and she bowed her head again, overwhelmed by tears.

'Poor thing,' said the young woman. 'Listen, come with me just for now. Let me take you to where I live. We'll get you warm and dry and then you can think again.'

She reached out to take Rosamund by the arm. For a moment Rosamund resisted. 'Where?' she asked. 'Where do you live?'

'Southwark,' the copper-haired girl said with a cheerful smile.

Southwark. The one place in London a well born lady would avoid at all costs: a place where all the women were whores, though not all the whores were women.

'My name's Anne,' said the girl encouragingly. 'Will you come? Come with me, do. You need some rest, something to eat. I was alone in London once, it's terrible.'

Everything she said was true. And besides, her face was kind and friendly. Rosamund knew she should not go, but she could think of nothing else that she could do. She let Anne take her by the hand and lead her down the street towards the waterfront and the river, and the thin, cold rain fell on her face until you could not tell which drops were raindrops and which were tears.

Chapter Eight

Mistress Alice was the manager of the Fountain of Love, a bath house and brothel in a relatively smart area of Southwark. She was a woman in her thirties, still handsome, with a strong, capable face and clothes that showed that her business was a success. She dressed like a well-to-do gentlewoman, and only the fact that she painted her face revealed that she was not as respectable as she seemed.

She was standing now in an upper room of the bath house, looking down with deep concentration through a small crooked window in the wall at a small room below her. 'A noble lady, you say,' she murmured in a thoughtful undertone to the man standing behind her. 'I would believe it, her skin is as smooth as cream. She has never had to labour for her living. But what makes you think that she will survive the life here? Most noblewomen would curl up and die at the thought.'

The man came forward and the little glow of light from the squint caught his face, revealing the sober features and close-cut beard of Walter Plaseden. 'Are you questioning Sir Ralph's judgement?' he asked, his soft whisper very cold.

Mistress Alice swung swiftly around. 'No, no indeed. Question the owner? I would not dream of it. But a noble lady becoming a whore, that is a rare thing.' She hesitated and frowned, her hard determined face revealing a little reluctance and distaste. 'Or,' she asked cautiously, 'is it perhaps Sir Ralph's intention that she, ah, succumb to despair?'

Walter shook his head. 'I think not,' he said, looking down. What he saw caught his attention; his lips parted and he slowly put out his tongue and licked them, his breathing hoarse and laboured.

Beneath them the girl Anne was undressing Rosamund, coaxing the clothes from her with honeyed words. 'Come, sweetheart, you are soaked to the skin. Come, off with everything, a hot bath will do you the world of good. You are frozen, feel how cold you are. And wine? A glass of sweet Malmsey? Here, drink it down.'

'This girl knows her business,' commented Walter.

'She loves it,' said Alice. 'I set her to break in all our new girls.' At this moment Anne gently drew off Rosamund's shift, leaving her naked in the warmth of the little tented room.

'Ah,' Alice breathed, 'there is a body. What breasts! A waist to span with your hands; an arse a duke would be pleased to rest his cheek upon. Thighs like white satin. By God, Walter, Sir Ralph has chosen a fine specimen for me, whatever he intends me to do to her.'

'She may surprise you,' said Walter, looking down at Rosamund's white body with consuming attention. Small beads of sweat began to start upon his upper lip. 'She was in Sir Ralph's possession for two weeks, and he tells me that in all that time there was not one thing that was done to her which revolted her.'

Mistress Alice raised her brows, clearly surprised and impressed. 'Did you sample her wares, Master Walter?' she enquired.

'Alas, no.' Walter leant forward as if he would suck Rosamund in with his eyes. 'I was compelled to remain a stranger to her.'

'It was clever, to bring her to London and then

abandon her,' nodded Alice. 'How much did you have to pay the lawyer to turn her away?'

Walter shrugged. 'My lord holds her dead husband's lands. Money is not a concern to him any more.' He swallowed thickly. 'Did you say,' he asked tentatively, 'that once your young woman has, er, warmed her, that she will be given the opportunity to try a genuine customer?'

'Not a *genuine* customer,' Alice corrected him. 'Piers will have her. He is a young man I keep on the premises for just these occasions; and for myself, of course.'

'And will we be able to watch?'

'We must. I must be certain that she will be able to do the work.'

Walter put his hand around Alice's nipped-in waist and lifted it slowly to cup the swell of her breast where it showed over the edge of her velvet gown. 'Perhaps,' he said, 'if you were to bend over, we could indulge ourselves in a little fleshly amusement while we keep an eye on proceedings.'

Mistress Alice looked at Walter and raised her elegantly plucked brows. 'Master Walter,' she said, 'you astonish me.' But she bent obediently, resting her hands on the ledge of the little window through which they could watch events below them unfolding. Walter fumbled with his points and drew out his cock from his hose, already stiff and scarlet with excitement. He lifted Alice's heavy velvet skirts, piling them round her waist. Beneath the skirts she was naked above her gartered stockings, and the pink, swelling pouch of her sex was moist and inviting between the white columns of her thighs. Walter put the head of his cock against the fleshy, glistening lips and held tightly to her white haunches as he thrust himself into her. Their breath hissed in and out as he swived her, their eyes fixed on the little glowing window.

'Come, sweetheart,' said Anne, holding out her hand to help Rosamund up the steps and into the bath. 'I'll join you, you don't want to be lonely.'

174

Rosamund gingerly climbed the little wooden steps and lowered herself down into the steaming water. It was deliciously warm and scented with lilies and roses, and so deep that it lifted her breasts into perfect cones and lapped tantalisingly around her coral nipples.

She knew well enough what the place was. It was a brothel, a place where men came to bathe with compliant, willing girls and then take more pleasure if they wished. She had guessed, too, why Anne was being so kind. The knowledge should have filled her with revulsion, but it did not. She felt numb.

'Anne,' she said, as the copper-haired girl shed her clothes and clambered into the bath with the jug of Malmsey in her hand, 'do you work in this place?'

'That's right,' said Anne, refilling Rosamund's glass with the dark, sweet wine. She had a pretty, curvy body, with tiny breasts like rosebuds and a pert, rounded backside, and Rosamund gasped to see her mound of love. It was plucked and polished until it was quite bare, as smooth as alabaster, so that the delicate pink lips were visible to the most casual eye. Anne smiled to see her surprise and leant back a little, thrusting her hips forward, showing off her naked sex.

'You're a whore, then,' said Rosamund hesitantly.

Anne made a rueful face, as if she did not like the word. 'Well,' she admitted at last, 'I suppose I am.' She set down the jug and her glass on a little ledge handily set into the side of the tall, linen-lined wooden tub, and pushed her way through the deep water towards Rosamund. 'Come,' she said, 'let me wash you. It's my job, I'm good at it.'

She rubbed the scented soap between her hands and lifted one of Rosamund's white arms from the water, stroking along it, making the skin slippery with soap. Rosamund closed her eyes. The feel of the warm water, the soft soap and Anne's deft little hands was utterly delicious. All the fear, the cold, the wretchedness of the day began to seep away into the steam.

Anne had not lied. As a bath girl she was shockingly

175

expert. Rosamund knew that she was being enticed into pleasure and she was certain that it was because Anne wanted her to become a whore too. But now she did not want to resist the delicate, sensual sensations which Anne's hands were giving her.

Small fingers dug gently into the soft flesh of her shoulders, easing away tension, coaxing out knots of worry. Rosamund sighed and let her head fall back to rest against the edge of the bath. Anne worked on her shoulders and neck for a little while, then moved down to Rosamund's white breasts. Her fingers slipped below the floating orbs, weighing them, fondling them, and despite the warmth of the water Rosamund felt a cold shiver run from the top of her spine all the way down to her loins, stirring her between her legs with an oily ripeness.

'Beautiful breasts,' whispered Anne, gently caressing the outer curve of the heavy globes. Rosamund shivered again, letting out a trembling gasp. 'So beautiful. Are they sensitive? Oh, I think they are. See how your teats stand up, sweetheart.'

It was true: the pink tips were stiffening, erecting into taut caps of sensation. Anne smiled and touched the hard peaks with her soapy fingers, trapping each eager point between finger and thumb and tugging, tugging, gentle and persistent. 'Have you ever come just from having your breasts touched?' she asked softly.

'Oh,' Rosamund murmured, turning her head. Her lips were soft and moist with desire and pleasure. Not even Geoffrey had touched her breasts as Anne was doing now, trailing her fingertips around the distended areolae, teasing at the tight nipples with fingers and nails until the delicious sharpness of the pleasure made her belly quake with urgency.

'Do you know what coming is?' whispered Anne, moving closer still and never, never stopping her delicious stimulation of Rosamund's aching breasts. 'Dying, some people call it. It is when the pleasure is so

176

great that you think it is the end of the world. Has a man ever done that to you?'

Geoffrey's image appeared before Rosamund's closed eyes, but she did not speak his name. She relaxed against the wall of the bath, accepting the waves of chilling delight that arrowed through her from her tense, rigid nipples, sighing with satisfaction as she felt Anne's soft body beginning to press against her. Her thighs moved apart and Anne slid between them, rubbing her thigh against Rosamund's mound of Venus.

Then a kiss, a delicate, gentle kiss. Rosamund moaned and responded eagerly, arching her back so that the lips of her flushed, pouting sex were chafing against Anne's slender hips. Their tongues touched and twisted and all the time Anne's fingers flickered against the stiff peaks of Rosamund's breasts. Every particle of Rosamund's body craved for pleasure, reaching eagerly out to seize whatever delight was offered, taking refuge against the world in sensual ecstasy. She began to cry out as the convulsions of orgasm materialised as if from nowhere, making her body jerk helplessly against Anne's rubbing hips and fondling hands.

'Well,' Anne whispered, supporting Rosamund in the warm water, 'you are eager, my dear, aren't you?' She took the soap into her hands again and continued to wash Rosamund from head to foot, drawing fresh cries of pleasure from her as her hands touched flesh that was still shuddering with echoes of orgasm. At last she said gently, 'Come, that's enough water, you don't want to turn into a wrinkled apple, do you?'

Rosamund trembled as Anne helped her to climb out of the bath. Her orgasm had been brief and ferociously intense, but it had gone as quickly as it had come and now she was afraid of the hungry emptiness that had replaced it. She caught quickly at Anne's face with her hands, turning it up to kiss her.

'What, more?' whispered Anne. 'More already? Why not, why not. Come over here, lovely Rosamund.'

Rosamund allowed herself to be led unresisting to a

177

couch spread with fine linen. Anne picked up a linen towel from a little basket and roughly brushed the drops of water from Rosamund's body, making her shiver. Then she guided her to lie on the couch and lay on top of her and set her lips to hers.

Oh, the pleasure, the sweetness, to feel that lustful kiss, to feel skilled hands squeezing at breasts, sliding between parted thighs to touch and probe deep between moist tender lips. There was nothing, nothing, to compare with the sweet security of sensual pleasure. As long as the sensations lasted there was no need to think of loss or grief or hardship, no need for tears or hatred. Rosamund kissed Anne back eagerly, wishing that the bliss would never cease.

'Let us please each other,' Anne suggested. She took Rosamund's hand and guided it gently over her naked mound and between her slender thighs, encouraging her to feel, and at the same time she slid one finger deep into Rosamund's damp, willing sex. 'Shall we, sweetheart? Have you ever given a woman pleasure before?'

'No,' Rosamund replied hesitantly. Then she gasped as Anne's finger began to move gently in and out. 'Oh,' she gasped, 'oh God, that is sweet.'

'Sweet,' Anne repeated, putting her other hand on Rosamund's breast and squeezing hard. She arched her white hips, rubbing herself against Rosamund's fingers. 'Do you like to be swived, then, sweetheart?'

'Yes,' Rosamund whispered, imagining that Anne's moving finger was replaced by Geoffrey's wonderful cock, so long and thick, so determined and demanding, filling her. 'Oh, yes. Please, don't stop.'

'Touch me,' hissed Anne, and obediently Rosamund tried to imitate the girl's skilful movements. 'No,' said Anne, 'not inside me, no, no. Touch my button, my pleasure point, here.' She let go of Rosamund's breast and moved her hand, taking one finger and setting it to the little proud bead at the front of her cleft. 'Oh, yes, that's it. Touch me there, sweetheart, and I will swive you with my fingers to your heart's content.'

Anne's sex was slippery with desire. Rosamund gently moved her finger over the swollen, hard nubbin of flesh, smiling as Anne reacted with a gasp and a sigh of delight. They kissed, and Anne thrust first two and then three fingers deep into Rosamund's aching mound. The lips of her vulva opened like a flower, begging to be filled, and she began to moan regularly as Anne's fingers slipped in and out of her moist flesh. They clung together, their hands squeezing at each other's breasts, pinching the tight nipples, their tongues thrusting deep into each other's mouths, crying out in unison as they drew themselves closer and closer to the brink of ecstasy with their working hands. Rosamund pressed her finger down hard on the taut peak of Anne's clitoris and felt the soft flesh begin to quiver and shake with the onset of climax. Anne arched her hips towards Rosamund's fingers, letting out a series of little shrill cries as her body tensed and quaked with frantic spasms of delight. Her fingers twisted and plunged within Rosamund's welcoming sex and as they slipped in as deeply as they could, Anne pressed the heel of her hand against Rosamund's clitoris, clutching at her soft, wet mound as if she would never let it go. A desperate moan escaped Rosamund's lips and she rubbed herself against Anne's shaking hand, drawing her fingers deeper inside her and closing her eyes as dark jets of pleasure raced through her body.

Presently they calmed and lay in each other's arms, kissing delicately. Anne's face was flushed and pretty with the heat of orgasm. She squeezed gently at Rosamund's taut, tender nipple, making her wince and sigh. 'That was wonderful, sweetheart,' she said kindly. 'Just imagine, if you were to stay here, how we could give each other pleasure like that all the time. And the other girls, too. Lots of us aren't too fond of men, you know: quiet days are what we look forward to. We lie in the steam room looking after each other, plucking each other, rubbing each other with oil until we are sighing with pleasure. And if we take the opportunity to love

179

each other a little, who can blame us? Wouldn't you like that, sweetheart?'

Rosamund let her head lie upon Anne's soft arm. She felt languid and heavy with ecstasy, but still desirous of more. Soon Anne would ask her to stay at the bath house and become a whore, she knew it, and she wanted to delay the moment as long as possible so that she would not have to make a decision. 'I like men,' she said at last, sleepily.

'Do you?' murmured Anne, sliding a little way down Rosamund's softened body to draw a taut nipple between her warm lips. She sucked at it, laving it with her caressing tongue until Rosamund tilted back her head and cried out. 'Do you like men? Well, there are plenty of them, too.'

'Anne,' Rosamund whispered, 'don't stop.'

Anne looked delighted. 'Why,' she said with a smile, 'you are insatiable. I thought I liked it! I never met a girl as eager as you. Come then, sweetheart, shall we give each other some more pleasure? Will you lick me with your hot tongue, Rosamund, and make me come?'

'Lick you?' Rosamund frowned uncertainly. She had often moaned with pleasure to feel warm mouths lapping between her soft parted thighs, but she had never tasted a woman. 'Me?'

'Fair's fair,' Anne murmured. 'Oh, don't worry, dear heart, I will lick you too. You won't mind, I promise you.' And without another word she got onto all fours and turned so that her head was by Rosamund's thighs. She glanced back along the white curving hills of Rosamund's body and smiled, then placed one knee on either side of her head.

'Oh,' Rosamund whispered, astonished, as she looked up into the gleaming folds of Anne's swollen sex. It was beautiful, naked, unadorned by a single hair, every convoluted curve and fold of delicate skin open to the searching eye and the probing tongue. Her clitoris stood up hard and proud, protruding from the hood of flesh that should protect it, begging to be stroked.

'Kiss me,' Anne whispered. 'Lick me.' She began to lower her hips, offering her open sex to Rosamund's lips. For a moment Rosamund hesitated, smelling the dense, musky scent of another woman's arousal. Then her reluctance evaporated and she reached up with both hands and caught hold of the round orbs of Anne's buttocks and pulled at them, drawing her close to kiss her.

She reached out at once, instinctively, to caress Anne's straining clitoris with her tongue. As she did so she felt a quivering gasp running through Anne's body and then almost at once a warm, delicious wetness between her own legs as Anne thrust her clever, searching tongue deep into her sex. Rosamund groaned with pleasure and lapped eagerly, quivering her tongue against the tingling bead, sucking wetly at the hood surrounding it, unable to prevent her own body from undulating like the surface of the sea as waves of pleasure swept over her. They lay together, bodies pressed close, thighs spread wide apart, tonguing, licking, sucking, driving each other inexorably towards another orgasm. As the pleasure increased their hands began to clutch more tightly at the soft swell of buttock and haunch. Rosamund pulled Anne's clitoris into her mouth and sucked at it as if it were a nipple and Anne cried out with sharp delight. She pulled Rosamund's cheeks wide apart and then drove her wetted finger into the tight ring of her anus, sliding it deep, and as the finger entered her secret passage Rosamund arched convulsively upwards, jerking with a paroxysm of pleasure as her climax possessed her. Anne cried out again and thrust the wet mound of her naked sex against Rosamund's quivering lips and Rosamund buried her tongue in the moist flesh, feeling it gripped by helpless contractions as Anne succumbed to the ecstatic heaves of orgasm.

After a few moments they separated and lay beside each other on the soft couch, head to tail, panting. Rosamund stared up at the painted rafters of the little room, her mind deliciously fogged with pleasure. She flung out her arms in joyous, wanton abandon.

Anne pushed herself up and swung around to lie beside Rosamund, propped up on her folded arms and smiling. 'Come,' she said, 'you are in trouble: all your money has gone, you said. Stay here and work for a while. We get paid, you know. I know they'll welcome you.'

'I don't want questions,' Rosamund said quickly. She could not bear the thought of people knowing her history.

'No questions asked,' Anne smiled, stroking her hand lasciviously down the curves of Rosamund's long body.

'Won't your master want to know something about me?' Rosamund sounded surprised.

'What, with your body?' Anne grinned broadly. 'It's a mistress, anyway, and she'll welcome you like manna from Heaven. Mistress Alice is our manager. There's an owner, too, but we never see him. No one knows who he is except Mistress Alice, and she never tells anyone anything. My guess is that it's the Bishop of Southwark. Clerics own nearly all of the houses of pleasure around here. So much for men of God, eh?'

'Well,' Rosamund hesitated, still uncertain.

'I tell you what,' Anne whispered, leaning forward. 'Let me get you one of the customers. A man. Perhaps you don't know if you could do it with a stranger. Wait here, sweetheart, I'll bring him to you.'

She slipped off the couch and disappeared before Rosamund had a chance to say yes or no. Rosamund lay back, stretching her arms above her head, luxuriating in the aftermath of her pleasure. She could not refrain from laughing. What would Anne say if she discovered that the girl she had taken such trouble to seduce had already been debauched, abused in every conceivable way, passed between one man and another for them to use at their pleasure? Obviously her sordid experiences had not left their mark upon her.

What was she to do? She had nothing, no friends, no

money. She knew no one in London to whom she could turn for help. Before she could help herself she found herself thinking of Geoffrey. She rolled onto her front and hid her face in her arms. Tears smarted bitterly in her eyes. If Geoffrey was alive, she would not care that Sir Ralph had taken everything she owned. Geoffrey was poor too, he had told her so, but it would not matter. They would walk together barefoot through England, hand in hand. She would beg his bread in the market-places, and they would lie together at night in a haystack beneath his ragged cloak, sharing their love, buried alive beneath the smothering weight of their desire. But he was dead, dead in the foul cell where she had last seen him, his poor naked body flung aside like carrion. She would never see him again.

So what point in hopeless grieving? She had no energy to resist what the world might fling at her next. She would stay here, in the brothel, until she felt stronger. Perhaps then she would be able to think of some way to revenge herself upon Sir Ralph. Vengeance was for men: but a determined woman might find some means to wreak her anger on the man who had harmed her.

The door opened and Anne entered. Behind her came a young man, four or five and twenty perhaps, tall and broad shouldered. He wore only a swathe of white linen, wrapped around his waist, and his shoulder-length hair hung in dark, wet curls around an olive-skinned, narrow-featured face.

'Rosamund,' said Anne with a smile, 'this is Piers. See what you can do for him. I'll stay and watch,' she added, smiling more broadly, 'in case you need any help.'

Rosamund got to her feet, suddenly conscious of her nakedness. Piers looked at her with liquid, dark-brown eyes and his face tautened with a surge of eager desire. He was handsome and well made, she did not think that it would be difficult to give herself to him.

'Oh, and by the way,' Anne said mischievously, 'if there's one thing Piers likes, it's a nice tight arse. If you don't mind, Rosamund.'

A jolt of apprehension and reluctance filled Rosamund's stomach, curling there. To be taken in her arse – she knew it could bring pleasure, but she did not believe that she could bring herself to permit it. In a single hot red flash she remembered how Sir Ralph had taken her there when she was bound, pinioned and helpless, her naked buttocks thrust upwards for his strong hands to part them, for his thick cock to press between them and take the virginity of her anus. She swallowed hard and was about to refuse, but already Piers was standing by her, lifting his hands to her shoulders. 'By God,' he said, 'you're a ripe one.'

He put his hands on her and ran them down to her breasts, drawing the white globes into his palms and squeezing them thoughtfully. His face was absorbed, preoccupied, taken up with the prospect of his own pleasure. He cared nothing for her, she was merely the tool of his lust. He did not expect her to refuse. Rosamund felt a tinge of the ferocious arousal that had seized her when Sir Ralph abused her, forcing her to satisfy his brutal lusts.

'Turn round,' said Piers shortly. 'We'll do it standing up.'

'Yes,' Rosamund said obediently, and found that before she could help herself she had added, 'my lord.'

She turned her back to him and he stood behind her, running his strong hands over her breasts and belly and onto the swell of her white buttocks. She stood shivering, her eyes closed, her breath coming faster and faster as she felt him touching her, impersonal, uninvolved, caring for his own arousal, not for hers. Suddenly she wanted to feel a cock, any cock, Piers' cock because it was there and available. She needed to be entered, to be taken, to be driven into forgetfulness by the urgent lunges of a man's thick shaft within her. She reached out behind her, sliding her fingers beneath the linen towel that wrapped Piers' hips, loosening it until it fell to the ground.

'Ah,' whispered the male voice in her ear. 'that's it,

darling. You're a natural.' The hand on her buttock slipped further down, tracing the dark length of her cleft, then pushed between her legs. She gasped and opened her thighs a little, allowing the edge of the hand to run along her wet furrow, gathering moisture, drawing it back to lubricate her tingling anus. A finger penetrated her there and she gasped with shock and pleasure. Her eyes still tight shut, she ran her hand down the taut flat plane of the young man's belly until her fingers found the warm curling hair of his groin, traced their way through it and encountered the thick, hot base of his rearing shaft. She licked her lips and took a quick deep breath as her hand locked around it, weighing it, feeling its length and thickness. It was a fine weapon, stiff and hard and of impressive proportions. She slid her furled hand up the whole smooth hot length, savouring the tense tightness of the rod, the swollen silky knob at its tip.

'All right,' hissed the voice in her ear. 'Let go. I want you to clasp your hands behind my back.' Rosamund hesitated and with a murmur of irritation Piers took hold of her wrists and pulled her hands behind him, fastening them in the small of his back. Rosamund gasped with sudden arousal: it was almost as if he had tied her.

'That's it,' Piers said. 'I like that, see how it makes these splendid tits stick out. Oh, I like that.' His penis slipped between the cheeks of her bottom, nudging its way forward. It found the taut dark rim of her anus and prodded there, checking that it was in position. Then Piers' hands slipped over her haunches and up her ribs and took hold of her breasts, clutching them hard, and he grunted as he tensed his buttocks and thrust into her.

'Oh,' Rosamund cried as the swollen knob of his stiff cock forced its way through her tight sphincter. 'Oh, oh God.'

'Christ,' hissed Piers, 'you are tight. Oh Christ, that's so good.' He pushed harder, driving the whole throbbing length of him deep inside her, his big hands working on

185

her aching breasts. When he was fully inside her, buried deeply within her, he stopped. His breath was hot on her shoulder and he stood very still, muttering to himself. She stood quietly, her hands locked in the small of his back, her breasts heavy in his hands, gasping with pleasure to feel him in her.

'Piers,' said Anne's voice suddenly, 'go on, swive her. Hold her tight, I will pleasure her while you do it.'

Rosamund opened her eyes, startled, and saw Anne dropping quickly to her knees before her. Anne's mouth opened and Rosamund shut her eyes quickly in the anticipation of ecstasy.

Oh, there it was, the sensation of Anne's hot wet tongue lapping and flicking against the quivering pearl of pleasure. Behind her Piers gasped and began to move, sliding his thick shaft in and out of her secret passage, moving faster and faster as he drove himself inexorably towards his climax. The feel of him moving within her and of Anne's tongue licking her drove Rosamund half mad with pleasure. Her head fell back and she would have fallen, but Anne's hands were firm on her hips and Piers' frantic gripping of her breasts held her on her feet.

'Oh, God,' Piers gasped as he worked his thick iron-hard penis frantically to and fro, 'oh God, that's good. Anne, make her come, I want to hear her scream. Push it up her, Anne, do it now.'

And Rosamund opened her lips in a yell of amazement and delight as she felt something, something hard and thick pressing between the lips of her sex, sliding up inside her. It slipped out and then in again, spreading her, filling her deliciously as Piers drove himself ever faster in and out of her quivering anus and Anne sucked at her clitoris, working eagerly upon it with her clever lips. Piers gripped more tightly at her breasts and snarled with ferocious pleasure as his climax seized him. He pushed himself into Rosamund as hard as he could and his thick cock jerked as it spurted his seed deep inside her. Anne thrust the hard object in and out of her frantically clutching vagina and the sensation drove

Rosamund over the edge, making her scream as her crisis clutched her with red-hot claws and shook her and left her shuddering and helpless.

Presently Piers withdrew, still holding her tightly so that she did not fall, and Anne got to her feet and kissed Rosamund on the mouth. Rosamund turned, gasping, a sheen of sweat gleaming on her naked skin, and said to Piers, 'Did you *pay* for that, my lord? Did you pay to do that to me?'

Piers wiped his hand over his face. 'Pay for it? Me? Certainly not. I work here.'

'Piers is Mistress Alice's, er, what would you call yourself, Piers?' asked Anne brightly.

'Her bodyguard, general assistant and professional stallion,' said Piers with a grin. 'I stand at stud for the whole place. She always lets me try out our new acquisitions.' He smiled at Rosamund and leant forward to kiss her on the lips. 'You'll do, darling. I'd recommend you to any customer. Welcome to the Fountain of Love.'

Chapter Nine

*L*ife at the Fountain of Love was not bad, on the whole. It was a stylish place, resorted to by the nobility and wealthy men who wished to rub shoulders with them. It was also extremely expensive, and the single common feature of the customers was that they were rich. They were of course also clean, at least by the time that Rosamund and her colleagues had finished with them. Some of them were still not the type of man that a beautiful young woman would choose for a sexual partner, but a surprising number were. The Fountain had recently become the resort of choice for the fashionable young men of London, the sons of dukes and earls. They would arrive in gaggles, dressed in silk velvet doublets, samite shirts and skin-tight hose, posturing and laughing with each other as if the whole of the English nobility were not lurching inevitably towards war.

Rosamund learnt her duties quickly. They were not onerous. For four days in the week she worked in the bath house. This meant lying with the other girls in the steam room, dressed in linen so fine that it showed the nipples and the triangle through its gossamer folds, waiting for the customers to enter and make their selection. Then, if chosen, she would take the man to his bathing-tent, a sumptuous little cubicle equipped with tub and couch, help him to bathe and then perform any services he required. She had to report his requirements afterwards to Llewellyn, Mistress Alice's Welsh clerk, who would draw up the bill accordingly. For two days in the week she worked front of house, welcoming customers ('guests', Mistress Alice called them, but none of the girls were fooled) and sitting in one of the upper chambers with those whose pleasure was only to dine in female company and who had perhaps brought some business colleague with them to be impressed by the richness of the Fountain's provisions and the beauty of its girls. And the last day was her day off, during which she might if she chose sleep the day away in the girls' dormitory, or cross London Bridge to amuse herself in the shops of the City. She might have visited her family on that day, if she had had any. As she had no family and no desire to spend the small sums which she was earning, she would stay within the Fountain's buildings, lying in the arms of one of the other off-duty girls, giving and receiving lazy, gentle bliss. Her favourite lover among the girls was always Anne, but if Anne was engaged nearly all of her colleagues were acceptable as substitutes, skilled with their hands and tongues and eager for pleasure.

A noble upbringing gave Rosamund the grace required to excel at hospitality and after a few weeks, Mistress Alice said that if she wished she might work only at front of house, since she did the job so well. To her surprise, Rosamund replied that if she had the choice she would work only in the bath house. When Alice asked her why she only shrugged, not wanting to answer, and in the end Mistress Alice decided to continue with the status quo.

The truth was that Rosamund hated to work front of house. There were many reasons. When waiting for customers front of house she was alone, and then, when she dined with the gentlemen, they might well address not two words to her during the whole meal: for many of them she was a mere animate table decoration. This could mean that for hours at a time she was effectively alone with her thoughts, and this was what she dreaded above all else. When she was alone she would think of Geoffrey, and the grief which she kept locked within her would beat furiously at the doors of its prison, demanding to be let out.

And, furthermore, she feared to be recognised. Working in the bath house, her thick chestnut hair loose upon her shoulders and her body more naked than nudity in its gauzy gown, she felt camouflaged. Nobody who had known her would recognise her, she was sure of it. But front of house she wore fine clothes, a lady's clothes, and her hair was dressed and concealed beneath a headdress: she looked like herself. If a man she had met in Lincolnshire should come in one day and see her and recognise her, she felt she would die of mortification.

She hid her grief, but to do so required constant effort. She was not herself. Her spirit was pervaded by a settled melancholy. The girls knew that her sadness was real, though they did not understand its cause. But the young men who came to the Fountain thought it affectation and found it uniformly charming. They called her *La Dolorosa* and she became a fashion with them. They would leave calling out to one another, 'And did you make *La Dolorosa* smile today?' 'No, but I made her squeal.' 'Better than a smile!'

Surprisingly often, Rosamund's customers did give her pleasure. Many of them were young courtiers with a high opinion of themselves, who took justifiable pride in their performance. Even with ordinary customers she could find pleasure. She sought pleasure, she craved it. She would let herself slip into the strange, erotic trance that had possessed her when she was captive at Murthrum Castle. Within that self-induced trance she was open to every sensation, her whole body sensitised and eager, hungry for stimulus. When she was rising towards orgasm or sinking down afterwards as if she flew through clouds, she could forget her grief, and she developed the capacity to arouse herself so that the slightest touch, the first thrust of a man's body within hers was sufficient to begin her climb to ecstasy.

Her pleasure of the body did not involve her mind. Her thoughts were closed off, remote, while her beautiful body tensed and heaved in bliss and her voice sounded in smothered moans. Nothing, she thought, could penetrate the shell of her self protection.

One day she was lying in the bath house steam room with her head in Anne's lap. Anne leant forward over her, holding a tress of her thick copper hair. She brushed the soft hairs over Rosamund's nipple, making it stand up dark and proud through the filmy linen of her gown. Rosamund shivered and lifted her hands above her head to caress Anne's breasts. Their breathing began to deepen and Anne was just stooping her lips for a kiss when one of the girls said softly, 'Customer ahoy, watch yourselves.'

Anne and Rosamund separated quickly and sat up. Not one man but two came through the curtains, naked but for linen towels. The first was a young nobleman, the son of a lord, who was a regular visitor to the Fountain. Rosamund privately believed this was because no decent woman would stand his company. He was a raucous, guffawing youth, who thought that because he had broad shoulders and a shapely leg he was God's gift to women, though all that he could talk about was dogs and horses. When he was engaged in one of the cubicles his lusty yells of pleasure could be heard all around the bath house: he bellowed like a ram and then boasted like a fool. Fortunately his taste ran to 'girls who like to have a bit of fun', which meant that he had never found Rosamund attractive.

Behind this unsavoury specimen came another man, younger and slighter than the first. They looked a little alike, both blond and high coloured, and Rosamund was not surprised when the first one said in his habitual half-shout, 'Right, then, girls. Here's my little brother Johnny

191

come among you for a bit of tuition. Which of you wants to be his first pony? Show yourselves off, my darlings.'

God in Heaven, Rosamund thought to herself, poor boy. What an introduction. The other girls began to do as they had been bid, their bodies undulating as they presented to the two young men whatever part of them they thought most beautiful: a pair of white, rounded shoulders, a slender calf, a shapely thigh, breasts like shallow snow-covered hills, swelling buttocks that asked to be slapped. But Rosamund sat looking at the young man in silent sympathy. He had a pleasant face and he looked more intelligent than his older brother, though that would not have been hard, but now he was flushed scarlet, first with embarrassment and then with sheer astonishment at the wealth of riches laid before him.

'Right, then, Johnny,' said the elder, clapping his hands together and rubbing them eagerly, 'which d'you fancy?'

The young man's eyes cast over the gently shifting sea of flesh and fixed on Rosamund's face. She did not move, but she knew that her sympathy for him showed in her eyes. She saw him swallow hard: then he said, 'That one.'

His older brother looked and frowned. 'What, her? *La Dolorosa*? You don't want her, Johnny, she's too serious – '

'Her,' the young man repeated, setting his jaw.

'Please yourself,' said his brother, and he snapped his fingers at Rosamund. She detested being treated like a servant, but she got to her feet and came towards the young man, her white body glimmering through the thin folds of her gown. She dropped a gracious little half-curtsey and held out her hand to him. 'My lord,' she said, 'will you accompany me?'

The young man looked astonished and delighted. His eyes kept leaving her face and running down her body, then returning with an effort as if he had dragged them. 'Gladly,' he said, and took her hand.

It was obvious that he had not visited the Fountain

before. As she led him through to the bath house she explained quietly, 'We will go to one of these cubicles, my lord, and you may bathe. And then afterwards, at your pleasure.'

She led him into one of the cubicles, let go of his hand and turned to face him. She reached for the linen towel around his waist, but he caught her wrists and held her away from him. His hands were trembling. 'Why do they call you *La Dolorosa*?' he asked her, and his voice was trembling too.

'Just a nickname,' Rosamund said lightly. She stood very still, afraid that if she made another move she would frighten him. He seemed as nervous as a stag: his bright blue eyes, fringed with golden lashes, were blinking rapidly. He stood holding her hands and gazing at her, quite silent. At last she said gently, 'What is your pleasure, my lord?'

He let out an angry laugh and dropped her hands, turning away from her. His arms folded tightly across his chest, tense and defensive. His back was slender and elegantly muscled, showing the ribs through the silky skin. 'Oh, come,' he replied, 'don't flatter me. You heard Simon introduce me: here's my little brother the virgin, girls, which of you wants him?'

'Does he always act so coarsely?' Rosamund asked. 'He is always the same here, but it is a shock to see him embarrass his own brother.'

The young man spun on his heel and stared at her. 'You do not talk like a – whore,' he said after a moment. 'You sound like a lady. What are you doing here?'

'I work here,' Rosamund said. She did not want to encourage his questions, and so she put her hands to the fastenings of her gown, one on each shoulder, and unclasped them. The soft gauze slithered down her body to pool at her feet.

Now he was shaking. The towel around his waist began to lift into a little tent as her nakedness worked on him. 'Christ,' he hissed, 'you're beautiful.' He took a step towards her, then suddenly hesitated. His right hand was clenched into a fist before his mouth. 'Listen,' he blurted, 'I'm here because I'm getting married next month, to a woman older than me, she's a widow. My father ordered me to come here, he made Simon bring me, he said he wouldn't be able to face my wife the morning after if I didn't – if I couldn't – I didn't want to come – ' His voice faded. 'Please,' he whispered, 'show me what to do.'

Rosamund came a step closer. She was fascinated by the thought that this young man, this boy, had never had a woman, and that he had chosen her to be the first. She was flattered and moved. She said, 'He called you Johnny.'

'John,' said the young man, tearing his eyes from her naked body to look into her face. 'It's John. I hate being called Johnny.'

'John,' Rosamund said, and she smiled. 'What do you want to know?'

He was trembling from head to foot, his whole body shaking with a mixture of excitement and fear. He shrugged helplessly and said, 'Whatever there is.'

'Come,' said Rosamund, catching hold of his hand, 'come and get in the bath with me. It's a nice start, I promise you. Come on.'

She put her hand to the towel around his waist and twitched at it, pulling it away. He took a quick deep breath, his stomach pulling in sharply beneath his ribs. He was slender and well made, with fine muscles and delicate skin. Golden fur curled crisply in his groin and his penis was already desperately erect, stiff and shining with excitement. He looked at Rosamund as if he were afraid that she would laugh at him. She smiled reassuringly and said, 'You're handsome.'

'You're just saying that because I'm a customer.'

'You are,' she assured him. 'I don't have to say it. Most of my customers don't care whether I think they're handsome or not.'

She took him by the hand and led him into the bath.

As they climbed in she asked curiously, 'How old is your widow, then?'

'Thirty, she tells me,' said John, 'but I think she's older. She was married fifteen years to her first husband.'

'*Thirty?*' repeated Rosamund in astonishment. 'How old are you?'

'Eighteen next month.' John sounded suddenly defensive. 'She's rich.' He lowered his voice. 'My family are getting poorer all the time. Simon spends everything Father gives him on places like this. We had to have a good match for me. She's got no children, maybe if she dies she'd leave me all her money. So Father wants her to be pleased with me. That's why he told Simon to bring me here.'

Rosamund caught herself about to say, 'My husband was sixty when we wedded,' but she held the words back. Instead she picked up the soap and advanced on John through the warm water. He retreated until he was trapped against the side of the bath. Rosamund said reassuringly, 'Let me look after you,' and set her hands to his shoulders, rubbing the liquid scented soap across his chest and into the hollows of his collar bone. He opened his mouth as if to speak: then her hand moved lower, running down the flat plane of his abdomen towards his groin, and he gasped and shut his eyes tightly. She very gently took hold of the hot, quivering shaft of his penis. It jerked in her hand and John set his teeth against a little cry of shock and pleasure. She felt down beneath the strong proud bar of flesh to his tight, updrawn balls, fondling them, weighing them.

'Christ,' John whispered, clutching at the edge of the tub with both hands to hold himself up. 'Christ, oh Holy Mother of God.' Rosamund reached dexterously between his legs with her left hand and fondled his balls while with her right she began to masturbate him, ringing the glossy head of his cock tightly with finger and thumb and then slipping her hand up and down the length of it. As she aroused him she watched his face, his eyes shut tight and his mouth tense as if he were in pain, his nostrils flared and quivering. She was the first woman to do this to him. The thought filled her with avid arousal and a sense of shuddering power.

After only a few strokes, John began to shake as his climax built up within him. He clutched frantically at the wooden tub and opened his eyes, looking desperately into Rosamund's face. 'Stop,' he moaned, 'stop, or I'll – oh God – '

'Too late,' Rosamund whispered. She looked down. Below the surface of the warm, transparent water his cock was pulsing and twitching, forcing out long streams of white come that swirled slowly upwards.

John moaned and fell back against the tub, almost sobbing. 'God,' he whispered, 'that'll please my new wife, won't it? Three strokes. God help me!'

'Hush,' said Rosamund. She let go of his penis and pressed herself against him. He was trembling. 'Don't worry. Young men recover quickly.' She knew from the other girls that this was true. 'You'll be hard again in a moment or two.' She felt gentle, almost loving, and she reached up and stroked his face with her hand. He looked down at her, his blue eyes glittering with tears of shame. 'Kiss me,' she whispered.

He hesitated for a moment, tugging at his lower lip with his teeth. Then he leant forward and touched his mouth to hers. He kissed her chastely, almost like a sister, and when she gently touched her tongue to his closed lips he pulled back, flinching.

'Don't be afraid,' Rosamund said softly, concerned. She reached out for him again and ran her hand along the line of his jaw and then on to the back of his neck, holding his head firmly so that he could not escape her. He closed his eyes as she lifted her lips to his. Their mouths pressed together. Rosamund found that his lips were very slightly parted. Shuddering with excitement, she pushed her tongue into his mouth. His body jerked against hers and he gave a little moan. His hands hung in the air above the surface of the warm rippling water, opening and closing in helpless amazement. Then suddenly he seemed to understand and he gasped and put his hands to her face, cupping her delicate jaw like a jewel. He kissed her with desperate urgency, thrusting his tongue between her lips and exploring her mouth. He let go of her face after a moment and put his arms around her, first tentatively and then with glorious abandon, exploring her body with his hands, feeling, stroking, weighing her breasts as they bobbed in the warm water, and all the time he kissed her. His astonishment and delight lit him like a glowing candle. Rosamund arched her body against him in a fever of exhilaration, aroused beyond measure by the thought that she was the first, wanting to show him more, more, until he was no longer afraid.

At last John lifted his mouth from hers and drew back a little. He was panting, but now he was smiling too. 'There,' he admitted, 'now you can guess it. I never even kissed a girl before.'

'Why not?' Rosamund asked bluntly, intrigued. 'You're handsome enough.'

John let out a little bitter laugh. 'Where would you start if you were the son of the lord of the manor?' he asked her rhetorically. 'With the local girls, eh? Believe me, *Dolorosa cara*, there isn't one of them that Simon hasn't already had. If I took one of them he'd know about it the following morning and he'd laugh at me. Every three months or so he does the rounds and collects any maidenheads he missed on the last sweep.' He shook his head. Then he caught her face in his hand and looked into her eyes. 'You looked at me as if you understood,' he said, 'and then he said he didn't like you. Has he – '

'No.' Rosamund smiled slowly. 'No, he never had me.'

'I'm glad.' Impulsively John flung his arms around her, squeezing her so tightly she gasped. 'I'm so glad.' He pulled back, looking earnestly into her face. 'Promise me you won't tell him anything, no matter what he asks you.'

'Of course I won't.' He was so young, so solemn. It would have been impossible for her to be unkind to him.

197

She took his hands and pulled them from around her waist. 'Come,' she said, 'let's get out of the bath before we turn into raisins.'

'Another kiss first,' he said urgently, catching her hand and tugging her towards him. She let her head fall back and closed her eyes, waiting. Nothing happened, and after a moment she opened her eyes again.

He was hanging over her, his face close to hers, staring down into the dark pools of her eyes in disbelief and rapture. 'You're so beautiful,' he whispered. 'You're the most beautiful woman I ever saw.' His hand hovered trembling above her cheekbone as if he did not dare to touch her and his eyes glittered. Was he weeping? His lips moved hesitantly and suddenly Rosamund was afraid of what he would say. She did not seek declarations of love. Quickly she broke the moment, drawing back and saying, 'No, I must get out, it's bad for my skin.'

She clambered out of the bath and picked up a linen towel, holding it ready to dry him when he emerged. For a few moments he hid his face in his hands and stood silent, his shoulders heaving. Then he tossed back his blond hair and wiped the back of his hand hard over his face and got out of the bath.

As she towelled him down he was silent. Then, when he was nearly dry, he said, 'I suppose you have men falling in love with you all the time.'

'I can't say that I do,' said Rosamund, kneeling to brush drops of water from his calves. For a few seconds she stared into nothingness, remembering the dungeon at Murthrum Castle, the cold damp stone, Geoffrey's body warm and softening beneath her lips, his face as brilliant as the sun rising and his caressing voice telling her that he loved her. An icy hand seemed to clutch at her heart and she bowed her head and returned to her work.

To business. She forced away the memory of Geoffrey, thrusting it back into its little cell within her mind, slamming the door and turning the key in the lock. She dried John's legs thoroughly and then put her hands on them, sliding her soft fingers up towards his groin. He looked down at her with a frown of surprise and she lifted her face and made herself smile. His penis was long and soft, hanging between his legs over the cushion of his balls. It seemed entirely exhausted. Rosamund took a long breath and licked her lips, then slowly reached up to take him in her mouth.

'God on the Cross,' he gasped as he felt her lips on him.

Rosamund closed her eyes, concentrating entirely on the sensation of John's penis within her mouth. For a moment it lay still, apparently stunned with amazement. Then the gentle pressure of her lips and tongue began to work its magic and the soft cock began to swell, growing, stretching, the satin-soft skin tautening as hot blood poured in to stiffen the spongy flesh. Rosamund lapped delicately at the expanding tip, her mouth fastened around the shaft in an O of warm, succulent tightness. With her hands she stroked between his thighs, feeling his testicles lifting and tautening, tugged snugly upwards beneath his loins as his cock engorged under her deft attentions.

Within moments he was fully hard. He had a fine penis, long and well shaped, hot and smooth within her mouth. She drew back and looked up at him, smiling. He was shaking as he looked down at her and again she felt the rush of desire and arousal, the sense of extraordinary power. Between her legs she was slippery with lust. Her breasts ached, longing to feel his hands.

She half expected him to lead her to the couch, but he did not. He was her pupil. She got to her feet and took his hand, drawing him after her across the room. She lay down on the couch and parted her legs and held out her hands to him.

He got onto the couch, moving in hesitant jerks. His cock stuck out before him as straight and stiff as a cannon. He knelt upright between her open thighs, trembling and uncertain, and Rosamund smiled with affectionate patience and caught hold of him, pulling him down onto her.

She took his hand and put it between her legs. His face was close to her, gazing at her, his eyes stretched wide. 'Feel,' she said, guiding his fingers. 'Feel me. Here, do you feel?' She put one finger at the entrance to her sex and pushed it into her. Pleasure made her gasp and shut her eyes. Her vagina closed tightly upon his finger in a lurch of excitement and John took a quick, startled breath.

'It's so small,' he said hesitantly, 'it's as small as my finger. I won't – '

'Please,' Rosamund whispered, 'put yourself inside me, John.'

He licked his dry lips and withdrew his hand, then began to fumble to put himself in position. She did not smile, because now she was full of urgency. She wanted to feel him moving inside her. Reaching down between them, she took hold of his staring cock and lodged the bulging head just between the lips of her sex.

Then she waited, looking into his face. He was breathing in quick, regular pants. Rosamund gently rested her hands on his naked buttocks and gave a little, encouraging squeeze. She felt the strong muscles begin to tense and she held him more firmly, wanting to feel the hot, glossy head of his cock slipping up inside her.

John whimpered as he began to move. His lips parted and his breath became ragged. He thrust gently, steadily, his eyes wide and transparent with disbelief, and gradually his long phallus pushed its way inside her, sliding all the way up into her moist, welcoming flesh, filling her vagina with hot quivering hardness, penetrating a woman for the first time.

He was inside her now, lying quite still, buried in her to the hilt. His balls nestled tightly against the roundness of her buttocks. He breathed softly, 'God have mercy on me. It's unbelievable.'

Rosamund passed her tongue over her lips. She wanted to lie still until he was ready to move, but she could not prevent her head from arching backwards, pushing her taut aching nipples up against him. She wanted to feel him moving inside her. She wanted to watch his face as he spilled himself within the body of his first woman. She wanted to come. 'John,' she murmured, 'swive me.'

His face changed. The expression of astonishment left it, replaced by a look of determination, of challenge. His buttocks swelled as he withdrew from her, then hollowed as he pushed himself in again. The movement made him close his eyes and draw his lips back from his teeth in a snarl of pleasure. Rosamund sighed with delight, watching his face as he moved, offering the soft mound of her sex to him, pleasure mounting and surging within her as he thrust and thrust. She was almost there, poised on the brink, but his movements were becoming jerky and uncoordinated as his own crisis approached. Suddenly she was filled with panic: She clutched at him, moaning, 'Not yet, not yet, don't stop,' and he stared at her and set his teeth and lunged into her with frantic strength and she was there, her body pulsing with ecstasy, her eyes wide open, fastened on his face. He cried out as she spasmed convulsively around his plunging cock and with one last desperate thrust he flung back his head and shouted aloud as orgasm seized him, draining him, and his deeply imbedded penis throbbed and jerked in her still quivering flesh.

After a few seconds in which he hung above her, tense and rigid as unfamiliar sensations flooded through him, he fell forward onto her and buried his face in her shoulder. She lay beneath him panting, looking up at the tented ceiling of the cubicle and gently stroking his hair. She felt affectionate towards him, protective. After a little time had passed and he still lay with his face hidden she kissed his ear, then used her hands to turn his head so that she could look into his eyes. They opened slowly, wide and blue and awestruck. She smiled at him.

'Thank you,' he said at last. He began to move away

from her and then winced. She hushed him and gently shifted her hips so that he could withdraw, though she would have liked to hold him longer. He sat up between her parted thighs, frowning intently, and reached out one hand to stroke her body.

For a little while he touched her, exploring her with his hand, and she lay still and watched his absorbed, fascinated face. Presently his expression changed: he looked suddenly like a chastened child and turned his head away.

'What's the matter?' asked Rosamund quickly, sitting up.

'I have to go,' he replied, folding his lips together as if he were trying to hold back tears. 'Simon was very clear on the subject. He said I could only have you once. He said that's all he could afford.' He looked back at Rosamund with a guilty, unhappy face. 'I'm really sorry.'

'Is that all?' Rosamund laughed. 'Listen,' she said, reaching out and catching hold of his hand, 'if I told our clerk everything that has gone on, you'd already have been charged extra twice. What makes you think I'm going to?'

His lips parted in amazement. 'Won't you get into trouble?'

'They'll never know,' Rosamund said with a smile, shaking her head. Her hair lifted and settled over her shoulders. She ran her hand up John's arm, feeling strong slender muscles, and passed her eyes over his body. He was still partially erect: everything her friends had told her about the powers of a young man was obviously true. Her hand began to move downwards, over the ridges of muscle on his narrow abdomen. 'We could do it again, if you wanted,' she whispered temptingly.

'If I wanted?' he repeated, laughing in disbelief. 'Of course I want to.'

'No hurry then.' She let her fingers trail very gently up the length of his half-hard cock, feeling her own moisture softening the delicate skin. He shuddered and his buttocks tensed, making his phallus and balls twitch under her hand. She looked up at him and asked softly, 'What would you like to do?'

He hesitated, his eyes travelling over her body as if embarrassed by riches. 'I want,' he said at last, 'I want to learn how to please a woman. You know how to touch me, how to – God, take me in your mouth. You know what to do. What should I do to please you?' His face was suddenly alight with eagerness. 'Let me look at you,' he asked breathlessly, catching her shoulders between his hands. 'Let me look at you and touch you, and then you can tell me what to do.'

Now it was Rosamund's turn to hesitate. Many men had told her that she was beautiful, but the thought of lying naked to be examined made her stomach coil with nervousness and need. But after all, what was wrong with it? She said after a moment, 'All right,' and then gently lay back on the pillows of the couch, lifting her hands above her head and closing her eyes so that she would not have to watch him looking at her.

He knelt beside her, she could feel him, his knees by her chest. 'Your breasts,' he said after a moment, 'they're lovely.' She started as she felt his hands on her breasts, cupping them, lifting them. 'They fill my hands,' he whispered. 'Does it please you to have them touched?'

'Yes,' Rosamund whispered. She felt intensely disconcerted. In her life so far men had not asked her what might give her pleasure. They had either seemed to understand instinctively, as had Geoffrey and, most horridly, Sir Ralph, or they had not cared. It was hard for her to articulate anything more. She stumbled for words, then managed to say, 'The – the tips are, are very sensitive.'

'Your nipples,' John whispered. His hands moved on her breasts, centring on the taut peaks, touching them very gently. Rosamund's breath hissed and she shifted on the cushions, arching her back, unconsciously pressing her breasts into his hands. 'Kiss them,' she whispered thickly.

There was silence. Then she felt his mouth on her

breasts, his lips fastening on the nipple like a child's, suckling gently. She gasped in ecstasy: sharp, pure pleasure began to radiate through her body, settling in her loins, making her writhe.

The sensation suddenly stopped. 'Are you all right?' said his anxious voice.

She opened her eyes. He was kneeling still beside her, his face taut with worry. 'I'm well,' she said softly. 'It's the feeling, it's so good. Please don't stop.'

Reassured, he leant forward again and again she closed her eyes, luxuriating in the wonderful sensation of his mouth on her aching nipples. He sucked at the tip of each breast and then extended his tongue and began to lap, flicking the warm stiff wetness against the erect, distended peaks, moistening them, tormenting them. At the same time his hands squeezed and fondled the soft mounds of her breasts. Her head began to move and she moaned aloud, twisting on the cushions. The pleasure was sharp and piercing, making her sex long to be filled, to feel a man's hard cock sliding up inside her.

John grew bolder. He shifted to kneel between her legs and began to kiss his way down her white belly, delving with his tongue into the darkness of her navel, brushing his nose against her soft curling fur. She felt his breath between her legs and she whimpered and shifted her thighs further apart.

There was silence. Rosamund shut her eyes more tightly, imagining him lying there, staring up into the heart of her, seeing every secret fold and whorl of flesh gaping moistly open, aching. Then his hands were on her thighs, sliding upwards to frame her sex. A blinding flash of memory seized her: she was bound and helpless, naked, lying with her ankles forced up to her buttocks and her knees dragged open, and Sir Ralph's hands were on the insides of her thighs, pulling the labia apart, opening her vagina to Geoffrey's tortured gaze. Something touched her, a finger, pushing delicately through the lips to slide up inside her, and she jolted with shock and pleasure and the delicious horror of the memory.

How could she have enjoyed what Sir Ralph had made her do, humiliating her before her lover, humiliating him with his desire for her? But she could not resist those strong hands, that vicious imagination.

Memories threatened to overwhelm her. She tore herself away, dragging herself back to the present, immersing herself in the sensation of John's exploration of her body. He had two fingers in her now and was moving them in and out, gently and persistently. She let her hips lift and lower a little, encouraging him. 'Does this please you?' he whispered.

'Yes,' she replied after a moment. 'But there is another place you can touch a woman which will please her just as much. Look here.' She put her hands between her thighs, shivering at the shamelessness of what she was about to do. 'Have you ever – given yourself pleasure?' she asked him.

There was a little pause. His voice sounded ashamed. 'Well,' he said, 'well, yes.'

'If I wanted to please myself, I would touch myself here.' Rosamund caught her lower lip in her teeth and with two fingers of her left hand drew back the hood of her clitoris, exposing the little pink pearl of flesh. With the middle finger of her right hand she touched it and instantly gasped and moved helplessly, her vaginal muscles clenching with delight.

'There? That little bud?' She took her hands away and he moved his fingers, exploring delicately, touching her there with delicious gentleness, delicious sensitivity. She shivered and moaned. 'Oh,' he whispered, 'you like it.'

She lay back, luxuriating in bliss as his finger very gently stimulated the throbbing bead of her clitoris. She arched her back and began to caress her breasts with her hands, pinching the nipples to full hardness and then scratching at them with her nails. He learned fast: already he was stroking her with a gentle, regular rhythm, drawing her into agonies of pleasure. Then he paused and she felt him shifting position. And then, without warning, without prompting, he pressed his face close between her thighs and began to lick her there, lapping with slow tormenting strokes of his tongue against her engorged, quivering clitoris, his fingers squeezing at the soft insides of her thighs. At once she began to orgasm, her white flanks heaving as she lifted her mound towards his face. He did not withdraw, but licked her harder, and she cried out as the pleasure of her climax grew even greater, possessing her, maddening her, making her beat her head up and down on the soft pillows of the couch, crying out like a beast as his warm wet tongue trembled against her spasming body.

At last she was reduced to helpless twitching. He sat up, his face glistening with her juice, smiling proudly. 'Good?' he asked.

She opened her eyes and held out her hands to him. 'Your wife will love you,' she said as he came into her embrace. 'She will adore you! What made you want to do that?'

'It was beautiful,' he said simply. 'I wanted to kiss it. And it gave me so much pleasure when you did it to me.'

That made her think. His cock was almost fully hard again now and she heaved her languid, exhausted body from the couch and stooped over him, drawing him in. He lifted his hands and put them in her hair, stroking and gently controlling the speed of her caresses. After only a few minutes he was restored to full erection, stiff and eager, and Rosamund sat back and licked her lips. 'Well, my lord,' she said, smiling at him, 'what is your pleasure?'

He looked at her, bright-eyed, and shook his head. 'I don't know,' he said. 'Suggest something.'

'Perhaps,' Rosamund said thoughtfully, 'you might like to, er, have a better view? To watch, while you do it?'

His face changed, becoming tense with arousal. 'Yes,' he said instantly.

She caught hold of his arm and steered him quickly off the couch. She arranged herself on the edge of it, her thighs spread wide and hanging loosely down, and lay back. 'Now,' she said, 'you can see what you do.'

He moved up to kneel between her thighs, the tips of his fingers gently caressing her white skin. She shivered as she felt the head of his cock prodding into her vulva. This was his third time in less than an hour, he would be sure to last, to give her a swiving to remember. He lodged the bulging glans in the entrance to her sex and then hesitated. His hands took hold of her hips, holding her still, and his breathing began to deepen. Rosamund opened her eyes and watched his face as he held her and began to thrust himself into her, watching his penis as it penetrated her, disappearing into her coral-pink flesh until it was sheathed to the hilt.

Rosamund's earlier climaxes had left her sensitised and delicate, and now as he entered her she shivered and moaned. She wanted more, she wanted him to take her, to service her, to swive her so soundly that she screamed. His face was quivering with tension as he watched himself slide into her and then withdraw, over and over, while the stiff hot shaft of his cock glistened with her copious juices.

She lifted her feet from the floor and rested her heels on his thrusting buttocks, letting her knees fall open so she did not block his view. His grasping hands tilted her white hips up towards him so that her mound was completely exposed, offered to him lewdly for his possession. His taut bollocks slapped snugly against her buttocks and he gasped as he moved.

'Beautiful,' he hissed. 'So good, it's so good, I can see myself going in and out of you.' Rosamund arched her hips towards him, eager to receive his strong lunges, and she gripped at him with her inner muscles, watching his face contract in sudden ecstasy. As she lifted her hips he drove himself into her. They were perfectly positioned for total penetration: his strong, rigid shaft slid right up inside her without obstruction, without hesitation, filling her and then withdrawing smoothly to thrust again. She wanted to feel him closer, deeper. She wanted to feel his weight on her, holding her down.

His eyes had slipped shut; he was moving regularly against her, his penis sliding in and out as smoothly as a pendulum. The sight of her no longer mattered to him, he was consumed by the sensations of possessing her. Rosamund twisted her hips upwards, freeing herself from his hands. She untwined her legs from his waist and lifted her legs to rest her ankles on his shoulders. Anne had told her about this position as being good for a customer with a small cock to feel that he was doing her properly. John's cock was not small, but if the posture meant that he entered her deeply then she wanted to try it.

He opened his eyes, surprised. She reached for his arms, drawing them on either side of her lifted thighs. 'Lean forward,' she said, 'press me down. Oh, please.'

Slowly, uncertainly, John began to lean his body forward. Rosamund's hips were tilted up towards him, her whole sex open and gaping and filled by his cock. He rested his hands on either side of her head and looked into her eyes and she put her hands on her breasts and stared up at him. When he thrust she thought it would pierce her completely through, she was so open to him. His weight held her down and forced her thighs apart, exposing her utterly. His penis was still and hard inside her, driving her mad. 'Please,' she whispered again, 'do it to me. John, do it.'

'I'll hurt you,' he replied, hardly more than a murmur.

'I don't care. I want you to do it.' She tried to move her hips, but his body held her down. She was trapped, pinioned, her legs held on his shoulders by his constricting arms, her body open to his ravaging. 'Please,' she gasped again.

And he began to move. If his cock had been any bigger she thought it would have burst her in two, it filled her so deeply, touching the neck of her womb with every thrust. The sensation was so wanton, so abandoned, that it drove her wild with pleasure. She tugged ferociously at her erect nipples and panted desperately, the breath sighing out of her whenever he slid his stiff cock into her moist, gaping sex and gasping back into her lungs as he withdrew.

'You're filling me,' she muttered in a shuddering whisper. 'Oh God, it's good.' Her eyes slid shut and she abandoned herself to the pleasure, to the sensation of his body entering her over and over again. He began to groan and pant as he thrust, no longer caring that he might hurt her, but driving himself into her with terrific force. He grabbed her knees with his hands and pushed them even further forward, spreading her thighs agonisingly wide, plunging himself into her as if determined to batter her down. Rosamund took her hands from her breasts and raised them above her head and suddenly imagined that they were chained there, fastened to the couch so that she could not even strike the man who was ravishing her so vilely, and as the fantasy took shape in her mind she began to spiral upwards to climax.

'Do it,' she gasped, 'harder, harder, oh God, that's it,' for John was nearing his own crisis. His thrusts were short and deep and determined and he cried out. Rosamund twisted against her imaginary bonds and gave a long, shuddering cry of ecstasy as the seed pulsed through his jerking shaft and his weight fell upon her, pressing her down, helpless and abused and enraptured.

After a moment he withdrew, suddenly anxious and concerned. 'Christ,' he whispered, 'are you all right?'

'Hush.' She was still shaking with orgasm, but she pulled him close and held him. Geoffrey emerged again from the prison of her mind: she felt his glossy hair and his strong, hard body.

Suddenly the curtains opened to reveal John's brother Simon, naked, his thick penis dangling limply down between strong legs thatched with blond hair. 'Blood of the Devil, Johnny,' he said, 'we all heard that. Making the most of it, eh?'

Rosamund sat up quickly and turned away, afraid that her face would show her anger. John got up from his knees and squared up to his brother furiously. 'Get out of here,' he spat.

'Now now,' said Simon, unperturbed. 'If I leave you alone you'll probably want to have this lovely another time, and we can't afford that. Time to go. Was she good, by the way? Should I give her a try?'

John stood still for a moment, shuddering with fury. At last he said through his teeth, 'I doubt she'd be to your taste.' He bent to pick up the towel from the floor and wrapped it around his waist. Then he went over to Rosamund where she sat with her head bowed, hiding her face, and put his hand on her arm.

She looked up at him, not smiling. His lower lip quivered as he watched her. Then he glanced once at his brother as if he was afraid, stooped quickly and kissed her on the lips. 'Thank you,' he said again, soft as a breath.

'It was my pleasure,' said Rosamund. It was what the girls always said: but this time she meant it.

He looked as if he wanted to say more, but Simon shifted impatiently and John's face became hunted. He turned and went away without a backward glance.

Rosamund watched the curtain fall over the door and slowly got to her feet. She had thought of Geoffrey twice while the boy had been with her, when often she could keep her mind from him from one day to the next. It was dangerous, it seemed, to enjoy oneself too much.

She slipped on her gown and went back to the steam room. Anne was still there, rebraiding her hair. 'Well?' she asked curiously, 'did you get his maidenhead?'

Rosamund smiled. 'You could say so,' she said. She sat down beside Anne and was about to take over the braiding when the entrance curtain swung open and a young man entered, a nobleman in a fine embroidered doublet, high boots stained with mud, doeskin gloves tucked into his belt, sword and dagger and a feathered hat. It was not until he came and stood before her and caught her hand that she recognised him as John.

He stooped over her hand and kissed it. 'Simon is in

the jakes,' he said quickly. 'I took my chance.' He was concealing something in his left hand: now he pressed it into her palm, looking around quickly at the other girls watching him wide-eyed. 'Accept this,' he said, 'please. I'm sorry it's not more, it's all I had on me. Thank you, *Dolorosa cara,* from my heart. My wife to be is not lovely, but I know I will be able to please her if I close my eyes and think of you.'

Rosamund could think of nothing to say. John kissed her hand again, then looked into her eyes and very gently touched his fingers to her face. Then he was gone.

'What is it?' demanded Anne eagerly. 'What has he given you?'

Rosamund was not venal: she did not share her colleagues' frenetic desire for gifts and largesse. She would have liked to examine John's gift in privacy, not share it with the whole steam room. But there was no chance of that. She slowly opened her hand.

It was a brooch, a man's brooch, such as might fasten a cloak or adorn a hat, a plain band of gold set with cabochon garnets and topazes. Anne curled her lip. 'Not much,' she said, 'if you were as good as all that.'

Rosamund shook her head, remembering that John's family were growing poor, that they depended on his marriage, remembering how much he was in awe of the ghastly Simon. He would get into trouble for giving away the brooch. She sat back against the wall, her hand clutching the jewel and resting against her heart, and closed her eyes.

Why did John's kindness bring Geoffrey again before her? Why could he not fade from her mind? She sat holding the brooch so tightly that its clasp hurt her, squeezing her eyes shut against the tears.

Chapter Ten

*F*ebruary brought great events. London was without a king: the witless King Henry was in the North under the control of Queen Margaret. And on the penultimate day of February Londoners flocked to see Edward, Earl of March, son of the dead Duke of York, entering the city in state, accompanied by every friend, companion and servant he could muster.

The staff of the Fountain were at work, and had to content themselves with snippets gleaned later from customers who had been present. From this they learned that the Earl was young, not quite nineteen, six feet and three inches high, broad shouldered, blond haired, handsome, and in all other respects the pattern of male perfection.

'He deserves to be King just for that,' Anne said. 'Kings ought to be handsome. Don't you think, Rosa?'

Rosamund remembered the Earl of March well. He had visited de Verney manor with his father the Duke a few years since. He had indeed been very tall, a little skinny at that age, and handsome, so handsome that some people might fail to notice that he was also extremely intelligent. She thought the intelligence might fit him better to be king than the appearance. But she said nothing. As far as her colleagues knew, she had no

212

history before that freezing day when Anne had brought her back to the bath house, shivering with cold and tears.

It was announced that in a few days' time the Earl would address the citizens of London. They all knew what he wanted: he wanted to be King. Noble supporters who had not accompanied him began to trickle into the city, and business at the Fountain was brisk. Rosamund reflected that if Lionel were still alive he too would be riding down to London to support the son of his patron. Perhaps he would have taken her; she had begged him to let her accompany him to London more than once. Lionel had not kept a London house, but on his visits he had stayed at the White Hart, a splendid inn on Cheapside, and he had often told Rosamund of its luxuries. She would have enjoyed herself, taking Margery to and fro to see the sights, making new friends, shopping until she dropped in Cheapside and Cornhill.

And instead she was a whore in a Southwark bath house. Had Lionel ever come to Southwark when he was in London? She found it hard to imagine, but when she saw one member of the peerage after another striding or slithering through the door of the Fountain hell-bent on pleasure she could not help wondering.

At the public meeting the citizens of London and the assembled nobility acclaimed the Earl of March as King. All of London was there, including the Fountain's people, all craning their necks for a better view and shouting. Piers hoisted Anne up onto his broad shoulders so that she could see over the heads of the crowd. She ignored the scandalised glances of respectable matrons nearby and called down to her colleagues, 'He's there. Oh, girls, he's gorgeous! He's amazing! and the Bishop is asking if we want him for King – '

And all around her the crowd flung up its hats and roared, 'Long live King Edward! *Vivat Rex!*' and Edward Plantagenet, son of the Duke of York, was King Edward IV of England.

* * *

'It's such a shame,' said one of the girls in the steam room a couple of days later, 'that that lovely young man has to go off to fight.'

There were no questions about which lovely young man she meant. Since the acclamation the talk at the Fountain had been of nothing but King Edward, his youth and beauty, and the enviable status of whatever woman managed to secure the first appointment as the new king's mistress.

'He has to fight King Henry and Queen Margaret,' said someone else. 'We can't have two kings. And he's bound to win. He's so strong and handsome: and he has won all his battles so far. He's a better soldier than his father was.'

And I wish that Lionel had been with him, and not with his father, Rosamund thought with a sigh.

A customer entered, drawing political speculation to a halt. He did not choose Rosamund, and she was composing herself to rest when Anne appeared at the curtain and hissed, 'Rosa!'

'What?' Rosamund got to her feet and went to the curtain. Anne caught her hand and towed her through. They went quickly between the bathing-tents, occasionally sidestepping to avoid the porters who toiled to and fro with jars of hot water, and towards the stairs to the apartments at the front of the bath house, where Mistress Alice slept and where rooms were provided for the most exalted customers to disport themselves in private.

'What's going on?' Rosamund repeated.

Anne turned, her face glowing with excitement. 'Rosa,' she said eagerly, 'do you remember I told you about Ralph Huntley?'

'The one who skipped without paying? Yes, I remember.'

'He came back,' Anne explained, rubbing her hands with glee. 'He slipped past the doorman and he was going to try it again! And they caught him and took him up to Alice's room. She said she was going to make him

214

sorry. I want to watch, I thought you might like to as well.'

'Watch? How?'

'There's a squint,' said Anne, catching Rosamund's hand again and hurrying up the stairs. 'All the upper rooms have got one. People pay to watch, you know.'

'What will she do?' Rosamund asked, resisting. 'Is she going to hurt him? I don't want to watch if she is.' She was assailed by memories of Geoffrey crying out in pain as Sir Ralph's girls tortured him.

'Hurt him? Ralph Huntley? Rosa, don't you remember what I told you? He's the most beautiful young man you could imagine. That's the only reason he's got away with skipping his bill for so long. If she hurts him at all, it's only as a prelude to something else.'

Rosamund's mouth opened in a soundless sigh of understanding. From Mistress Alice's example she knew that older women could desire, enjoy and satisfy very much younger men. 'I'll be glad to see young Huntley get his come-uppance,' Anne was saying. 'He fancies himself too much, if you ask me.'

They came to the little service corridor above the main chambers. A figure was already stooped over one long, narrow slit in the wall, looking down. 'Piers,' Anne hissed crossly, 'don't you have work to do?'

'Don't you?' retorted Piers, also under his breath. He looked at Anne and Rosamund with a challenging smile. 'I wanted to see what she has lined up for the poor devil. If she likes it, I'll probably be in for it next time I'm done for slacking.' His smile became wider as he looked at Rosamund. 'Anyway, Rosa darling, *you're* welcome,' he said. 'We haven't really got any better acquainted since you arrived.' He stepped back, holding out his hand. 'She knows I'm up here. I tied him up for her,' he hissed as Rosamund came forward to look down.

They could see down into an opulent bedchamber. The bed was a four-poster and the curtains were drawn back, but there was nothing happening within the bed. By the end of the bed, however, stood Mistress Alice,

215

dressed in a loose silk robe over her stays, resting her chin on her hand as she observed a most pleasing sight.

Before her stood a young man, quite naked. His body was extremely beautiful and he was tied by his wrists to the top of the post at the foot of the bed. The position showed off the strongly developed muscles of his arms and lifted his chest so that the fine skin tautened over the ladder of his ribs. He was breathing fast and his abdomen swelled and tightened with each breath. He was dark, and fine dark hairs spiralled around his flat nipples and gathered in the centre of his chest, tracing a delicate line down his taut belly to his navel and on to his groin. The soft nest of hair protecting his balls was pure black and glistening, and his slack penis was long and thick. Rosamund could not see his face below the shining waves of his dark hair.

'Listen,' the young man was saying. There were overtones of panic in his voice. 'Alice, you know I meant to pay. It was an oversight. You could have sent me a bill.'

'And you'd have wiped your arse with it, same as you have with all the others,' said Alice sternly. 'No, Master Huntley, it is time you learnt your lesson.'

'If you hurt me,' said Master Huntley urgently, 'I'll sue.'

'*Sue?*' Alice flung back her head and laughed. 'It'll be too late then, won't it?'

She walked slowly towards her prisoner, her eyes travelling over him from head to foot. He stood still, but his jaw was quivering. Alice extended one hand: it had long fingers and long nails which were stained as pink as coral. She licked her lips thoughtfully, placed the tip of her nail in the centre of Master Huntley's chest and then pressed it into his white skin. He winced and turned his head and Rosamund saw his face, a high-boned, aristocratic face, thin-nosed and fine-lipped, with straight dark brows over heavy hooded eyelids. His eyes were closed and his lips folded tightly in a concentrated frown of fear. Mistress Alice began to move her fingertip, leaving a bright red line on the white skin as she trailed

216

the nail's sharp edge down towards Master Huntley's right nipple, and his mouth and eyes opened wide. His eyes were blue, crystalline, with a dark ring around the iris that made them sparkle more brightly than icicles on a gable. He seemed to look straight up into Rosamund's face and she withdrew a little, gasping.

'Scared shitless,' Piers whispered in her ear, 'but it pleases him too. Look at his cock.'

Rosamund took her eyes from the young man's face and looked obediently at his crotch. The soft rod of flesh was beginning to quiver with a life of its own, lifting, thickening. Rosamund's lips were suddenly dry and she licked them. It was so easy to imagine herself there in the bedroom, naked, her wrists fastened above her head, shivering as she felt that sharp nail leaving a red furrow in her pale skin.

'Alice,' whispered Ralph Huntley as Alice's finger moved down, skirting his nipple and leaving a long even scratch down his ribs and onto his abdomen, 'Alice, Alice, listen, I'll pay you, I'll pay you double, I'll – '

'You'll be silent,' said Alice, 'or shall I gag you?'

'*Gag* me?' echoed Ralph, his jaw dropping. There was a little pause in which he stared into Alice's face and she looked calmly back at him, her plucked eyebrows archly raised, her fingertip digging into the soft skin just below his navel. After a moment he shut his eyes tightly and Alice smiled in triumph and began to move her finger again.

She ran it down to where his thickening cock was beginning to defy gravity, lifting skywards. Ralph winced and breathed roughly and turned his head aside as the sharp nail drew closer and closer to his tightening balls. Alice suddenly moved her finger quickly and he gave a little shocked cry and tried to pull away, his cock wilting with fear.

'Now then,' said Alice, smiling and moving away, 'what have I here?' She went beyond the bed and returned carrying a little table. On it were some pots and jars, a small glass flagon that was beaded with condensation, and a little heater with a candle beneath it. Alice began to spoon something from one of the jars into the heater. It hissed and bubbled.

'Christ,' whispered Ralph, tugging at his bonds, 'Christ, what are you going to do?'

Alice did not reply. After a moment she dipped a little ladle into the heater pan and lifted it out. It steamed. She brought the ladle across the room and Ralph began to pant and writhe, hissing desperately, 'What is it? Alice, Alice, for God's sake, don't, I can't – ' And then Alice lifted the ladle and tilted it to pour its contents onto his shoulder and he gave a smothered howl of fear and looked away.

Golden liquid trickled down onto his white naked skin. Rosamund flinched, expecting the poor young man to scream, but he did not. His howl cut off into a whimper of shock and he began to gasp with relief. The liquid pooled in the dark hollow of his collar bone, filled it, brimmed over and began to trickle down his muscular chest. Alice licked her lips lasciviously, leant forward and opened her scarlet mouth. She extended her tongue and began to lap up the golden thread and Ralph moaned and shuddered.

'Honey,' Piers hissed. 'By God, she's a wanton bitch.'

Rosamund breathed quickly, infinitely relieved that Alice had not hurt her captive. She shivered as Piers pressed up more closely behind her, looking over her shoulder. His cock was erect: she could feel it through his hose, fitted snugly into the curve of her buttocks. He began to move against her, rubbing up and down very gently as if he thought she would not notice.

Below them Alice had trickled another ladleful of honey onto Ralph's lean abdomen. The sticky thread rolled down, kept liquid by the warmth of his skin, and she dropped to her knees to lick it up. Ralph groaned deep in his throat and his head fell back, showing his fine face tense and distorted with the agony of waiting. Alice burrowed her tongue into the curls of dark hair, searching out hidden morsels of honey, and then dribbled a little directly onto the head of Ralph's growing cock. It twitched like a live thing and she smiled and leant forward and flicked her tongue over it, coaxing off the viscous strand of sweetness. Instantly Ralph's phallus reared upwards, its head becoming glossy and swollen, its shaft thickening and darkening, and Ralph opened his lips and moaned.

'Lucky bastard,' Piers hissed.

Yes, Rosamund thought, he is lucky, tied up and tormented by a woman who desires him and doesn't want to hurt him. That would be real bliss, to be compelled by someone you love. She shifted her feet on the floor and pressed her thighs together. The sight of Alice diligently licking at Ralph's straining cock was arousing her. The lips of her sex felt swollen and tender as she closed her thighs upon them, clenching her inner muscles, suddenly very conscious of the thick shaft of Piers' cock snugly concealed beneath his hose and rubbing, rubbing through her flimsy gown at the crease of her bottom.

Beside her Anne suddenly whispered, 'Has anyone ever tied you up, Rosa?'

Rosamund answered without thinking, a little groan of wanton need. 'Oh, yes.'

Anne caught her tone instantly. 'You liked it,' she hissed, 'didn't you?'

A hot blush crept up Rosamund's cheek and she turned her head away. She had not meant to respond, her lips had replied of themselves. 'No,' she whispered, 'no, I didn't mean it. Nothing, nothing.'

Ralph cried out as Alice at last took the whole of his throbbing cock into her mouth. She sucked him for a moment then got to her feet and brought the glass flagon across from the table. He stood with his chest heaving, watching in wary apprehension. Alice smiled at him and lifted the flagon to touch his cheek. He winced and flinched away.

'Cold, isn't it?' said Alice with a smile. 'It's been in the ice house all day. Lovely muscat wine. I believe I shall take a mouthful.' She lifted the flagon to her lips and took a deep draught, then began to drop to her knees.

'No,' Ralph whispered hopelessly. He knew what was coming. 'No.'

Alice said nothing, but she gently, delicately pressed her lips against the glossy head of his rigid penis and absorbed him into her mouth without spilling a drop of the icy liquid that filled it. Ralph's whole body jolted with reaction and he made a sound that was half way to a scream.

'You liked it,' Anne hissed in Rosamund's ear. Rosamund shook her head in feverish denial, but Anne would not be denied. She wrestled her flimsy gown over her head, revealing her naked body. Her nipples were erect, standing up sharp and proud from her little breasts. She twisted the fine linen into a thick rope and caught at Rosamund's hands, dragging them behind her back and roughly binding them together. Rosamund knew that she should struggle, but she did not want to. A heavy, aching languor filled her body as she looked down through the narrow squint at Alice tormenting her captive. She tried to move her hands, but she could not. Her blood raced through her veins, scalding and singing with eagerness.

Anne seemed to sense the hot excitement that filled her. 'Come on, Piers,' she hissed, 'you want her, take her. Rosamund, lick me.'

'No,' Rosamund protested. She wanted to go on watching what was happening in the room below. But Anne dug her little fingers hard into the coils of Rosamund's thick chestnut hair and pulled back her head, thrusting her silken, plucked mound towards her lips. Rosamund could not stop herself from shuddering as she felt her head dragged around, the tug of fingers on her scalp, the delicious agony of force. 'Lick me,' Anne repeated, pushing her hips lewdly forward against Rosamund's mouth.

Rosamund closed her eyes. Her lips felt incredibly swollen and sensitive. She tried to move her hands and could not, and the sensation of captivity poured through her like wine, arousing her beyond measure. Obediently she extended her tongue and lapped delicately at Anne's naked sex, finding the little stiff bead of her clitoris and licking at it with exquisite precision.

'Ah,' Anne whimpered, holding Rosamund's head still with her hands and forcing her vulva closer to her working mouth, 'ah, God, that's sweet. Piers, don't wait, you silly fool, swive her.'

Rosamund felt cool air on her naked skin. Piers was lifting her gown, revealing her round buttocks and the damp plumpness of her sex between her white thighs. She was wet and ready, aching to be filled, and when she felt the thick, hot head of his cock nudging its way between her swollen labia she moaned with pleasure as she serviced Anne with her mouth.

Piers crouched behind her, clutching at her hips. He thrust and his long, thick cock slid up inside her, making her gasp with ecstasy. Her breasts dangled before her, hard nipples chafing against the thin scratching of her linen gown. She would have liked to have fondled her breasts, teasing the points with her nails, but her tied hands prevented her. She clamped her mouth to Anne's sex, thrusting her tongue up hard inside her, imitating Pier's movement within her. His hard cock slid in and out of her, a regular driving rhythm, and his tight bollocks thumped against her aching clitoris with every stroke.

'God,' Piers grunted as he shafted her, 'Christ.' He lunged into her, his body slapping against hers, and as he took her and she licked and sucked Anne's melting sex they heard below them the sound of Ralph, crying out in a desperate mixture of pleasure and pain.

'Next time,' Piers hissed, driving himself deep into Rosamund's willing vagina, 'next time, darling, I'll tie you up. You want to be tied to a bedpost? Is that what you want?' and as he asked the question he caught hold of her bound hands and jerked them upwards, dragging her shoulders back so hard that it almost hurt her. He wrestled with her bound wrists and she gasped and shuddered and was instantly overtaken by an orgasm as strong and vivid as it was unexpected. She cried out, the sound smothered by Anne's body, and her tongue quivered in ecstasy and drove Anne over the peak to her climax, and as he saw Rosamund's white buttocks clenching in frantic pleasure and Anne's breasts heaving with her gasps Piers came too, grunting as he thrust his jerking penis deep into Rosamund's shivering flesh.

After a moment Piers withdrew and began to put himself away. Rosamund collapsed onto the floor in a trembling heap and Anne stooped over her to untie her hands.

'That's what you need, Anne, darling,' said Piers softly. 'A good swiving by a man who knows his business.'

'Excuse me,' said Anne with barbs in her voice, 'I'd rather die. Women for me, Piers darling.' She helped Rosamund up. 'Are you all right, Rosa?' she asked solicitously.

'I don't know,' Rosamund whispered, feeling herself still trembling. She looked anxiously up into Anne's face. 'Why?' she asked, her dark eyes wide and frightened. 'Why do I like it? It should be horrible.'

Anne shrugged, smiling gently. 'Don't worry about it, dear heart,' she said. 'Lots of girls like it. If someone makes you do it it's even more exciting. Is that right?'

It was right, absolutely right, so right that Rosamund shivered even to think about it. She closed her eyes and turned her head away.

'Look at that lucky sod,' Piers hissed, and Anne put her arm around Rosamund's waist and helped her to stand at the squint. They stood looking down, copper and chestnut head side by side.

Ralph was groaning and flinging his head to and fro. His white muscular torso was patterned from neck to hips with scarlet bite-marks, the marks of Alice's teeth and tongue. Alice was on her knees before him, worrying with her teeth at the tender flesh in the hollow of his loins, ignoring the thick quivering rod of his penis which bounced and twitched only a few inches from her face.

'For God's sake,' Ralph was saying again, 'Alice, please, no more.'

'No more?' asked Alice, releasing him and drawing back to admire the circular red weal. 'I've barely started.'

Then all of them jumped as a knock sounded on Alice's door. She stood up and swung round and snapped angrily, 'I don't want to be disturbed!'

'But Mistress Alice,' said a voice outside the door, 'Sir William Hastings is in the hall – '

'Sir William Hastings?' repeated Alice disbelievingly. Hastings was the new King's closest friend.

' – And he's got King Edward with him!'

Alice froze, then let out a helpless squeak of incredulity. She shouted, 'I'll be there straight away. Take them wine, sweetmeats, amuse them, get all the other customers out of the house, I'll be down in two shakes of a lamb's tail.' She rushed to her mirror, looked at her disordered hair and her face stained with trickles of honey, and moaned.

The three above stared at each other. 'The *King!*' exclaimed Anne. 'The King himself! My God, things have changed in this country. Poor old King Henry wouldn't have known what to do in a place like this.' She caught Rosamund's hand eagerly. 'Come on, dear heart,' she said, 'back downstairs for us. By the Magdalen, if he has you and likes you he might take you out of here and make you his mistress!'

They dashed into the steam room, which was flurrying like a hen house when the fox gets in. 'Anne,' squeaked one of the girls, 'is it true? Is it true?'

'The King is here,' Anne confirmed. 'Alice is running down to see to him right now. Come on, girls, fast, make yourselves look your best!'

Rosamund withdrew into a quiet corner of the steam room, watching as her colleagues began to rebraid their hair and touch up their faces, every woman for herself.

None of them needed to be told about the possibilities which a king's patronage might offer them.

The curtain swept open and Alice entered. She was flushed and wearing less make-up than usual, but showed no other signs of unseemly haste. 'Well, girls,' she said, 'we have an important visitor. The King himself is here with a few of his friends. The bath house has been cleared, it is all to be for him this afternoon. On your best behaviour.' She vanished. Then Piers appeared, pale and anxious-looking, and held back the curtain with a deep bow. The girls rustled, glancing at each other and then at the door.

King Edward stepped into the steam room, cheerful and self-assured, smelling of some costly perfume. He was a fine looking young man, with the strong bones of his family and bright hazel eyes under his heavy fringe of golden hair. His air of composure was striking, far beyond his years. He was dressed in scarlet velvet and white satin hose, with long boots cuffed in scarlet silk reaching to his firm thighs. His sword and his spurs were richly made and inlaid with gold.

Behind him Alice leant through the curtain, gesturing frantically that the girls should get up from their seats and curtsey to his Grace. They began to obey her and King Edward tossed his golden head and laughed. 'I beg you,' he said, 'don't get up! Stay as you are, all of you, be comfortable.' His sharp, clever eyes began to flick around the room, inspecting, appraising, passing on.

Rosamund remembered his voice, a pleasant light tenor, surprisingly light for his big frame. She looked away from him and sighed, remembering herself three years ago when he had come to her manor: the young wife of the elderly lord, virtuous and cool, untouched by lust or improper desires. How she had changed. What Sir Ralph had done to her. She shivered and closed her eyes as the vile, delicious memories paraded before her.

'Madam,' said a voice immediately before her, 'are you well?'

'Oh,' Rosamund gasped, startled, 'I beg your pardon, your Grace.'

King Edward looked at her and narrowed his bright eyes. 'Your colleagues,' he said softly, 'evince interest in me, madam, and you do not.'

'Forgive me, your Grace,' whispered Rosamund, wishing that the earth would open and swallow her up. 'I meant no disrespect.'

'Then come with me,' said the King, holding out his hand commandingly.

Rosamund got slowly to her feet. She could feel the other girls looking daggers at her and resisted the temptation to beg the King to take someone else. What a fool she would look! She dropped a deep curtsey and said meekly, 'What is your Grace's pleasure?'

'A little pastime,' said the King, taking her hand as she got to her feet. 'Such as you show to all your guests, madam, I do not doubt. A bath, a little relaxation.'

She led him through into the bath house. The finest cubicle was already prepared, the bath filled with scented water, the couch laid with silk, a little side table prepared spread with dainties and a silver jug of cool wine, a stool set ready to receive the King's clothes.

Rosamund closed the tented door, leaving them in the faint light that filtered through the heavy fabric and the glow of five beeswax candles. 'May I help you disrobe, your Grace?' she asked humbly.

'In a moment,' said the King. He went to the candlestick and lifted it, then held it high and with his other hand took Rosamund's face by the chin, turning it to the light. She submitted, but was suddenly possessed by a shrinking feeling of horror. She remembered all at once what people said about the King's inhuman powers of memory. He could call to mind, they said, the face and the name of every man he had ever met, no matter how humble. There was a little silence, in which King Edward frowned. Then he said, 'What is your name?'

'They call me *La Dolorosa*,' said Rosamund disingenuously.

He drew down his blond brows. 'I know your face,' he said at last. 'That is one reason I chose you. But you confuse me. I do not remember you as a light woman, as someone I might have slept with.' He spoke like a man of many years' experience: well, perhaps he was, nearly nineteen and a Duke's son. 'Have we met before?' he asked at last.

'Oh, your Grace,' said Rosamund lightly. She did not like to lie, but did not want to tell him the truth. 'How could that be?' She tried to pull her face away from his hand, but he tightened his grip and his lips folded tight with thought. If he remembered her, what could she say? She could not ask him for help, it would be absurd, he would scorn her. Suddenly she was inspired. She said brightly, 'Perhaps it was in a dream, your Grace.'

That made him laugh. 'A dream!' he repeated. 'Well, perhaps. You are fair enough, by all accounts.' His face changed. The thoughts passed from it, replaced by a look of concentration that she knew meant simple lust. He put one big hand to her shoulder, took hold of her robe and jerked it down to bare her breast.

Rosamund stood very still and closed her eyes. Her nipple tensed and tautened, aroused by its exposure. King Edward looked at her breast for some time, then pulled the gown off her other shoulder so that it slipped down to her hips. He put his hands very gently on Rosamund's breasts and squeezed them, feeling their weight and softness. 'Snowy hills,' he whispered, 'twin lilies. Fair as day.'

His fingers moved lightly to the stiffening peaks and began to rub against them, teasing them out to their full length. The dark areolae began to swell with need. Rosamund stood quietly, her breath coming faster as King Edward pinched and tugged at the aching coral tips of her heaving breasts.

After some time the King took his hands away and began to unfasten his velvet doublet. Rosamund said earnestly, 'Oh, your Grace, let me.' She took over from him, quickly opening his doublet and laying it aside, then helping him off with his silk lined boots. His points were made of silk and capped with silver. She untied them deftly and he pulled his shirt over his head, revealing a body moulded like a young god's, broad-shouldered, broad-chested, with strong firm arms and a lean narrow waist. Beneath his satin hose his buttocks were tight and well muscled, flat sided and taut under her hands. She coaxed the costly fabric down his lean thighs, leaving him in nothing but his linen pouch. The ties yielded in an instant and he was naked before her.

Rosamund looked at his splendid phallus open-mouthed. Even half-erect it was massive, and as she watched it began to creep upwards to full erection, becoming smooth and shining and hard as wood. It was beautiful, too, sculpted with blue veins, ridged and taut, its broad head as dark and richly red as his velvet doublet.

The King caught Rosamund by her naked shoulder and pulled her up to face him. 'You have a mouth like a rose,' he said. 'Like a peony. Let me taste it.'

He bent his head to kiss her. He was expert and she became limp between his hands, responding urgently to his probing tongue. 'Sweet,' he said, after a moment. 'I should like to have you there.'

'Your Grace,' said Rosamund obediently, and she began to kneel at his feet. But he took her arm and held her up. 'No,' he said, 'if I am going to have a woman in her mouth I like to do it properly. Lie on the couch, *Dolorosa.*' He guided her across the room and laid her naked on the couch, her head propped on the silken pillows. 'Open,' he said shortly.

His terse, direct orders made Rosamund shiver with submissive pleasure. She closed her eyes and let her moist lips part. The King knelt over her, his strong thighs straddling her throat, his prick fiercely erect and pointing skywards. He guided the shining head between her lips and gasped as she teased the satin tip with her tongue.

'Good,' he said shortly. 'Use your hands, too. I like to feel you all over me.'

He propped himself on his hands and began to thrust into her mouth. She lay beneath him, her lips stretched wide to accommodate his massive shaft, her whole body stinging with sharp pleasure as she felt the hot, smooth rod sliding in and out. He made no concessions to the fact that he was swiving her lips: he pushed as if he filled her sex, thrusting himself to the very back of her throat. She moaned and raised her tingling hands, fondling his strong thighs, lifting and caressing the taut dangling sac of his testicles, and he groaned deep in his throat and the muscles of his flat belly tautened as he pushed his hips forward, shoving himself deep.

Rosamund's body began to heave as he swived her mouth. Her sex was empty, open and aching, longing to feel a man's hard shaft thrusting inside her. If only he had brought a friend with him, she thought, they could both have me at once. She remembered how Sir Ralph's minions had amused themselves with her, filling every orifice she possessed, sliding their thick tools at their pleasure into her sex or her anus or her mouth.

The King gasped and his working buttocks hollowed and tensed. The glistening glans of his huge cock moved between her lips, almost choking her. She tilted back her head in wanton abandon, wishing that she could take even more of him, wishing that she could open her throat so that he could push his throbbing phallus right into her mouth and let her caress the hairy pouch of his balls with her stinging, sensitive lips.

She was drooling with the pleasure of sucking him, her saliva flowing as freely as the juices of her sex. A sudden urge of wantonness gripped her. She put one hand to her lips and caught up a trickle of saliva on one finger, then traced her damp finger between the cheeks of his labouring arse until she found the tight puckered hole of his anus. Briefly she wondered if what she was about to do constituted *lèse-majesté*, but the urge was too strong to resist. She slipped her moistened finger into the little tight orifice, opening the strong sphincter, penetrating him as far as she could.

He cried out, a sudden sharp cry that revealed shock and desire and urgent lust. In her hot mouth his cock jolted and pulsed and he began to move more eagerly. Rosamund twisted her finger around in his anus, drawing it out and then thrusting it back in again with all her strength, and the King gave a yell and his working cock jerked and burst open like a ripe fruit squeezed in the hand, spilling his salty juice into her throat. She swallowed greedily, sucking him hard, feeling his body spasming around her piercing finger.

At last he withdrew himself with a curse. 'What did you do?' he demanded, staring at her wide-eyed and panting hard. He looked very young.

'I thought you might like it, your Grace,' Rosamund said meekly, hanging her head. The effect was somewhat spoiled by the fact that a trickle of his seed was running from her lips, and as she spoke she licked at it lubriciously.

'Well,' said the King, 'I did, I suppose.' He set his shoulders awkwardly, and Rosamund thought that perhaps he rarely had a woman who dared to do something for him without being asked. 'I think,' he said, 'that that bath seems like a good idea.'

She bathed him and rubbed him down with fragrant oil, on her best behaviour now. He lay beneath her massaging hands, sighing with pleasure as she rubbed the tension from his taut muscles, stretching and pushing against her like a great cat. Presently he had had enough and he rolled over, staining the costly silk with oil. His splendid cock was hard again, lying taut against his flat belly, swollen and straining.

'I am here to relax,' he said. 'I have a lot of work before me, and I don't have long to gather my strength. Ride me.'

With a shiver of obedient delight Rosamund spread her thighs over his lean hips and lifted his hot shaft with her hand. She was soaking wet, aching to feel him inside her. She lodged the shining head between the lips of her sex and leant back, resting her hands on the hard muscle of his thighs, pushing her breasts upwards as she sank slowly down onto him, impaling herself.

Few of her customers asked her for this: mostly they came to take a woman, not to be ridden by her. It was deliciously unfamiliar to slide down on that thick, stiff rod, feeling it moving up between the silken walls of her eager body. Unfamiliar: and yet unforgettable, making her remember how she had sat in Geoffrey's lap, her distended nipples rubbing against the smooth strong muscle of his chest, his arms around her, his face looking into hers with desire and delight and nascent love. He had lowered his head to suckle at her breasts and she had come at once, shivering and crying out, and then she had sat above him helpless while he held her with his strong hands and his body surged up into her, beating against her like the waves of the sea, undreamt-of pleasure, miraculous ecstasy.

Beneath her moving body the King gasped as she grasped at him with the muscles of her vagina, holding tightly to his rigid, thick penis as she slid down upon it. He lifted his big hands and took hold of her breasts, clutching at them, his face tensing with pleasure. 'Now,' he hissed through his clenched teeth, 'faster, sweet, faster. Take me there.'

He cared nothing for her, only for his own pleasure. But she obeyed him, receiving his body deep within hers with every lunge of her white hips, lost in the bliss of fantasy. She imagined that Geoffrey was still alive, that he came to her, that he found her lying weeping in the steam room: lifted her in his strong arms, kissed away her tears, carried her to a couch and lay upon her, blessing her with the weight of his beautiful body, ravishing her with his kisses, spreading her white thighs and putting his wonderful cock between her legs and entering her, his eyes the colour of a wood in springtime looking down at her, radiant with love. She imagined the sensation as he took her, the feel of his strong powerful phallus pulsing deep inside her, and she rose and fell frantically upon King Edward's throbbing cock and he grasped at her breasts with his hands and shouted as he spurted his seed inside her. She flung back her head and cried out Geoffrey's name and her whole body jerked as it spun into a desperate, consuming climax.

After a moment she recovered and lifted herself gingerly away from the King, her head bowed. He sat up, his handsome face glistening with sweat. He caught hold of a handful of her hair and tugged at it, making her look into his face.

'Geoffrey?' he repeated, and he did not sound or look in the least amused.

Rosamund swallowed, breathing fast. 'Your Grace,' she murmured, 'I am very sorry. I don't know – '

'Never,' said King Edward, 'in all of my life, have I met a whore who chose to give herself pleasure with *my* body while imagining that she is with someone else.'

What would he do to her? Rosamund resisted the urge to hide her face in her hands. She said again, miserably, 'I am very sorry, your Grace.'

King Edward shook his head, frowning. 'You are – unusual,' he said after a moment. 'I am intrigued by you. Who was Geoffrey, then?'

Rosamund shook her head, fighting tears. But one does not deny the King. She said at last, 'He was – my lover, your Grace. But he is dead.'

There was a little silence. The King's face was sombre: in recent days he had lost both his father and his younger brother, and rumour said they had been very close. 'I am sorry,' he said after a moment. He sounded as if he meant it, and Rosamund looked up, suddenly understanding why men loved this king and were glad to serve him. 'What sort of a man was he?' asked Edward, gently now.

'A squire,' Rosamund managed to make herself say.

'In whose service?'

She shook her head again. 'Please, your Grace, no more. I – cannot.'

The King raised his brows. 'As you wish.' His face looked heavy, as if he were an old man, and he swung his feet off the couch and stretched his hands high above his head, watching Rosamund acutely.

'You are weary of me,' he said, 'or of serving me, which is the same thing. Off you go, *Dolorosa*. Send me some more hot water. And another girl. Someone with imagination.'

'Your Grace,' whispered Rosamund, and she picked up her gown from the floor and fled. She hurried into the steam room, where the girls looked at her with angry jealousy, and said to Anne, 'Anne, he's finished with me. He asked for another girl. You go. And he wants some more hot water.'

Anne's face lit up and she jumped to her feet and scurried out. Another of the girls said to Rosamund, 'Alice wants you. Probably wants to check that you gave the King good service.' And as Rosamund turned and hurried away the girl made an angry, envious face behind her back.

Rosamund pulled on one of the loose robes that hung at the door and went out into the hall. Some of the King's household were there, knights and esquires and men at arms. They looked at her avidly, whistling and passing comments as she went to Llewellyn's desk and asked where Mistress Alice was.

'She's in her study,' lilted Llewellyn. Rosamund turned to go and he lifted one brow and asked archly, 'Aren't you going to tell me what to bill his Grace?'

'I imagine you'll bill as much as you want whatever I say,' Rosamund retorted acidly. 'For what it's worth, he's with Anne now.'

The men around her laughed raucously at this proof of their King's potency. They pressed close to Rosamund as she tried to make her way to the stairs which led to Alice's study, not threatening or ill-natured, just high-spirited. But she was feeling melancholy, and could not respond to their jesting with anything but irritation.

At last they let her through and she hurried to the door of the study, feeling rather sick. Normally girls were only called there for some misdemeanour. Could

Alice have been listening outside the cubicle? Could she have heard Rosamund insulting the King with her uncontrollable cry of pleasure? What would she do?

Rosamund bit her lip and knocked at the door. Alice's voice within said, 'Enter.'

The door swung smoothly open. Inside was a fair-sized room, well-appointed, with desk and chair, a couch with silk cushions, and tapestries on the wall, like the living-room of a well-to-do merchant. Alice was sitting at the desk, bolt upright, looking uncomfortable. Rosamund dropped her a curtsey. 'You summoned me, madam.'

'Not I,' said Alice. 'Our owner is here, on a brief visit, and he particularly asked for you.' She gestured with her hand to the shadows of the room beyond the door.

Rosamund turned, puzzled, and looked. From the shadows a big figure moved forward, stepping lightly, like a stalking beast. She knew who it was before the light fell on his face. Cold horror seized the pit of her stomach and she stepped back, her hand at her throat, speechless.

'Alice, you may go,' said Sir Ralph's gravelly voice. Its sound sent chill icicles down Rosamund's spine. 'Walter will do any business I need.'

Alice dropped a curtsey and went to the door. As she left another man emerged from the shadows and stood beside Sir Ralph, smiling at Rosamund. It was Walter Plaseden. Rosamund began to shake her head, the whole of Sir Ralph's vile plan exposed to her in an instant.

'You dog,' she whispered, unable to contain her rage. 'You filthy, calculating beast. You planned it all!'

'Everything,' admitted Sir Ralph with a proud smile. 'Every little thing. Did you never wonder why the sots in that inn didn't just hit poor old Walter here over the head and enjoy themselves with you? They wouldn't dare touch my steward.'

'Your steward,' breathed Rosamund. She remembered how she had almost worshipped Walter for his kindness, his generosity, his restraint, how she had trusted him and wept when he left her. She stared at him, unable to believe that a man could be so duplicitous.

Sir Ralph continued as if she had not spoken. 'But I have to admit,' he said ruefully, 'that here as at Murthrum Castle you have defeated me, Lady de Verney. I thought that this place would kill you. But Alice tells me you have already won yourself a name among the girls for your ability to enjoy yourself with every customer, no matter how unprepossessing. I suppose I should have guessed. There was nothing I did to you that threatened your composure, was there?' He looked narrowly at her tense, pinched face and smiled. 'Not to *you*. It was a different question where that young stallion of yours was concerned. But we needn't worry about him any more.'

He came closer to her, still smiling his cold smile. Rosamund closed her eyes and turned away from him. Perhaps her survival was a victory: but if it was, it was one she abhorred. She felt no gladness that she had inflicted defeat upon him. She hated him. But as he stood at her shoulder and she felt his breath warm on her ear she sensed her body beginning to shake with tension and a wicked, contrary desire, a desire for him to take her, to possess and abuse her as before.

'So,' said Sir Ralph from behind her, 'what am I supposed to do? I have never met a woman like you, Lady de Verney. Everything I fling at you you accept and turn to your own pleasure. You have defied me and succeeded. You have made me look a fool.' He put his hands on her shoulders. She flinched, wanting to pull away, but then she made herself stand still. 'Lady de Verney,' whispered Sir Ralph in her ear, 'would you not like to leave this place and return to your home? To de Verney manor?'

Rosamund's eyes opened wide and she turned and stared at him. His black eyes looked unwinkingly into hers, as opaque as a cat's. 'You are trying to torment me,' she said after a moment, breathing deeply. 'I will not listen to you.'

'No, no,' Sir Ralph insisted, his face lit by a cold smile. 'I do not jest. I hold your lands: yours and mine. They can be restored to you if you become my wife.'

'*What?*' Rosamund pulled violently away from him, shaking with shock and disbelief. His smile widened into a delighted grin. 'Your *wife*? Never.'

'Come,' said Sir Ralph, flinging his hands in the air in a parody of light-hearted banter, 'would it be so bad? Imagine, Lady de Verney, just imagine. As my wife you would have all the power I have myself: power to take your pleasure as you please, with whom you please. I am not a jealous man: I understand that a woman as sensual as you has desires that one man could not possibly fulfil. Imagine how you could amuse yourself. You liked my young servants, did you not? I watched you with them often enough, I know they gave you pleasure. Imagine yourself able to have one of them for your own, to do with him just as you liked. Take him, of course, but more, my lady, more, if you wished it. Torment him, torture him, see him writhe in exquisite agony. Kill him, why not? Take revenge for the debaucheries I wrought on you.'

His words filled her mind with burning images of lust and depravity, but although they aroused her they disgusted her too. She stepped back, her face showing her fervent scorn and loathing, her hands clenching in horror. 'What makes you think,' she said, brimming with indignation, 'that my revenge would fall on any man but you?'

'Oh, you are splendid,' laughed Sir Ralph, flinging back his grizzled head in vivid amusement. 'You are magnificent, Lady de Verney: a goddess in her wrath, Diana before Actaeon. You are the only woman I have ever met that I know I could marry. Come, Rosamund, will you have me?'

He had never used her Christian name before and it made her shudder with revulsion. She took another step back and drew herself up tall, setting her jaw. 'You think you know me,' she said at last. 'You deceive yourself.

You say I would not be content with one man. You are wrong. But you killed the man I could have been content with. I would never marry you, never. Not if you were the last man in the world. *Never.*'

Sir Ralph took one step towards her, then another. His dark eyes were glinting with the same hot glow of lust that had filled them when she was his prisoner. 'Lady de Verney,' he said through his teeth, 'you never disappoint. It is always so charmingly piquant to torment you. Do you remember how much you enjoyed it when I took you? And now here is poor Walter, who rode in close proximity to your voluptuous body for a whole week and never once felt the delicious tightness of your hot cunny. I think we should redress that wrong, my lady, and at once.'

'No,' Rosamund whispered, and she flung herself towards the door, eager to make her escape. She got her hand on the latch of the door and then Sir Ralph seized her from behind and dragged her away. She opened her mouth to scream and his strong hand clamped over her open lips, silencing her.

'Walter,' hissed Sir Ralph, 'off with her robe, come on.'

Rosamund writhed and fought, but even as she struggled she knew it was hopeless. She remembered the fierce possessive strength of his big hands, the determination that forced her down and made her his. She moaned with protest beneath his gagging hand as Walter grabbed her robe and pulled it from her, leaving her stark naked, her white limbs flashing in the gloom.

'Christ,' hissed Sir Ralph, 'I had almost forgotten your body. God in Heaven, it is lovely. You are flawless, you are a siren. Walter, you can have her mouth, but her cunny is mine.'

They dragged her across the room. Her struggles began to weaken. She knew she should fight Sir Ralph with every ounce of strength, but she could not. His hands were so strong, compelling, every line of his broad body pulsed with power. He forced her down crossways over the couch, her body supported from shoulders to hips, her legs and her head hanging into empty space. Walter seized her arms and pulled them outwards and she hung helpless, her head dangling back, her breasts and the mound of her sex thrust upwards. Sir Ralph drew his hand gingerly from her mouth and she moaned, a sound of delirious submission.

He put his hand on her breast. His fingers were strong and he squeezed the soft flesh hard, pinching her nipple so that she winced. Pleasure and pain coursed through her. 'Surrender to me,' he hissed. 'Admit it: I am your master.'

'No,' Rosamund whimpered, turning her head from side to side in desperate denial. But the hot, melting ache between her legs told her how far he had enslaved her to him. She knew that even if Geoffrey still lived, even if he stood before her, she could not prevent her body from leaping with startled pleasure at the touch of Sir Ralph's hand.

'Surrender to me,' hissed Sir Ralph again. He forced her legs apart and she gasped. Then, suddenly, he dropped to his knees between her spread thighs and his mouth clamped to her sex, hot and wet, his strong blunt tongue thrusting deep into her vagina, coiling and twisting within her like a snake. She arched her back and groaned with horror and delight as she felt him licking her, stirring her to eager, sensual desire.

'There has been a man there,' he said after a moment, sitting up and licking his lips. 'Well, my lady, is that a king's seed that I have just tasted?' She did not reply, and after a moment he plunged his head back between her legs, flickering his lips and tongue over her engorged, shivering clitoris, his hands squeezing at the softness of her inner thighs, lapping and lapping at her pearl of pleasure until she moaned.

'Surrender,' he whispered again, and she groaned and turned her head from side to side, denying him.

'If you will not surrender to my mouth,' he said, lifting himself above her, 'then by God, you will surrender to my cock. Walter, hold her,' he added quickly as Rosamund tried to resist him. Walter's hands fastened tightly on her wrists, holding her arms wide apart and flat upon the couch so that she could do no more than heave her hips upwards in hopeless protest as Sir Ralph entered her with his great thick penis, sliding it up into the heart of her moist sex, penetrating her so deeply that she gasped and arched her back. The points of her nipples thrust upwards, distended and aching, and Sir Ralph took hold of one swollen peak in his strong hand and squeezed, harder and harder, making her cry out.

'Surrender,' he snarled again, lying still and hard within her. 'Surrender.'

And as he lay unmoving she felt herself seized by desperate yearning, terrible urgent need, and her breath came in pants and her breasts and belly lifted and fell and she gasped, 'Yes, yes,' over and over again, submitting herself, knowing herself enslaved even as she hated the man whose iron-hard cock was filling her.

'You are mine,' said Sir Ralph, 'no man else's, mine. Mine! Walter, take her mouth.' And then he began to lunge into her, slow juicy strokes that made her groan and thrash beneath him. Walter grunted urgently and pushed his swollen cock between her open lips and began to swive her mouth, thrusting himself deep until she almost gagged. It should have revolted her, but she welcomed her shame and degradation, embraced the hot dark pleasure that rose in her loins and her breasts and her lips and surged up inside her, rising on the rhythm of Sir Ralph's massive phallus sliding in and out of her pouting, shuddering sex. If she had not been gagged by Walter's cock she would have begged him to take her harder, to ravish her.

In moments Walter was gasping and moving in irregular jerks and his cock began to pulse and shake in Rosamund's mouth as his hot seed spurted from it, slipping down her throat and trickling from her lips. He withdrew quickly and crouched behind her, holding her arms down, offering her white body as a sacrifice to his master's virility, watching greedily as Sir Ralph's thick shaft worked strongly to and fro in his victim's moist tender vagina. Rosamund felt Walter's eyes, hot upon her like thick fingers stroking her naked flesh, and she shivered as she felt her pleasure begin to overtake her. Her open mouth made words, desperate words, begging for mercy, begging for brutality, and as Sir Ralph drove his rigid eager penis in and out of her she began to spasm, her eyelids fluttering and her whole body shaking as a convulsive orgasm rushed through her like a tempest.

'Mine!' growled Sir Ralph as he felt her flesh shudder and quicken around his plunging shaft. 'Mine!' And he fell forward on her, snarling like a beast and catching her nipple in his mouth, sucking and biting so hard on it in his extremity of pleasure that she opened her mouth to scream with agony and delight.

Walter clamped his hand over her lips, smothering her. She writhed once more and then lay still, trembling with the echoes of dreadful pleasure, as Sir Ralph withdrew himself with a jerk from her still pulsing body.

'You are mine,' he said again, crouching over her. 'Admit it. Marry me.'

She lifted her head heavily, her hair trailing, her mouth slack with ecstasy. His black eyes looked into hers, cold and eager. 'No,' she said, 'no, never.'

'But you are mine,' he repeated. 'Mine. You are my slave. I have proved it.'

Rosamund rolled to a kneeling position on the couch and put her face in her hands for a moment. When she lifted it her expression was resolute. 'My body may be your slave,' she said, 'but not my soul. I loathe and detest you. You killed the man I loved.'

He was silent for a time, staring into her face and frowning deeply. At last he curled his lip and laughed as he got to his feet. 'Well,' he said, 'on that charming note I shall leave you, Lady de Verney.' He looked down at her with a bitter smile. 'I need not hurry, my lady. I will return here from time to time and remind you of the fact that you are my slave. And one day you will surrender. You will become my wife.'

'Never,' Rosamund said again. Sir Ralph gave her one long, hard look, then shook his head and turned away, summoning Walter with his hand. They went to the door and it slammed behind them.

Rosamund knelt on the couch shivering, staring before her. Her whole body ached and tingled with echoes of dark, infernal pleasure. She had not spoken a word of a lie: she did hate him, hate him with all her soul. But not with her body. She could not deceive herself. She knew for certain that as long as he lived, as long as he walked the earth, Sir Ralph would be her body's master.

Chapter Eleven

*P*alm Sunday, and a bitter dawn. Borne on a knifing wind, stinging flakes of snow swept over a broad, high plain above a steep Yorkshire river valley. On the windswept plain tens of thousands of men were fighting a deadly, vicious battle, the greatest battle ever to be fought upon English soil. The clash of steel and the cries of the wounded carried for miles on the wings of the wind. It was like the Apocalypse on earth. For generations men would speak in hushed voices of the myriad deaths at Towton field.

Geoffrey Lymington struggled on foot over the blood soaked earth. He had fought all day since before dawn and although he had escaped wounds so far he was near exhaustion. Long ago he had lost his companions. He had seen George fall, a spear in his throat, and he had lunged for the man that had done it, and when he had killed and turned back, Sir Thomas and what remained of his household were vanished. Now he was alone, afraid and confused. He had thought himself a seasoned soldier, but compared to the carnage around him his previous bloody fights had been no more than scuffles.

He heard cries that York was victorious, that the Lancastrians were broken and fleeing, and he broke into a stumbling run. Suddenly the ground seemed to give way before him and he staggered and fell, rolling down a steep bank, unable to stop himself, gasping as the white faces of slaughtered men flashed spinning past his eyes. At last he fetched up against the bole of a tree and lurched to his feet, panting, shocked but unhurt.

He had fallen half way down the edge of the river gorge. Through the snow he saw the army crowding towards the river and he plunged on downwards. His fall had brought him far up the Yorkist advance. He could see the front of the line and a sudden death-or-glory urge seized him. He shouldered in between men in King Edward's livery, pushing towards the enemy.

The Lancastrians before them were fleeing, but their resistance was not at an end. Geoffrey pushed towards the front rank, striving as if strife were an end in itself. His sword was notched and dull from fending off the desperate blows of the men they pressed back, back and back towards the glistening death trap of the river. The Yorkists on either side of him were fully armoured, wearing surcoats of the King's livery: he was in among Edward's household. Amid the fear and horror and fatigue of the battle he laughed aloud to find himself fighting close to the King.

A little way in front of him was a great tall figure, a gold coronet on its helmet, swinging a two-handed sword as if it were a feather. King Edward! Geoffrey felt some of the King's strength and courage enter his weary limbs and he pressed forward to draw closer. The King was forcing a path through the crumbling enemy, drawing away from the protecting screen of his household, and Geoffrey eagerly shouted his war cry and drove through his opponents to reach that glittering giant. As he came up beside the King, gasping with pride, a whirring shape in the snowy air became a mace and struck the crowned helmet and Edward staggered and fell to his knees. At once the retreating Lancastrians shrieked with triumph and pounced. Without a thought Geoffrey lunged forward, his dull sword flashing, shouting in wordless rage. He flung himself in front of the fallen king. Sharp pain burst in his arm and shoulder and he almost fell, but he stood firm and took the blows meant to kill King Edward on the blade of his whirling sword. He stood there only for a second: then the King's squires and household knights were around him, shouldering back the Lancastrians almost without effort, speaking urgently as they helped the King to his feet.

'Sire, are you hurt?'

'No.' Edward raised his visor. His face was grimed with sweat and blood from a cut on his brow. His men ignored Geoffrey, but the King caught his eye and said quickly, 'You, sir, find me after.'

'Your Grace,' Geoffrey replied, bowing his head, absurdly reassured that King Edward thought that there was going to be an 'after' among this utter chaos. Then the King had closed his helmet and plunged on towards the river, yelling his war cry: '*Dieu et mon droit!*'

The river Cock was running full, but the swelling of its waters was not caused solely by melting snow. Corpses lay packed between its steep banks stacked so high that they formed a ghastly bridge of chilling flesh. Geoffrey could not keep up with the king. He crossed the river on the bridge of the dead with the rest of the army. The Lancastrians were broken, running for their lives, and fresh energy was beginning to creep into the Yorkists as they spotted their chance to pursue for plunder.

Geoffrey was not interested in plunder. When resistance had ceased he stopped fighting and leant against a twisted hawthorn, his head tilted back to receive the cold snow full in his sweating face, panting. Blood was running from his wounded arm, soaking his thick padded jack and trickling down to melt the snow at his feet. He was cold and sick. The sights of the battle began to return to his mind like grim spectres, men pierced and broken and tossed aside like dolls, white skin torn with scarlet, the wounded writhing in the bloody snow, faces that were handsome on one side and on the other grinning naked bone. He closed his eyes.

For a moment there was silence. Then his soldier's sense of danger made him stand up, his limp hand tightening on his sword, staring through the snow at a single figure approaching him.

'Geoffrey Lymington,' said a gravelly voice he knew well.

He shuddered with disbelief and a sudden swift flowering of hatred so violent that it lit his blood as with a flame. 'You,' he said softly. His tongue was thick in his parched mouth. 'Why are you not fleeing with the rest?'

'I heard you were here,' said Sir Ralph Aycliffe, drawing closer. 'We have unfinished business. You called me coward. You will die for it.'

Fear settled between Geoffrey's shoulder blades. Sir Ralph wore full armour, he had the advantage, and he walked as though he were not wounded and bone weary. It would be hard to kill him. But Geoffrey's hate and his desire for revenge towered upward, fierce and tremendous, and he shivered not with dread but with the glittering prospect of vengeance. He looked quickly around him, checking the ground, and drew his dagger from his belt to hold in his left hand.

Sir Ralph said nothing more but snarled behind his visor and leapt at Geoffrey, his sword gleaming blue in the cold snow light. Geoffrey dodged, wishing vainly for his usual strength and speed. It was an ill-matched battle: if Sir Ralph landed a blow it would wound, while he himself moved securely in his cage of steel. Geoffrey's sword arm was weak and bleeding, there was no point in striking uselessly. He swung and ducked, every nerve on edge, waiting, watching for his chance.

It came. Sir Ralph took a long stride forward to land a heavy blow and his foot skidded on a patch of greasy mud. He tottered. Geoffrey yelled and rushed bodily at him, knocking him sprawling. He flung himself on top of the armoured figure as it struggled to rise and thrust hard with the sharp, narrow blade of his dagger. A hoarse scream sounded within the helmet and blood ran over Geoffrey's gauntleted hands.

'Curse you,' Geoffrey gasped, forcing back Sir Ralph's visor. The strong face behind it was contorted in pain, dark blood bubbling from its mouth. 'May the Devil carry off your soul.' He withdrew the dagger and thrust again, sobbing with the ecstasy of revenge like a man panting in the act of love. 'That's for Rosamund,' he gasped, and tears burst from his eyes and ran down his grimy cheeks. 'For Rosamund.'

The twisted face formed itself into a snarling parody of a smile. Thick words oozed from Sir Ralph's lips. 'You think she's dead,' he rasped. 'Wrong, you fool. She is alive.'

Geoffrey froze. 'What?' He dropped the dagger, grabbed Sir Ralph by his armoured shoulders and lifted him from the cold ground. 'What did you say?'

Sir Ralph began to laugh. With every heave of his belly blood ran from his lips. 'I didn't kill her.' The words emerged in halting jerks. 'It would have been – a waste. She was – too unique to waste.'

Horror made Geoffrey's hair stand on end. 'Where is she?' he shouted, shaking Sir Ralph ferociously. 'What have you done with her?'

Still Sir Ralph laughed, his black eyes fixed on Geoffrey's desperate face. He said thickly, 'Sweet,' and then he choked and twisted and was still. The blood stopped running from his mouth and the gaping wounds in his belly. His dead eyes stared out like glass.

Geoffrey staggered away from the corpse, his clenched hand pressed to his lips. His vengeance tasted as bitter as sloes. Sir Ralph had mocked him and defeated him even in death. Had he lied or told the truth? Did Rosamund live? Now he could say no more, and Geoffrey knew that for the rest of his life he would be the instrument of Sir Ralph's last revenge, for ever and hopelessly seeking for Rosamund.

In the middle of June, King Edward finally completed his grand tour of the kingdom he had won in battle and arrived back among the comforts and splendours of

London. He took up residence in his palace at Shene while the arrangements for his coronation were set in train.

A king requires a king's household, and Edward's friends and those who had served him well were rewarded by places about him. His remarkable memory was not a fable and he knew how to inspire loyalty with generosity. Among the newly appointed Squires of the Body was one Geoffrey Lymington, stunned by his sudden elevation and hideously afraid that his tiny income would be insufficient to keep him in a manner suited to his new station.

King Edward was much given to pleasure. He worked hard and had exhausted many of his men with his tireless attention to the detail of his new realm while travelling around the country. But he played hard, too, and liked his household to keep him company in his amusements as in his labours. When they were established at Shene Palace one of Geoffrey's first tasks was to work with Sir William Hastings to arrange a truly splendid, very private party, fit for a young king and his soldier companions.

Geoffrey did his best, but his heart was not in it. Fortunately Hastings was fond of parties and knew how to organise them. He left Geoffrey with the relatively less taxing task of providing food of royal splendour on a remarkably tiny budget while he sent out into London for dancers, musicians, acrobats, tumblers, fire-eaters and whores.

'This will be a chance for you to show the king what you're made of, Geoffrey,' said Sir William. He was in an excellent mood: after the coronation he was to be ennobled as Lord Hastings, and a rosy future glowed before him. 'All this time we've been traipsing around the country I have never seen you with a girl on your arm. You do like girls, don't you?' He gave Geoffrey a dark, suspicious, homophobic look.

'Girls?' Geoffrey repeated blankly. 'Yes, I like girls.' My own friends would not know me, he thought. Six months ago if you showed me a room full of women I would have been like a wolf among sheep. I had the best Yes rating among all the young men I knew. But that was before Rosamund.

'Good,' said William Hastings firmly. 'There'll be plenty of them.'

There were plenty of them, serving the wine, carrying trays of sweetmeats, sitting around King Edward in decorous yet voluptuous poses and making themselves available to the other young men of his household at their pleasure. Geoffrey wandered among them, receiving many welcoming looks and smiles, for after King Edward he was the handsomest man in the room. He returned the smiles but did nothing more, telling himself that he needed to concentrate on the arrangements for a while yet.

It was almost three months since he had killed Sir Ralph and fulfilled his vow, and in that time he had not lain with a single woman. His last sexual encounter had been with Rosamund de Verney in the dungeons of Murthrum Castle, a moment of such sublime sweetness, such distilled and desperate love that it still brought him close to weeping when he thought of it. If he had known for certain that Rosamund was dead, then after he had taken his revenge he would have been free to return to his old philandering ways, but if Sir Ralph had spoken the truth there was a chance that she was alive. With that hope in his heart he had not wanted any other woman.

He had not, though, found himself in the position he did now, surrounded by opportunity and men taking the opportunity. William Hastings, who was older than the king and an accomplished libertine, had already retired into a dim corner with a couple of girls. Geoffrey glanced that way and saw Hastings sprawled on a couch, his legs spread and his teeth bared in pleasure as both girls pressed their faces close to his groin, their delicate tongues flickering and darting against his exposed, erect penis. One of them drew her tongue all around the glossy head, drooling with obscene enjoyment, and then parted her lips and took the dark, shining glans into her mouth while her friend sucked gently at Hasting's hairy cods.

'By God,' said a voice at Geoffrey's ear, 'Will's not wasting any time.'

Geoffrey started and turned to see another of the king's close friends, a young man called Thomas St Leger, watching admiringly as Hastings enjoyed the services of the two women. Thomas smiled at him. 'Good party, Geoffrey. I think we're due for some entertainment?'

'Yes,' said Geoffrey, swallowing thickly. The sight of Hasting's libidinous pleasure had had an effect on him. He was warm and tightening with lust between his legs. 'The dancers should be starting –'

On cue shrill music began and half a dozen pretty girls dashed out onto the little improvised wooden stage in the middle of the hall. They were dressed as Amazons in little short, Greek tunics that left one breast bare. At their gold-belted waists they wore small stage swords. Their arrival was met with whoops and cheers of approval and they grinned at the audience and began a sort of warrior's dance, using the swords as props.

'Hey, this is splendid,' said St Leger cheerfully. 'Lovely girls. Where are they from?'

'I don't know,' said Geoffrey. 'Will Hastings found the girls.' He was watching them dance, feeling his throat stiffen with lust. They had been well cast: all of them had little, firm breasts, tip-tilted and pointed, pert and lustful, and the white pink-tipped flesh jiggled lubriciously as they moved.

'My father was at Court once when someone tried this sort of entertainment for King Henry,' commented Thomas. 'He told me about it. You can guess what happened. Poor old Harry jumped to his feet and spluttered out, "Fie, fie for shame, forsooth you are much to blame," and dashed away into the screens. Lost his wits the next day, my dad said.'

'Really,' Geoffrey managed to say. He could hear behind him Hastings groaning with lust and the smothered moans of the girl sucking him, and on the stage the girls had changed their dance. Instead of waving the swords as if they meant to use them they had turned them round and were now rubbing themselves with the thick pommels, lifting their tunics to slide the stiff wood eagerly between their legs, thrusting their hips forward and backward as if a man were shafting them.

'Christ,' said Thomas, 'look at that little blonde one. She's the one for me.' Without another word he marched to the stage, swung himself up onto it to a chorus of cheers, caught the girl of his choice around the waist and slung her over his shoulder. She squealed and drummed with her fists and feet but he ignored her protests. He jumped quickly down into the crowd, which parted for him, carried the girl to a couch, flung her down upon it and fell on her. Her naked legs opened, revealing her moist pink sex, and in seconds Thomas's stiff cock was in her, spreading the lips of her vulva and sliding deep into that moist, welcoming tunnel. He began to move in and out and her glistening pink lips clung lewdly to his thrusting penis.

As if this were a signal other men jumped up onto the stage, which was rapidly cleared of dancers. As yet there were not enough girls to go around, and several men were without partners. Some were economising, enjoying themselves two to a girl. Near Geoffrey a dark-haired beauty was moaning and throwing her head from side to side as she stood sandwiched between two eager young male bodies, both servicing her as thoroughly as possible. The one in front thrust himself vigorously in and out of her vagina, grunting as his long shaft slid into her willing flesh. His hands gripped at the cheeks of her bottom, pulling them apart to ease the task of his friend, who was rutting avidly in the tight secret passage of her arse. He had his hands on her breasts as he sodomised her, her erect, distended nipples tightly squeezed between his clasping fingers. She cried out again, her tongue showing between her quivering lips, her mouth slack and her eyes glazing as the two men pounded her energetically towards climax.

Geoffrey turned his attention back to the stage, wondering what would happen next. His penis was fully erect now, hard as an iron bar beneath his tight hose. He would have to have a girl soon, he knew it: the promiscuous fornication around him left him no choice. It was just a question of which one. Or more than one.

The stage was not empty for long. The musicians began a slow beat, a foreign, strange rhythm, accompanied by skirling flutes and oddly twangling gitterns. Those men who had no companion or who had already finished their appetiser lifted their heads eagerly, wondering what would come next.

What came appeared to be a bundle of clothing, flung onto the stage with some force by a huge figure that leaped up after it with athletic speed and power. It was a black man more than six feet high, dressed as a Moor in loose trousers and turban. His torso was naked, oiled and glistening in the candlelight.

The bundle of clothing moved. A fold was flung back to reveal the pretty cat-like face of a young woman under a pile of copper hair, looking upwards in what appeared to be the starkest terror. The black man stood over the prostrate girl and looked around the room, raising his clenched fists, his white teeth gleaming. 'Your Grace, my lords,' he intoned in a voice like a great bell, 'for your entertainment: *The Captured Pilgrim*.'

He reached down and seized the girl's outer garment and pulled at it. It unravelled, spinning the girl across the stage, revealing her clad from neck to ankles in a gown of coarse pilgrim grey, hung about with badges and crucifixes. The audience laughed and roared their approval and the music grew louder.

The black man lunged towards the girl. She mimed terror and tried to flee. He caught her by the arm and pulled her towards him, his big hand catching at the neck of her gown. With a single jerk it pulled open. She screamed and struggled as he dragged it from her, leaving her in a shift and crucifix. She fell to her knees at his feet, holding up her clasped hands, begging silently for mercy. She was a good actress: her pleading eyes would have melted stone.

Stone, but not the hearts of the watchers. 'Strip her!' someone yelled. 'Let's see her tits!'

The Moor grasped the girl's crucifix in both hands and jerked hard, breaking the string. She moaned and tried to clutch at it as he flung it away. Then he twisted her arm behind her back and dragged her to her feet, turned her to face the audience, and began slowly, slowly, to tear open the shift down the front.

Geoffrey stared, swallowing hard, as the girl's body was revealed inch by inch. It was a sweet body, perfectly made, small and fragile, with round high breasts capped with nipples like rosebuds and a delicately curving belly that looked as soft as satin. The Moor paused, grinning at the audience, wanting them to ask for him to reveal the girl's sex. His captive moaned again and writhed, her curling copper hair tumbling over her shoulders, her breasts heaving. The audience roared again and with a lascivious smile the Moor tore the shift open the rest of its length.

'Christ,' Geoffrey gasped. The girl's sex was plucked as smooth as an eggshell. The audience whooped and shouted as the Moor looked down over the girl's shoulder, miming astonishment and approval as he saw the bare, tender, trembling flesh. He put his big hand on the white skin of the girl's quivering belly and began to move it down, inch by inch, the black fingers creeping onward like a huge spider. The girl struggled, but it was hopeless. The hand slipped over her mound and opened her tender thighs, holding them apart, and the Moor jammed his knee into the girl's back to thrust her hips forward, displaying her hairless, glistening sex to the audience like a slave-master showing off his latest purchase.

251

'Swive her!' shouted a voice from the back. The black man grinned again, then forced the girl to the floor. From his belt he drew a piece of soft rope and with it he fastened her hands behind her back with quick, loose stage knots. The girl mimed horror and tried to wriggle away. He pushed her head to the floor and put his foot on her tumbling hair, holding her still as he began to open his loose trousers. She writhed and whimpered, gazing upwards with enormous terrified eyes as he drew out a cock so huge that the whole audience gasped. It was magnificent, black and shining, hard as an ebony staff, the glistening knob at its tip the size of the girl's clenched fist. She cried out and struggled as he leant down and caught her by the shoulders and pulled her to her knees.

'My God,' said someone at Geoffrey's shoulder, 'she'll never be able to get that into her mouth.'

He was wrong. The audience watched in astonishment as the black man dug his hands into the girl's hair and jerked back her head. She moaned and opened her mouth, and without hesitation he thrust his enormous phallus between her parted lips. It entered her, going on and on, and she closed her eyes and took him in, inch by inch, inch by inch until the whole stiff length was buried in her throat and the dangling purse of his balls brushed her lips.

'God,' said the voice, 'I've heard of this but I've never seen it. God's shit.'

The Moor was swiving the girl's lips now, moving in and out. Geoffrey expected her to choke at any minute, but she remained passive, accepting the movement of the great shining member as it slid deeply into her mouth. Her nipples were erect, little tight buds of sensation, and her bound hands were clenching tightly.

After a few minutes the black man withdrew his penis, wet and gleaming with the girl's saliva. He pulled her backwards until she lay on the floor, propped on her bound hands and her knees. Then he spread her thighs, wide, wide apart, so that her loins tensed and hollowed and every man in the audience could see the pouting, glistening lips of her sex, like the petals of a heavy pink flower moist with dew.

The music stopped and the drum began, a single, pounding beat. The audience licked its dry lips and began to stamp on the floor, to pound on the tables, in time with the drum. The black man knelt down between the girl's widespread thighs and stroked his hand up and down his shaft. Then he nudged the great glossy head between the naked lips of her sex, holding her thighs apart with his hands so that everyone in the audience could watch as the huge black tool slid up into her. The girl cried out and arched her back as the thick shaft penetrated her, stretching the soft lips, filling her to the hilt. Then the Moor began to swive her in time with the drum, his strong haunches hollowing as he thrust, and the beat quickened and quickened as his broad shoulders and smooth chest became shiny with sweat. He panted and moved faster and faster, the drum always keeping time, and the sight of that column of ebony flesh sliding smoothly in and out of the girl's hairless sex made Geoffrey's head spin. At last the Moor withdrew with a jerk and caught the girl by the hair, dragging her head towards him, and with two practised strokes of his hand he spurted his white seed between her parted lips and let out a cry of satisfaction.

The audience erupted into cheers. Geoffrey took a step back, haggard and shaking with astonishment and arousal. The Moor and the girl jumped to their feet, suddenly absurdly theatrical as they bowed and smiled and made their exit.

'Good stuff, Geoffrey, eh?' said a voice. It was William Hastings, finished with his first entertainment, smiling broadly as he contemplated the stage.

'Incredible,' Geoffrey agreed, though it was hard to speak. 'What's next?'

'Just some more dancing,' said Hastings. He was holding two cups of wine in his hand and he thrust one at Geoffrey. 'Tamer this time, I think. Have a drink, Geoff, find yourself a girl. Relax: you've done your bit.'

Geoffrey nodded and tried to smile. He drank the cup of wine in one draught. It was good and strong: the vintner had not cheated him. He put his head in his hands for a moment, his brain spinning with heated images of lust and desire.

The musicians began to play again, this time a stately, courtly dance. From the curtain at the back of the stage dancers began to emerge, stepping hand in hand. They were all women, dressed in a curious, erotic parody of Court wear, tall head-dresses and complex gowns made of a myriad translucent scarves, which were deployed to reveal the swell of a breast, the edge of a pink nipple, the flash of a white thigh. Unlike the Amazons and the Captured Pilgrim these women were tall and splendid, queenly in their bearing. The audience catcalled and cheered as they came in but they ignored it and stepped proudly forward, poised and elegant. They were all masked, masks of black fabric trimmed to match their exotic clothes. There were eight of them. They formed a square and began to pace through the steps of a court dance, curtseying gracefully to each other.

Geoffrey stood still, gazing up at them. Their hands moved elegantly, as if they should be glittering with jewels. Each of them turned and as she did so caught hold of the clothing of her neighbour and pulled a scarf free, showing a little more of the white flesh beneath it. The audience howled with delight, realising that all this formality was no more than the prelude to a languid strip tease.

It was strange to see the bodies of the women begin to be exposed while their faces were hidden behind black masks and their hair beneath heavy head-dresses. Geoffrey watched, intrigued, and as he watched he found his gaze fixing more and more on one link in the chain. She was tall, statuesque, with a high, deep bosom. A gauzy scarf, floating free, disclosed a breast tipped with a nipple the colour of watered wine. Her legs were well shaped and as she turned the scarves lifted to show a glimpse of her white belly and the dark triangle of her sex, opulent and tempting.

She looked like Rosamund. The sight of her body trapped Geoffrey in nets of invisible steel, holding him riveted. He could see nothing of her face. If only he could have seen her mouth he would have known her at once: those soft, full lips, redder than roses, would have betrayed her to him among a thousand women. But he could not see her face, only more and more of her splendid, insouciant nakedness, appearing scarf by scarf before the enthralled audience.

Someone pushed in front of Geoffrey, obscuring his view. He scowled and pushed the man aside and stepped closer to the stage, gazing eagerly upwards. The dancers turned: the woman who looked like Rosamund faced him, raising her arms gracefully. The heavy orbs of her breasts lifted and tightened, the proud erect nipples dragging at his eyes. She turned her head, and the dark glitter of her eyes behind the mask swept over his face.

'Geoffrey!' called a voice. Geoffrey started and turned, for it was the voice of the King. He hurried over to the cushioned couch where King Edward lay with a cup of wine in one hand and a pretty girl in the other, beaming.

'Your Grace,' he said, bending his knee, 'how can I serve you?'

'No service,' said Edward with a grin, 'Christ, look at me, what more could a man want? I just wanted to congratulate you on the arrangements. I know good old Will did the entertainment, but you have managed the money very well, he tells me. You are a natural at this sort of thing. I shan't forget. You have had no gift from me yet to show you my thanks.'

'You gave me my place, your Grace,' said Geoffrey, feeling uncomfortable. 'I could ask for no more.'

'Hmph,' said the king. 'Tom says you're as poor as a church mouse. Well, the cupboard is bare at present,

Geoffrey, but when I get around to parcelling out the spoils from Towton you won't be forgotten.'

'Thank you, your Grace,' said Geoffrey, very pleased indeed.

'Edward,' said King Edward, 'at times like this.'

Geoffrey smiled into the king's face and Edward grinned back, then pulled the girl in his arm around in front of him and began to kiss her lips. Geoffrey turned away, beaming. Then he remembered the dancer and hurried back towards the stage.

She was gone. The dance continued, the dancers now nearly naked but for their masks and headdresses, but a link in their chain was missing. Geoffrey frowned, puzzled and perturbed.

'Hello,' said a voice beside him. He looked around and saw the girl who had danced the part of the Captured Pilgrim, wrapped in a white robe and smiling up at him.

'Hello,' he said. He did not smile at her as welcomingly as he might have done, for his mind was full of Rosamund. He looked back to the stage, frowning still. Had he been imagining things? He had longed for her so much that he had started to see her face where it could not possibly have been. Was he now projecting his memory of her body onto other women? Was he deceiving himself?

'My name's Anne,' said the little copper-haired creature before him. 'A friend of mine has a bet with me on your name.'

'My name?' Geoffrey repeated, puzzled.

'She says she thinks you're another Edward, like his Grace the king,' said the girl with a cheerful smile. 'I said I didn't think so.'

'My name's not Edward,' Geoffrey told her. It was charming that she should come out to court him: he felt favoured. The image of the dancer began to slip from his mind.

'I said I thought you looked like a Henry,' said the girl called Anne.

'Wrong again,' said Geoffrey. 'My name's Geoffrey.'

She pouted, disappointed. 'I've lost my bet, then,' she said. She turned as if she would leave, but he reached for her shoulder and caught hold of it, holding her back. She stopped and looked at him with an arch smile.

'What you did on stage,' he muttered thickly. 'Could you do it for me?'

She raised her brows and without a word pushed the robe from her shoulders. Beneath it she was naked. Geoffrey looked down at her curving, rounded body, at the pristine nudity of her pubic mound, and swallowed hard. There was a couch nearby unoccupied, and he took her hand and drew her towards it.

Her small hands busied themselves in his clothing and within moments his doublet was off and his hose loosened so that she could reach inside. He gasped as she sat on the edge of the couch and pulled him close to her so that her mouth was poised before his crotch. She said nothing, but she opened her lips and licked the tip of his erect penis and then gently tugged his hips towards her.

Slowly he thrust, expecting her to protest and hold him back. She did not. The throbbing head of his cock touched the back of her mouth for an instant; then her throat spasmed as if she was swallowing and he slid in further, deep into her, and her delicate lips began to caress the coarse, silky skin of his balls. The sensation was unprecedented, incredible. He closed his eyes and let his hands rest in her hair as he thrust gently into her mouth, relishing the strange feeling of her lips on his testicles, shuddering with pleasure and relief.

For a few moments she sucked him. Then his cock began to pulse and twitch in her throat and she drew back, releasing him. 'You don't want to come in there,' she said, looking up at him meaningfully. 'There's a better place for that, handsome.'

She lay back on the couch and parted her legs. Geoffrey put his hands on her hips and moved them slowly, experimentally, gliding his fingers over the silken, naked skin of her mound, intensely aroused by the naked sex, the way its soft lips showed without concealment, lewd and obscene, asking to be parted and filled by a man's body. She was wet and she shivered as he put one finger inside her. He did not hesitate, but replaced his finger with the head of his cock and thrust it deep.

A skilled, expert whore, that Anne. When he had penetrated her to the hilt, until his balls rested against the bare smooth skin of her thighs, she began to work at him with her inner muscles, clutching him with velvet fingers, milking him. He shuddered and lifted himself on his hands, looking down so that he could watch his cock plunging in and out of her, glistening with her juices. He was highly aroused, and the sight of his thick stiff shaft sliding again and again into that hairless pouting sex drove him quickly to the edge of ecstasy. He panted as he shafted her, moving faster and faster, strong determined thrusts until he flung back his head and yelled in pleasure as his balls tightened and pulsed and his cock shivered and jerked and spurted inside her. She held him hard as he came, sucking the seed from him so that he shuddered and moaned. When at last she relaxed the sensation was almost one of relief. Geoffrey let his head fall forward, his eyes closed tightly, trembling with the aftershock.

In the red darkness behind his eyes he saw again the moving figure of the dancer, her full high breasts, the dark smudge of her pubic hair, smoky with promise. Was he mad? Had she not looked like Rosamund?

The girl beneath him began to wriggle away, her business done. He let himself withdraw from her, but as she got up to go he touched her arm and looked up into her face.

'Anne,' he asked hesitantly, 'the girls here tonight. Are you all from the same place?'

'A couple of places,' she replied, tossing back her curling hair.

Geoffrey paused, wondering if he was setting himself up for misery. At last he swallowed and said, 'Which places?'

Chapter Twelve

The day after the King's party Rosamund sat front of house beside Mistress Alice, dressed in her best and quite silent, staring blankly before her.

Alice did not pay much attention to her. There was practically no business and while she waited for customers to come in Alice sat and wrung her hands, expressing her anxieties aloud. 'Ever since I heard about the owner's death I've been worried. We're in the King's hand now, you realise that, Rosamund? He can give us to whom he pleases. I'm really worried he might let the Bishop of Southwark bid for us. You know what those clerics are like as owners: always interfering, and always sending friends around for free rides. Whatever you say about Sir Ralph, he was the best sort of owner: hardly ever here, and then he hardly ever asked for anything. The time he had you was the first I remember.' She hesitated as if suddenly curious about what had occurred on that day, but then she shook her head. 'You see,' she went on, though Rosamund had not responded to her by look or by word, 'you see, I should really like to buy the place myself. I've got a bit saved, a bit put by. But I – '

The curtain to the steam room corridor opened to reveal Anne, in her working clothes with a towel wrapped around her shoulders. She looked pasty-faced and puffy. 'Mistress Alice,' she said, 'may I speak to Rosamund for a moment?'

'What, out here?' asked Alice crossly. 'I suppose so. Rosamund, step into the corridor.'

Rosamund got to her feet and went through the curtain. She looked down into Anne's little cat-like face with cavernous eyes. Anne said quickly, 'Well, you were right. Geoffrey it is. Good-looking young man, I thought, if you like that sort of thing; nice body. But excitable, though, hardly gave me a run for my money. Anyway, you know me and men: I'd as soon forget the whole thing.' She frowned up into Rosamund's face. 'Rosa, are you all right? Who is he?'

'It doesn't matter. Thank you, Anne. I'd better go back.' Rosamund turned and went back through the curtain. She sat down, white-faced and composed, and folded her long fingered hands in her lap. Her eyes stared at nothing and her face was quite emotionless, concealing her shock and distress beneath a veil of artificial calm.

Geoffrey. Geoffrey, alive, and in the service of King Edward. There had been nobody at the party but the King's friends and household. Alive, alive. Conflicting emotions threatened to tear Rosamund in two. She was full of joy, simple gladness that he had not been killed. But adulterating her happiness was pain so exquisite that she thought it might truly kill her. She had rejoiced to hear of Sir Ralph's death at Towton. It had seemed to grant her her freedom from the shameful thraldom that he had imposed on her. She had thought that perhaps, in time, she might form herself a new life, a new purpose, when she had grieved for Geoffrey and laid him to rest in her soul. But Geoffrey was not dead. He was alive and within her reach: and she was a whore.

What was he doing in the King's service? What was his place? Perhaps, she thought with eager yearning, perhaps he would accept me as his mistress, perhaps we could live together. But as the thought crossed her mind she forced it aside. He had seen her dancing a lewd dance before a company of his friends. How could he ever respect her after? Her spirit cringed at the thought. He was a rising man at Court now. It would demean him to associate himself with a Southwark whore. He would not want her. She would be to him as Anne had been last night, a mere receptacle for lust, taken and forgotten.

'Rosamund,' said Alice, 'are you well? You're very pale.'

'I have a slight headache,' Rosamund said coolly. She came to a decision. She would excuse herself from further attendance upon the King's pleasures. She would not go where Geoffrey might be, would not speak to him, would not be tortured by his closeness or show herself to him to be a cause for discomfort and regret. She loved him too much to impose herself upon his good nature. Perhaps she would see him by chance, she told herself. She closed her eyes and imagined a hot summer's day by the Thames, herself standing on the banks waiting for a boat to cross to Saint Paul's. There, floating past her, came one of the royal wherries, all scarlet velvet and gold paint, and in it a few of the King's household, dressed for their leisure in bright thin shirts and drinking wine. Among them, Geoffrey, his head bare, the hot sun glowing from his heavy mop of gleaming hair, a silver cup in his hand. He flung back his head and laughed. The brilliant sunlight glowed on the carven bones of cheek and jaw, touched the sharp curves of his arching brows with gold, gilded the pale skin of his strong throat. He was the most beautiful creature on God's earth, and he floated by her in a cocoon of silence as she stood with the ache of her heart filling her eyes with tears.

There was no business that morning, and Rosamund sat beside Mistress Alice as noon came and went. She began carefully to accustom her mind to the idea of Geoffrey alive and well and to her necessary sacrifice. Piers brought them some food, but she did not eat it.

A little after noon the doorman bowed as he opened the door. Alice had been dozing, and she got to her feet with a start and said, 'Good day to you, my lord.'

Rosamund raised her eyes incuriously to see who had come. She saw the young man standing in the doorway, taking off his hat and cloak, and her heart stopped beating and then began to thump in her chest as if she had run a race. She got to her feet, trembling, and he lifted his eyes and looked at her.

Those eyes, golden green as the sunlight in a beech-wood, wide and wondering! Rosamund stared for a second in desperate delight. Then she remembered her decision and with a sound that was half way between a gasp and a sob she turned and ran, shouldering through the curtain to the steam room.

'Rosamund!' cried a strong voice. 'Rosamund!' And she was running through the steam room, watched by the gaping, astonished faces of the girls, through and into the bath house. Chaos behind her, the doorman's voice and Piers' voice shouting, 'You can't go through yet,' and Geoffrey's voice crying out furiously, 'Let me go, you dogs!'

She was in the bath house proper, surrounded by the silent tents of the cubicles, gasping and weeping as she hesitated, uncertain which way to run. Her brain urged her onwards, her body hung back, unwilling, reluctant. She heard quick footsteps in the steam room and cried out in misery and lifted her heavy skirt in her hands.

'Rosamund!' Geoffrey burst into the bath house, dishevelled, his sword in his hand. She glanced over her shoulder and saw him and wept as she ran. In a few paces he had overtaken her, caught her, whirled her to face him. He stared into her eyes, panting, his brows tight and hurt. For a moment they did not speak. Then he said, shaking his head, 'You ran away from me. Why did you run away?'

She was weeping and could not speak. With her free hand she gestured at herself, a single gesture showing her shame, her wretchedness. Geoffrey's face changed, overcome with desperate tenderness. 'Oh, Rosamund,' he whispered, 'how could you think that I would care?' He frowned irritably at his naked sword and thrust it back into its sheath then pulled her into his arms. She was shaking with her tears. He held her close, his lips in her hair, her face pressed against his throat. She felt his arms around her, strong and firm, his muscular body warm beneath his clothes, the wonderful, subtle smell of his skin. Shivers of pure ecstasy ran through her from her nape to her toes. Even if he rejected her when he understood what she had become, she could not deny herself this moment of bliss.

After an infinite second there was a voice beside them. 'Go upstairs,' it whispered. 'Go to one of the private rooms. Go on.'

It was Anne, tugging at Rosamund's clothes, smiling at her. Rosamund lifted her face from the hollow of Geoffrey's throat and nodded. He stooped over her, anxious, holding her close as she guided him through the bath house to the servant's stair that led up to the private chambers.

In a moment they were alone, the door closed behind them. Rosamund glanced apprehensively up at the squint in the corner of the room. Geoffrey saw the direction of her gaze, snorted with laughter and released her for long enough to shrug off his doublet and stuff it into the hole. Then he turned back to her and opened his arms and she ran across the room to him, weeping again with love.

'Rosamund.' How well she remembered his voice, tender and caressing. 'It was you last night, dancing. Where did you go?'

She looked up into his face, her eyes fleeting over the perfection of every feature. 'I saw you,' she whispered. 'I thought you were dead, Geoffrey. He told me you were dead. When I saw you I – I was ill.'

'You didn't speak to me,' he said in gentle reproach. 'Why didn't you?'

She shook her head. 'I couldn't. I didn't know if – if I was imagining you.'

He smiled as if he understood. Then he took her face between the palms of his big hands and tilted it up towards him. For a long moment they looked into each other's eyes. Then, very slowly, he lowered his lips to hers.

As they stood wrapped in the ecstasy of their kiss she gently put her arms around him, feeling his warmth, his solidity, the comforting realness of his body. No dream: it was no dream, she stood broad waking, exchanging soft kisses with the man she had grieved for. Her hands slipped up his strong shoulders and dug into the shining mass of his heavy hair; it slid like silk over her searching fingers. Beneath his mouth she gave a little cry of wonder and bliss and tugged at him, pressing his lips down upon hers as if only the feel of his strength would allow her to believe in him.

At last he drew back. His face looked suddenly chastened and ashamed and she frowned at him, puzzled. 'That girl,' he said, 'Anne. She's your friend.'

Rosamund nodded and Geoffrey pressed his lips together and looked at the floor. When he raised his eyes he looked hunted, and he swallowed hard before he spoke. 'Last night,' he said hesitantly, 'at the party, I – I had her. I'm sorry.'

'Oh, Geoffrey.' Rosamund smiled with sweet, gentle amusement at his plea for pardon. 'Geoffrey, since I came here I have been a whore, and you apologise to me for having a girl?'

'I love you,' Geoffrey said suddenly, jumping forward and catching hold of her arms, speaking with sudden burning eagerness. 'Rosamund, I love you. Since I last saw you that's the first time I've had a woman. I vowed I wouldn't until I had avenged you. He told me you were dead, Rosamund, I thought you were dead.' He caught her face again in his hands and kissed her, forcing his mouth onto hers with a desperate urgency that made her gasp. 'I love you,' he said again, his mouth pressing to her cheek, her eyelids, her throat. 'I love you, I want you. Now, Rosamund, now.'

Already his hands were tugging at her gown. So many clothes, so much damask, so much cotton, laces to be untied, buttons on her tight sleeves to unfasten, the rustle of the gown as he forced it down to her feet, her stockings rumpling at her ankles, his breath hot and hissing as he kissed her neck, her shoulder, the swell of her breast over the edge of her stays. They were flurried, panting like children, clumsy with haste. Her head-dress was next, the tall cone of silk pulled from her, the black velvet band around her forehead loosed and dropped, and Geoffrey laughed as he began to tug out the bone pins which held up the shining sheaves of her chestnut hair. It fell at last around her shoulders and he caught it up in his hands and kissed it as she fumbled with the laces on his shirt and tugged them open to reveal the delicious, tender hollow of his strong throat.

Her stays were loose, unlaced, falling from her; his points were all unfastened and he was jumping from one foot to the other as he feverishly pushed his hose down to his ankles. They were giggling, eager, like a pair of country fools in a hay rick. Then, quite suddenly, they drew breath and faced each other. He wore his shirt alone, its hem held out from his body by the length of his erect penis, and she was in just her shift, her tight nipples showing through its fineness. One flimsy garment each between themselves and lovers' nakedness. They stood very still, gazing, tasting the moment of blissful discovery.

At last Rosamund stepped forward and took the hem of his shirt in her hands. He lifted his arms and she drew it up, trailing her fingers over his smooth skin. Up above the hard ridges of his hip-bones, revealing the glossy curling fur of his groin and the beautiful, eager hardness of his phallus; up the taut plane of his abdomen, the muscled corrugations of his ribs, the broad smooth expanse of his chest, up over his head, his strong arms, up to the tips of his long fingers, until he was quite naked. She let the shirt fall and touched her hand softly to the perfect line of his jaw, then stood back.

He dropped to his knees before her and lifted the hem of her shift, stooping down to kiss her bare feet. He stole the fabric upwards, furling it between his strong fingers like a sail, and as it revealed her body so he kissed her, setting his wonderful firm lips to her ankles, her calves, her thighs, brushing softly against the dark fleece of her loins, kissing her belly, her breast bone, her throat, and then, when the shift fell to the floor and she was naked too, kissing her peony mouth. She opened her lips to receive his kiss and he moved into her arms, his hard body pressed against hers, the hot smooth shaft of his penis trapped quivering between them.

They moved together towards the bed, swaying as the wind of their desire buffeted them. He seized the covers and drew them back, then put his hands on her waist and lifted her to sit on the edge of the high bed, her thighs spread to admit his body between them, their mouths locked together. She lay back, pulling at him, and he lifted himself onto the smooth sheets and lay down beside her.

They kissed and touched, lying close together, his thigh between her thighs, his arms around her. Hot June sunshine poured through the casement of the room and warmed their feet and ankles and their curling toes. She pressed her lips to his, feeling love and bliss deepening into passion and need as his strong smooth body moved against hers. She trembled with wanting him. She needed no force, no restraint or compulsion, nothing to urge her to arousal: his presence, his love was sufficient. His erect phallus was pressed against her belly, scalding her with its hardness. If she did not feel him inside her she would die. She lifted her thigh and hooked it over his hip bone, moving her body even closer. The velvety, swollen tip of his cock slipped between her legs, gliding over the lips of her sex, rubbing against her engorged clitoris until she moaned into his open mouth. Then it was at her entrance, and as she gasped and caught his face in her hands to kiss him harder she felt him beginning to move, to penetrate her, filling her, soothing away her emptiness.

He thrust, very gently and slowly, until he was sheathed inside her to the hilt. Then he lay still, his body buried within her, and stroked her face with his hand. They lay quietly, looking into each other's eyes and breathing deeply, their thighs interwoven like the decorated initial of a manuscript.

He drew back a little and looked down at her body and their locking thighs, the conjoined darkness of their pubic hair, mingling in the sweet closeness of penetration. He put his hands on her shoulders and ran them down to her breasts, trapping her nipples between his fingers and squeezing gently. A pulse of pleasure darted through her and she closed her eyes and took a deep, strong breath. Her body shifted slightly against his and his lean, muscular thigh pressed against the shivering pearl of her clitoris. She caught her lip in her teeth and her inner muscles spasmed, clutching at the thick, hard length of his penis as it lay deeply imbedded in her tender sex.

Slowly, so slowly, he began to move, the slightest pressure of his hips on hers, pushing himself into her oh-so-gently, just letting her feel that he possessed her, that his phallus was within her, stirring deeply as his thigh rubbed against her pleasure point. She began to shudder and moan. His hands closed more tightly on her breasts and the muscles of his belly and buttocks tensed as he withdrew again, a little further this time, and thrust back. His fingers teased at her distended nipples and she gasped. Gradually he increased the speed of his movements, watching tensely as his thick shaft slid out of Rosamund's sex and then firmly back, breathing fast as he saw himself pleasure her.

She could not bear it. The feel of his powerful cock moving deep inside her, his warm body stimulating the epicentre of her desire, his hands on her breasts, lifted her to an agony of bliss. She opened her eyes to watch his face, his beautiful face set in lines of the deepest concentration as he took her. The pleasure was too much. She would have liked to lie there for ever, surrounded by his love, moaning as his iron penis glided in and out of her quivering sex, feeling herself consumed utterly by his loving fervour. But waves of sensation began to flow through her, making her arch her back and gasp, making her cry out in desperate need as his steady, forceful movements drew her to the edge of orgasm, held her there, and at last broke her like spun glass, shattering her into fragments of ecstasy. She cried out and clung to him and he thrust again and again into her convulsing body, harder and harder, gasping her name as he ravished her. At the moment of his crisis he lunged forward and kissed her, his tongue trembling in her mouth as his cock jerked and shuddered within her body, his groan smothered by her lips.

They lay together as their breathing slowed. She rested her head on his chest. His body was outlined with a golden rim of sunlight and she smiled and traced the bright glow with her finger, listening to the steady pounding of his heart. As their bliss ebbed slowly away reality returned, pressing coldly in on her, and she shivered.

He held her tightly and kissed her bowed forehead. His penis was still within her, warm and wet, slowly softening. 'Hush,' he whispered.

'Geoffrey.' She wanted so much to say that she loved him, but how could she? It would seem that she was trying to keep him, when all of her knew that she must release him.

He sighed heavily and pulled her closer still. 'Did he make you come here?' he asked at last. 'Did he force you?'

'He tricked me.' She drew back a little so that she could speak. 'He let me believe that you were dead and he tricked me over and over. There was nothing else I could do.' Her lips tightened, losing colour. 'When I heard he had died at Towton I thanked God on my knees for it.'

Geoffrey began to say something, then hesitated. After a moment he said, 'You know that I am one of the King's men now. I did him some service at Towton and he doesn't forget. If I ask him, Rosamund, I know he will restore your lands. Aycliffe died a traitor: he forfeits everything.'

Rosamund looked up at him wide-eyed, hardly daring to believe. His face looked sad, as if he had lost something. 'Would he truly restore them?' she asked tentatively.

'Oh, I think so. He likes gestures like that, and after all it would cost him nothing. And once he sees you, he won't be able to resist – '

'Geoffrey,' Rosamund said faintly, 'I think I should not see the King.' He looked at her, frowning, and she felt herself beginning to blush, her insides hollow with shame. 'A little before Towton he came here, to the Fountain, and he, he . . .'

For a moment Geoffrey was silent, his brows a tight hard line. Then he said slowly, 'King Edward had you?'

She nodded, unable to speak. He turned his head away from her as if he did not know what to say and his face showed his hurt. She said timidly after a moment, 'I did not please him. I, I called him by your name.'

'You did what?' His eyes were wide. 'You called the King by my name?' There was a little tense pause, then he caught his lip in his teeth and began to chuckle. The chuckle became a laugh; he laughed himself right out of Rosamund's body. 'Oh, Rosamund,' he said, touching her cheek, 'you know how to soothe a man's jealousy!'

He had forgiven her. She moved forward again into his arms, luxuriating in his closeness. 'Anyway,' he said over her shoulder, 'it doesn't matter whether you see him or not. The widow of a man who died fighting for his father, robbed of everything by a Lancastrian: of course he will restore your lands. I'll ask him tonight.' He swallowed hard and his jaw swelled against her skin as it clenched with tension. He went on determinedly, 'And then you will be free to marry again. You can make a good match, you know, Rosamund. A nobleman, of course. Probably someone young and good looking, and rich, with the lands you have. King Edward will be bound to take an interest.' He fell silent, holding her.

'Geoffrey,' she said softly, 'you can't believe what I have been thinking all this time.' He stayed where he was, his head on her shoulder, not looking at her. 'I have been thinking that to know me now would demean you, hold you back from your advancement. That's why I ran from you.' He murmured in protest and shook his head, his glossy hair sweeping over her white skin. She closed her eyes, drawing up her strength. 'If the King returns my lands to me,' she said, 'if you are prepared to ask him for them, would you not ask him if, if he would let you marry me?'

'Me?' He drew back now so that he could look into her eyes. 'But I'm nobody. I serve the King, but I'm still just a squire. I'm no one, Rosamund.'

'But I love you,' she said. Her lip began to quiver with tears and she chewed at it to keep herself in control. 'I love you. I couldn't marry anyone but you.' He began to shake his head, to deny it, and she plunged on regardless. 'If the King refuses,' she said eagerly, 'tell him I will have you anyway. I will keep you as my lover whenever you are not at Court and scandalise the countryside. In the name of common decency he will have to let you marry me.'

His face was soft with love and surrender. 'You'll ask him,' she said, weeping openly now. 'Promise, promise you'll ask.'

'Hush, hush,' he soothed her. 'I promise.'

On Sunday the twenty-eighth day of June, King Edward was crowned at Westminster Abbey with all conceivable pomp. To celebrate his coronation he granted many titles and made many knights, and he restored to Lady Rosamund de Verney the lands that had been extorted from her by the deceased traitor, Sir Ralph Aycliffe.

On the following Sunday one of the King's men, Geoffrey Lymington, married Lady Rosamund de Verney at a very small ceremony in the private chapel of the Palace of Westminster. Thomas St Leger stood as groomsman and a couple more of the King's household were witnesses. After the priest had knotted his pallium around the joined hands of the couple and pronounced them man and wife they walked from the chapel in a daze of happiness, blinded by love and the blaze of the summer sun through the bright painted glass.

Geoffrey caught hold of Rosamund and pulled her close to kiss her. 'Well,' he said, 'you have to say that this is an unusual match. Most men make ladies of their wives when they marry them. I have unmade a lady.'

'I would rather be plain Mistress Lymington than the highest duchess in the realm,' Rosamund told him, holding him tightly. She reached up to take his face in her hands and pull his lips down onto hers.

'Geoffrey,' said St Leger's cheerful voice, 'here's an uninvited guest.'

They separated and turned to see who had come. Geoffrey took a quick breath and went pale and Rosamund moved closer to him as if he would protect her. The uninvited guest was King Edward.

The King's handsome face was smiling as he said to Geoffrey, 'Did you think to do it without me? I would not – ' and then he turned his eyes to Rosamund and fell silent. His smile vanished, replaced by a look first of shock, then of louring anger, then of slow understanding.

'Lady de Verney,' he said after some time. 'I knew that I knew your face from somewhere. I came once to your house, I remember it.'

'Yes, your Grace,' Rosamund whispered, bowing her head. Blood was burning in her cheeks like a fire. She risked a glance upwards and saw King Edward's eyes fixed on her, very cold and stern.

'Well,' said the King slowly, 'does your new husband

know that we met each other more recently than that?' He glared at her, making it clear that he would protect the men of his household if necessary from the machinations of gold digging whores, whatever they might have been in the past.

Geoffrey tightened his arm round Rosamund's waist. 'Your Grace,' he said, 'my lady has told me everything that happened to her after her lands were stolen. It makes no difference to me.' He smiled at Edward. 'Though I thank you for your care of me, your Grace.'

Edward raised his brows. Then he said, 'So you are *the* Geoffrey.' The others looked puzzled and Rosamund and Geoffrey both looked at the floor and tried not to laugh. 'Well,' the King went on, 'Mistress Lymington, I congratulate you on your taste. If I must come second in a race, I prefer to lose to a worthy opponent.'

Rosamund looked up into the King's eyes. As she did so she remembered his body, his height and strength, the glorious length and hardness of his erect phallus, and she shivered. He smiled at her, a smile full of dark meaning, and at once she looked down, discomfited.

'Well,' said the King, 'my lady, your lands were restored to you as a gesture of appreciation for your deceased husband's faithful service to my father. That would have been sufficient in itself, without Geoffrey's pleading for you, once the matter had been drawn to my attention. I am surprised you did not mention it when we met.' Rosamund's eyes flicked up briefly, but she could not endure the sharpness of the King's gaze. She was glad for Geoffrey's arm around her waist, holding her up. 'In any case,' said Edward, 'I do not feel that what I have done for you is sufficient reward for Geoffrey. I do not like my men to be beholden to anyone for their living, not even their wives, and I promised him a reward for himself.'

'Your Grace,' Geoffrey protested, 'there is no need.'

'Tut.' Edward waved his hand, then reached into the bosom of his doublet and drew out a parchment from which hung his seal. 'This,' he said, 'grants to you in your own person, Geoffrey, the lands and revenues of the traitor Aycliffe.' Geoffrey swallowed hard and Rosamund put her hand to her mouth. 'I could not resist the opportunity to redress the man's wrongs in such a satisfying way. And since the previous holder of the lands enjoyed the rank of knight, you too will have that rank. It would be a shame not to make your lovely wife a lady, since she was one before.'

Geoffrey stood for a moment silent, then let go of Rosamund and fell to one knee before the King, grasping his hand and kissing it. 'Your Grace,' he said, looking up with tears in his eyes, 'I can offer you nothing except my faithful service.'

Edward looked down at him with a kind smile. 'And not even that for a while,' he said. 'Your wife will have a more urgent claim on you than I, Master Lymington, for a few weeks at least, and you must set your hand to the reins of your new possessions. I give you leave of absence from Court until Michaelmas. Then I shall expect to see you both around me once again.' He stooped and drew Geoffrey to his feet, put his arms about him and kissed him firmly on each cheek, and pressed the parchment into his hand. Then, releasing him, he went to Rosamund, took her hand and kissed it. She felt the power of his sexual energy like a sudden chill in her spine and withdrew her hand as soon as she could.

'For now, farewell,' said the King. 'Enjoy your honeymoon. I will see you both at Michaelmas. Tom, will you come? There is a game of bowls afoot on the green, and I have a bet with my lord Hastings – ' He caught Thomas St Leger by the arm and piloted him away and the other men of his household followed him.

Geoffrey and Rosamund stood looking down at the parchment in Geoffrey's hand. After a moment he unrolled it and read the good clerk's script carefully, shaking his head slowly from side to side in disbelief. 'Well,' he said, 'my guardian angel was watching over me at Towton, my lady, for both our sakes.'

'Aycliffe stole some of his lands from good people,' Rosamund said, remembering how Sir Ralph had terrorised their shire. 'You might give them back, Geoffrey, if you wanted to do good.' He nodded, still looking half-stunned. Then another thought struck Rosamund and she put her hands to her mouth to hold in a spurt of laughter. Geoffrey looked up, puzzled, and she shook her head, still laughing.

'What?' Geoffrey demanded, smiling to see her laugh. He caught her hands and pulled them away from her mouth. 'What is it? What's the joke?'

'Geoffrey,' Rosamund whispered, 'you will never guess. Oh, Geoffrey, you are now the owner of the Fountain of Love!'

They spent a joyful night in a guest chamber at Court and the following day set off with blue streaks under their eyes to travel back to Lincolnshire. The journey took six days, for they did not hurry. Each day they stopped at a welcoming, well-appointed inn, bespoke the best chamber, ate and drank the finest that the landlord could offer and then retired to bed and fell into each other's arms and made love until sleep conquered them. They travelled alone, and in the morning each would act as servant to the other. Rosamund shaved Geoffrey and fastened his points; he would braid her hair and lace her gown. They moved through the days in a glowing cloud of joy, and as they passed by people would smile at them, touched by their radiance.

As they drew closer to de Verney manor on the last day of their journey Rosamund became still and silent, afraid of what they would find there. She had written as soon as her reinstatement became certain, informing the steward, whoever it now was, that she would soon be returning: but she did not know what horrors Sir Ralph and his people might have wrought in the few months they had held the manor. Geoffrey knew better than she the depravity of which soldiers are capable, and he could offer her no comfort. He kept his mouth firmly closed in case he should say something untoward.

They rode through a beautiful, calm summer's day, and the lands around Rosamund were familiar as breathing. The corn was high and shading to gold, the new hay was stacked into fragrant ricks, starred with the drying stems of summer flowers. The peasants working in the fields turned to stare as they rode past, but she was wearing a broad-brimmed hat and veil to protect her creamy skin from the strong sun, and nobody recognised her.

They crested the brow of a little hill. Beneath them lay the manor, its mellow bricks glowing in the sunshine. The gardens on either side of the gravel courtyard were full of tumbling roses. Rosamund caught her breath and glanced at Geoffrey, her hope and her fear showing in her face. He smiled encouragingly at her.

The last mile flowed past like the water of a stream. The gravel of the courtyard crunched beneath the horses' hooves. Geoffrey dismounted and came to help Rosamund down, holding up his hands to take her by the waist and swing her lightly from the saddle. She trembled as he set her on the ground and he looked anxiously into her face and kissed her.

Suddenly the door burst open and a figure emerged like a stone from a sling, racing across the gravel, hands extended. 'My lady!' it cried shrilly, 'my lady!'

'Margery – ' Rosamund opened her arms and caught her maid into them, tears springing to her eyes and pouring unheeded down her cheeks. 'Oh, Margery, are you well? I have been so worried. What happened to you all?'

Margery's face changed, her smile shadowed like a cloud covering the sun. 'Oh,' she said, 'my lady, they killed Hugo. He tried to stop them from taking my lord's will. And Matthew, they – ' She broke off and turned her face away.

'I know,' Rosamund whispered, 'I saw it. Are you – all right, Margery?'

Margery tossed her head angrily. 'It would take more than a bunch of filthy soldiers to bother me,' she said. 'And apart from Matthew and Hugo they didn't hurt anyone. They took a lot of things, though, my lady: all the silver and all the money, and your jewels, my lady, I'm afraid. I doubt we'll ever see them again.'

As she spoke Margery had been giving sideways glances at Geoffrey, glances of speculation, eager intense curiosity and unconcealed appreciation. Rosamund smiled at her now and said, 'Well, Margery, you must meet my new husband, Sir Geoffrey Lymington. I am Lady Geoffrey Lymington now. You remember my lord Geoffrey, I am sure.'

'Oh yes, my lady,' said Margery, curtsying deeply. 'Many congratulations,' she went on, 'and my service to you, Sir Geoffrey.'

'Geoffrey has been given Sir Ralph Aycliffe's lands by King Edward,' said Rosamund, delighted to see the expression of amazement that spread over Margery's face. 'So no doubt all will be set right again very soon.' She looked lovingly at Geoffrey and took his hand. 'My lord,' she said, 'will you come into your manor and greet your household?'

It was not until late that they retired to bed in the great bedroom at the front of the house. It had been aired, freshly painted, strewn with sweet herbs and the bed made up with the finest linen. Rosamund had been afraid that Lionel's ghost might be in it, but if Lionel saw her he was pleased, for the room felt warm and welcoming. She let Margery disrobe her and dress her in a loose silk gown, then kissed her and shooed her away.

'As you wish, my lady,' said Margery. She jerked her chin towards a corner of the room as she closed the door, saying, 'I forgot to tell you; there's a little chest there came from London with one of the messengers, my lady, and it's just over there. The messenger said none but you should open it, so I left it in here away from prying eyes.' She gave Rosamund an odd, bright, significant look and retired.

Geoffrey and Rosamund looked at each other, then went over to the corner of the room that Margery had indicated and looked down at the little chest. After a moment Rosamund stooped and unbolted it, then lifted the lid.

Upon a piece of white linen lay a folded letter. Rosamund lifted it and opened it and read aloud in tones of growing amazement, 'To our friend Rosamund, with all our good hopes for a joyful future, from Alice and the people of the Fountain.'

'A wedding present?' Geoffrey laughed aloud. 'From a bath house? Oh, Rosamund, open it up. Let's see what they've sent you.'

Rosamund hesitantly drew back the linen a little way, saw what lay beneath it and hastily pushed the covering down again, breathing fast, a hot blush staining her cheeks. She began to close the lid of the chest, her fingers shaking with haste.

'Why,' asked Geoffrey, 'whatever's the matter? What's wrong?'

'Nothing,' she said, trying to shoot the bolt. 'I – '

'Let me see.' He knelt down quickly and pushed her hands aside and tried to lift the lid. Rosamund elbowed him aside and sat firmly on the chest, challenging him with her eyes.

'What is it?' Geoffrey demanded, frowning. 'What's in there? Rosamund, get up.' She licked her lips and did not move. 'Get up,' he repeated, his voice taking on a tinge of harshness. 'Did you not hear me? Must I order you as your husband? Get up!'

Rosamund turned her face helplessly aside and got up from the chest. Geoffrey opened the lid and whipped the linen away to reveal the contents. He was silent and his eyes widened and then contracted in a frown of disbelief.

Soft ropes made of silk, covered in silk and velvet. Manacles clad in velvet, but steel beneath. A whip with a long, soft lash. Even – Rosamund's face was crimson from chin to brow – even a collection of dildoes, phalluses made of wood and ivory and padded leather.

Rosamund tried to swallow, but her throat was closed up tight with fear and sudden wrenching excitement.

Geoffrey sat back on his haunches, staring down into the chest, still silent. His loose woollen robe fell open to the waist: he ignored it. Presently he put out one hand and lifted the leather phallus and gazed at it in speechless incredulity.

'Is this a joke?' he asked at last. Rosamund gasped with astonished relief: if she could make him believe that it was intended as a joke – But before she could frame a reply he looked up and saw her face. 'It isn't,' he said at once. 'It's serious.'

'Geoffrey,' Rosamund said helplessly.

He continued speaking over her. 'I never asked you about that place,' he said in an odd strong voice, revealing no emotion. 'Is this what they did? Was this your – business?'

'No,' she said. 'Everything was very, ah, straightforward. At least, my customers were.'

'Aycliffe owned the place,' Geoffrey went on deliberately, his face taut and set. 'Who there knew what he had done to you?'

'I think only Alice, only the madam. And even she didn't know exactly what had happened. But – ' Rosamund swallowed and pressed on, determined to be honest with him. 'But Anne, Anne guessed that – sometimes I – that things like that could, could give me pleasure.'

His face had become very heavy. 'I remember that what Aycliffe did to you gave you pleasure. Christ, I remember.'

'*Bodily* pleasure,' she corrected him timidly.

There was a long silence. His face revealed nothing, and Rosamund gradually realised as she watched him that she did not know him well. They had spent less than a month together, and she did not know how he would react or what he was thinking. He looked at the leather phallus as if it had a bad smell and replaced it in the box, then withdrew one of the soft ropes and held it between his big hands, playing it gently this way and that, frowning at it. At last he said without looking at her, 'Did what he did to you give you more pleasure than – than what I do?'

'Geoffrey,' Rosamund said in gentle, sad reproach.

He looked up at that, still frowning. 'Well,' he said, holding out the rope, 'would it please you if I – tied your hands with this?'

Rosamund closed her eyes, trying to fight down a shudder of arousal so extreme that it threatened to overwhelm her. Her breathing deepened and her breasts felt suddenly tender as the dark nipples began to tense and harden. She swallowed hard, then said with difficulty, 'Yes.'

Geoffrey got to his feet and came towards her. His expression was strange, both excited and oddly self-contained. He held out the rope and she saw with a shock that his hands were trembling. 'It would please you,' he whispered, 'if I bound you? If I – forced you?'

'You wouldn't be forcing me,' she said truthfully. 'I love you. I want you.'

He stood before her, his breath shaking in and out. 'But,' he said, and his voice was trembling too, 'but we could pretend. We could – play.' He reached out suddenly and caught hold of one wrist, pulling her harshly towards him. She gasped and came to him, bent awkwardly forward to take the pressure from her arm. 'When I – had you,' he said, low and urgent now, 'that first time, when I was rough and then I was so ashamed, you liked it, didn't you?'

'Yes,' she breathed into his face, shivering with excitement and desire. 'Yes, I did, you know I did.'

'By God,' Geoffrey breathed, 'you are a woman of strong sensual appetite, my lady.' He did not let her go, but with his other hand he roughly tugged open the front of her gown, pushed it from her and reached out to grasp her breast. Rosamund staggered and almost collapsed as the quick, chill pleasure shot through her. Geoffrey laughed with disbelief and ran his hand down her belly, pushing it between her legs, feeling her. He looked into her eyes. 'Hot,' he said, 'hot as a glowing coal.'

The sensation of his strong fingers stroking the soft dampness of her sex was unbearable and delicious. 'Geoffrey,' she whimpered, hanging from his hand, 'my lord.'

Suddenly he seemed to be caught up in a whirlwind of passionate excitement. He took both her wrists in his hands and pulled them high, towed her across to the bed and with the soft rope fastened her hands securely above her head to the bedpost. She looked up into his face as he tied the knots, speechless at the sight of his fervent beauty. When her wrists were secure he stepped back and slowly, slowly stretched out his big hands to cup her breasts. His robe had fallen open to reveal his naked body, glistening in the evening sunlight, his strong eager cock lifting from the nest of his groin, stretching its swollen head questingly forward like a blind beast seeking a haven. His hands kneaded and stroked her breasts, scratching against her distended tender nipples, and the trickle of pleasure swelled to a stream and she moaned.

'I can do anything to you,' he whispered, looking into her face with his lips parted and his eyes bright with wonder. 'Anything. I can have you how I want, whatever I want. You are my prisoner.'

'Your prisoner,' Rosamund repeated, shaking with desire. 'Your handmaid, my lord.'

'I can take you in your lovely arse if I want,' Geoffrey hissed, his eyes lighting up. 'I wanted to do it before, do you remember? And you said no? Do you remember, Rosamund? Will you deny me now?'

'No,' she breathed in bliss. 'No, my lord, nothing.'

He flung himself to his knees before her and kissed her body in a wild fervour of hunger, like a starving man throwing himself upon his food. She could not move her hands; she arched her back and laid her head against the bedpost and cried out with bliss as his lips and tongue and teeth caressed her, tormented her, teased her, drew her moaning to the tip of ecstasy. She was so aroused that his slightest touch made her shudder with pleasure. All the bitter rapture of force was there, but surrounded, sheltered, cushioned with her knowledge of Geoffrey's love, like a house built upon a rock and battered by storms. Within ten breaths she was at the point of climax, but he sensed it and pulled back, grinning fiendishly up at her.

'Not yet,' he said, 'not yet.' He got up and made her turn, twisting the ropes on her wrists so that they clung tightly to her skin, pressing her face against the bedpost. 'My God,' he hissed in her ear, 'you have the most beautiful arse in the world. Look at it, look how beautiful it is.' His hands were running over her haunches, fondling them, squeezing them. He pulled the cheeks of her arse roughly apart and began to feel between her legs, using her copious juices to moisten her dark, secret crease. 'I am going to have you there,' he gasped, fitting the velvet tip of his hard cock against her tight rim. 'I am going to have you, wife. Christ, I have always wanted – ' and his words broke off into a groan of pleasure as he thrust and the hot glans opened her and pressed inside her and the thick shaft slid up after it, spreading her.

'Oh,' Rosamund moaned, leaning her head helplessly back on his shoulder. 'Geoffrey, my lord, my lord, I love you.' He stood behind her and with one hand grasped her breast, pinching and pulling at her nipple, and with the other felt between her legs for the engorged stem of her clitoris. He began to stroke at the tiny pearl of sensation and Rosamund instantly gave a desperate, anguished cry and bucked against him as her orgasm convulsed all her body, filling her brain with shimmering stars and her flesh with surging waves of rapture. He did not stop, but continued to stroke her, to touch her, drawing her ever deeper into the abyss of climax as his stiff eager penis slid in and out of the tight aperture of her arse.

At last her spasms began to fade and she hung from

the ropes around her wrists, savouring, cherishing every moment of his movement within her. His breath was hot on her neck and his wonderful soft lips brushed her throat. As she hung there, a powerless captive in her husband's embrace, a picture came suddenly to her mind: a picture of Geoffrey lying upon the great bed, spreadeagled and crying out in pleasure as she slid a hard wooden phallus deep into his anus. The image burned before her closed eyes, lifting her towards a second climax, and as she gasped she laughed with joy to think that he loved her so much that if she wanted to do that to him he would let her, he would not fear her, he would welcome whatever pleasure she chose to bestow upon him.

He was shaking now, almost there, driving himself into her with desperate force. His polished body was pressed against hers, slick with sweat, sliding deliciously over her damp skin. 'Rosamund,' he moaned, clutching at her soft flesh with his long-fingered hands. 'Rosamund.' She cried his name and felt him jolt and pulse inside her and she spun again into shuddering orgasm, pinioned by his strong hands, prisoner of his desire.

After a moment he reached up, unfastening the ropes around her wrists. She relaxed into him and they slipped together to the ground at the foot of the bed, a damp tumbled heap of love. He drew her into his arms and held her cradled in his lap like a child, kissing her forehead and her hair and murmuring her name over and over.

She reached up and clung to him, her arms around his neck. 'I love you,' she whispered, 'my lord, I love you.'

'My lady,' he said softly. He gathered her closer into his arms and laid her head on his chest and got slowly to his feet, holding her against him, looking down into her face. He placed her on the bed and climbed in beside her and laid his body against hers. He was smooth and hard as polished wood, warm as wax, strong and fair as burnished steel.

'My lady,' he whispered, 'enough of play.' His hand

traced the line of her body, touching her as gently as a summer breeze, and his voice caressed her, revealing the depths of his infinite tenderness. 'Enough of play. Now it is time for love.' And he leant slowly forward and smiled; and then he set his lips on hers, and she lifted her arms to draw him into her embrace.

LOOK OUT FOR THE ALL-NEW BLACK LACE BOOKS – AVAILABLE NOW!

All books priced £6.99 in the UK. Please note publication dates apply to the UK only. For other territories, please contact your retailer.

MIXED SIGNALS
Anna Clare
ISBN 0 352 33889 X

Adele Western knows what it's like to be an outsider. As a teenager she was teased mercilessly by the sixth-form girls for the size of her lips. Now twenty-six, we follow the ups and downs of her life and loves. There's the cultured restaurateur Paul, whose relationship with his working-class boyfriend raises eyebrows, not least because he is still having sex with his ex-wife. There's former chart-topper Suki, whose career has nosedived and who is venturing on a lesbian affair. Underlying everyone's story is a tale of ambiguous sexuality, and Adele is caught up in some very saucy antics. **The sexy *tours de force* of wild, colourful characters makes this a hugely enjoyable novel of modern sexual dilemmas.**

Coming in July

WICKED WORDS 10
Various
ISBN 0 352 33893 8

Wicked Words collections are the hottest anthologies of women's erotic writing to be found anywhere in the world. With settings and scenarios to suit all tastes, this is fun erotica at the cutting edge from the UK and USA. The diversity of themes and styles reflects the diversity of the female sexual imagination. Combining humour, warmth and attitude with imaginative writing, these stories sizzle with horny action. **A scorching collection of wild fantasies rounds up this series.**

THE SENSES BEJEWELLED
Cleo Cordell
ISBN 0 352 32904 1

Eighteenth-century Algeria provides a backdrop of opulence tainted with danger in this story of extreme erotic indulgence. Ex-convent girl Marietta has settled into a life of privileged captivity, as the favoured concubine in the harem of Kasim. But when she is kidnapped by Kasim's sworn enemy, Hamed, her new-found way of life is thrown into chaos. **This is the sequel to the hugely popular Black Lace title, *The Captive Flesh*.**

Coming in August

SWITCHING HANDS
Alaine Hood
ISBN 0 352 33896 2

When Melanie Paxton takes over as manager of a vintage clothing shop, she makes the bold decision to add a selection of sex toys and fetish merchandise to her inventory. Sales skyrocket, and so does Mel's popularity, as she teases sexy secrets out of the town's residents. It seems she can do no wrong, until the gossip starts – about her wild past and her experimental sexuality. However, she finds an unlikely – and very hunky – ally called Nathan who works in the history museum next door. **This characterful story about a sassy sexpert and an antiquities scholar is bound to get pulses racing!**

PACKING HEAT
Karina Moore
ISBN 0 352 33356 1

When spoilt and pretty Californian Nadine has her allowance stopped by her rich Uncle Willem, she becomes desperate to maintain her expensive lifestyle. She joins forces with her lover, Mark, and together they conspire to steal a vast sum of cash from a flashy businessman and pin the blame on their target's girlfriend. The deed done, the sexual stakes rise as they make their escape. Naturally, their getaway doesn't go entirely to plan, and they are pursued across the desert and into the casinos of Las Vegas, where a showdown is inevitable. The clock is ticking for Nadine, Mark and the guys who are chasing them – but a Ferrari-driving blonde temptress is about to play them all for suckers. **Fast cars and even faster women in this modern pulp fiction classic.**

THE BLACK LACE SEXY QUIZ BOOK
Maddie Saxon
ISBN 0 352 33884 9
£6.99

- What sexual personality type are you?
- Have you ever faked it because that was easier than explaining what you wanted?
- What kind of fantasy figures turn you on – and does your partner know?
- What sexual signals are you giving out right now?

Today's image-conscious dating scene is a tough call. Our sexual expectations are cranked up to the max, and the sexes seem to have become highly critical of each other in terms of appearance and performance in the bedroom. But even though guys have ditched their nasty Y-fronts and girls are more babe-licious than ever, a huge number of us are still being let down sexually. Sex therapist Maddie Saxon thinks this is because we are finding it harder to relax and let our true sexual selves shine through.

The Black Lace Sexy Quiz Book will help you negotiate the minefield of modern relationships. Through a series of fun, revealing quizzes, you will be able to rate your sexual needs honestly and get what you really want from your partner. The quizzes will get you thinking about and discussing your desires in ways you haven't previously considered. Unlock the mysteries of your sexual psyche in this fun, revealing quiz book designed with today's sex-savvy girl in mind.

Black Lace Booklist

Information is correct at time of printing. To avoid disappointment check availability before ordering. Go to www.blacklace-books.co.uk. All books are priced £6.99 unless another price is given.

BLACK LACE BOOKS WITH A CONTEMPORARY SETTING

☐ SHAMELESS Stella Black	ISBN 0 352 33485 1	£5.99
☐ INTENSE BLUE Lyn Wood	ISBN 0 352 33496 7	£5.99
☐ A SPORTING CHANCE Susie Raymond	ISBN 0 352 33501 7	£5.99
☐ TAKING LIBERTIES Susie Raymond	ISBN 0 352 33357 X	£5.99
☐ A SCANDALOUS AFFAIR Holly Graham	ISBN 0 352 33523 8	£5.99
☐ THE NAKED FLAME Crystalle Valentino	ISBN 0 352 33528 9	£5.99
☐ ON THE EDGE Laura Hamilton	ISBN 0 352 33534 3	£5.99
☐ LURED BY LUST Tania Picarda	ISBN 0 352 33535 5	£5.99
☐ THE HOTTEST PLACE Tabitha Flyte	ISBN 0 352 33536 X	£5.99
☐ THE NINETY DAYS OF GENEVIEVE Lucinda Carrington	ISBN 0 352 33070 8	£5.99
☐ DREAMING SPIRES Juliet Hastings	ISBN 0 352 33584 X	
☐ THE TRANSFORMATION Natasha Rostova	ISBN 0 352 33311 1	
☐ SIN.NET Helena Ravenscroft	ISBN 0 352 33598 X	
☐ TWO WEEKS IN TANGIER Annabel Lee	ISBN 0 352 33599 8	
☐ HIGHLAND FLING Jane Justine	ISBN 0 352 33616 1	
☐ PLAYING HARD Tina Troy	ISBN 0 352 33617 X	
☐ SYMPHONY X Jasmine Stone	ISBN 0 352 33629 3	
☐ SUMMER FEVER Anna Ricci	ISBN 0 352 33625 0	
☐ CONTINUUM Portia Da Costa	ISBN 0 352 33120 8	
☐ OPENING ACTS Suki Cunningham	ISBN 0 352 33630 7	
☐ FULL STEAM AHEAD Tabitha Flyte	ISBN 0 352 33637 4	
☐ A SECRET PLACE Ella Broussard	ISBN 0 352 33307 3	
☐ GAME FOR ANYTHING Lyn Wood	ISBN 0 352 33639 0	
☐ CHEAP TRICK Astrid Fox	ISBN 0 352 33640 4	
☐ THE GIFT OF SHAME Sara Hope-Walker	ISBN 0 352 32935 1	
☐ COMING UP ROSES Crystalle Valentino	ISBN 0 352 33658 7	
☐ GOING TOO FAR Laura Hamilton	ISBN 0 352 33657 9	

To find out the latest information about Black Lace titles, check out the website: www.blacklace-books.co.uk or send for a booklist with complete synopses by writing to:

Black Lace Booklist, Virgin Books Ltd
Thames Wharf Studios
Rainville Road
London W6 9HA

Please include an SAE of decent size. Please note only British stamps are valid.

Our privacy policy
We will not disclose information you supply us to any other parties. We will not disclose any information which identifies you personally to any person without your express consent.

From time to time we may send out information about Black Lace books and special offers. Please tick here if you do <u>not</u> wish to receive Black Lace information.   ❏

Please send me the books I have ticked above.

Name ....

Address ....

....

....

....

Post Code ....

Send to: Virgin Books Cash Sales, Thames Wharf Studios, Rainville Road, London W6 9HA.

US customers: for prices and details of how to order books for delivery by mail, call 1-800-343-4499.

Please enclose a cheque or postal order, made payable to Virgin Books Ltd, to the value of the books you have ordered plus postage and packing costs as follows:

UK and BFPO – £1.00 for the first book, 50p for each subsequent book.

Overseas (including Republic of Ireland) – £2.00 for the first book, £1.00 for each subsequent book.

If you would prefer to pay by VISA, ACCESS/MASTERCARD, DINERS CLUB, AMEX or SWITCH, please write your card number and expiry date here:

....

Signature ....

Please allow up to 28 days for delivery.